FOR GEORGE MANN

Dear Everyone,

Welcome to the ongoing adventures of that transdimensional adventuress, Iris Wildthyme!

It's an absolute pleasure to be back with you here again, at the start of another romp through space and time with everyone's favourite Aunty and her best friend, Panda. Here we are again aboard the time-travelling double decker bus – the Number 22, which is still – and forever – bound for Putney Common.

This time we find Iris with a whole new crew aboard her rackety home from home. Firstly there are a number of humans she has picked up from Darlington, in the North East of England. One of them is Simon – a youngish fella who has recently inherited an amazing place known as 'The Great Big Book Exchange.' Although sitting at the heart of that splendid labyrinth of used books has always been his idea of heaven – he has been distracted by the possibility of a life of adventure with a certain drunken cosmic ratbag he met at someone's party.

His best pal Kelly, isn't quite so convinced that travelling with Iris is a good idea. Kelly is sceptical about the whole business… but Kelly has her own problems. She has started an affair with the famous poet and seducer, Anthony Marvelle – a mumbling nincompoop whom she can't resist. But, as Iris knows well, Anthony Marvelle (plus his ferocious poodle chum, Missy) is an out and out villain. He has stolen a glass jar from the Great Big Book Exchange. It is an ancient glass jar that contains the mortal, still-living remains of a tiny, alien Empress called Euphemia…An Empress who has been kidnapped from a world at the other end of the galaxy from Darlington. The world of Hyspero is a deeply perplexing, magical place – and it lies at the very brink of the universe. Alongside it in space there sits the cosmic Ringpull – a sealed barrier into a smaller universe known as the Obverse. Galactic legend has it that the Obverse contains fabulous wealth and riches…

Only Iris knows what the Obverse is like. Only she has been there. And that's because it's where she comes from..! Poor Iris is about to undergo a confrontation with her own past! And this present volume contains a number of Weird Episodes detailing queer events from her very beginnings…

And so our story begins on the world of Hyspero… in its baking deserts, where Iris's beloved Celestial Omnibus has deposited our heroes. Also among them is the incredible Barbra – a sentient vending machine who has been to hell and back in the course of her adventures. She recently found herself almost killed off (in a huge explosion on the wintry world of Valcea) – and now, as our new tale unfolds, we find her narrating, bless her…

So – welcome all! Here we are again, in further adventures aboard the Number 22. I hope you'll find surprises and thrills in store… as we open up the

Multiverse once again and eavesdrop on what life can be like for a baglady forever caught between dimensions…

With best wishes,

Paul

Manchester, March 2012

PART ONE

Beginnings

1.

Barbra the Vending Machine speaks…

When I was given the chance of riding on this bus, I leapt with both hydraulic feet.

I gathered myself up and flung myself headlong aboard the Number 22.

Well, that's putting it rather glibly. You have to understand what a huge deal this was for me. I don't get asked to do exciting things. Not very often. And also, clambering aboard was physically more complicated than that. I'm hardly nimble enough to fling myself or leap forth. Of course I had to be lifted and eased aboard the celestial omnibus, onto the step, and through the doors. Everyone had to lend a hand to get old Barbra on the bus. I run on castors, you see, and couldn't take a running jump anywhere with both feet, no matter how keen I am.

But nevertheless the sentiment was there. There was nowhere else in the Multiverse that I'd rather be. My electronic heart was beating madly at the very thought of setting my own little wheels aboard and becoming a fellow traveller.

A traveller and companion on the Number 22 to Putney Common!

I had seen her come and go, you see. That magical lady whose unsteady hands gripped the wheel and piloted that bus through the nooks and crannies of space and time. I had met Iris before and watched her amazing vehicle arrive with a flash and a bang. I had been enthralled every time and I delighted in her fleeting presence as she sallied forth into adventure.

Then I had watched the old bus fade away again, in a marvelous shower of glitter, as she took herself off to cosmic pastures new. And I was just a humble onlooker in my adoptive town of Darlington, somewhere in the North of England. I was standing rather near the back, feebly attempting to contain myself. I could only look on in tamped-down envy as Iris came and went and swooshed up into the galaxy once more. And in my heart I longed to go with her. Fat chance, I always thought. You're too cumbersome and servile. Why would she ever take you along for the ride?

No, Barbra, your days of journeys between the dimensions are at an end at last. That's how I thought.

And yet… and yet… I believe in wishes and dreams. I do. I do. What else has a living vending machine got in her life besides crisps and pop, but silly dreams?

And somehow… somehow… I have lived to see my dreams come true! And here I am! In space and time! A traveller on the Number 22 with Iris Wildthyme and friends..!

My name is Barbra. Hello, there, everyone. You might have noticed this about me already. But I feel I must explain myself. You see, I am a walking, talking vending machine. I hail from the far, far future. Far from the time you're living in. Far, far from here. I was settled in Darlington for a bit. But I was never content. Not deep down.

Now I am living in my wildest, strangest dreams.

*

I've had a lifetime tending and serving and vending and dispensing my cans of pop and packets of crisps. A mechanical task: money in the slot, exact change only. Making sure the right comestibles get whooshed down the chute to my bottom slot. Easy, really. Too easy, actually, for an inquisitive, sociable nature such as mine.

My job has always been to provide nourishment for the human beings in whose world I live. I keep their bodies and souls together – with my snacks and fizzy orangeade. This is a vital service and one that the human race hold in high esteem, even at the very fringes of their space empire. Out on the furthest edges of the unfriendly universe, they still like to indulge in snacks. Nibbles can make you feel human again through the simple act of chewing and swallowing and filling of organic bellies. I can provide you with ample nourishment and thus assuage that nagging ache of space sickness and hunger and cosmic heimweh.

In Outer Space creature comforts are even more important. I should say so. Chilly and nasty, space is. Not very welcoming at all. I know all about it, of course, having once or twice navigated my way through the more unfriendly fringes of settled space. Plus, I once vended in an orbital shopping mall and it was utterly devoid of atmosphere.

I have fled from the unconvivial places. On occasions I have taken my life into my own hands and fled. I have jumped down spatio-temporal anomalies out of sheer desperation. Do I look like a brave woman to you? Hmm? Because that's what I am. I've flung myself into the wild, tossing seas of fate. I've given myself up to the gaping maws of wormholes and set myself free upon the whims of the infinite time winds. Oh, it's been such a to-do some days. Each time I've prayed to be delivered into a better life.

A life in which I would be a servant no more. A liberated woman. I could choose the company I kept. I would be a helper and a friend to someone who respected me. I would be a stout companion when the going got tough. I have longed to be the sort who gave her comestibles away for nothing, upon request, rather than having all that rigmarole with the correct change. I have wanted to give freely with all my heart, so long as I belonged to a group, a gang, a family – of which I was an equal and respected member.

Here aboard the bus, I think I have found that place.

Not that it hasn't been dangerous and tricky. Already we have baited death and fled from fate. No sooner had I joined Iris' merry band that I found someone had planted a terrible bomb inside my malfunctioning chiller cabinet.

I almost blew us all sky-high.

I almost blew my dear, dear friends into smithereens.

But I didn't.

I escaped that potential disaster on Valcea and then we came here – another world altogether.

Iris and her friends have been reunited here, on the dazzlingly hot and colourful world of Hyspero. Iris tells us that it is one of the most ancient and bizarre places in the galaxy.

Well, I'm up for that, aren't you?

2.

There were a great number of double decker buses at the Haymarket. Sammy's bus pulled into its bay and he was sitting on the top deck, watching all the others. Saturday afternoon in Newcastle was always busy like this, with everyone milling about the Metro station and the back of Marks and Sparks. It was easy to get swept up in all the confusion and mayhem. Yes. Mayhem. That was just the word for it. Everyone else was so purposeful, carrying their bags and parcels from the shops. Striding about, where they wanted to go. Did Sammy ever look that purposeful and smart? He guessed not.

He was a kind of a shambling brute, really. That's what Aunty Viv had called him at Christmas when he was bringing chairs down from upstairs so that everyone could get round the dining room table. He was in the hall. Struggling with two chairs at once and he heard Aunty Viv say it to his mum. At least Mum hushed her. It wasn't quite standing up for him, but it was something. He was clumsy, he knew, and he never looked like anything much, even when he was smartened up. This winter coat of his was only a couple of years old, ordered from the catalogue, but it was scuffed and marked already, with a hole in one arm that leaked some kind of stuffing. His mum had said he was like a great big teddy bear with his stuffing coming out.

Today it was spitting on to rain under a sky the colour of dirty tea towels. He should have been happy, with his pocket money and his free afternoon. All he had to remember was fetching some of those lattice sausage rolls from Marks and Sparks because that's what Mum fancied for tea. And some bread and their fancy fruit juice with the bits in. Apart from those few messages, Sammy was free to indulge himself and do whatever he wanted. He had his return ticket, his brolly and twenty pounds in three notes, five from his mum and fifteen left over from his birthday.

Mum had asked him what he was going to get, and was he going to treat himself? Top Man had some nice slacks in the window, she had noticed. Or maybe he could find himself a smart shirt? It was October and he could do with something a bit new for the work's Christmas party. It wasn't too early to start planning. You always had to have something dressy in your wardrobe, ready for work's do's. This was the kind of thing he would have to be thinking about, just like she had, when she still worked in Binns' the big department store. They always had fancy do's there, and really, she supposed that the Post Office would be the same. So, he had to buy smart things to have ready when the invitations got passed round. Parties and being able to cut a dash and look smart were important things. Sammy needed to learn to mingle more. To socialize. All those kind of things.

Needless to say, Sammy wasn't keen on spending his money on expensive items of apparel from Top Man or anywhere else. The notes were tucked up the left sleeve of his coat and they were damp from his fingers, as he kept checking they were still there. The bus shunted to a halt and there was noise as the doors downstairs flew open and everyone started hustling out. Sammy transferred his cash to his inside coat pocket and waited to go down the spiral staircase last. He would feel a bit nervous with folk coming down behind him.

Anyway, bugger the new shirt and the fancy Christmas do's. He didn't want to socialize and mix. He didn't want to be going round, being false. That's what those kind of people looked like to him. The ones who spoke with such assurance, who looked so slick and admirable, as his mum always put it. 'Oh, if you could be a bit more like that, our Sammy,' she would say, pointing to some slick bugger on the telly. 'If only you could make something of yourself.'

Sammy wasn't interested in that.

What was Sammy interested in?

There was a shop, quite near the Haymarket. Over the road from the bus station. He crossed over quickly, patting his pockets all the way. He felt as if he had dropped or lost something. Which was just the kind of thing that would happen now, wasn't it? Just as he was coming to the front window and the doorway of his shop. His favourite shop. The only shop he really cared anything for, apart from the newsagents' shop near to his mum's house. But this shop was the platonic ideal of all shops. It was shabby with flaking paint and part of a row of what were essentially prefabs, hidden in the lee of a huge multi-storey car park. But this was Timeslip and, when Sammy stepped inside Timeslip, it was as if the whole world outside was put suddenly on hold.

The door jangled when he opened it. Today he was keen not to waste a second of his own free time, and so he didn't even stop to examine the window display. He had to be inside straight away because it was twenty four minutes past one and the advertised signing would already have begun. Sammy wouldn't have a good place in the queue. He'd be right at the back and, as he stepped inside this dusty domain with its bare wooden boards

14

and that wonderful scent of yellowed comics and brand new paperbacks... he found that he had very little room to manoeuvre. He was right at the back, wedged between two paperback carousels and the cash desk. The bloke serving at the desk looked vexed and bored, wearing a black heavy metal t-shirt. Sammy felt hot and steamy inside his coat. Everyone was damp from the rain. But he was inside at least, and he had made it. He got here in time. Now he could ask them. He could get his stuff signed and ask them the things he wanted – no, he needed – to know.

*

By the time the queue had moved a bit he was sweating. The man behind the till had put on some whining guitar music, with that sort of singing that was more like screaming. It was filling up Sammy's ears, the noise stuffing itself so rudely into his head. His tongue felt thick in his throat and it was all down to nerves, he knew. Perhaps, he thought, when he got to the front of the signing queue he wouldn't be able to make himself heard by the two eminent authors who were sitting there today. Perhaps he would be so shy that his voice would come out all creaky and too quiet, like his mum said it sometimes did. 'What are you mumbling for?' she'd say. 'No one listens to a mumbler, Sammy. And put some life into your voice! You sound so bloody depressed all the time!'

Maybe, he thought, all things considered, he'd be better off not saying anything at all when he got to the front of the queue. He could feel his nose starting to run and he didn't have a hanky. His spine felt itchy and his face was flushed. His heart was pumping hard like the rock music and Sammy decided what he would do was just put his books on the table and make a kind of gesture, like a mime of writing, indicating that he'd like the two of them to sign their names inside his books. No message, nothing special, just their names. And it didn't matter about his questions. They were silly questions, anyway. Not questions about anything serious and real, oh no. Just the sort of questions that a geek or a nerd or an anorak-type person would ever care about.

Those two writers would probably laugh at him if he asked them what he truly wanted to. Now he was only about fifth in the queue, shuffling forward on the dusty floorboards. Now he had a glimpse of them. Two fellas, quite a bit younger than him. One in a smart suit jacket and stylish glasses, the other was wearing a fancy shirt with black spots on it. They were smiling at the punters and exchanging pleasantries, and laughing now and then. They bent their heads over the desk and scribbled their names and personalized dedications inside the books.

But who were they really? These two writers weren't the real and actual thing, were they? They were just two young blokes, really. It was quite a surprise to Sammy. There they were, looking just like anyone. Both had haircuts that Sammy assumed were probably expensive. Both had gel keeping their hair in style. But was I expecting anything different? Sammy wondered. How could they be anything other than just ordinary blokes?

So... they wrote books for the book series he loved more than anything in the world. It didn't mean they were touched by magic. It didn't mean they understood anything. It wasn't like they lived in those worlds that Sammy loved. They had only written about five books between them for that series. Only five out of the three hundred and twenty four that Sammy had collected and read again and again. In fact, the ones they had published weren't even Sammy's favourites. But he would never be as impolite as to say that.

He had taken their previous books about Iris Wildthyme from his bookcase this morning and brought them to town in a carrier bag, ready for signing.

3.

Mary sometimes felt sorry for the girl.

The other servants at Wherewithal House said, 'Don't be ridiculous, Mary. The girl is a beast, a frightful creature. She is spoiled and savage, the very worst combination possible.'

It was as if, in her earlier life, her life before Wherewithal House, the girl had been made to feel like a princess. But she had been none of the charms and airs and manners that a true princess would have. Would a real High and

Mighty scream like she did? And hiss and scream and fling her chamber pot around her room?

Mary, after all, had the most to do with the little demon and still she felt sorry for her. The bad-tempered mite had lost everything in that crash. She had escaped with her life, it was true. Miraculously she had crawled out of that ruptured shell of the craft and there hadn't been a mark upon her. Yet she had lost so much. Everyone else aboard had been incinerated or smashed to pieces in the disaster. Perhaps the girl's parents had been aboard. Probably they had, and she had seen something horrible happen to them. No wonder the girl was difficult. She was traumatized, even a year later. It was a wonder she wasn't a basket case, after surviving all of that carnage on the Highway.

To hear some of the other servants at Wherewithal Hall talk, you'd think Lilith really was a basket case.

Mary knocked and let herself into the rooms where the girl had been living for all these months. The air was stale and no lamps were lit. Mary shoved open the window overlooking the gardens and breathed in deeply.

'Morning, my little one,' she said, turning to see the kid sitting at the end of her bed, with her hair sticking up, looking just about feral.

Lilith scowled back at her. 'I heard the screams again last night.'

Mary bit her lip. She knew she looked nervous. She felt she had been found out in a lie by the child, or that she was deliberately concealing something. But she wasn't!

She knew nothing. 'There were no screams, Lilith. You were dreaming again.'

The girl jumped out of her bed and went to rummage around in her wardrobe. The new clothes the Aunts had bought for her were tangled and strewn, mostly dangling from their hangers. Lilith set about choosing herself an outfit for the day. Her tastes tended to involve brightly clashing colours and lots of layers and jangling accessories. For a child of no more than ten she had an uncanny knack of dressing just like a baglady.

These screams she claimed to hear in the night, though... Was it any wonder that she did? She must dream about the Highway crash every time she slept... But she was quite insistent that the screams woke her up. For several weeks now she had sat here, cross, sleepy and demanding answers. But there was nothing Mary could do. Mary didn't live in the main house at Wherewithal: she lived in the grounds in a small cottage with her family. She had never been woken by the blood-curdling screams Lilith had imitated for her.

'Who can it be? Who else lives here that I don't know about?' Lilith demanded.

But there weren't many who lived and slept in Wherewithal House. Only Lilith, the girl who had been dragged from the wreckage on the dusty plain only a few miles from the house... and the three Aunts, who lived in the attics.

Then there was the rest of the staff. They gathered together in the scullery at breakfast, lunch and supper and Mary knew everyone's faces and timetables and their duties. Mary had high hopes for one day taking over the Housekeeper's job and ruling over the whole lot of them.

Could one of the Aunts be screaming in her sleep, perhaps? None of the three were particularly happy with their lot in life, and the smallest was a martyr to her bunions. They were so bad that she had them on her hands, her back and even her face, as well as her poor, twisted feet. Maybe she was wracked with pain at night and screaming so loudly she could be heard right across the building, even in the turret where Lilith had been settled.

Settled, indeed. Really, Lilith was a prisoner here.

Even though her survival had been reported to the High and Mighties of the Clockworks in the great Saga City, no one had ever come for her. There had been no delegation from the authorities sent to collect her. No mourning family members had arrived at the front door of Wherewithal House and demanded their youngest heir back. It was as if no one in Saga City even wanted the miraculously still-alive little girl. The Clockworks were happy to do without her, it seemed.

Lilith never alluded to this fact any more. In the early days she had stamped her feet and demanded to know when her people would be sending for her. When may she return to the beautiful city, half a world away? She didn't belong in this stinking old house. This dump. This dreadful place, set in acres of red earth with its scrubby trees, its fungoid gardens and crumbling walls. She wanted to be returned home at once!

But nobody came, and nobody came. And eventually Lilith stopped asking. The facts sunk in at last and she went quiet. Nobody was coming to take her home. She was stuck here forever now, dependent upon the charity of the three Aunts in the attics and the care of tender-hearted Mary.

None of us belong here, little one, thought Mary sadly. That's the thing. You're just the same as all of us, really. We all ended up here by accident and no one thought to fetch us back. Wherewithal House is a place where the people and things that nobody wanted end up jumbled all together. Knocking about together within its decrepit, chilly walls.

*

Lilith gained permission to walk about in the gardens around Wherewithal House. Mary saw to it. She consulted the three Aunts and one day stuck her head around Liliths' bedroom door and nodded quickly. Yes, she was allowed to go out and get some fresh air and exercise. Hm – whatever fresh air there could be found out there.

It was a blistery, smoky heat that rolled in from the scorched planes. It caught at the back of the child's throat as she skipped and scurried between the tall hedges. Also, the gardens smelled brackish and horrible, as if the vegetation was dead and rotting. There were nasty-looking fruits dangling from twisted vines and the flowers that jutted from the undergrowth were thorned and forbidding.

But at least it was outside. She hated being cooped up inside the House. She had exhausted all the books in the Sunken Library of the house, and longed to explore the other rooms filled with books, but permission for that was unforthcoming. The girl felt her education had been halted. She was to grow up stunted – an indoor orchid, with nothing else to read.

Out in the gardens she would go in search of Mary's younger brother, Dick. He would bring her a packet of coarse, evil-tasting cigarettes and they would find a walled garden out of sight of the house and smoke them together. The grasses and dead tree stumps were so dry in their hidden garden that Lilith often felt tempted to let her fag ends fall into the tinder box and cause a panic as the Wherewithal gardens were caught up in a conflagration.

Dick was a boy somewhat older than she and, though she'd never actually admit it, she was rather in awe of him. He was brawny and mucky and he moved across the barren countryside with native skill. In Mary's family it was Dick who kept them alive – foraging for food and stealing riches from the travelers who unwarily took their carriages across the wasted lands. Dick was a highwayman and Lilith adored him in his cloak and mask, his dusty tricorn hat and his magic goggles that could see for miles

'I've found something strange, and even I don't know what it is.'

This made Lilith stare at him suddenly, one afternoon as they relished their purloined smokes. What could there be that Dick didn't know about? The girl took it for granted that he was cleverest soul hereabouts.

'It's in a valley, not too far from here. I don't know where it came from... or even what it really is. But I know it's something important. Will you come and see it with me?'

4.

From *The Ajai'ib – Apocryphal Tales of Hyspero*

That year Simon and I were sure we were going to find a mysterious gateway that would lead us into another world. We checked out every doorway and shady corner near our houses. We even looked in the bins and skips at the back of the shops. Mysterious gateways could be absolutely anywhere! Where you least expect them to be. We had to stay on the alert for them.

And yet... the mysterious gateway to another land slipped away from us every time. Cupboards stayed cupboards, wardrobes remained wardrobes and bins were just bins after all.

Now it was nearly Christmas and things looked pretty hopeless. Even I was starting to think that we'd never get to go off on some fantastic adventure. Even me!

My name's Kelly, by the way.

Of course, it's often when things seem most hopeless that stuff starts to happen.

And it was that Christmas that me and Simon first managed to get to our other world. It was when we first got ourselves across to Hyspero.

Toward the end of that year I was pretty miffed because I was just about twelve and I was starting to think that the grown-ups had got it right after all.

Maybe it was true, and there aren't any other worlds apart from the deadly dull one that the grown-ups live in. I'd have to settle for the kind of lives they had. Waiting in supermarket queues and watching programmes about current affairs on the telly. That was a terrible thought!

So I was starting to think that maybe they were right and I was wrong. All those books I'd read that told me that there are other lands out there and adventures waiting for me... and magic and mystery and monsters... well, maybe they were just kids' stuff and I'd got it all completely wrong.

Maybe I would have to grow up and just forget about it.

There are three things you need to know right at the start:

1. The fact that me and Simon had always hoped that somewhere like Hyspero existed and that we would get to go there one day. One day soon. It was like time was running out.

2. How Aunty Iris was the black sheep of my family who I'd never met but who sounded really fantastic. And how she turned up that Christmas. Something terrible happened to her during the party at my house, but before it did, she still said and did some pretty amazing stuff.

and 3. How I got the most embarrassing present ever that year. How I'd have died if anyone at school found out I'd been given something as pathetic as that. But also, how that embarrassing

present turned out to be important. How it was Make Up Girl,
really, who was the one that got us into Hyspero...

So this is the stuff you need to know before we set off into
that other land with all the monsters and magic and adventures
and stuff. I guess you've read the same kind of fantasy books
as me and so you're expecting quests and villains and talking
creatures who will help out. Well, it's kind of like that. But at
the same time, it's nothing like that. It's madder than that. It's
much, much madder than that.

5.

Dear All,

Hello, it's Panda here. You may remember me from the
first book?

Well, here I am in the sequel (hurray! cries everyone),
and wouldn't you know, I survived? I'd call that a bloody
good piece of luck, actually, what with all the goings-on.
Sometimes I have to pinch myself to check that I'm still all
in one piece. Yes, it's that confusing and odd.

Time for a little update, methinks. (Methinks? Where
did I get that from? I never say that!)

Here we are on the wonderful, faraway world of
Hyspero. Iris reckons that this world is somewhere very
near the edge of our known universe and, lying very close
by, is the entrance portal to the next universe, which is
where she belongs. Well, I must say, all of this is news to me.

And not altogether good news. I've heard her muttering in the past about the mysterious place she hails from. And nothing she ever muttered about it sounded very good.

Anyway, the cosmological stuff and the astronomy was never her strong suit, to be honest. I think she pilots this old bus of hers on a whim. Though she did seem rather sure of where we are, and its proximity to something she calls the Ringpull – a strange aperture that leads directly into the Obverse.

This cosmic talk is making my poor little stuffed head swim.

Oh yes.

I am a ten inch tall stuffed, talking, sentient, erudite Panda.

Get over it.

I'm sitting on the very top deck of the bus, writing this today. On the front seat, which gives a terrific view of the blistering sands and glowing horizons of the Hysperon desert. Downstairs on the lower deck there's all this palaver going on. Raised voices. Thrown objects. The occasional tinkle of broken glass. Iris has really got her dander up, and so have her companions. Hardly any surprise, after three weeks cooped up together aboard the good old Number Twenty Two, trundling slowly over the shifting sands…

Hyspero is a huge world. Sometimes it seems like we'll never get out of this barren place. We could go on trundling forever. The bus is working as well as any terrestrial bus would, but that is all. Somehow it has temporarily lost its ability to slip into other dimensions and times. Something has wormed into its workings and made it unable to function as magically as it usually does.

This has put a terrible strain on our passengers, as well it might. Even Iris has been looking a little frayed and anxious, this last week or so. At first she was full of gumption and brio. 'So what if we can't travel in all time and space, loveys? This is only a temporary hitch! Something to do with the local atmospherics! You'll see, we'll be all right!'

But – old friend as I am – I could hear the strain in her too-bright voice. I could tell she was imagining the worst.

Downstairs on the lower deck there is a slash in the Very Fabric of Time and Space. It's usually hidden, but if you hunt around, you can find it. It leads straight through to a particular evening in 1972 in London. Step through it and you step into the toilets underneath the Hammersmith Odeon. When I gave a sudden shout, remembering this fact, Iris cried out in triumph like a gaudy old crow. 'Of course! Of course, Panda! You're right! We're saved!'

But search as we might, we couldn't find that portal through the dimensions. It was lost forever to us, as was 1972. Either the gap had sealed up, or London wasn't there any more.

We realized that we are well and truly stuck here on Hyspero. Someone or something has deliberately disabled the bus, Iris claims. The bus couldn't fail on its own account. Whenever we stop for the night she opens its bonnet and explores the complicated engines and its intestines and she can find absolutely nothing wrong. 'No, no...' she whispers. 'This is some kind of evil influence taking over my dear old bus...'

We make a small encampment each night quite close to the Number 22, building up a blazing fire, and we huddle around it, telling tales and comforting each other. Each night our suppers become less lavish. We are eking out our supplies and we are not sure if we'll have enough to see us through.

Barbra the vending machine went hunting. She came back with a creature that looked a bit like a rabbit and a Tasmanian devil. Luckily, I never get hungry. I can survive off a packet of Haribo sweets and the occasional ciggy. But the others roasted that poor desert creature. Barbra was the heroine of the hour. What a surprising machine she is! Hidden talents, indeed! She was wasted peddling cans of pop and standing in shopping malls and suchlike. Iris is very pleased that Barbra has come along for the ride, even if the robot does grumble about the sand in her joints and the chilling night winds freezing her telescopic limbs.

Here's Iris now, stomping up the staircase to the top deck. She's rummaging through the racks of outfits, glamming herself up for the day. She is determined to keep up a good front. She doesn't want the others to know how worried she actually is.

'Oh, you're here, Panda,' she cries.

'Keeping my journal up to date,' I tell her. I don't tell her I'm talking to you, in case she starts to think I've gone crazy.

'Journals,' she says, remembering how a certain enemy of hers recently stole a lifetime's worth of her diaries. Luckily, our friend Simon had managed to retain one single volume of her tremendous oeuvre. Quite by chance it was one that contained accounts of her earlier misadventures on this world of Hyspero. 'And what's more, Panda, I drew maps! Very clever of me, eh? You see, I've been lost here before!'

'Lost?' I bark. 'Are we lost, then?'

'No, no, chuck,' she smiles wearily. 'But it wouldn't hurt to check that old diary out, would it? Look, why don't I stay up here this morning and start digging around in my past… and you can take the wheel today?'

I leap out of seat on the top deck all excitedly. She's going to let me drive!

6.

'Don't build up your hopes, Sammy,' his mum was always saying. Especially about things like this. She knew how worked up he could get, in a mixture of excitement and panic. She knew that he set too much store by things such as this. Even when it was just an ordinary Saturday, even when there was no one doing a Timeslip signing, he would still build up his hopes that the new book in his beloved series would be in stock. He fervently hoped that it would be on the shelf and waiting for him. And that it hadn't sold out.

Sammy knew there were other fans out there. They would be dashing in ahead of him, buying the stuff up before he could get there. They would race home and read the books from cover to cover and then post a full, spoilery review on the fan forums before he could even buy his own.

Like this lot today. Where did they come from? And were they really fans of the same thing, in just the same way, as him? Could that be possible? He had never seen them before, other fans. This was, to his knowledge, the first signing there had every been for this series, at least, in his town. He looked at the others around him, trying to work out what he had in common with them. Nothing, he thought, rather miserably. There were punks and hippies and middle-aged women and Goths and students and all kinds. No one here looked or felt like he did. He reckoned that they must be much more causal fans than he was.

And then it was Sammy's turn. He was standing by the desk all of a sudden. He had arrived before he had known it. Here were the piles of fresh new books, with their lurid covers. Their newness set his heart beating quicker than the relentless death metal. Here were the new books! They were here! Just a few more minutes of this… this ordeal of having to meet people and talk and stuff… and then he would have them in his grasp. He could go and read them at once. Too cold to sit in the park or on a bench by the university buildings. He would have to find a warm, cosy café somewhere and have a scone or some cheese on toast and some sweet and milky tea. And then…

Sammy realized those two writers were looking at him. Friendly, maybe – they were smiling at him. But he could sense their impatience too. He looked around and saw that there were lots more in the queue behind him now. It had formed at his back as he waited and he was surprised all over again.

All these people had come to buy the books! This month's new releases! They were queueing for the books containing the latest adventures of Iris Wildthyme.

'Can we sign those for you?' asked the writer in the spotty shirt. He watched as Sammy tried to pick up the books, one off that pile, one off the other, without damaging them or the ones underneath. No fingerprints or creasing of covers. He had to keep them mint. 'Iris Wildthyme and the Deadly Incursion' and 'Iris Wildthyme and The Unicorn's Camper Van.'

He pushed the two books to their respective authors and there was something of a muddle as he guessed wrongly who was who. The two young men chuckled at that and good-naturedly set about their task. Sammy shook his head when they asked about a dedication, something personal. All at once he saw that these two were just ordinary people, even a bit shy themselves. He could feel his bravery getting stronger and all at once he was speaking aloud. He cleared his throat gummily and asked them: 'Have you always wanted to write books about *her*?'

They looked at him. Spotty shirt first, and for longest. He smiled. 'I think I have, really. I've read the series since I was a kid. That's how it gets you. You start it when you're little and it hooks you in.'

The one in a suit looked up and shrugged. 'Not me. I'm new to this whole thing. Writer for hire, me. I'll do you anything, any tie-in. There's nothing I'll not stoop to.'

There was polite laughter from the staff member standing by them and some others in the queue. Not spotty shirt though, and not Sammy. Sammy was frowning, not quite understanding this attitude.

'But you've read all the Iris stories,' Sammy said. 'You've read them all, haven't you?'

The young man in the suit snorted at this, and pushed Sammy's book at him, turning to the young lady who was next in the queue. Spotty shirt looked up apologetically. 'Even I haven't read the whole lot. I've read a fair few though. And I must have dozens of the things knocking about, all over the house!'

'Dozens?' said Sammy. He had all three hundred and twenty four in his room, all in precise order. That meant canonical order – the strict ordering of when novels *happened*, rather than publication order, which would have been something quite different. Sammy realized that they were trying to catch his attention. It seemed like he had been standing there for too long. 'But… how can you write them if you haven't read them all?' He was talking and taking up too much of their valuable time, he could see that. Spotty shirt was looking a little anguished with embarrassment, and the bearded staff member was seeming cross.

'Look, move along now,' said the staff member. 'You've got your books signed. Now, if you'd like to make a payment at the till...'

But Sammy was standing there, aghast. He hadn't finished shopping yet. Plus, he hadn't finished talking. This was all aggravating, having the staff member cutting across his flow of thought like this, and then there was all this murmuring starting up behind him. The other fans were getting impatient. But this was important, this, couldn't they see? It was as if Sammy had uncovered a strange misdemeanor. It was as if something dreadful had gone wrong. With the fabric of reality and so on.

'But how can you know? How can you know about *any* of it?'

Spotty shirt cast a glance at his fellow writer, who seemed content to carry on signing and forget the presence of Sammy completely. But spotty shirt was caught in the headlights and it seemed that no one was going to be able to shift Sammy without physically manhandling him. No one seemed to be prepared to do that; to cause a scene just yet.

Spotty shirt looked embarrassed. He tried to answer Sammy's questions. 'Well... really, you know, you don't have to know everything about her. Not in order to knock out another paperback, you know.'

'Knock out...?' Sammy echoed hollowly. 'Another paperback..?'

'It's not rocket science, is it?' Spotty shirt said. 'They're just stories, aren't they? And they're not even really proper novels, are they? Just a silly series?'

Sammy started chewing the inside of his cheek until it felt numb. 'Silly series? Proper novels?'

At this point his colleague in the suit joined in again. 'Hey, I'll have you know that I write proper books, too. Not just this tie-in franchise tat. My limited edition novella with Charnel House Press was nominated for four and subsequently won three awards from the British Horror and Fantasy Association last year!'

Sammy looked at him, and then back at Spotty Shirt. He thought they meant there were better books than Iris Wildthyme in this world. That the Iris books were not real books somehow. He took a deep breath, struggling with this thought.

'What would Iris say about this?' he said.

They were signing again by then, however. The impatient queue had surged forward and Sammy had to fight for his footing as they took his place by the table. He tried to say it all again – everything that was in his head:

'What would Iris say about this business? You don't care. You don't really care about her at all, do you?'

But he was talking to the backs of the other fans. But how could they be fans? Any of them? If they were content to listen to rubbish like this. If they could trust men who didn't really believe in Iris at all.

7.

'I've found something strange, and even I don't know what it is.'

This made Lilith stare at him suddenly, one afternoon as they relished their purloined smokes. What could there be that Dick didn't know about? The girl took it for granted that he was the cleverest soul hereabouts.

'It's in a valley, not too far from here. I don't know where it came from... or even what it really is.'

'What kind of thing? Is it big or small?'

'Big,' he said, 'and made all of metal. Battered about, with bits hanging off. It's got wheels... so it's some sort of carriage. Bigger than any I've ever seen. It's come a cropper somehow and fell into that valley...'

'Something to do with the High and Mighties?' Lilith asked, breathing in sharply at even mentioning the names of that ruling elite. Even though the likelihood that she actually belonged to that fantastic caste had been intimated to her by those who had taken her in – Lilith was never at ease whenever they were mentioned.

'I don't know about that,' murmured Dick, who shared her mixed feelings about the people from the city. 'There's words on the front of the thing and they say something about *Punty Connom* or something like that. That doesn't sound like anything from the Clockworks that I know about.'

Lilith shrugged. They knew so little about the Clockworks and the people there anyway. This large carriage labelled *Punty Connom* must be to do with them! Suddenly she knew she wanted to see it.

'I don't know about that,' Dick said, looking severe. 'It's a whole day's walk from here, you know. And they don't like you being out more than a couple of hours, do they? And Mary would have my guts if she knew I was leading you across the wasted lands...'

'I don't care about all them,' Lilith snapped, stubbing out her cigarette in the ashy earth. 'I want to see this Punty carriage. Somehow I just think I need to go and see it.'

'It's just a wreck.'

'Exactly! And that's how I came to be here in the first place, isn't it? Another wreck.'

'So?'

She shook her head. 'I don't know. It's important somehow...'

'It's in a right state. Still smoking. It could blow up at any moment.'

'Do you think it crashed recently?'

'It's hard to tell.'

Now they were leaving their hidden smokers' garden and walking together back towards Wherewithal House, where Lilith knew that a dull stew with mouldy dumplings was awaiting her. And it was true about the mould. The nasty damp had got into the cook's store of flour and, since there would be no more supplies till at least Magnarok Eve, they had to make do. The mildewy bread had already

36

sent the butler mad, Lilith had heard. He had grown fur and fangs and had had to be tranquilised.

'I don't want to go back there,' Lilith huffed, gazing up at the many storeys and the snide, narrow windows of Wherewithal House.

'Ah, you've got a great life,' Dick told her. 'Lap of luxury.'

She turned to him crossly, tears standing in her eyes. 'But I don't belong, Dick,' she said. 'They let me know it every single day. And I already know that. I belong to somewhere else. I don't know where exactly... just *somewhere…*'

His heart relented and he gave her one of those warm smiles. The ones that made her feel a bit peculiar, though she wasn't sure how or why. 'All right,' he said, 'you've won me over again, Lilith. We'll go tomorrow. Crack of dawn. You be out of your bed and ready before Mary comes in with your porridge. I'll meet you in our smokers' garden at first light. Got that?'

She beamed at him. 'Of course!' And she could hardly believe that he was letting her do this. He was a true friend. But Lilith also knew that, had he refused, she would have found a way to go on this trip alone. She had to find this strange, ruined carriage. Maybe it was just a diversion she was wanting, from her long and repetitious days.

But she also felt there was more to it. This was another piece in the jigsaw of her life. A survivor, an orphan at Wherewithal House, she felt she only had a few edge pieces of her jigsaw and the rest was yet to be filled in.

*

The next day Lilith went further afield than she could even remember. Dick's strides took him much quicker across the ruinous terrain and the girl felt herself having to adopt an undignified scurry in keeping up with him. The ground underfoot was rather squelchy and uneven and so it proved to be a good idea to watch were you were going.

When they paused for a rest, or so that Dick could survey their horizons for landmarks or possible pursuers, Lilith stared at her surroundings in dismay. What had happened to this land? What kind of blight had taken it over? They had seen so little vegetation, and no clean water. Surely something catastrophic had lain waste to it all.

Amongst the few memories of her earlier life that she still retained, was the safe, warm feeling about being in the Woods inside the Clockworks. At the very heart of the cities there were these spectacular forests, kilometers deep. Easily big enough to get lost in forever. And, because they were maintained by the faultless Clockworks, they were the healthiest, most verdant forests in the universe. They were much nicer wildernesses, it seemed, than any of the true outsides.

'Come on,' Dick urged her. 'We shouldn't hang about on the plains.'

She turned to follow him. She felt even younger than she was when she asked him questions. She hoped that he didn't think of her as some irksome younger sister. He most probably did, because here she was again, tagging along behind him. 'Are there dangerous beasties out here, then? Mutants and monsters?'

'Oh, yes,' said Dick breezily, pulling his tricorn hat to protect his eyes against the orange sun. They were walking straight towards it as the morning brightened mercilessly. 'Awful things. Creatures that will rip off your head and limbs, given half a chance. And then guzzle down all your sloppy innards like you were a great delicacy.'

Lilith howled in enjoyment as he regaled her like this. She figured that, if Dick saw fit to joke about this stuff, then the danger couldn't be too bad. And he was there to look after her, wasn't he? She believed in his gallantry as much as she did his invincibility.

It took them several hours for Dick to lead them to the particular valley he had told her about. Some time after noon they came within sight of the ugly, jagged crack in the earth. It was about a hundred metres across and steep. Steeper than Dick remembered, and he wondered now whether it had been such a good idea bringing the child along. 'I've got your hopes up, haven't I?' he said, as she gazed down into the sharp canyon. She was trying to look brave enough to climb down into it. 'I should never have told you about this. It's too dangerous.'

'No!' Lilith shouted, more violently than she intended to. 'No, I'm not scared. I can climb. I can do this. And I do want to see it. This carriage...'

Dick grinned at her. She really was brave, he saw. This was why he spent time with such a kid. This was why it was worth it. She had a very old head on her skinny shoulders. Everything she did surprised him. And then, all of a sudden, she was over the lip of the rock, and starting to lower herself down. He shook his head ruefully at the sight of her – in what looked like a frilly party dress and a tiny old woman's overcoat. Lilith was grimacing in terrible concentration as she held on for dear life and lowered herself into the unknown.

'Hang on, daft girl,' Dick shouted. 'Let me help you.'

And so he did. She went first, dropping down from ledge to ledge, a little too carelessly for Dick's nerves. He held just one of her hands and it was so tiny, he thought. So hot and determined, grasping his own hand like a vice.

Down and down they went, until they were so deep they could hardly see the midday sun anymore. At this point Dick produced a small pink pistol which he said was his present for her today (he often brought novelties he had stolen on the highway.) The pink pistol emitted a surprisingly bright torch beam and, with it, they saw that they were close to the bottom of the strange ravine.

After a final few metres of scrabbling against the chalky yellow rock the two explorers found themselves right in front of their quarry.

And it was a carriage indeed. It was quite unlike any kind of vehicle either of them had ever seen.

Lilith stared up at it in wonder. 'It...it's beautiful,' she said. 'Bright scarlet... like blood!' She whirled round to look at Dick's reaction, poking the torchlight in his face. 'D-do you think it could be from another planet? Do you think? It has to be, doesn't it? I mean… we have nothing like this in the Clockworks. Nothing…'

She shone her torch lovingly over the whole expanse of the mysterious craft. She saw the sign at the front that Dick had reported. But it didn't say what he'd said – and Lilith realized that the boy-man couldn't properly read and write. She spelled out the legend carefully, telling him that what it actually said was: '22 Putney Common.'

It was utterly meaningless to both of them.

8.

There was one last, late arrival at the Christmas party. She was exhausted and snowblind from driving south through all the weather.

She was squawking loudly in the kitchen: 'I'm here! I'm here at last! I bet you thought I'd never make it! But Aunty Iris is here at last!' She took one look at me in my party dress and started screeching her head off. 'You look ridiculous! You look terrible! What on earth have they done to you? What's that awful frock and tiara? You look like a sickly, saccharine, awful doll! My god, Kelly, I expected better than this!'

I just hung my head in shame. I wanted to shout out and tell her that this dress and everything, how it wasn't really me. But I couldn't get the words out. I couldn't tell her what I was really like.

Then Nanna Euphemia's nurse, Jenny, shoved herself forward and broke into the tirade: 'I beg your pardon, lady...' Nurse Jenny was looking worse for wear by now. Her paper hat was crumpled and skew-wiff and her lipstick was all over her face. 'It was me who chose this party outfit for the darling child. Everyone here thinks she looks simply delightful. We all think she looks like a fairy princess.'

'Pah!' Aunty Iris shouted in her face. 'That's as maybe, and that's all very well. But it's not good enough for my Kelly.'

Others were trying to push into the kitchen, coming to see who was causing the commotion. They were coming to see my Aunty Iris. I was still mortified and embarrassed - but I thought that Aunty Iris was magnificent. I was staring at her.

She was a lot smaller than I had expected, yet she still managed to fill our whole kitchen with her presence. No one's eyes left her as she shook the snow off her fur coat and flicked out her tangled blonde hair. She was completely unfazed by all of this attention. In fact, she seemed to drink it in with great relish. She liked being looked at and causing a rumpus.

Now she was grinning. She looked like someone who had been living in the wild. Perhaps that's what mum and dad had meant, when they said she'd been up in the wilds of Scotland. Aunty Iris had been living in a cave.

She was, however, wearing a very sweet and flowery perfume that came off her in gusts as she flung open her arms and cried out: 'Kelly, my darling! Come and give your long lost aunty a great big hug! You might look like a nasty little fairy princess, but you're still my beloved Great Niece! Come to Aunty!'

'Ehm ...' This was dad, awkwardly stepping in at mum's prompting. 'Actually, Aunty Iris, our Kelly is rather shy, I'm afraid. She's too old for hugs these days and she won't go to strangers...'

'What is she?' Aunty Iris bellowed. 'A cat? A pet dog? Don't be ridiculous, boy! She's her Aunty's favourite niece, aren't you, dear?'

Then I was being gathered up in the most powerful hug I had ever experienced and I was just about smothered in waves of flowery scent. I held my breath and I still couldn't believe it. I was being singled out and hugged by someone who looked like the Wicked Witch of the North! I was being petted and primped by the long, bony hands of a maniac! This was terrific. I couldn't wait to tell Simon.

'They kept me away from you all this time, Kelly,' Aunty Iris whispered in my ear. Her voice was scratchy, as if she wasn't used to speaking quietly. 'I always thought you would be my favourite... I knew you would be... and I haven't seen you since you were a toddler! Since you were the size of a stunted newt! And now just look at you..!'

'She's almost a teenager,' Mum pointed out. 'She's a proper, sensible young lady.'

Aunty Iris held me at arms' length and gave a very solemn look. 'Yes, indeed she is.' Then she blinked very slowly.

For a second I felt like I was being mesmerized. No one was letting me get a word in edgeways. I was still gobsmacked by Aunty Iris's presence, but I was wanting to ask questions of my own.

Then Aunty Iris was whirling around, scattering droplets of melted snow off her ratty fur coat and her flying hair. 'I've got a bottle of gin and some tonic water somewhere! Where did I put my plastic bags, hm? I've got party supplies!'

9.

Driving was harder than it looked, thought Panda.

The others kept a wary distance and tried not to distract me as I wrestled with the wheel. I was sitting on a pile of five embroidered cushions, which were a special gift from someone… an Emperor, I believe. Iris got him out of a spot of bother with his revolting populace. It was before my time aboard the bus.

I was starting to wish I hadn't been so gung-ho about taking the wheel. We were rattling and bouncing across the rocky road. Twice I had skidded into the slippery sands and almost tipped us over. The poor old bus herself was groaning in protest, missing its mistresses' particular touch.

I rang the bell and cranked up the sound system and pretended that it was all very easy. I couldn't have our passengers thinking I was scared! I'm Panda, aren't I? I'm not put off by anything!

Simon came to join me in the cab, and he too pretended that I was fully in control. He was a good boy like that. He stared at the bleakness ahead and the distant mountains and whistled to himself.

'This is really it, isn't it? Another alien world...'

I nodded enthusiastically. Simon was a new member of our merry crew and everything was fresh and amazing to him. I was determined not to sound jaded or flip. But really, seen one rocky alien terrain, you've seen the lot. He asked where Iris had got to and I told him.

'Doesn't she remember being here before then?' he asked.

'You've got to remember that she's been knocking about the cosmos for a great many years,' I shouted over the noise of the engines. 'More than she'd ever admit to. Even I don't know how long she's been at this business. And her memory can be a bit... unreliable at best.'

She had crept up behind us, just as I was saying this. 'Is that true, Panda, love?' she bellowed, right in my ear, making me swerve across the rudimentary road. 'Unreliable, is it? Older than I'd ever admit, am I?'

Her breath was hot with gin and Sobranies and for a moment she actually seemed threatening. It was hard to decide if she was really irate or not, especially when I was trying to steer at the same time.

'Oh, come out of the way, love, and I'll take over,' she said, hopping into the cab. For a second I was vexed, but then remembered that I didn't actually know how to stop the thing.

Iris was wearing a black and witchy ensemble, complete with a squashed-looking velvet hat. It hardly seemed the thing to wear in the midst of a blistering desert, but you'd only point that out at your peril.

Simon went off to mix some drinks and I leaned close to Iris as she lit up a ciggy. 'Did you find anything, then?'

'Of course!' she nodded. 'And it turns out I've been here rather a lot over the years. More than I ever knew! And I've even got a kind of base, a hideout, hidden somewhere here… What about that, then? It's in the shape of a giant head. My very own head!'

'Amazing!' I gasped.

She pulled a face. 'But don't you think I'd remember that? If I spent as long as all that, visiting here? Virtually living here?'

'Perhaps,' I murmured. But really, her memory was awful. It wasn't just the transdimensionalism or the drink, there really was something bizarre about the way Iris's memory worked. In fact, there was something bizarre about the way her whole life worked…

'Do you know what I think, chuck?' she said. 'I'm starting to think I've been tampered with!'

'Surely not!'

'I do. And I think I've been robbed specifically of my memories to do with being here on Hyspero. Someone doesn't want me to remember what I know about this place.'

I frowned. 'But couldn't it be a feature of the planet itself? You did say that it had some very unusual properties…'

She mused on this, hunching over the wheel and chewing energetically on her cigarette. 'Hmmm. You may well have a point there. The Scarlet Empresses ruled this world for many thousands of years – that much I do remember. And their powers were very deep and very strange. They had mystical powers that could change the very nature of the landscape and its inhabitants' minds… Nothing was ever fully stable here… it was always shifting and morphing… Nothing was ever nailed down, nothing was ever as it seemed…'

I asked her: 'Was… was I ever here, Iris? I just told Simon that I never was, that I had no memory of being on Hyspero, even though I've heard you mention it before…'

'But Panda… of course you were here! We both were!'

Simon returned to us up the gangway, bearing a silver tray of skillfully mixed drinks. My head was swirling about even before I'd tasted mine.

This was all very perplexing indeed. I didn't like the idea of anyone or anything messing with my clever old noggin. How could anyone get inside of there and change my memories around? Only the most potent magic could do such a thing… I'm not showing off here, I'm really not. If you opened up my head all you'd find is a lot of old stuffing… It would be so hard to pin down exactly where my genius resides…

But could the Scarlet Empress know? Could she have been looking down into my mind – into all of our minds – right at that moment? Could she have been eavesdropping and switching things about? What a terrible thought that was…

'Where's Jenny, by the way?' asked Iris.

'She's having a nap on the chaise longue,' Simon told her.

'She isn't sulking again, is she?' Iris chuckled. 'Poor Jenny. Being forced to join us on board the old 22 again. She must be furious!'

10.

Sammy moved away from the signing area, and cast a forlorn eye over the shelves of bright new comics. Mum had made him stop reading comics. He was still okay to read paperbacks, that wasn't so bad. It didn't look childish like comics did. She was embarrassed by him, she explained. It wasn't appropriate for a man of his age, to be interested still in comics. But as he perused the shelves with his mind still spinning, he longed to be caught up in comics again. He loved their intricate, overlapping, endless narratives. They would be moving along without him, now that he'd stopped. He would never be able to catch up again.

The small shop was starting to feel oppressive – with the wet smell of coats and hair and wool, and the scorching dusty smell of the radiators. Sammy took a look at the shelf reserved for fanzines and his heart leapt up when he noticed the crudely photocopied cover of his favourite publication in the world – Pandamonium – the foremost Iris Wildthyme fanzine. Issue fifty seven. He added it to his pile of things to pay for and, when he did so, he realized that most of his spending money was gone. But that was okay. There was nothing else he wanted, was there?

*

The fanzine was written by people who really cared. Lots of them, going by the number of names on the contents page. They all lived in the south, a million miles from where Sammy lived. The thought struck him that all those names might not be different people at all. It could be one single editor, spreading himself thin, creating alter-egos to swell the ranks of a lonely fandom.

I feel like a lonely fandom, Sammy thought.

He couldn't even interact with the online Iris fans in the faceless world of the internet. For saying intemperate things on the discussion boards, he had been blocked out. He was blacklisted everywhere online. And it was so unfair. He had been right, in each of those of those silly arguments that had somehow turned personal.

'Get a grip, get a life, don't take it so seriously. That was the chorus he kept getting in response to the stuff he was saying. He was too obsessed with it all. He lived it ate it lived it slept it. And he wanted to know what was so wrong with that? Part of the problem of the modern day world was apathy, wasn't it? Nobody cared enough about anything. Nobody tried hard enough. There was no commitment, no backbone – no enthusiasm. Nothing real, anyway. Look at them all – everyone had become a grinning service industry idiot, speaking in platitudes and clichés. It was all about being professional – which, as far as Sammy could tell, in reality added up to being blandly polite and completely unhelpful.

What was so wrong with passion and obsession and real commitment?

They should be qualities that made him feel closer to the heart of life. I have passion, I have strong feeling. Oh, but but but… the things I *feel* strongly about are silly things. Daydream things… impossible things that no one really values. Not in the real world.

He was out in the Haymarket again, having crossed the street from Timeslip. Today it had disappointed him. They had jostled him and shut him up. The magic shop hadn't been any kind of sanctuary today. Now he felt cast out and exiled again, and it was ironic, it was cruel almost, because the place was still filled with people who were supposed to be fans of Iris Wildthyme.

Have we been reading the same things? he wondered. And living in the same stories?

Maybe not.

He went for a mug of tea and some cheese on toast, not too far from the bus station. The rain clattered against the window and each new customer came in brandishing a wet brolly. The café was his favourite one, with sugar cubes in paper wrappers and ketchup in plastic tomatoes. There was steam and chatter and a reek of vinegary chips. Sammy flicked avidly through his fanzine, Pandamonium, and sipped his ultra-sweet tea.

He didn't get the novels out of their brown paper bag. He might have got grease on their pages if he looked at them while he was sitting there, and that would never do. He read the letters pages of the Fanzine and frowned intently as he moved onto reviews of novels published last spring.

And gradually he became aware of somebody trying to catch his attention.

'Yoo-hoo,' she said, in a rather dull tone of voice and an Eastern European accent. 'Is this side of your table taken?'

Sammy stared at her in surprise. He was jolted out of his reading with an almost physical sensation. He could nearly hear the 'thoom' as he fixed his attention on a person in the actual café before him. He smiled but felt that it was inauthentic. 'Course,' he said, pulling his plate and mug closer. Really, he resented her joining him. But then he felt bad for thinking that, because she was in a wheelchair. It was a rather old and clunky model, and she was having some difficulty getting herself in the right position in front of the table.

Sammy got up and awkwardly tried to help her, grasping the worn handles and nudging her forward.

'Oh, thank you, thank you.' It sounded more like 'zhank' you, the way she was saying it.

When he sat back down he studied her briefly. She was an oldish woman, over sixty, probably, with a pale complexion and dark glasses on. Her hair was smoothed beneath a green silk headscarf, darkened by the rain. She was wearing some kind of fur jacket of the richest, darkest chocolate brown and she had a red and green tartan blanket drawn over her knees.

'There we are,' she said, comfortable at last, and reaching for the tatty menu. She perused it vaguely, all the time watching Sammy as he returned to his fanzine and those too-forgiving reviews. 'My name is Magda, by the way,' she added.

Sammy realized that she was still talking to him. 'I'm Sammy,' he said, and saw that she was holding out her bony hand for him to shake.

He wiped his hands on his napkin and squeezed her fingers.

'Pleased to meet you, Sammy,' said Magda. 'This is fortuitous, huh?'

He shrugged, and wished that she'd just get on with ordering her food and stick to her own company. Why were old people so rude? Always pushing their conversation on you. Making very personal remarks.

'Oh, come on,' she giggled, and he noticed something odd about her teeth. Did they look a bit sharp and pointed? No, he must have imagined it. Maybe they're a funny colour? A sickening kind of green..?

But then Magda was pursing her lips and she lifted up her glasses, in order to reveal that the lights in her brilliant sea-green eyes were dancing with glee. Sammy was feeling clammy by now, without knowing why. He felt that this old woman was being a bit insinuating with him. She was being a bit weird. If he ran outside now, leaving his tea half-finished, he'd get away okay, wouldn't he? She could hardly come after him in her chair, could she? He could have done it right then and been away from all this. Whatever 'all this' was… this curious atmosphere that hung about in this place… with the rest of the noise and steam and hurly-burly dying away… and just this old woman sitting opposite him, staring into his eyes.

'Don't you think it's a big coincidence, this, huh? Us sitting here in this selfsame Greasy spoon?' Her smile broadened, and became friendlier. Then she added, 'We have friends in common, don't we, Sammy?'

He didn't have a clue what she was talking about. Until she said:

'Oh, we do indeed, Sammy. I think you know who they are, too.'

*

When he had been out for a whole afternoon, say, or a few hours, it was always a surprise when he came back into Mum's house. He put his Yale key in the lock and took a deep breath in the porch, which always smelled of gladioli and standing rainwater. Inside there was a musty smell, of things coated in dust and probably termites and mice burrowing their way through the landslides and cairns of sheer stuff.

Mum was a hoarder. Sammy was too, he supposed. He had the same kind of instincts for picking up bargains and hunting for treasures; and for bringing them back to his home and stowing them away safely. These Comic Annuals and teapots, stuffed toys and candle holders... posters and toy cars and half-empty tins of paint. Sammy's mum had been collecting and hoarding for decades, much longer than Sammy himself, and so it was she who had filled the passageways and individual rooms with so many cast-off belongings. Secretly Sammy thought his mum had a problem, because she was gathering up useless stuff. He had opened a few of the wrinkled carrier bags and found very strange things inside – rusted spinning tops and banana skins. Nothing anyone sane would really want to keep. Not proper treasure, like Sammy's first edition Iris Wildthyme novels, cd's, action figures and comics. Or his vast collection of Pandas.

11.

'It's damaged beyond repair,' Dick said. The wheels were burned away and the sides of the machine were thoroughly buckled. Many of the windows were smashed and there was only a few lights still glowing inside. An ominous, nasty-smelling smoke came curling up from underneath the wreckage.

'I bet we can fix it,' Lilith said, moving closer. 'I bet we can, you know. Look at it! It's a beauty!'

Dick started forward to grab her. 'No! Don't get too close...'

She looked back at him and said witheringly, 'If it hasn't blown up yet, it surely won't do right now. That would be pretty unfair, wouldn't it?'

With that she reached out and touched what looked like two tall doors near the front of the carriage.

'It's okay, Dick. It's cool enough to touch.'

Lilith relished being the bravest one; becoming the one in charge.

Before Dick could stop her she had done something to the doors. All of a sudden they gave out this great gasp of air. Then they whooshed open like the jaws of a subterranean beast.

'Lilith…!' he bellowed, dashing towards her.

But the girl had fallen inside the machine. She gave a quick yelp before toppling through the doors. And then she shouted more coherently, 'Dick… come and see! It's fantastic in here!'

*

And it was.

Days later Dick was still marveling at what they had seen within the carriage.

At first glance it had seemed nothing more than a pile of old junk. He remembered when his grandmother had died and her nearest and dearest had, in compliance with age old tradition, dragged all of her belongings and clutter out of her tiny house and set fire to it all in the lane, with his grandmother's corpse set on top.

The inside of the carriage looked just like that. Except there was no dead body surmounting these heaps of funereal clutter.

The girl was fascinated, stumbling through the mess of rags and wrecked furniture. Several times he had had to call out a warning as something toppled and fell towards her. Dick's light beam flashed around erratically as they stumbled through the debris down some kind of gangway.

'Watch out for all this broken glass,' Dick urged. 'Bottles, look. Smells like… alcohol.'

But it was a smoother kind of alcohol than the rotgut that his family sometimes indulged in during festivals or at weddings. Each item of furniture, clothing or decoration that lay about in tatters and ruins seemed to have once been rather luxurious. The burned and ripped bits of apparel were gaudily-coloured and well-made. All of them belonging to a woman, he realized, as he carefully picked up a soaked and slashed coat with green fur around its collar. What kind of person would wear these things? And what kind of a person would travel and seemingly live aboard a carriage like this?

'Not one of the grown-ups,' Lilith said, 'That's for sure. No one in the Clockworks would have things like these… They would never dress like this! They're all so drab!'

Now the girl was examining the parchment blinds that were supposed to cover the windows of the travelling machine. They had come unrolled and they were torn in places. As Lilith looked at them by torchlight she saw that they were covered in what first looked like scrawl and ragged drawings. Dick came to examine what had caught her attention.

'I know what they are,' Lilith gasped. 'I've seen these once before… in the Woods. There's an ancient tree, right in the heart of the woods…. And its huge trunk has been ripped apart… by forces unknown, the High and Mighties always say. And, on all the soft wood inside, all furled out like pages in a vast book… there are these charts. These very charts. When I ran into the woods one day and stayed there… it must have been about seven days… I happened upon that tree. Eliot the tree, they call him. And the clockworks think he is alive and that we must keep away from him…'

Dick was looking at her, amazed. What had this child seen in her time? What other surprises and secrets had she been privy to? The likes of Dick and his family only ever dreamed of one day visiting the Clockworks – if they were deemed to be of the right sort. But here was this child, who had fled into the fabled Woods, and she had seen the tree…

'The Atlas of all Time,' she smiled, making the phrase sound silly and melodramatic. That's what I saw that day. Everything, everywhere, and everything that's ever happened. It was too much to take in. But… these canvas blinds… they are bits of it, I'm sure. Fragments of those charts… Or maybe someone has copied them out for themselves…'

'So this belongs to one of the High and Mighties after all?' asked Dick.

Lilith shrugged. 'I dunno! How should I know?'

'It's just… with everything you say, you seem to know more about the world and stuff, and secrets, than you ought to.'

Lilith looked at him fondly. He was quite right. But most of this stuff she had forgotten. It was just coming back into her agitated mind now because of the sight of these convoluted charts. And maybe it was something to do with this carriage, too…Somehow it seemed more familiar. It was awakening strange, unbidden ideas in her mind…

But maybe that was simply down to all the excitement.

They found a narrow spiral staircase that took them up to the second, sloping deck. This area was in even more disarray, with linens flung everywhere and clothes rails toppled over, strewing their contents all over the place. There were books, too. Diaries bound in leather, with each and every page covered in tight handwriting.

'Can't read in this light,' said Dick. 'Come on, let's get back up to the surface. We've got a real climb ahead of us.'

'Hm?' Lilith had forgotten about the climb back up to the surface. The thought of it impinged on her only distantly now. She was trying on a ridiculous, wide-brimmed hat made of scarlet silk. It was decorated with a flower not native to this world. It was still giving off a rather powerful scent that caught her breath. All at once the girl found herself wanting to cry.

'What is it?' Dick came over to see.

'It's nothing… I… I don't know…'

'You're crying.'

'I know. But I don't know why. It was this flower that started it… the scent…'

Dick rolled his eyes like this was typical girl's stuff. 'Come on. Here, you take this book. I'm no reader. I'll never make head nor tail of it. We've got to get back, though, Lilith. Your Aunties will fret, and Mary will make mincemeat out of me…!'

'All right,' she said, shakily. She took the small volume of cramped writing from him and stowed it with the flower she had removed from the hat, into her bag.

As Dick and the girl left the top deck, clattering down the spiral staircase, they never realized that they were being watched. From behind one of the still upstanding clothes rails and its musky freight of fur coats, two button-bright eyes were watching them intently.

When they left the bus, a small figure stepped out from his hiding place and gave a soft, feral growl.

These were the first living creatures he had seen in ages. He had forgotten how to communicate with them. All he knew was that they were violating this sacred place by crashing around and taking things away.

They must be followed.

12.

'But you were in Aberdeen, in Scotland,' I said. 'And that's miles away.'

Aunty Iris shook her head. 'I wasn't in Scotland all of the time.'

'Where were you then?'

For a moment Aunty Iris looked very serious and distant. Those reddened eyes of hers, surrounded by their clods of black mascara, seemed to be looking at somewhere that wasn't our downstairs hallway. Then she glanced down at me. 'I'll tell you. But first, I want to ask you a question.'

'What?' I looked at her expectantly. What could she want to know about my boring life? But there was something strange in the air. I knew that this was one of those special moments. Something was about to be said that would change my life forever. Aunty Iris's gaze was all mesmerizing again.

'Have you been on any adventures yet?'

I stared back at her in astonishment. 'Adventures?'

Aunty Iris nodded. 'It's a simple enough question. I want to know whether you have been Elsewhere yet... And whether you have managed to find one of the mysterious gateways that lead into Hyspero...?'

It was as if something clicked inside my mind. Here I was, in this moment, sitting with my Aunty on the stairs at the end of Christmas Day. Everything had changed. Just like I always knew it would. I knew instantly that my life was going to stop being ordinary. I wouldn't have to settle for a life that was normal and dull.

My adventures were about to start.

Things were about to start coming true.

'You can tell me, Kelly. I'm your Aunty Iris. I won't say that I know all about everything, but I know a damn sight more about it than that boring lot through there.'

I was still dumbfounded. I must have been sitting there with my mouth hanging open, looking dopey.

'Maybe,' smiled Aunty Iris. 'Maybe you're not very interested in adventures in other lands, hmmm?'

It was possible that Aunty Iris was just drunk. She had necked a fair amount of the gin bottle she'd brought in her plastic bag. I didn't want to go spilling out my heart to someone who was just humouring me, or who would laugh at me. Slowly I pulled the fake tiara off my head and fiddled with it. The thing is, when you believe in impossible things and you believe that, some day, your adventures will begin for real, you have to get used to being ridiculed. People are going to laugh. If you keep on believing until you're my age that you can still find a gateway... well, you have to be very careful about who you talk to. And even then, talking with Aunty Iris, I was still being careful.

Even though she seemed to be telling me that everything I'd ever imagined could be real.

'They all laugh at me,' I said at last.

'Who does?'

'Mum and dad. Everyone else. All the rotten kids at school. I know they do.'

'But why?' Aunty Iris was frowning deeply, as if she was prepared to duff up anyone who laughed at her niece. This made me feel braver. Aunty Iris believed it all too! She wasn't going to laugh at me.

'They think I'm childish because I believe in other lands. I do believe in them, Aunty Iris. I always have. They must exist, is what I think. They have to.'

Aunty Iris was nodding and smiling mysteriously.

'Simon thinks so too. But he'd say anything to stay my friend. He hasn't got any others.'

'Who is this Simon?'

'He's my best pal. He's okay.'

'I see. Go on.'

'Well,' I said. 'Mum and dad say I should grow up. They say that I let my imagination go mad and that it's embarrassing. And they've made me start to think that maybe they're right. That's what I'm thinking. Simon and me, we've searched everywhere for the... magic gateways... that might lead to another land. But... no luck.'

'Hmmm,' said Aunty Iris. I looked at her, still checking to see if she was laughing.

She wasn't.

'That must have been awful for you,' Aunty Iris said. 'To be so sure of something and not find it.'

I nodded. 'What do you think? Do you think it's silly as well?'

Aunty Iris sounded very serious. 'There's nothing silly about the imagination, dear.'

Oh, I thought. The imagination. So she thinks I'm just imagining it, as well.

But Aunty Iris's eyes were sparkling. She went on: 'And besides...'

'What?'

'I don't think the other lands and the gateways are just in your imagination. I think everything you've been saying is absolutely true!'

'You do?'

Aunty Iris let out one of her great loud laughs, which made me jump. 'Of course I do, dear! It is all quite, quite, quite true! Everything you ever thought about and imagined! All those places, those other lands! All those gateways into adventure and excitement! All of it! Why, I myself have been on COUNTLESS adventures!'

Aunty Iris was on her feet, jumping up and down in her striped tights.

Maybe we're both daft in the head, I found myself thinking. But my insides had turned to water. My heart was going twenty to the dozen. Somehow I just knew my aunty was telling me the truth. No matter how wild it sounded. No matter that everyone thought she was a maniac. I just knew that it was all true!

'And I'll tell you something else!' Aunty Iris cackled. 'I'm not the only one who went on those kinds of adventures in other lands when they were young! Oh, I'm not the only one, not by a long chalk!'

'W-what?'

Aunty Iris flung out her arm accusingly in the direction of the living room. 'Oh, I'm the only one who'll talk about it, of course. The rest of them have shut their minds to it and they pretend they've forgotten. They reckon I've gone mad and made it all up and we're not even supposed to mention it! But I'll tell you, Kelly love, there's something very odd about people in this family. We all get drawn into the other lands before we hit a certain age. Only some of them are determined to blot it all out.'

'E-even Mum and Dad?'

Aunty Iris looked very severe. 'Do you mean to tell me that they've never sat you down and explained all of this to you?'

I shook my head. 'Never.'

'Ha!' cawed Aunty Iris. 'There's something weird and nefarious going on here. Some kind of mystery to sort out!'

I was clutching my knees. I couldn't believe what was happening. I wanted Aunty Iris to slow down, to stop shouting and not to get so worked up. I wanted her to explain things to me more slowly and carefully.

'Do you mean to tell me, that before this night, before this very conversation that you're having with me - you've never even heard of the Land of Hyspero?'

I stared at her, wide-eyed. 'H-hyspero?' I faltered. 'I've never even heard that word before tonight.' But even as I said the word for the first time, that didn't seem quite true. All of a sudden, it seemed like the most familiar word in the world. It seemed just as familiar as my own name.

'But that's where everything went on in the past! That's where I went when I was your age! And that land is still there, Kelly! That's where everything STILL IS GOING ON! HYSPERO, Kelly! The land where ANYTHING can happen!'

13.

She was the oldest - therefore the smallest and the most obscure - Empress of Hyspero.

Her reign had been so long ago that hardly anyone remembered it. There were monuments to her everywhere, including within the Scarlet Palace itself, but no one ever thought about Euphemia much any more.

Certainly no one thought she was still alive.

But I am, I am! She cackled triumphantly inside her glass jar. Not only am I still alive after so many millennia on this world, I'm currently sitting at the back of a double decker bus on a road trip across the inhospitable sands of Hyspero!

Never in her previous life had she travelled so widely. Reigning Empresses had a rather dull time of it, actually. They crouched inside their jars in the throne room and various supplicants and officials would shuffle in to ask them things and whatnot. No one ever thought of the Empress as a real being inside her glorious jar, no one really thought of her as a woman. It was a dreadful life, really. And then, at the end of it, they took out your withered, exhausted body and crammed it into a different, much smaller jar. They took you down into the labyrinths beneath the palace and stored you away like winter fruits in the furthest, driest corner they could find.

Euphemia had lived there for many thousands of years, seething with boredom and a horrible feeling of betrayal.

She had watched the internment of the Empresses who had followed in her path, and she saw them installed in their own hidden niches. Dozens and dozens of Scarlet Empresses, long past their sell-by dates.

Out of all of them, it was the original who had kept her marbles and her wits most about her. While the others sunk into misery and inactivity Euphemia managed to keep that spark of life glowing inside her. Somehow she always knew this wasn't the end for her.

And one day she was proved right, because she was rescued from that subterranean obscurity.

A thief stole into the passageways beneath the palace. Euphemia was aware of him at once. A man! There was a man down here! Her mind came alive with possibilities. She used her mental powers to reach out and investigate this terrible thief... he probed the gloom and tip-toed towards her, intent on stashing her away in his bag. She was secretly thrilled and longing for the touch of his hands on the glass jar that contained her...

And this was the way she had been set free upon the universe once more. So long after she was meant to have died.

After that there were all sorts of complicated events to do with being taken to a distant world called Earth, and ending up in the hands of a young man who had inherited a bookshop. And Euphemia had passed into the hands of the members of a secret Earthling society known as MIAOW. And then she had been ineluctably drawn into the orbit of a space and time traveller known as Iris Wildthyme.

It was her bus that Euphemia was now travelling aboard, feeling much happier than she had in ages. Also, she was in the care of a youngish, rather snappy woman called Jenny. There were other companions too, all of whom Euphemia found more or less interesting, including Simon, the said owner of the book shop, Barbra - a kind of living machine, and Iris Wildthyme herself, who seemed a rather difficult figure to pin down. Sometimes she was incredibly happy and excited at the prospect of traversing the face of Hyspero in her bus, and other times she went off in the most incredible sulks about it all.

Euphemia sat in her jar and mulled it all over. Occasionally she would issue out through the lid and manifest herself fully, into her favourite form – a kind of very glamorous dwarf. She liked to do this in order to feel fully part of the quest.

Oh yes, it was a quest they were on. And Euphemia was quite glad to hear that she was at the heart of it.

So far they had skimmed across the forest floors in some region or other Euphemia had never heard of. They had navigated a murky and terrible swamp inhabited by uncouth reptiles she had never come across before. There had been some kind of ravine thing that the bus had to be carefully driven through and everyone had had to pipe right down in case a single sound dislodged a deadly avalanche. And now they were in the blazing desert, driving through the day and camping at night. Iris spent long hours consulting maps, charts and her single remaining volume of her diaries and her friends did the best they could. Barbra the machine jollied everyone along, in a way the Empress Euphemia found grating to her nerves. She was tired of being offered something called 'crisps' and 'pop.'

The Empress got the idea that they were taking her back to the City of Hyspero. At least she thought that's what they were intending. Her memory had become slightly fuddled recently – probably something to do with the time she was spending jumping in and out of the jar. It might be bad for her – so used to seclusion – to be as active as this, but she didn't care. Yes, the idea, surely, was to return her to the palace and the city she herself had created… and there to… and there she must…

No. No use. She couldn't remember. She didn't know why it was so essential she return. It was a troubling thought, too… the very idea of going back to that place and possibly being placed far underground again, back on her dusty shelf. Why, it hardly seemed any time at all since she had been liberated by that thief – that fabled man with two plastic arms – and she was loathe to give up that freedom now.

Euphemia had fallen into the hands of travellers. She was in the company of adventurers. She wanted to tell them – I'm happy like this! I'm content to stay on the road with you forever! Please don't take me home! Not yet… please! Let me stay with you, aboard this double decker bus…!

14.

Sopping wet, Sammy slipped into the house, walking sideways down the hallway, careful not to dislodge mum's slippery piles of magazines (*Look and Learn*, *The People's Friend, Hello.*) He was lugging with him the shopping from Marks and Sparks, as instructed. Scooting round those aisles and chiller cabinets amongst all those snooty-looking people was the most strenuous and tiring bit of his whole trip out. He found the fluorescent lighting of Marks and Sparks very hot and exposing. Even the bright colours of the fruit and veg somehow appalled him. He liked food to come ready-prepared, ready to microwave, so you never had to know what actually went into it.

'Mum?' He stood in the kitchen, emptying his carrier into the fridge.

No reply. The kitchen was dowdy, cramped and filthy. There were broken eggshells on the side by the tea-making stuff. Trails of the albumen from inside were hardening on the formica and the kettle like snot. Mum must have raced out in a hurry, he thought. She was probably off to the community centre to meet her cronies. It was Kick-Fighting and Naked Yoga day, he seemed to remember.

She hadn't left a note on the pine kitchen table. Just three opened cereal boxes, some empty dishes and mugs, a filled ashtray, a Virago classic ('*All Passion Spent*'), money for Clive the milkman, a bowl of rotting pears, the whole weeks' newspapers, a saw and a hammer, and…

And a stuffed Panda. About ten inches tall. Sitting by the silver candelabra, wearing an orange cravat and a very sullen expression. His ears looked very flattened down.

Sammy stood there, staring at the new arrival. It wasn't one of his. It certainly wasn't one of the pandas he had rescued and collected over the years. Had his mum bought it for him, he wondered? Had she discovered this somewhere and left it out for him as a surprise? Why, not so long ago she had been telling him off, telling him he was weird. He'd better get rid of all those dusty monstrosities out of his room. They were taking over the whole top landing and they gave her the heebie-jeebies. 'It's like Planet of the Frigging Pandas in here!' she'd yelled, sticking her head round the door of his room one night as he lay in bed. He'd been watching the extras on the box set of 'The Iris Wildthyme Show', the single series of TV episodes produced by Tyne Tees all those years ago.

His mum had disturbed his viewing. He remembered how frustrated he'd been to have his viewing of the brand new dvd interrupted like that. There was new behind-the-scenes footage in the extras. Amazing things he had never seen. And Mum was interrupting. Sammy had found himself yelling and screaming at her to leave him alone.

Nothing more had been said about the plethora of Pandas in his room.

It wasn't as if any of those rescue Pandas were anything like the real Panda. They were all differently proportioned and wore a very different expression to the particular Panda immortalized by the 17-episode legendary Tyne

Tees serial from 1979 and the three-hundred-and-twenty-four novel cover paintings since. The short-lived show had never had any official merchandising, and so an exact Panda was impossible to come by, naturally.

Except… this one.

On the kitchen table, today, seemingly looking at Sammy, straight in the eye. This one was just like the Art Critic Panda who accompanied Iris Wildthyme on her rackety progress around the Multiverse aboard her double decker bus. He was *exactly* like him. He even had a reddish scorch mark on his right arm, just like Panda from the series – the legacy of some or other hair-raising escape from danger.

Where had Mum found this curious little fellow? Was this her way of saying sorry for something? She had clearly left it out for him. Nobody else came and went into their house.

Sammy picked up the unresisting Panda. He felt the polystyrene balls inside shifting and trickling about as he hefted the toy in both hands. The thing felt a bit floppy and worn out, as if he had been played with too roughly by an over-enthusiastic owner. The brown eyes stared back dully at Sammy, who cursed himself for even checking them out for signs of life.

I'll have to Google it, Sammy thought. Someone somewhere is manufacturing *real* Pandas, just like out of *The Iris Wildthyme Show*. Someone either had a licence, or maybe there was a Panda pirate operating somewhere out there?

Or just maybe... *She* was coming back.

This was new merchandise. A new Panda toy, exactly as shabby and scarred as the real thing. If someone was making them... perhaps secretly, quietly, impossibly, there were plans afoot to revive the Iris TV series? Could that even happen? So many other, classic genre shows had been revived in recent years, as TV people ran out of ideas and looked to the past to fire their imaginations. Nostalgia was still big business. Could it be... Might it be possible that someone had seen fit to dig out that old ITV series about the mad old woman, her panda and her transdimensonal bus?

That series that had been like a stellar flash in the pan. It hadn't even been broadcast in all the ITV regions. Seventeen episodes watched by the nine year old Sammy and a weekly strip in *Look-in* magazine which had lasted a year (and broke off halfway through a story! Sammy thought ruefully) – and all those many, many novels since.

No one could revive it. No one with any clout really cared enough.

But besides all of that... where on Earth had this Panda come from?

In that moment he flashed back to the thought of that odd woman in the Greasy Spoon in Newcastle. In her wheelchair, coming out with all that stuff. She hadn't been making much sense, though, had she? She was just a random dafty, going on at him, disrupting his peaceful tea.

He took the new Panda upstairs to his room, where he stood before his bookcase and looked at his collection. He felt like he was standing before a shrine. He put Panda on his candlewick bedspread, from where the newcomer could see the windowsill lined with lookalikes (or not-very-likes) and then Sammy set to work, trying to figure out where the two new novels fit into the sequence on his bookshelves. When did they actually *happen*?

Only when he knew that would he be able to sit down and actually read them.

15.

The climb and the journey back turned out to be less arduous than either explorer had imagined. Both Dick and Lilith were so buoyed up and excited by what they had discovered, the whole thing went by in a flash.

'Nobody else on this whole planet will have seen such amazing things,' Dick said.

Lilith was thinking hard about where the crashed vehicle must have come from. She knew that alien beings were sometimes brought to the Clockworks: species with faster-than-light capability who found themselves straying in the land of the High and Mighties. For a while there would be celebrations in the Clockworks and all would flock to see the strange off-worlders. Much would be learned from them and public access TV was turned over to programmes solely about them. But then, generally, there would be some sort of fracas before the month was out. The off-worlders would start saying things like, they wanted to invade, or they wanted to go home, and it really couldn't be countenanced by the High and Mighties and so, sooner or later, they were publicly executed. Such events were a huge draw…

Lilith realized with a shock that she could remember first hearing about these killings. She had cried and asked why such things should happen… But who had she said this to? A parent or a guardian…? Who had shushed her in case anyone in the crowd took notice of the child's protests? Who had scurried away with her before she made a scene?

She couldn't remember. Anything prior to her being found in the wreckage of a Clockworks capsule in the desert was a blank in her mind. She had resigned herself to never remembering her family or her past. And yet… here was a tiny fragment reappearing in her consciousness: this memory of the slaughter of aliens in Sagacity.

Yes, that was the name of her city. That was where she had been brought up. Sagacity, the greatest metropolis within the Clockworks.

Perhaps the blazing sun on the walk back was seeping into her brain and melting its defences. The heat and the exertion had freed up her mind, after many months of being kept indoors, within the gloomy walls of Wherewithal. Or perhaps these recollections had been triggered by her curious reaction to the interior of that machine... that off-world vehicle...

That Omnibus.

The *22 Putney Common*.

Something very odd had happened to her whilst she was aboard. Like when she smelled that flower... and got covered in dust from the toppled and scattered old objects. And when she peered into that ancient book...

She had the book now, snug in her pocket, for later study.

Lilith had been changed by her day's adventure, and she knew it. Walking ahead of her, perplexed and a little worried, Dick knew that too. If anything bad happened to that girl – or if it already had – then he was too blame. Dick believed in evil magic, vapors and phantoms, just as all his family did. Perhaps he had exposed Lilith to the influence of a devil's graveyard out in the hinterlands today...

They hurried home to Wherewithal, stopping only once at a fetid oasis where Dick said they shouldn't drink the water. They paused for breath and both had the uncanny sensation that they were being watched. There was something or someone coming after them. But when they looked back the almost featureless landscape, there was nothing and no one to see. So neither mentioned their suspicions.

It was almost supper time when they reappeared in the grounds of Wherewithal House. Mary and the servants were frantic in the grounds, going round and round in circles, calling the girl's name. Thirteen of the housemaids were in the labyrinth, lost in its twists and turns calling the child's name, just in case Lilith had strayed and couldn't get out again.

When the missing girl marched up to Mary on the gravel drive she received a stinging slap that knocked her speechless. Dick, too, received a blow from his frantic sister that he simply took, hanging his head, alarmed by her anger.

'You idiots!' Mary raged. 'Do you realise what you've done here today? Everyone's been frantic. The Aunties have been beside themselves…!'

Lilith found herself speaking up, 'They're just scared of losing me, in case the day comes and the High and Mighties come calling for me…'

Mary looked as if she was about to strike her again. 'How dare you say that? How dare you? They took you in and healed you and mollycoddled you and gave you a home…'

Lilith felt a wave of resentment rising inside her. 'And they've kept me a prisoner! Those crazy old ladies! They don't care about me… all they care about is one day getting a reward maybe, from the Clockworks, when they find out who I am…'

'Lilith!' Dick said warningly. 'Don't shout at Mary. She's been worried about you all day.'

'Where have you been…?' Mary demanded. 'I've got to answer to them, you know. You'd better tell me what you've been up to.'

But neither Lilith nor Dick would tell her. Where they had ventured and what they had examined in the ravine wasn't something they wanted to talk about.

Dick was sent away by his sister. She threatened never to speak to him again, though Lilith knew that she would never do that really. Lilith was beaten and sent to bed with nothing to eat.

She lay inside her musty four-poster bed in the mildewy room she had been allotted. High atop a turret in Wherewithal House, where no one could hear her shout and protest, and where she really was a prisoner. She felt like something put away safely, ready for the day when she might prove valuable. She was an investment, she realized. The Mistresses had tucked her away like old bonds and stocks and shares.

Her head was thumping with the day's excitements and exertions. The beating and the confinement didn't feel so bad tonight. Underneath she was still excited about exploring the… Omnibus in the desert. She even loved the sound of the curious word that had popped into her head on the long trek home. *Om-ni-bus*.

During the darkest hours of the night she was still thinking about her finds when she remembered the small book, which she had tucked away in her bedside drawer, away from Mary's eyes.

Mary's eyes: since Lilith's return they had been brimming with tears. The maid was furious and she felt betrayed. She had been scared Lilith was gone for good. The Aunties might be interested in Liliths' possible monetary value, but Mary's feelings were real and Lilith regretted upsetting her.

Her thoughts returned to the purloined book and, just as she rolled over and opened the musty curtains round her bed, stretching to fetch open the drawer – she heard something from the window….

A storm had blown up out of nowhere. It was nothing unusual, here at the edge of the wastelands. The fierce winds blattened against the distorted glass; the acidic rain pounded down almost every night. But tonight there was something else. A muffled thudding against the window pane.

Lilith hauled herself out of bed, pulled on her dressing gown, and very bravely went to see.

The noise came again once, and then stopped. She reached the window and opened the rich curtains to their fullest. She squinted at the glass, which was black as patent leather. Silver beads of rain and busy rivulets were all she could see. More bravely than she felt, she found herself grasping the brass handles and shunting the sash window open.

Something was out there, she was sure of it. Spying on her. Watching her. Banging on the window so that she would hear.

The wind and rain took her breath away, and soaked her nightgown in the first few seconds. It was exhilarating, though, that sudden cold that greeted her. She remembered what Mary had told her about the poison rain and not letting it touch her skin, but tonight she didn't care about that. It was cold and thrilling.

Just then something jumped into her room from outside. It wasn't so big, but it was fast and soaked through. It made Lilith scream out in terror as it flew past her, showering her in freezing droplets as it went.

She whirled around to see it land heavily on the carpet.

It was making horrible noises. Growling noises. Curses. Sounds of appalled dismay.

The creature rolled over soggily and turned on his hostess a look of fury. His glass eyes burned indignantly in his furry face.

'It's a filthy night out there! It's like all the storms in Hades rolled into one! I've been out in that disgusting tempest for hours! Running through that godawful desert and even when I get here it isn't all over, is it? I had to scale the walls of the castle! In the midst of a ghastly gale and torrential rain I had to clamber up the ivy just to get to your window! Well, I hope you appreciate it, young madam!'

Lilith just stared at him. He was filthy and matted with rain and dirt. When she looked more closely she could see that he was in rather bad shape, with one of his ears partly singed away, and a nasty-looking bald patch on one of his arms. He was nothing more than ten inches tall – he had stood up to address her mid-rant – and yet his voice filled up the room. It was a cultivated, somewhat fruity voice, raised to its highest pitch of annoyance.

'Well?' he growled. 'What have you got to say for yourself?'

Lilith really didn't know. But she was slowly realizing that this visitor was far from the hideous ghoul she had been expecting. She had felt something was following her through the wastelands, and she had known it was climbing up the tower where she was virtually imprisoned. Now she was somewhat relieved, feeling sure that this small, noisy creature wasn't about to do her any harm. Lilith turned to the still-open window and pulled it closed. Immediately it was quieter in her room.

'Well?' he repeated, crossly, staring up at her.

'Y-you're a bear…' she gasped.

He almost fell over again. 'BEAR…??!'

'A-aren't you?'

He drew himself to his full height and started brushing his fur down. 'Well, perhaps I'm a bit mucky and you can't see my distinctive and handsome markings. I, my dear, am not some common-or-garden bear…'

'I'm sorry…'

'I am a Panda. *The* Panda, as a matter of fact. Art critic and bon vivant extraordinaire. Cosmic traveler and gentleman adventurer.'

Lilith grinned at this. He seemed so conceited and plucky she had to conceal a laugh.

'What?' he barked, noticing this.

'Well,' Lillth said. 'Where did you come from? I've never seen anything like you in all my life. And why are you here?'

Panda had started exploring the room where Lilith had been living for these past few months. He poked and prodded at a few dull-looking books and a nasty doll. He found a folded towel and started dabbing at his fur. 'Lots of questions, eh? An enquiring mind, eh? Well, we don't have time for all that now.'

'Don't we?' As far as Lilith could see, it was the middle of one more gloomy night at Wherewithal House. One night in a season of many. She wasn't going anywhere, was she? Sometimes she felt like she'd been put away in this tower forever.

'Time is of the essence,' Panda snapped, rubbing briskly with the towel. 'I'm here to rescue you.'

Her heart started beating fast. 'You? How?'

He looked piqued. 'Thanks a lot! Don't you think I'm up to the job?'

'Oh, yes, of course, Mr Panda. Of course I do! I'm sure you're a dab hand at... rescues and so on. It's just... the Aunties and their servants are completely in control of this whole place. No one can get out... I'm stuck here forever.'

'Rubbish,' he grumbled. 'I'm not leaving you here alone.'

'But why? Why do you care so much?' A sudden, alarming thought gripped her. 'Are you from the Clockworks?'

Panda waved a dismissive paw and flung down his now-soaked towel. 'The Clockworks? Do I look like I belong to that miserable lot, eh? Did you ever see a panda like me when you lived in Saga City?'

Lilith had to admit that she never had. Not even when she was lost in the Woods at the heart of the city. 'This is the first time I've ever clapped eyes on someone like you,' she said. There was, Panda noted in a pleased sort of way, a touch of wonderment in her tone.

'I have to tell you,' he replied, 'that this is not the first time I have ever seen the likes of you, Lilith.' His fur was standing up in damp spikes. Suddenly Lilith longed to brush him, but thought this might be an affront to his dignity.

'What do you mean by that?'

'I mean… I've seen you before, Lilith. And, by the way, that's just a name the old Aunties gave you. It's not what you're really called.'

The girl gulped. She didn't like the way this interloper seemed to know so much about her. 'Well, what is my name, then?' she asked.

Panda strode up to her, as if this were a moment of grand ceremony. He fixed her with his glaring, amber eyes. There were dancing lights inside the glass – and she somehow he looked both amused and proud at the same time.

'I don't think I should tell you. *Yet.* The time isn't right. Now, come. Wrap up well. We must flee this very night!'

16.

This is how we went to Hyspero…

All we did was light some candles and stuck them around the plastic head and shoulders and tumbling tresses of Make Up Girl. She was my most hated Christmas present, but she was turning out to be useful now.

Then we burned some incense sticks that I had bought in a hippy shop. The scent was jasmine and soon it was stinking up the place with white smoke. We turned down the lights and the place was filled with flickering shadows. Suddenly Make Up Girl was looking quite spooky and fierce.

'Now,' said Simon excitedly, 'We should get on our knees and chant and pray to the Great Goddess of Cosmetics and Beauty: Make Up Girl the Magnificent.'

I stared at him witheringly. 'What on earth for?'

'For the tortured soul of your Aunty Iris,' he said solemnly and, next thing I knew, he was kneeling on the carpet and making up all these weird chants. I tutted, but I joined in because I didn't want to be left out.

It was about then that the golden nylon hair of Make Up Girl caught light. Now, I had been warned time and again never to play with matches and naked flames, and now I could see why.

Suddenly Make Up Girl went up in a blue flash. The whole of her altar was awash with fierce flames. Nylon burns very easily.

I let out a squawk of fright and Simon's eyes were wide as the fire went licking up the wall.

We were both frozen, staring at this great sheet of flame that had started to engulf the doll's head. Well, I thought frantically: now we can see what a dangerous kind of present THAT was, anyway.

I knew I had to leap into action.

I seized up a half-emptied glass of orange juice from the bedside cabinet and dashed it into the flames. There was a horrible sizzling noise and then the most diabolical smell: melting plastic and burnt orange juice.

I realised that I was shouting at the top of my voice as black smoke started to fill the room. 'That's put the worst of the flames out!' I yelled. 'Quickly!'

As I dashed from the room I could hardly see through the stinking fog. I grabbed a towel from the bathroom, ran it quickly under the cold tap and carried it back. Without pausing to breathe, I threw the sopping thing heavily at Make Up Girl.

There was a loud hissing noise.

'My mum's going to kill me,' was all I could think, as I grabbed hold of the whole thing and took it smartly through to the bathroom. 'She must have smelled the smoke by now...'

'Open the windows!' I told Simon.

In the bathroom I set both bath taps running hard and dumped the towel-wrapped Make Up Girl straight into the water.

I stood there, waiting to hear Mam shrieking from downstairs.

But there was nothing. Yet.

I looked into the bath where Make Up Girl was lying like some awful experiment in a horror film. 'She should have coolled down by now,' Simon said and I turned off the taps.

I was thinking about the dreadful scorch marks on the pink wallpaper.

Together we lifted the soggy parcel out of the bath and started unwrapping the filthy towel.

I almost screamed when I looked at the face underneath.

One half of Make Up Girl's face was melted off. What was left of her hair was black and dropping out. Simon was patting at her face with another fluffy towel.

'Look, she's all right,' he said vaguely. 'We've rescued her. Maybe your parents won't even notice...'

I rolled my eyes at him. 'My Mam and Dad are a bit dopey. But they're not THAT dopey.' I took hold of the ruined toy and sighed. 'Poor Aunty Iris. This was her present to me! The last present she ever gave anyone! This is SO ungrateful! Look at what we've done to Make Up Girl!'

I looked at Simon and now he was really worried as well. In fact, I thought he was going to cry. He hates being in any kind of trouble.

Mind, there was worse trouble coming.

We went back to my room and saw that the smoke had cleared. There was a chilling breeze coming in from the open windows. Still there was no noise from downstairs. With a heavy heart I set Make Up Girl back on the chest of drawers which was, by now, a real mess of ash, melted candlewax and sticky orange juice.

'She looks horrible,' I said, sitting down on the bed.

'She looks ghastly,' Simon said. 'That's the word for her.'

Together we sat staring at the melty-faced, hairless goddess.

And that was when her eyes turned funny.

All by themselves. They lit up a fiery orange. She wasn't one of those toys that required batteries. She wasn't supposed to light up or make noises or anything. Neither me nor Simon said anything in that moment, but we both saw the same thing.

Make Up Girl's eyes were shining out of her melted face and she was staring back at us.

We both knew that something absolutely fantastic was about to happen.

'LOOK INTO MY EYES!' came a high-pitched warbling voice.

Make Up Girl's plastic melted lips hadn't budged an inch, but we knew it was her talking. Simon made a choking noise and this reminded me to breathe.

'KELLY AND SIMON! LOOK INTO MY EYES! LOOK! WHAT DO YOU SEE?'

Those glowing orange points of light were flickering now: they were silver, then emerald green and sapphire, then a deep, bloody scarlet. They grew and grew in size and they were turning around in a gorgeous flicker, like a kaleidoscope.

Me and Simon were being hypnotised. Two tunnels of strange light were opening out from the eyes of Make Up Girl and reaching out for us.

I managed to look across at Simon for just one second.

He was rising up off the edge of the bed. He was lifting off like a helicopter, floating gracefully. As I watched he started swimming down the tunnel into Make Up Girl's left eye.

From downstairs there came muffled shouts at last: 'Kelly? What's going on? What's that smell? Kelly!'

I shouted at Simon, but there was no way of breaking the spell. And I realised that I was floating by now as well.

It was like the bedroom was fading out around us in the swirling, spangling light. All my stupid girly stuff was fading away: the pastel pink furniture, the poodle bedside lamp. But my good stuff was vanishing, too: the bookshelves crammed with notebooks and favourite fantasy novels, Goth band CDs and posters. Everything was crinkling up and losing all of its colours.

It was all turning into one huge tunnel.

It was becoming a gateway.

'Kelly!!' Now there were heavy footfalls on the stairs.

I was swimming through the air just the same as Simon had done, and all those spirals of mad colours were widening out in front of me.

There came an awful clattering and banging on my bedroom door: 'Let us in at once!'

But I was being drawn after Simon through the brilliant lights: right into the left eye of Make Up Girl's ghastly melted head.

We were going somewhere and we didn't know how or where we'd end up.

We were completely at the mercy of a mysterious and magical fate.

AT LAST!

17.

That night the Empress called Euphemia came out of her jar in time for her new friends' evening meal. They were sitting at a rough encampment outside the bus, sheltered by rocks as the brilliant sun was setting and melting the horizon into mercury. Euphemia felt herself turning corporeal and glamorous, stretching her tiny limbs and making her new dress shimmer. She knew they were all looking at her by now.

'Good evening,' she said, trying not to sound too imperious. It could be a problem, that, in mixed company, away from the palace. She really was doing her best to muck in and be one of the gang.

They had a kind of barbeque going, roasting various bits and pieces that Iris had fetched out of the freezer. The spices and marinades smelled delicious as they laced the evening air.

Euphemia could see that her friends were being somewhat muted tonight. Their greetings weren't quite as enthusiastic as usual. There was a tremor of tension in the air between them. As they talked amongst themselves – and Simon brought the Empress some kind of barbequed wing to nibble on – she realised that they were all a bit cross with Iris.

They were lost.

They were lost in the trackless Hysperon desert and it was all Iris's fault.

She had miscalculated. Her diaries and her memories were wrong. She had wound up leading them into disaster. Now she was looking rather flushed and ready to lash out at anyone who moaned at her.

'Look, you lot,' she snapped, 'I can't be held responsible for everything! You've got to understand… it's a long time since I've even been to this planet!'

It appeared to be the gruff Jenny – currently chewing on a whole roasted leg – who was behind the murmurs of rebellion. She was scowling at the mistress of the bus.

Panda was up on his feet, spoiling for a fight. 'Now look here, you people. You're all relatively new to this business. You don't know what it's like for Iris! How should she know all the answers all the time, eh? Why do you all look to her?'

Even Simon was frustrated. 'But you said it was a doddle, Iris. You said you knew this world like the back of your hand…'

'I do!' Iris cried. 'Well, I did…'

'Oh, dear, Iris,' Barbra the machine said tremulously. But even she sounded as if she was having a dig. 'I think you've brought us to the middle of nowhere. And all our supplies and everything are dwindling now!'

'Oh, belt up the lot of you!' Iris stormed, and jumped up off the rug and stomped away.

Empress Euphemia felt that she ought to speak up. 'What none of you understand – including Iris is that…'

Jenny rounded on her. 'Sssh. Don't interfere. You'll only make it worse.'

'Yeah, let her go off and feel guilty for a bit,' Simon said, which rather shocked Euphemia, who knew already how fond the boy and Iris were of each other.

But it was the machine, Barbra, out of all of them, who decided that they ought to listen to what the first Empress of Hyspero had to say, 'After all,' Barbra warbled, 'She should know more about this planet than any of us.'

Thanks very much, Euphemia sighed. At last someone's talking sense. 'You see, my dears, Iris isn't too blame for getting us lost. If anything, her mistake was to even *try* to find the older routes she used when she was here last.'

'Oh, do talk sense, dearie,' snapped Panda.

'Hyspero is a changing land,' Euphemia told them, and something in her tone gathered them in and made them attend. There was a hint in her voice of the endless millennia she had lived and all of the experience she had gained in that long life. 'The world turns and twists about and recreates itself. Deserts and seas change about and forests turn inside out. Nothing is stable, nothing eternal. And it switches about according to the whims of the reigning Empress. She never leaves her palace but her mind roves all over her planet, reinventing things, improving them, toying with the least little thing... You see, nothing is in the same place as it was when Iris was last here. It isn't her fault that we're lost...'

Her companions stared at her, lost for words for a moment. Then Panda coughed loudly and said, 'Typical!'

Euphemia realised that she was feeling worn out suddenly, so she issued back into her jar and asked Jenny to slide the lid over.

Simon hurried to rescue the burning meat, saying, 'Poor Iris. We misjudged her.'

Panda was running up a tall dune, after the deep footprints Iris had left. He wanted to tell his friend what the Empress had said. She needed to know she wasn't at fault. (He knew how badly the old dear took criticism…)

When he reached the top of the dune he realised he was quite high up, looking down on the bus and the camp far below. By then he was cursing Iris for leading him on such a merry dance.

She was standing glaring down the other side, squinting her eyes in the last of the sunlight.

'Iris! You're not to blame!' he shouted.

She yelled back, 'Never mind about that now. Come and look at this!'

The multi-hued sand was slippery and unfathomably deep. It took Panda twice as long as anyone else to toddle through it. But he persevered and was soon standing beside his impossible friend.

She was pointing to a building, standing alone at the foot of the rise on the other side to the bus. It was a two storey building with dark windows and some kind of signage over its front entrance.

'Tell me, Panda old chum,' she said, musingly. 'Does that look anything like a pub to you?'

Panda squinted through the wavering heat. 'It must be a mirage!'

Iris felt around in the deep pockets of her green-fringed, zebra-striped coat. Producing some sort of bronze and cherry wood device and waggling it in the direction of the mysterious building.

'Nah, that's no illusion, my old partner in crime. That's definitely what's known as a public house! Come on! Last one down there is a) a numpty and b) buys the first round!'

Already she was plunging down the steep declivity, sending up spumes of sand.

'Wait! What about the others?' he cried.

'Bugger them!' her voice drifted back to him.

Panda set off happily after his best friend.

18.

After their book-signing they were taken to a nearby pub. The owner of Timeslip had offered the two guys a pint and a pie as a thank you for turning up and doing the biz. Both writers were pretty local (Bill was in Gateshead and Terry lived in Darlington) so it hadn't been a big deal for them to turn out for no money. And it was all good publicity for the new books, wasn't it?

'And it was a chance to meet your fans, eh?' asked Mike – the Timeslip staff member who'd been delegated to take them out to the pub. He was the only Iris Wildthyme fan on the staff, and so he'd been looking after the guys all day.

'Oh yeah, great,' said Bill, chuckling into his ale. 'Loved meeting them. Where the hell did you dig them up?'

Mike and Terry both laughed at him. Bill was funny. He'd been funny all day long, actually. He was quick-thinking and witty – and he had this very professional air about him, like nothing ever touched him. Like he belonged to a wholly different atmosphere to the people who came shuffling up to get their goodies signed. He went on like he was a bit better than all of them, Terry thought. Look at that suit. That never came out of Primark, did it? Not even out of an Austin Reed outlet store, like Terry's favourite spotty shirt had done. There was a glamour about Bill. He had something about him that made him seem famous.

It was evident in the way that the Timeslip guy, Mike, kind of sucked up to him as they had their pints and waited for the pies and chips to come. It was an old-fashioned town pub, with regulars sitting alone at their usual spots, the match playing on the telly above the bar, and a juke box going non-stop. Now it was playing 'Fernando'. Terry made a very conscious effort not to sing along or start miming the words to ABBA. He didn't think his company today would appreciate it. Maybe they wouldn't even notice. Right now Mike – who'd said he was a fan of Bill's non-tie-in and award-winning work in the small presses – was listening intently to Bill.

'I was a bit surprised to see as many women in the queue, actually,' Bill was saying, frowning. 'I thought it was all blokes who read stuff like these books. But there were a few Goth girls and some older women there. Amaze!'

Terry shrugged. So Bill didn't know much about the readership. Really, you could tell that from the Iris books he had written. Too many guns and too much pomposity for Terry's taste. Too much real science fiction stuff with fighting and supposedly mind-bending concept stuff. Nevertheless, Terry had told Bill earlier today what he'd liked about his book, and Bill had grinned and said, 'Thanks, fella. Can't say I've read yours, though. It's too much like work, innit? Reading more of the bleedin' things?'

Terry had smiled and nodded ruefully then, and he was doing so now as the two others proceeded to send up the people who had come to see them in Timeslip this afternoon.

'I thought they'd just come in to shelter from the rain, to be honest,' Mike said. 'There were people there I've never seen before! Certainly not our regulars.'

Then the cute waitress came with the pies. Three plates balanced on her pale arms and, as she set them down on the upturned barrel they were using as a table, she made it clear she was taking no shit from these tipsy blokes.

'Actually,' said Mike shyly, as they examined their homemade pies. 'I've brought my own books along, if you don't mind, eh? Signing them later? After you've had your scran, of course.'

'Yeah, sure,' Terry smiled. 'It'll be a pleasure. It's good to hear you're a reader.'

'Yeah, yeah, yeah! That's why I got you two invited along. I'm a huge fan of the whole thing. I'm one of those who had the old cassette tapes of the sound from all eighteen episodes of the show back in 1979. And I campaigned online along with the local group for the DVD release…'

'Hey, that's cool,' said Bill, lifting the thick pastry off his pie. It looked way too carb-heavy for him to even touch. 'You're a geeky twat too, eh?' He gave an offhand laugh.

Mike twisted in embarrassment. 'Well, I guess so… though I haven't read *all* the books, of course. I haven't read any of the ones you two have written, but I'm sure they're really great!'

'Yeah, they're fucking fantastic,' Bill nodded, spearing a chunk of steak with his fork.

Terry was looking at Mike. 'Erm, you mean seventeen episodes, don't you?'

'Huh?'

'You said you had tapes. Of the soundtracks.'

'Yeah. I still do. Even though I've got the DVD box set that came out last year. I've still got a box of the nine tapes. I recorded them myself when I was eight or something, on my dad's tape recorder. Holding it up to the telly and shushing everyone while it was on!'

Terry was frowning. 'But there were only seventeen episodes made, weren't there?'

Bill laughed through a mouthful of kidney. 'Shit man, you're geeking the fuck out. What's wrong with you?'

'Well, I recorded eighteen episodes,' said Mike. 'That's what I've got.'

'It must have been a repeat of one,' said Terry. He had put down his knife and fork and he was sounding too urgent, he knew. It was bad – sounding like he cared as much as this. But he needed an answer. 'Don't you have one episode recorded twice?'

Mike from Timeslip was looking at him like he was feeling a bit uncomfortable now. 'I didn't live here then. We lived in south Manchester back then. Different TV region. Maybe Granada had more episodes?'

'That's impossible,' said Terry. 'Only seventeen were made. I know…'

Bill shook his head. 'Christ, Terry. You're sounding like one of them fucking fans…'

Terry knew it. And Bill had effectively shut him up. He returned to his dinner, but his stomach was roiling and turning over inside him. He felt very odd indeed. And Bill was quite right. He was geeking the fuck right out over this.

19.

Panda soon discovered the brutal fact that Lilith had realized many weeks before. And that was that there could be no escape from Wherewithal House in the middle of the night. The doors that sealed Lilith away from the outside world were innumerable and very firmly bolted. The two of them couldn't even get outside of the small suite of rooms at the top of the turret and onto the stairs.

'I see,' grumped Panda. 'This is going to require some extra thought.'

The girl looked down at him as he paced about on the priceless but faded carpet. She felt a twinge of fondness already for her rescuer. He truly thought he was like a handsome prince, flying in through the topmost window of the castle in order to rescue her, the damsel.

'Can you climb?' he asked her suddenly.

'I'm not clambering down all that ivy,' she said firmly.

'It was fine going up!'

'For you,' she said. 'And you must weigh next to nothing, even soaked through. If I tried it, I'd fall to my death. Anyway, look, why are you so keen on rescuing me? You don't know me. What are you after?'

Lilith flopped back into her bed, pulling her comfy pillows all around her. To her surprise, Panda came to join her, and lay quite close.

'Let's just say you remind me of someone, hmm?' he said. 'Someone I knew a long time away from here.'

She frowned, and started combing her hair again, back into its ponytail. During all the kerfuffle it had turned to frizz. 'You know, hardly anything you say makes any sense.'

'It will do,' he sighed. 'Eventually. Look, my dear, do you mind awfully if I grab forty winks here? This rescue attempt has made me so very tired. I could do with a little snooze…'

And with that the small, stuffed creature fell into a heavy sleep which lasted until first light. Lilith remained awake and watched over him for a while, turning over the strange events of the evening. She took note of his various scars and threadbare patches, and of the ragged cravat about his neck. Once he must have looked quite dapper, she thought. But who or what was he? And where had he come from?

Then, just on the point of sleep, an answer came to her.

He had come from the magical omnibus in the desert. He had followed her home from that ravine. By the looks of him he had been aboard the strange machine when it careened out of the sky and crash-landed.

How long had he lain waiting there? And why had he fixated on her? Was it because she was the first to venture down into the omnibus? Had she been the first living being Panda had clapped eyes on when he came back to life?

Too many questions. Lilith gave herself up to sleep quite contentedly, reassured rather than disturbed by the small being laying curled up at her side. I've got to look after him, she thought, before drifting off. We are both survivors of something awful… and we must both look after each other.

20.

All I could think was: I was right! It's all true! We're on our way to a different world!

Even when we were flying down those tunnels of spangling green and purple and gold I knew we'd end up somewhere fabulous and new at the end of it. And that it would be somewhere completely unlike home.

We were tumbling head over heels and we were both screaming fit to burst. I could hear our two voices bouncing off the walls of spiralling colour.

Then there was an almighty THUMP and all the spinning round suddenly stopped.

We were spat out at the other end.

We landed with a jolt and a thud and, for a few moments, everything was silent and completely still.

And red hot. I could feel the heat on my back. It was blazing through my black dress.

All this light! It was burning into my eyes and making them water. Even after all the shining lights of the gateway and the kaleidoscopic tunnels, this brilliant daylight came as a shock.

I was lying on the ground. Outside. On something soft and grainy. Slowly I was regaining my wits and starting to take proper notice of where we'd landed. Very slowly and carefully I lifted up my head. There was sand in all my frizzy hair and my ears were ringing and popping like I'd been on some mad kind of fairground ride.

The sand was a weird kind that was more like shards of multi-coloured glass.

Inside I was calm. I was prepared for this. I'd been waiting for this all my life.

Oh, Aunty Iris! Why aren't you here to see us? Why can't I tell you about this? I wanted her to know that I'd made it after all.

I'd been sucked up out of the normal world and flung right into ... THIS!

The sun was blazing down from an enamelled blue, perfect sky. The only details I could make out in all the miles of sand were a few outcroppings of bright red rock, peeping out. Then - further in the distance - grand crags of pinkish-red mountains.

Everything was swathed in shimmering heat waves.

I'd always known that some day I'd end up in a place like this. A place that isn't home. A place that isn't the ordinary world. And here I was! Here we were!

There was a whimpering groan just beside me then and I turned to see Simon, sitting up groggily and rubbing his eyes. He looked very small and startled, all crumpled up on the side of the dune.

'Don't rub sand in your eyes,' I told him. 'You'll only make them worse.'

The sound of my own voice surprised me. It was so calm. There was no echo to it, either. It came out flat, as if my words were being whisked away on the hot, empty air.

Now Simon was blinking at me. He gulped. 'It's happened, hasn't it?'

I didn't say anything to that. I was trying to stand up. The gritty sand under my silver moon boots slithered and shifted. It was as if the ground underfoot in this new world wasn't sure about us. I was struggling to keep my balance.

'It's true, isn't it, Kelly?' Simon asked again. 'We've really gone and done it!'

I looked at him and grinned. 'Yes,' I said. 'Even though everyone laughed and said we were stupid. Even though my mum and dad laughed at me and said I should grow up. Well, I'd like to see them laughing at us now. Except we can't see them and they can't see us, because we're in a different dimension!'

I was gabbling, I knew. I couldn't stop.

And it was at that moment that I realised I was wearing my backpack. When I looked inside I saw that I was carrying my black velvet notebook and my silver pen with me.

'Hey,' Simon said. 'They've come with us!' He looked proud, because they were the presents he'd chosen for me. His eyes were wide. 'They must be, like, important on this adventure!'

'Do you think that's what we're on, then?' I said. 'An adventure?'

Simon looked as if the very words coming out of his own mouth were surprising to him. 'Of course we are! Look! We're in a whole different ... land..!'

He gestured around hugely, with both arms flung out. 'This isn't your street! It's not our town! It's not even our country! There's nothing but sand ... for miles and miles.' Simon was getting up like a newborn giraffe and tottering towards me across the dune.

I was squinting into the receding dunes, thinking: that's why there's no echo to our voices. We're in an endless desert.

Me and Simon looked at each other. We gulped, both daunted by all the space and grandness around us.

We were lost in all of it. Probably millions of miles from everywhere. And no one knew we were there. And we didn't know what we were there for.

Was there a purpose? We hadn't just been dumped there, surely, just to be lost and to die of thirst? Make Up Girl had sent us there. Aunty Iris had meant us to be there. We were here because we were ... well, us, and there was some kind of adventure waiting for us.

'This is Hyspero,' I told Simon, with absolute certainty.

'It's what? How can you know --?'

'I just do,' I said.

Simon's eyes lit up and he grinned. 'This is where your Aunty Iris said you needed to go. This is the other land! We made it, Kelly! We made it!'

Our sudden screams and shouts must have been heard for miles. That's if there was anyone to listen in that whole dust bowl. But we didn't care who was there, or how much noise we were making. We were hugging each other and dancing around, kicking up the glittering sand.

'We've done it! We went through a gateway! We've found the other land! We've found Hyspero!'

The two of us went on like this until we both got really tired in all the heat.

And, at that point, neither of us noticed that, of the gateway that had dumped us there, in the middle of nowhere, there wasn't the slightest sign.

It had vanished. Its job was done.

We were in Hyspero and there was no way back home.

But at that point, getting home was the last thing on our minds.

21.

'Helloooo?'

The heavy doors took some pushing. Panda lent a hand and Iris had to give them a hefty wallop to open them up.

The bar inside was silent and mostly in darkness. There was a rank smell of old cigarettes and slopped beer. Iris bundled the two of them towards the scarred wooden bar and found the optics and the glasses covered in dust.

'Give them a wipe, they'll be okay,' she said, and hastened to pour them both a drink. 'No ice.'

'Never mind.' Panda was up on the bar, staring around. 'How very odd. An old boozer in the middle of the desert.'

'Some mirage,' Iris grinned and handed him a glass of gin. 'Tonic's flat so I didn't bother. Hey, look what the others are missing out on!' She laughed and knocked back her drink.

Panda was investigating the walls. There was a portrait of Queen Elizabeth the Second from the time of her Coronation. 'This can't be right!' But when he looked closer the Queen's face was Iris'. Then he looked at the peanuts hanging on a cardboard sign. There was the usual picture of a naked girl underneath. Panda blinked and saw that, hidden under the remaining bags of nuts, the portrait was of Iris in her silver mackintosh. He turned to her quickly. 'Have you seen...?'

'Someone's expecting us,' she frowned. 'Someone is toying with us.'

Panda hopped off the bar and jumped from bar stool to bar stool, thinking hard. 'Do you know what this pub reminds me of?'

'*The Gryphon*,' she nodded. 'Yes, I clocked that as soon as we saw it. Our old drinking hole.'

It was true. Every detail was correct. Everything here was a perfect match for the London pub where, back in the Seventies, Iris and Panda had whiled away many a happy hour. This was back when they were working for MIAOW in a full-time capacity, fending off criminal masterminds, loony spies and alien invasions on a weekly basis.

'Happy days,' Panda sighed.

Iris shrugged. 'I suppose they were. But then we were betrayed by that awful woman. The woman behind MIAOW. Mida Slike. I'll never forget what she did. And I've never felt the same about blummin' MIAOW and what they get up to, ever since.'

Panda could see that Iris was getting irate as her memories flooded back. He didn't want her going off on a cross tangent just now. He distracted her with a more relevant thought, 'But why would the *Gryphon* be transported to Hyspero? What would anyone do that for?'

Iris turned to fiddle with the optics for another gin. She cried out suddenly. 'I know why! It's that Empress! They can see everywhere, you know. It's the current Empress in her throne room in the city. She knows I'm here. She's taunting me with that fact.'

Panda frowned. 'Oh dear. If she knows we're here, then do you think she knows we have her ancestor with us?'

The two of them boggled at each other. 'But she should want Euphemia back!' said Iris. 'She should thank us! Reward us!'

'I hope so,' said Panda. 'Perhaps there'll be a reward.'

'Maybe she can show us the way?' Iris brightened up.

'Wouldn't that be grand?' said Panda. 'We totter off up the sand dune, go to the pub, and find a solution to our being hopelessly lost all at the same time! What heroes we would look if we went back and told the others…'

His words were interrupted by a resounding clang.

'There's someone or something else in here,' Iris whispered.

'It sounded like some kind of machinery…' Panda gulped.

'Quickly…' Iris opened up her carpet bag on the bar and started filling it with as many bottles as she could. 'Before we get disturbed.'

Panda knew that it wouldn't do to accuse her of thieving. It would only cause bad feeling between them, plus he'd forfeit his share of the drink.

Clank, again.

'I think it's downstairs,' Panda said. 'In the cellar.'

Sure enough, a door slammed beneath their feet. The floorboards trembling, sending up a puff of old dust.

'Shall we go and see what it is?' Iris smiled broadly. Sometimes she really enjoyed nothing more than getting into something dangerous. Panda's nerves could hardly stand it. He thought she courted danger, gadding about like she was doing now. She found the door to the cellar behind the bar and, pausing only to stash that picture of herself with all the peanuts in her bag, she plunged fearlessly into the dark.

Panda had no choice but to follow.

He knew that her interest was aroused by those graphic representations of herself. The silly woman was flattered, he could tell. Her pride and vanity had led them into a great many lethal situations over the years. He just wished they could take the stolen drink back to the bus and forget they'd ever been to this queer facsimile boozer.

It was cool in the cellar. Colder and colder with every step. Panda could feel the chills creeping up his limbs as he struggled down the stone steps. After the blasting oven heat of outdoors this cold felt sickly and supernatural. Impossible.

Iris found a light switch. Ping.

There was a red curtain in front of a door. There was a little table with a lamp and a set of brochures. Iris picked one up.

'Oh! It's a cinema. These are times of screenings and so on.'

'A cinema under the *Gryphon*?' Panda frowned.

'They must have done it up,' Iris mused, flipping through the brochure. 'Gone a bit upmarket…'

'But it's not the real *Gryphon*,' Panda said. 'It's a copy on another world.'

'Good point.' She handed him the booklet. 'This is useless, since we don't know the local date. But the films they're showing seem very interesting.'

Panda almost dropped the thing in shock. 'They're all about you!'

Iris nodded firmly. 'Isn't that great?'

'B-but that's impossible, isn't it? How can… every single film they're showing be about you? I never knew there were *any* films about you!'

Her eyes were gleaming. 'Can you hear voices?'

Indeed he could. Beyond the red curtain and the door there were loud, muffled voices. A soundtrack, too, swooping and soaring around the voices. A film was playing through there. Next door.

22.

Iris Wildthyme – in the old show and in the many original paperback novels published over the years – is a bit camp.

In the story she is an enigma, with no beginnings and no roots. The first time we encounter her she is already travelling through the Multiverse in her celestial omnibus with her best friend, Panda. She is a transdimensional lush, with an eye for the boys and an outrageous dress-sense. She looks – as Panda memorably said in episode two – like she has purposefully covered herself in Velcro and rolled straight through a church hall jumble sale. She drinks, smokes, swears and attempts to put right cosmic wrongs. Even trying their level best, she and Panda tend to cause more chaos than anything. But above all, they always have a whale of a time.

Where did she come from? Where is she going to? And who came up with the idea of her in the first place? Nobody truly knows. The paperwork pertaining to the creation of the original 1979 series was destroyed in a warehouse fire shortly after production ceased in late 1980. All props and costumes were chucked almost immediately and rumour has it they were used as landfill, somewhere near the site of the brand new Metro Centre near Gateshead. Nothing more had been heard from the actress who had played the eponymous heroine. As far as anyone knew, Suzy Kendall had never worked again, following the rolling credits on the final episode of that late night show.

The six writers of that single season had never spoken a word about their year on that show. Even those viewers who still remembered watching it only vaguely recalled what they had seen. In the non-fictional books and almanacs celebrating the history of British Telefantasy the show was treated with a certain amount of mockery, even disdain, by the overly-earnest authors.

The show took thirty years to gain a new life on DVD, when those who remembered it fondly or otherwise got the chance to measure their memories against the truth. And most people thought it looked awful, seeing it again in the cold light of day. Panda was obviously a stuffed toy. The woman playing Iris wasn't just acting drunk. The sets of alien and historical locations were clearly painted cardboard, and the supporting artists were acting as if they were in a pantomime. The stories themselves were curiously meandering and often lacking in a plot of any kind at all. Each show ended in a ludicrous cliffhanger that was never satisfactorily followed up in the next instalment.

And the series itself climaxed in the most unsatisfactory situation yet – with Iris and Panda aboard the bus, with a bunch of friends they had met during the course of their adventures. One of them was a living vending machine called Barbra ('The not-very convincingly realized Barbra,' said Dreamwatch Bulletin in a typically venomous 1990 restrospective of the show.) The characters were left at the end of the first and only season driving into an arid desert on a far distant world called Hyspero. The bus trundled off into the shimmering distance, towards new adventures. With a great many plot threads dangling behind it.

Most fans of genre TV and science fiction in general regarded the whole thing as a disaster. Not only was it inconsistent and unrealistic – it was camp. It seemed to poke fun of the genre it was supposed to belong to.

In recent years, novelists contributing to the book series had tried to change that a bit. They gave Iris Wildthyme and Panda what they felt were proper adventures. Beginnings, middles and ends. Story arcs. Guns and derring-do. Iris became a darker, even drunker, tragic, lovelorn figure. She was a kind of Cassandra, spouting awful truths about the coming disasters the universe must endure. Panda became a gnomic, godlike being who messed around with the time-lines and manipulated cosmic events... sometimes for his own benefit.

That was the way the novels were going. Bleaker, darker, more nihilistic. As if the Wildthyme franchise was moving away from its ludicrous roots and was coming up to date. It had – in the hands of writers such as Terry's colleague Bill Fordyce – even become a bit gritty.

And a lot less gay.

That wasn't the way Terry liked it, though. He liked Iris the old way and he tried, in his own contributions to the series, to turn things back, as best he could. He loved the anarchy and the inconsequentiality of the original show. That's what people remembered. That's what the surviving fans really liked, wasn't it? Not all the blood and guts, surely. Not all that sententious moralizing...

Or maybe Terry was kidding himself.

The three of them said goodbye outside the pub. The rain had cleared for a bit in the late afternoon. They were thanked again by Mike from the shop, and he waved his bag of books signed by both of them as he dashed away, back to Timeslip.

'Ok, matey,' Bill said, clasping Terry's hand and giving it a firm shaking. 'I'm off to get the Metro. I'll see you again, soon, yeah? Are you going down to Manchester in December for the convention?'

'Oh,' Terry said, remembering. 'Yeah, I am, actually.'

'Should be good,' Bill grinned. 'It's always a laugh. I haven't been back to Manchester in ages. Last time was back when I was writing tie-in shit for '*Menswear*', that daft soap opera.'

Terry remembered '*Menswear*' well. It had been the world's first and last porno soap opera, based in a posh department store. That had been sometime round the millennium and it had starred ageing hottie Lance Randall, and that famous lady vamp, Karla Sorenson. 'You wrote tie-in novels for '*Menswear*'?'

'Yeah, sure,' Bill nodded. 'It was great. They had me down to the studios to meet everyone. I loved that job. It was my first! Happy memories. Anyway, fella – see you there, right? I think we're doing an Iris Q&A panel together.'

And then Genre Tie-in God Bill Fordyce was dashing off, into the bustling crowd of shoppers.

*

Terry took the train. Since Timeslip were paying his travel he'd decided the much- quicker train was a far

111

better bet than the bus. Even the Express coaches stopped at various little towns for ages between Newcastle and Darlington. Terry just wanted to be home. He felt bloated and woozy from the pints of ale, plus he also felt obscurely humiliated by the whole thing. The crowd had been mostly there for Bill, he had realized pretty early on.

He had a quick coffee as he waited for the train, sitting on a concrete concourse on a cold metal chair, with the hideous smell of pasties wafting by from a concession stand that sold nothing but.

Bill was famous in that SF world for his Zombie Hooker series of books, and his Dark Magus books, all that other stuff. He'd been optioned for movies and won awards from the Science Fiction, Horror and Fantasy communities. And good luck to him, Terry thought. But he wished he hadn't felt such a fool, sitting next to him. Terry had proved himself terminally uncool and way too into Iris. And worse than that, he had pretended not to be. Like when that bloke in the anorak had stood before their table he had tried to act casual and uncaring. He had even been snitty, putting the Iris series down. He had said they were just silly, really. Nothing proper. Not like real books at all. And he had watched the anorak bloke with the thin, greasy hair look appalled. He had watched his blubbery face fall. Terry had felt immediately guilty and wanted to take back all his silly words. But he heard Bill beside him grunt with laughter and turn away. Terry had felt like a shit.

He'd wanted to run after the anorak bloke. Tell him he had been just messing on. Of course Iris meant just as much to him. Of course she did. She was just as real and vital as she was to the anorak bloke. She always had been.

And now he found he wanted to tell the anorak bloke what Timeslip Mike had said about an eighteenth episode. Could that be right? There had been rumours of course, for a long time amongst hardcore fans, that an eighteenth script had been written – by the revered, long unheard of Denis Grice – but no one had ever suggested that it had gone into production. This was the kind of thing that a hardcore fan would simply die to hear. Terry should have been telling the anorak bloke all about it, rather than sitting in that dreary pub with Mike and Bill, both of whom seemed keen to seem so nonchalant, and even keen to let the subject drop.

There was a kerfuffle of noise and movement then, and Terry looked up to see that his train had pulled in.

There was a surge of movement and pushing at every open door, as travelers tried to get on board before others got off.

Terry found himself hanging back, not really caring if he had to stand all the way. It wasn't that long a trip.

'Hey,' said a voice from below.

He looked and saw the woman in the wheelchair. She had pulled up beside him, looking ridiculous in a transparent rain hood. She was pulling on his shirt sleeve.

'Any chance of you helping me aboard? I can't see any of those porters.'

He took a second to react. 'Yes, of course, Magda. Of course!'

'HUH! Recognise me, do you? I thought you were miles away, honey.'

He smiled ruefully. 'Yes, I was, really. Look, the crowd's thinning, here, we need a little ramp, don't we...'

Mercifully a porter came running to help them at this point. Terry stood awkwardly as Magda, his neighbour, was hoisted aboard.

When they were safely installed in the open compartment used for storing prams and bikes, the train lurched on its way. Magda asked Terry, 'What brought you here on a Saturday?' She was peering at his green carrier from Timeslip. It had a picture of Spiderman on the front, hanging upside down from his webs. The bag was stuffed with books and comics he had bought for himself.

'I was doing a signing. You know, the new book.'

'Oh! Is it out yet, then?' Magda looked genuinely enthusiastic. 'And when do I get to read a copy, Terry? You know how I enjoy your things.'

'I've got my author copies in,' he shrugged. 'I can let you have one when we get home, if you like.' Then, he thought, gloomily – pretty soon she'll have a whole stock of them anyway. Magda was the manageress of a remainder book store in the darkest, dimmest corner of Darlington's indoor market.

Back in the 1980s when Terry had been a kid, Magda's had been the place to go for proper American science fiction and fantasy novels. The young Terry had become hooked on those slightly yellowed novels with the weird covers and the even weirder contents. Magda had watched with amusement as the boy came back each Saturday with his pocket money – avid for books by Tim Powers, James P Blaylock, R. A McAvoy, Jonathan Carroll, Jon De Cles…

It hit them both at the same time, as they sat there, bumping along on the train home from Newcastle: they had known each other all that time. Magda and her bookshop and Terry the teenager in the foppish charity shop ensembles and his taste for Dark Fantasy. All that time! And here he was, a published author, all these years later.

Magda had played no small part in fanning the flames of his ambition. He remembered a writing contest she had organized for the local library. Terry had won – with a piece of Iris fanfic no less – and Magda had presented him with a book voucher and his picture had been in the Northern Echo.

All that time! He looked at Magda and saw that she was gripping her wheels hard and her chair was shifting about on the lino stuff on the carriage floor. Terry reached forward and grasped the brake handle. It was way too stiff for the old lady to use.

She said, 'Oh, you and that Iris Wildthyme. Ever since you were a boy, eh? Always with the Iris stories.'

He felt himself blushing.

'And now you have made her into your career.'

'I suppose I have,' he agreed. He imagined that any moment she would weigh in with how he ought to be writing his own work, about his own characters and situations. How he should give up writing for other people's series. He had his own mark to make on the Multiverse, surely…

But to his surprise Magda didn't say any of that. She simply stared out of the windows at the houses and tower blocks of south Tyneside giving way to lush green fields as the rain spattered against the windows.

Terry thought he heard her mutter, 'She still needs you, Terry. Iris needs you more than ever…'

But he must have been mistaken about that.

23.

In the morning there came Mary's bright and cheery knocking at the door, and then her merrily irritating singsong voice as she bustled in. Panda was awake in an instant, scooching down under the bedclothes so that he couldn't be seen.

Lilith woke feeling less cross and mithered than normal and Mary noticed it at once.

'You've got colour in your cheeks this morning.'

'It's after all that exercise, going into the desert yesterday,' Lilith told her brightly.

'I hope it's not any kind of, you know, radiation sickness.'

'Hardly,' Lilith tossed her head and clambered out of bed, careful not to reveal Panda to her housemaid. 'We Clockworkers are hardier than you countryfolk.'

'Clockworker now, are you?'

'Well, that's what everyone says, don't they? That's what the old Aunties are hoping. They want to make a profit on me, don't they? When my people come looking, one day.'

'I wouldn't know about that, you cheeky thing,' Mary set about her morning tasks brusquely. 'My job is to see that you are clean and fed and behaving yourself. Do you think you can manage that today?'

Lilith skipped over to the wardrobe and flung it open. 'Of course, Mary.'

The girl was definitely sparkier this morning, Mary thought. Maybe her foray into the frightening outside world really had done her some good. Or maybe she was growing up a little at last, and feeling more grateful for her situation here at Wherewithal House.

*

'I do hate it here,' Lilith sighed. She was dawdling through the ornamental gardens later that morning with Panda. For safety she had popped him into the baby carriage that was meant for her nasty-looking doll, Miranda.

Panda hadn't been insulted at all by the offer of the push. His old legs were rather tired after the previous day's efforts. He lay under a frilled blanket and observed the exotic gardens keenly. He was also very interested in the tall, foreboding exterior of Wherewithal House. 'I think anywhere becomes hateful if you're confined there,' he opined wisely.

'But it's hideous here as well. These gardens stink of mildew and rot. The ponds are all black and so are the trees. Frogs the size of dogs, all slimy and purple. There are eels swishing out of the water and hurtling through the undergrowth. Foul things.'

'Someone must have thought it was beautiful once, I suppose,' panda said. 'All this decadent style was very much the *in* thing on this world, in an earlier period.'

Lilith was alert to his every word. '*This* world? So you've been to other ones?'

'Oh yes,' he said complacently, lolling in the pram. Today he was looking much more chipper. His ears had firmed up somewhat and they were much less matted. 'I've been to many worlds and times, Lilith.'

'Just like the Clockworkers,' she said. 'The High and Mighties always said travel between other eras was possible, and other worlds were a doddle. They even said the same about other dimensions and universes.'

Panda nodded sagely, fiddling with a doll's bonnet. The sunlight today was pinkish and sticky. He really thought he ought to protect his ears. Lilith was wearing a frilled purple monstrosity of a dress, leaving not a scrap of skin exposed to the sun. Her golden hair was tucked up inside what looked like a top hat and she wore heavy black goggles, so that he couldn't see her expression at all.

'Your world is in a very small universe indeed, Lilith,' he told her gently. 'It's a kind of adjunct to the one I know. Your place in the world is really quite small.'

'That's how I've always felt,' Lilith sighed. 'As if… there's no elbow room here.'

Panda smiled. 'That's why I'm here, you know. I came here especially for you.'

'In the… omnibus? *The Twenty Two Putney Common*?'

'Oh, indeed.'

Now they were at the secret door under the tangled black vines that led to the garden where Lilith went to smoke. She felt around inside her clutch bag for the ancient key.

'*The Twenty Two* was wonderful,' she said. 'It was like something I felt I already knew.'

Panda simply nodded, and waited to follow her into the garden where she felt most at home, here within the shadows of Wherewithal House.

*

Dick cracked out in loud laughter when she presented Panda to him.

'What the devil's that meant to be?' he gasped. He was holding his sides and actually rolling about on the overgrown grass.

Panda hopped down lightly onto the ground and stood glowering at the young man in the tattered highwayman's cloak.

'And who, may I ask, are you?' he bellowed.

The smile faded from Dick's face. 'Your stuffed bear talks!' he shouted at Lilith. 'Is this some kind of magic thing from the Clockworks?'

Lilith rolled her eyes and grinned at them both. 'He's a new friend. And you should be more polite to him. Panda, this is Dick.'

Panda boggled his eyes at the young man, and when he thought he'd boggled enough he turned to look at the rampant garden around them. It was walled in by crumbling brickwork and every square inch of the place was choked with fecund plantlife. It was the liveliest part of the gardens, and indeed of Wherewithal House itself. Flowers and thorns tangled promiscuously along the ground, through the twisted trees and up the orange walls. All the plants were striving upwards to catch the smouldering sunlight. All the vegetation was frozen in an attitude of supplication.

It was Lilith's little wilderness. It was the only part of her new home that felt like it had anything to do with her.

Panda wandered off, exploring. Strange insects slumbered through the warm air.

'He's from the omnibus,' Lilith told Dick. 'He followed us all the way back here yesterday. Last night he climbed up to my window and demanded to be let in. He's here to rescue me, he says.'

Dick laughed again, and there was something in that laugh that Lilith didn't like. Something sardonic and beyond his years. 'What's an omni… bus?'

'The Twenty Two Putney machine we found yesterday. After we were home the word just came to me. It popped into my head. It was familiar, Dick… I already knew it.'

'Must be something from the Clockworks then,' Dick frowned. 'They must have these omni things in Saga City.'

She shook her head. 'I don't think so. This is something else.'

'And how's this little toy going to rescue you, huh?'

'I don't know. But he says he will. He says I don't belong here.'

'We can all see that,' Dick said, with another hint of bitterness. Lilith stared at him. Could it really be that he was jealous of Panda? Was he being like this because Lilith had made another friend in her lonely captivity?

Now Panda was back, surveying the two of them with great interest. 'A remarkable garden,' he muttered. 'Now. Let's consider the matter in hand, hmm?'

'What's that?' Dick shrugged. He was happy to spend the day lazing, hiding from his chores at home and regaling Lilith with tales of his derring-do. She noted that he had his pistols with him today. Clearly he was ready for some highway robbing later on. She longed to go with him, one day, on one of these forays. She had even wondered about making a mask and cloak of her own out of bedsheets. But Dick had solemnly refused to listen to her suggestion. The mistresses would have him hanged and quartered if he led the young miss into a life of crime.

'You,' Panda looked at the young robber beadily, 'are going to do what you did yesterday, and help Lilith here, and my good self, to escape from this dreadful place. You are going to take us back into the wilderness to the bus.'

'The bus?'

'The Celestial Omnibus,' said Panda grandly. 'The Number 22, Bound for Putney Common. You should remember, man, you were there yesterday! Breaking in and rummaging about in other people's property!'

Lilith looked excited at this plan. It was on the tip of her tongue to start begging the older boy, but she managed to prevent herself in time. It didn't do to seem too needy.

'I don't fancy going back there,' yawned Dick. 'What more is there to see? Anyway, I've got things planned for today. I'm headed for the Highway and rich pickings.'

'You will help us escape!' thundered Panda.

'It's easy, escaping from here,' Dick said. 'Lilith here has been beyond the bounds of Wherewithal house many times. That's not the problem. It's having nowhere to go, once you're out. That's the problem. If you keep walking the wilderness, you'll be dead in three days. There's nothing out there till Saga City and that's thousands of miles.'

Panda looked thoughtful. 'I know what I'm doing, Mr Dick. You'll see. But Lilith and I will need your help. And we ought to work together, you know. Lilith has a destiny far beyond this gloomy old house.'

'She does, does she?' Dick grinned.

'Yes,' said Panda, looking very serious all of a sudden. 'And you are one of those chosen by destiny to help Lilith and myself on our way. We are all tangled up in this, and we need to get on with the adventure laid out for us.'

Both Dick and Lilith stared at the small creature, slowly taking in his words. Though the young highwayman would never have admitted it, something in Panda's words was striking a very deep and resonant chord in him. He knew Panda was speaking the truth. Somehow he had seen all this coming, from the very first day he had ever met Lilith. He knew that she was bound for some amazing destiny. He had always known that. She wasn't just some orphaned brat. She would grow up to become… somebody incredible.

'All right,' Dick said at last, his voice quite different now; lacking that mocking tone. 'I'll lead you out of here. I'll show you the way back to your alien carriage. But I'm not walking all that way again.'

'Then how will we get there?' asked Lilith, hope rising in her chest.

'We go to the Highway,' Dick announced, jumping up from the grass. 'Just as I planned, but all three of us. And we steal a car. And we'll be there before we know it. How does that sound?'

Panda rubbed his ears thoughtfully, a gesture which Lilith would soon come to learn meant that he was trying to conceal his excitement and glee while maintaining a calm exterior. 'I think, Mr Dick, that sounds like a very good idea indeed.'

24.

That night, when it had all gone quiet in the desert wastes, the Vizier who had captured us tried to steal my notebook. His chubby arm came sneaking and snaking its way between the bars of our cage. It would have been more straightforward for him to send in one of his tattooed soldiers to simply grab the book off me - but, oh no. He was more sly and cunning than that. He wanted to lay his hands on the book himself. It was somehow valuable to him.

Simon leapt into action. As soon as he noticed what the Vizier was up to, he jumped up and grabbed hold of the Vizier's fat hand and wouldn't let go. 'Quick, Kelly! Help me!'

There was a bit of a confusing struggle in the dark then, with both me and Simon trying to stamp on his hand, and me trying to keep a tight hold on my black notebook and stow it away in my backpack again. At last the Vizier snatched his hand back through the bars, hissing at us. Behind him, round their fire, his three soldiers were chuckling at this scene.

The Vizier glowered as he blew on his smarting fingers. 'You can't be allowed to run about with an object like that,' he gasped. 'A small creature like you. It could lead to all kinds of disaster. You don't know the powers an object like that has, here in Hyspero. Why don't you just hand it over to me, hmm? That would be safer all round...'

I narrowed my eyes at him, suspiciously. 'Which object would that be?'

'Don't mess me about, girl. I mean your... your... book. You know what I mean. I think it best that you hand it over to me.'

Simon tried to stand in front of me protectively. 'Well, she won't! That book was a present from me! And so was the special pen! And she won't just give them away to a creep like you! Will you, Kelly?'

The Vizier's arched brows went up a notch in surprise and greed. 'She has a pen as well, has she? A special pen..?'

'What's it got to do with you, anyway?' I snapped. 'Why all this fuss?'

His face darkened. 'It is very clear that you know hardly anything about our land.'

'That's true,' I said. 'We haven't been here long.'

'Then let me explain one or two things,' said the Vizier. His voice was oily and menacing. 'Only the Scarlet Empress has the power to Write Things Down. Only she has the right and might to turn thought into written language. Only she may Write Things Down and Have Them Come True. Such is her magic.'

Simon and I were listening very carefully. We had learned to pick up every clue we could about how this world worked. No matter who the information came from, and however untrustworthy they may prove to be, we still had to be alert to clues about the laws and rules of Hyspero.

'Anyone else even attempting to read or write is committing a very grave offence,' the Vizier went on. 'Possession of a book is unheard of. So ... perhaps you can see why it is best if you simply hand your book and your pen over into my custody...'

'No way,' I said. 'I don't care if it's against the law. You're not having them.'

The Vizier smirked. 'Then, when we arrive in the central city of Hyspero itself, it will be all the harder for you.'

I shrugged. I was putting on a pretty brave face, but inside I was shaking a bit. I didn't like what we'd got into at all.

'You have a very nasty future ahead of you,' sighed the Vizier. 'To be found in possession of writing materials! And to be captured and Selected, too! Why, things can't really get any worse for you, can they?' He whistled through his small, square teeth.

Simon broke in, 'We still don't know what this Selection business is.'

'Your life essence is required by the Empress,' said the Vizier. 'It is a small price to pay. Hyspero has the most marvellous ruler. She is eternally marvellous, of course - but to keep her that way, she needs to absorb life essences. Each village and town and city in this land donates two of its people each and every season to keep the Empress alive. It is, as I say, a very small price to pay.'

'She's like some kind of vampire!' Simon cried out. 'She drinks their blood? She's after OUR blood to keep her alive?'

'Not blood,' the Vizier shook his head. 'The life essence is rather harder to get at. Why, we could get blood simply by cutting you open, couldn't we? No... this magical ingredient is harder to come by. The Empress's willing volunteers have to be... smelted down. And that's what you, Kelly and Simon, have been selected for. SMELTING!'

It was me shouting out this time. 'I don't like the sound of that!'

The Vizier shrugged. 'You have no choice in the matter. Now you are in Hyspero, and you are subject to the divine will of the Scarlet Empress.'

With that, he swept away, with his cloak swirling darkly behind him.

Next to me, Simon was rigid with horror at the very idea of being smelted down.

I lowered my voice, and tried to reassure him. 'We'll escape, Simon. We have to. Don't worry.'

The Vizier's voice came drifting over to us from where he was sitting with his soldiers. They were mocking and jeering at us from their place by the crackling fire.

I saw Simon's eyes flash with determination. 'I know, Kelly,' he said. 'We're a team, yeah? And we can do anything.'

25.

They travelled quite companionably and, within the hour, they were emerging from the train as it paused briefly under the arches of Darlington station. The train and its passengers were about to zoom off down south, to London, and the two of them felt harried getting Magda and her chair safely onto the platform.

'All this rush, rush,' Magda sighed. 'I am glad I now live out in the countryside. You know, don't you, that is where I live now?'

'No, I didn't,' Terry said. Magda had once lived quite near to his flat, in a maisonette of her own. In fact, he'd assumed she was still there, within easy reach of her book shop and everything she needed in the town centre. How she was managing in some place in the wilds was worrying to him.

'You must come and see me,' she said. 'Yes, I will cook a meal for you, like I used to do, remember? And we will watch some TV and talk. This is very fortuitous, this running into you...'

Terry found himself trying to wriggle out of the commitment. He wasn't sure why. All he wanted to do was hole up in his own apartment and not see anyone for a few days. Maybe get on with some work. The only real thing he had to do was teach his writing class at the Arts Centre, on Monday evening. Now this woman was breaking into his solitude. She was kindly but she wouldn't be dissuaded.

As he pushed her chair down the long, sloping road from the station, through the streets towards the town centre, passing the old Civic theatre and the Magistrates Courts as they went, she was talking as if it was all settled. He would come to hers on Sunday evening for a good, home-cooked meal. He was too skinny and sallow and needed feeding up. And it would be good for her to hear about all his successes and plans...

He groaned inwardly, but then decided that he'd better perk up. He'd best look keen. He owed her a lot. She had encouraged him when school had failed him. She was interested in his daft, nonsensical tales when his parents were not.

'Okay, okay,' Terry laughed, as they waited for the lights to change on the main crossing. 'I'll bring us some drink and I'll tell you what else…'

'Absinthe!' Magda burst out. 'Oh, let us have absinthe again! Through the little spoon with the sugar cubes, eh? Its taste reminds me so much of Paris before the war…'

'Absinthe, then,' he smiled, quite sure that she was making it all up. How old was she if she'd been in Paris before the war? 'And shall I bring my boxset?'

'Your what?'

'It's just recently come out from Network DVD. '*The Iris Wildthyme Show*' – the complete series. We could watch it together!'

'Oh,' she said, uncertainly. As he pushed her along, he couldn't see her expression, but he had a feeling it was troubled. 'Oh, all right then.'

'Well, you've read my stories and books about the old bat, ever since I was a kid! I thought you might like to see some of the actual episodes at last.'

'Yes, you're right,' she said, her voice brightening. 'And I would love to watch them with you. My TV set is very old though…'

'They're very old episodes,' he smiled.

All of a sudden he found he was really looking forward to tomorrow evening now. Magda wasn't such bad company after all. A few drinks and she'd start off on the crazy reminiscences. She would talk about her years in New York and Paris and Cologne. She'd talk about the book trade and some of the scandals she knew of, surrounding various writers and publishers. It'd be great.

He waited with her for a while at the bus stop. There was one particularly rural service that ran every hour to her new neck of the woods. She filled him in on instructions for getting to her cottage, and she even drew him a map on the back of a crushed packet of fags unearthed from her bag.

'Now go,' she told him. 'You're waiting here won't bring the bus faster. You look beat, my boy. Go home to your luxury apartment and leave an old woman in peace!'

Indomitable, he thought. That's what she was. And so he felt all right about leaving her waiting in the drizzle on Queen Street, and hurrying home to his apartment on the fringes of the town centre.

*

That night as he tried his hardest to sleep, turning this way and that on his memory foam mattress, Terry couldn't get the events of the day out of his mind. Just when he thought he was falling asleep and the dreams started, he'd see faces looming out of a spectral mist. They were lowering down on him, saying words he couldn't hear. Trying to tell him… warn him… but for some reason nothing was breaking through. Just some discordant, cheesy music… which he soon realized was a nightmare version of the Iris Wildthyme theme tune… It was playing hurdy-gurdy style, as if at an old fashioned fair.

The faces revolved about him, gurning and shouting silently… Bill Fordyce Tie-In Genre Legend in his sharp suit, looking very pleased with himself. Timeslip Mike, looking shifty somehow. Magda had a greenish tinge to her face and her hair was plastered back and wet, with seaweed tangled through. Here were other faces, of the people queueing up for his autograph in their books – they came back to him now… the pasty-faced man who'd bought three copies of both books (one for reading, one for mint and a third for Ebay) and a mumsy-looking woman with two teenage kids in tow. The skinny Goth bloke with all the tattoos and his frazzled-looking girlfriend in the leopardskin macintosh. And lastly here was the face of the man in the anorak. The man he knew he had disappointed. Terry had disavowed Iris. He had dismissed her. Betrayed her. And this man's face had crumpled as if he was about to cry.

I was talking just like Bill Fordyce would, Terry thought. Just like anyone would. And it wasn't true. I don't even know why I said it. I'm sorry, anorak man. She's real to me, too. She is! And ordinarily I would never say things like that.

But the anorak man's face was still glaring at him, still on the verge of tears.

26.

Lilith couldn't believe how quickly things happened after that.

It seemed that, when her two companions put their heads together, they could act pretty swiftly. Under the blazing noonday sun they absconded once more from the wretched grounds of Wherewithal House, knowing full well that there would be angry eyes behind those dark windows, watching them go. But what can they do, Lilith wondered? The mistresses can't come running out after us. The servants wouldn't want to pursue us through the wilderness. Suddenly she saw that she had always been free to roam, and to take off by herself. There were no bars or tall fences around stately Wherewithal.

Up until now though, she had had no objective. There had been nothing to run to. But now there was the Celestial Omnibus and Lilith looked back barely once that morning.

Dick took them to the Highway, which Lilith had never been to before. It took more than an hour to get there, but when they did it was worth seeing. It turned out that the Highway was a plastiglass tube, taller than a house, stretching far across the sands. Infinitely far, in fact. Dick explained that these tubular roads ran like veins across the entire world, connecting the major conurbations. He pointed down the silvery length of the road, to where it went hazy and melted on the horizon. 'Follow it all the way and you'd eventually come to Saga City, Lilith. That's your way home.'

The girl shook her head firmly. 'Not any more it's not.'

Dick set to work on a narrow doorway in the highway. Panda and Lilith both expressed surprised at his expertise. Neither of them had even noticed there was a doorway there at all. Dick grinned and looked every inch the old hand, crying out in triumph as he made the door slide open. A wheezing cacophony burst into the desert. The raucous noise of heavy traffic echoing through miles of pipelines. Straight away Lilith started to choke on the fumes.

'It's a filthy way to travel,' Dick said. 'Only a tiny proportion of the Clockworks folk are allowed to commute between cities, and they all die young. But they have no choice in the matter.'

The more about life with the High and Mighties Lilith heard about, the less she liked the sound of it. She didn't belong with them. She couldn't. Somehow she knew all her instincts were wrong. It was no accident that her only memory of living in Saga City was of escaping into the Woods.

She and Panda watched with baited breath as Dick stepped into the noxious interior of the Highway. He was in full robber's regalia – his tattered black cloak, ruffled shirt, and a tricorn hat that was singed all over. His masklike goggles were in place as he listened for the first car heading his way. He stood resolute in the tunnel and prepared to flag it down.

'I don't approve of people carrying guns,' Panda said sniffily.

Lilith didn't say anything to that. She agreed, really, but she also wanted Dick to succeed. He wouldn't hurt anyone, she knew.

But he would.

Lilith didn't really know what Dick was like in his work. She didn't know how brutal he sometimes had to be. She didn't even know that the reason he had chosen to break through this particular access point in the highway was that, even though there were other, closer ones, they were littered with evidence. There were bodies in Clockworks finery, still melting and becoming skeletons in the desert sands. There were smashed and pillaged vehicles that he'd driven off road. There was plenty of evidence for what Dick got up to.

Lilith and Panda watched helplessly as Dick went about his business.

He flagged down the next car that came along. It was an executive class vehicle, with and important-looking man and woman carrying a cargo of fancy-looking paperwork. Dick dug through the boxes of scrolls and exclaimed in frustration – there was nothing worth stealing here. He pressed his blaster to the temples of the passenger and driver. Both were periwigged and dressed for the city. Out here in the desert in their pearls and their ruffles they looked ludicrous. Lilith couldn't stand watching Dick terrorize them. She marched over.

'Let them go, Dick. We just want their car, remember?'

He nodded grimly, half listening to her, half staring greedily at the podgy, frightened faces of his victims. He instructed the woman to bring the car out of the Highway and onto the desert sands. Out here it looked so pristine and new. Within minutes of travelling across the wilderness, that beautiful bodywork would be destroyed.

The man was staring at Lilith as his counterpart and Dick were fussing with the car. He ignored the Panda in her arms and he was staring into her face with a curious expression. Lilith felt more uncomfortable than she already was and returned his questioning gaze fiercely. 'What is it? Why are you looking at me like that?'

The fat man shook his head and looked away. Lilith hated that. She hated that he was afraid of her. She wanted to ask him, to beg him… Why had he been staring? What could he read in her face? What had he seen there? Did he recognize her? Her individually, or her provenance? Did he see the face of a Clockworks child?

But Lilith was never to know what he saw.

Dick had turned away from the car and shot the fat man in the back of his skull.

He did it without a by-your-leave or a comment or anything. The Clockworks woman screamed and the sound died in her throat as Dick whirled about and shot her too. He shot her in the heart and she collapsed at once to the sandy floor, her vast skirts billowing out around her.

Panda and Lilith didn't say anything. He froze in her arms. They both stared at Dick. They couldn't believe what they had just witnessed.

Dick slid away his pistols and frowned at them. 'What?'

Lilith gripped Panda hard. 'You shouldn't have done that.'

There was a pause. The fat man's legs were jiggling about in the dust. Twitching. He was slow dying.

'It's easier,' Dick said. 'They can't rat on us. They can't describe us.'

Lilith had tears down her face. 'They were people!'

He shook his head. 'High and Mighties. They aren't normal people. We're nothing to them. Desert rats.'

Lilith felt Panda squeeze her arm. Not to reassure her. Not to be nice. He was warning her. Don't rile him. Don't set him off again. She looked down at Panda's eyes and realized what he was communicating to her.

The boy is mad. Don't fall foul of him.

'Now,' said Dick. 'If you're ready – our carriage is waiting.'

27.

On Tyneside that night it so happened that the anorak man was dreaming of the licensed fanfic author. Sammy lay in a welter of sweaty sheets and duvet, having horrible dreams. He had seen to his own tea, microwaving a fish pie from the fridge. It was something that should have been cooked from the freezer. As he ate them the prawns seemed to fizz against his palate and he'd thought it was because he'd just brushed his teeth. But the funny taste had haunted him and he went to bed expecting to be wracked with food poisoning at any moment.

His mum must have gone straight from her yoga class out on the town. Meeting the girls perhaps, bingo and a dance. His mum had a very active social life. Sometimes he thought she stayed out so much, and got herself involved in so many activities simply to be away from him. She felt crowded at home as much by his presence as she did the mounds of rubbish and stuff she and her son had collected. Sammy preferred to be at home, even with the musty smells of bat droppings and old, stained carpets, undone washing and dishes steepled in the sink.

This wasn't food poisoning, thank goodness. There was nothing untoward happening downstairs as he turned over and over in bed. It was his head that was spinning with ideas and images. Too many to keep up with. Occasionally he would sit up and shake his head, and then his whole torso. He realized that he was behaving like he was an Etch-a-Sketch. One of those silvery screens that you covered with scribble by turning the dials. They worked like magic, those toys. And when you had created a mess on the screen and covered it with scribble, all you had to do was give it a good shaking, and it would all become clear again.

Sammy wished he could do that with his head. With his home. With his whole life tonight.

He sat up and clambered out of bed, thinking maybe some hot milk would do him some good. But that meant stumbling down the stairs at night, heavy-limbed and groggily trying to avoid bashing into the several hostess trolleys on the top landing, the heaps of old letters and flyers piled on each step. He could slip and fall and lie twisted and dead on the hall carpet. A fine sight for his mum to see when she eventually came home.

Sammy looked at the window sill and there was his Panda collection, staring out at the rooftops of the estate outside. They were silhouetted against the sherbet colours of the streetlamps. He moved closer to examine the latest addition to his collection. This was where he had placed him – the new, lifelike Panda – right before going to bed. But he wasn't there now.

That couldn't be right. Sammy rubbed his eyes and stared harder at the line of toys. Sure enough, there was the small gap he had made, pushing apart Rubbish Tip Panda and Amanda Panda. That was where he had wedged the newcomer, some time before midnight. But the interloper was gone.

Sammy's heart was thumping like crazy.

What if it wasn't a real Panda? What if it was a tiny homicidal person he'd unleashed inside the house? Or what if it was a toy possessed by some malign kind of spirit?

But none of these things were possible, Sammy told himself. Those things are what would happen in a book. In a book of the sort Sammy loved, those kind of things – tiny serial killers and displaced souls – were quite permissible.

But not in Sammy's everyday world of muddle and trash.

He negotiated the cluttered landing and staircase like someone who was expert at living in a warzone. He took the copy of the fanzine he had bought that day with him, clutched in one hand as he made his way to the kitchen. Once there he put a small pan of milk on the hob to heat, and swept an arm across the pine table so he had some space. It was silent down here, apart from the occasional rumbles from the heating. The pilot light on the boiler would suddenly ignite and set all of the pipes rumbling. Sammy leafed through the A5 photocopied pamphlet, pausing to read some fanfic and tutting at various errors the author was making.

The typing was a mess, too, with letters out of kilter with each other. There were smudges and capitals and flecks of punctuation in the wrong place. Someone was still using a typewriter! This was incredible in this day and age, Sammy thought. Even a fanzine ought to have better standards. Though there was something heart-warming about it, he had to admit. And actually, as he read on, the story wasn't that bad either. It was one of those Iris tales set in the time that she operated out of a South Kensington address, above a swanky shoe shop. She and Panda had an office there, and were regularly brought in by MIAOW – a secret government agency – to solve strange mysteries usually to do with time and / or monsters and showbiz.

The author seemed to have a good grasp of the main characters. Sammy could believe in those voices as they bickered and quibbled in their usual way, through this odd fragment of an adventure. He flicked back to the first page to see who the author was, but he couldn't find a credit.

It was rare that Sammy found fanfic that he really approved of. His standards for Iris stories were very high. Authors really had to enter the spirit of the thing. They had to give themselves over into her world...

That's why he approved of Terry Kelly, in the spotty shirt. His Iris Wildthyme books really captured something. They weren't perfect. But he was closer to the essence of the old dame than most were. Bill Fordyce's were pathetic. He had his own agenda and no understanding of Wildthyme's world. He was someone Sammy expected to be disappointed by. But not spotty shirt. Not Terry Kelly. It had cut him to the quick that Terry Kelly had been as dismissive as he was today.

It had put Sammy off reading both their books, actually.

The milk spilled over with an angry hiss. Sammy jumped up and started mopping round immediately. When he drank the milk it tasted singed.

There was a crash and a clatter and Sammy almost choked on the skin of the milk. He thought it was someone at the front door. Perhaps his mum was in the porch, fumbling with her keys. But the noise came from the kitchen door. Sammy held his breath and fought his impulse to flee. He remembered the woman down the street who'd been sitting drinking coffee in her back kitchen, in broad daylight. And some gangland criminal had come at her back door with an axe. Some of them had no fear at all. And now it was – what? – five a.m and Mum was still out and surely there would be robbers coming through the back garden. The grass was waist high and the back fence broken. It wouldn't take much effort to get in here. Sammy felt like he was having a heart attack.

He cried out as the clattering noise came again. But he found himself being brave, all of a sudden. Crazily brave. He stepped forward on the old kitchen tiles and peered around the corner of the table. Now he had a full view of the back door.

The cat flap was rocking back and forth, and letting in an icy chill.

It had been years since they had had a cat. When Muffit died just after the millennium Mum had said no more. No more strays, cos they wind up breaking your heart, they do. She refused to go through all that again. And Sammy had been devout, obeying his mum. He had never let another mangy moggy through the catflap, or up the back steps from their wilderness of a garden. He hadn't put out milk or bits or scraps of raw bacon. He hadn't let those little faces and begging paws sway him. The catflap had been nailed up. Sammy had done it himself – messily, ham-fistedly, as he did everything. But at least the flap wouldn't let in any more creatures who might steal his mother's heart.

It's been a lonely house ever since, Sammy thought. Somewhere at the back of his brain he happened upon this clear thought. The shock had jolted it out of him. Yes, that's what had gone wrong here. We don't have anything or anyone, do we? Mother and son – neither of them – had anything to love.

But could this really be a cat? What kind of cat could pull out nails with his teeth or claws?

Sammy watched as the catflap swung outwards again, very slowly.

Horror movie slowly, and with an agonizing squeal.

Something was opening it from the outside.

A head suddenly popped through the square hole. A small, furry white head with tufted black ears. The face glanced around crossly, inquisitively. And then those button bright eyes fixed on Sammy.

28.

Steeling ourselves bravely, Simon and I started to climb the rope ladder, with the three foxes following nimbly behind.

We didn't dare look down, because we knew that we were extremely high up by now. And when we looked up, all we could see was the endless blue of the alien sky and - directly above us - the ominous inky black of that nostril. It loomed closer and closer as we heaved our worn out bodies into the unknown.

We were all scrapes and scabs and cuts and bruises. We were covered in dust and sweat and sand and blood.

But we were clambering into the palace and we were going to meet the woman who the foxes worked for. We were going to meet their mysterious mistress...

'Just keep going,' Frank Fox called jauntily from below. 'Go up to the very top where it narrows and you'll find yourself in a kind of corridor.' He made it seem as if he scampered up people's noses every day.

We hauled ourselves over the chin, across those pouty lips and, after what seemed like ages, up into the nose itself.

My arms were aching. I could hear Simon scrabbling and complaining on the green ladder behind me. Apart from that it was weirdly quiet in the nostril.

On trembling legs, I took another step and another and another, my feet struggling for purchase, my knuckles and knees grazed and stinging and sticky with blood.

Then it was getting lighter. Near the top of the nose, where it all became narrow, there was a soft radiance in the air. There was also a curious smell. Before Simon or I even knew what it was, our stomachs were rumbling.

'That smells just like bacon,' Simon shouted excitedly. 'Someone's frying bacon!' This made me look down and the view I got was very disorienting. All I could see was an oval of searing sunlight and the silhouettes of the others coming up after me. Far below were the red rocks.

Why was someone frying bacon up Make Up Girl's nose? There was another smell too. Someone was baking cakes.

At last I came to the top of the ladder and there was indeed a sort of corridor there. It led straight into what should have been the giant head's brain. There was a green door at the end, waiting for us. But there was no sign of whoever had thrown the rope ladder down. I stayed where I was to get my breath back, pausing while the others caught up.

The delicious smells of cooking and baking were almost overpowering here in the corridor to the brain. It was tortuous, having to hang on.

Simon lay down on the gritty floor and he was exhausted. 'Can we go for a less tiring adventure next time?' he moaned.

'I think it's only just starting, Simon,' I said.

Then the three foxes were springing up onto the ledge. 'Oh, good,' grinned Frank. 'She must be making a little snack for us.'

'Yip!' said Muchless.

'She'll be very glad you're here,' Notso told us. 'She's been waiting for you.'

'You foxes haven't told us anything about why your mistress wants to see us,' I said. 'You could be leading us into awful danger...'

'Don't you trust us?' asked Frank. Even in the dim light Simon and I could see that he looked hurt.

'Yeah, we do,' I said. 'But why does it all have to be mysterious?'

Frank looked shifty. 'Because the mistress is here secretly. Nobody knows she is here. Only friends are allowed up here in the nerve centre. If word got out this is where she lives... well...'

Now my interest was really piqued. Someone important was hiding herself away inside her own palace? Who would need to hide away like that? 'What would happen if people knew she was here?'

Frank looked very uneasy. 'I'll let her tell you herself,' he said. 'But there are spies everywhere in Hyspero.'

Frank and his brothers led us quickly down the empty, glowing corridor to the green door. 'This is the way into the nerve centre,' he whispered, licking his black lips nervously. 'Only trusted friends get in here.'

'We're friends,' Simon said.

'And we're trustworthy,' I added. And we were both ravenous. Frank carefully opened the door.

Inside we found ourselves inside a large, circular room crammed with banks of electronic gadgets and futuristic computers. Everything looked like it had come out of a science fiction film. The computers were the sort that lit up different colours and had spools of tape going round and reams of paper coming out of everywhere. There were screens on the walls but all they showed were snowstorms. The very air was alive with the chattering and whirring of the machines.

Simon and I were quite impressed. The nerve centre looked exactly like it should. Every machine had buttons and levers that cried out to be pressed and flicked and switched. It was that kind of place. The computers looked like the type that would talk in droning, stilted mechanical voices.

'Don't touch anything,' Frank instructed as he led us through the humming room. 'This is the nerve centre, and the mistress's nerves are extremely sensitive...'

'Isn't it grand?' said Notso.

'I bet you don't have gear like this at home, do you?' Muchless said boastfully.

'Hmm,' said Simon. He was quite keen on science-fictiony things and I knew he would have liked the chance to have a poke around, but the foxes were urging us on, deeper into the secret base.

Frank was holding open another door - a purple one this time - and ushering us through. 'The mistress would like to see you in her private apartment.'

We had to step down another corridor. This one was beautifully and elaborately tiled in ice cream green. There were strange sculptures everywhere. There was no telling what they were supposed to be.

Down the other end, Frank knocked politely on yet another door. The smell of baking and cooking was strongest here.

'Is this it?' I whispered. 'Who lives here?'

At that very instant we heard a voice from within this inner sanctum:

'Come in! Hurry up, you lot! I've been waiting AGES!'

It was a loud voice that I recognised immediately. But it couldn't be...!

I grabbed at Simon so hard I almost knocked him into one of the weird alien sculptures.

'What's the matter with you?' he squealed, steadying himself. But I was rigid and frozen to the spot. I couldn't get my mouth to work properly.

The door flew open and there before us stood the woman that the foxes called their mistress. She was wearing a floor-length flowery housecoat and she had curlers in her hair. She looked absolutely delighted, and she flung out her arms to embrace us all.

'I knew you were coming,' grinned Aunty Iris. *'So I baked us a bloody big cake!'*

29.

Lilith remembered very little about the journey across the sands that day.

Vaguely she thought about the expedition she and Dick had made yesterday, along the same route. It had all seemed so simple then. No tinge of brutality and death. Dick had been a hero to her, plain and simple. Unlike the other adults she knew, he had time for her. He was willing to spend a whole day trekking into the wilderness with her, purely to keep her entertained.

Today it was like he had changed completely. Another person was hunched at the wheel of this stolen car, driving recklessly and ignoring his passengers. He was a killer, stuffed full of greed, ambition, impatience.

Lilith hugged Panda to herself all the way there.

They arrived at the ravine when the sun was at its hottest. She recalled the blazing heat of yesterday, and the sheer effort it had taken to climb down to the omnibus in the deep shade.

Panda stood at the lip of the hole in the desert and stared down.

'What does he even want with it?' he asked Lilith, sotto voce. 'He can't pilot the bus. He doesn't have the knowhow.'

'Perhaps he just wants to loot it,' Lilith frowned. 'That's why he stole a car. To fill the boot with treasure...'

'Oh, how awful,' Panda sighed. 'That it should all come to this.' After everything. After so many years on the bus.' He turned angrily on the girl. 'Why are you so rubbish at making friends? Couldn't you see he's a bad'un?'

Lilith looked as if she was about to cry. Her protective clothing billowed in the noonday breeze and she lifted her goggles to see Panda more clearly. 'But I thought he was good... I never thought he'd... he'd actually k-kill anyone.'

Across the other side of the ravine Dick heard them conferring. He was busy sorting out ropes and pulleys and attaching them to the stolen car. He glared at his companions and said, 'You better not be discussing me.'

'No, no...' Lilith said.

'There's stuff down there, aboard that machine,' Dick said, fervently. 'Important stuff. Techno stuff. I just know it's valuable. There are people who'd pay a lot for the stuff that's down there. And it's your job to help me get it out.'

Lilith said, 'What stuff? All I saw were old journals and clothing and bits of ornaments.'

'She's right,' Panda added. 'A load of old rubbish! Just the junky remains of a mad old woman with no sense or taste!'

'Don't lie to me,' Dick snarled. 'It's an omnibus. You said so. I know what they are. They come from the Clockworks. They come from the High and Mighties.'

'Rubbish!' jeered Panda. 'You don't know what you're talking about! What are you? A servant boy! What would you know about the High and Mighties?'

'Don't rile him,' Lilith warned. Then she shouted at Dick, 'You were my friend! My only friend in the whole of Wherewithal House, apart from Mary. Now I can see what you're really like!'

Dick tossed his head and laughed crazily. 'Mary? She's not your friend. Mary can't stand you either. Don't kid yourself there. You're just some whining, moody little brat that no one could give a damn about. We just pretended to be your friends. We knew it'd be worthwhile in the end. That's all.'

Panda watched Lilith as her face crumpled. She stifled a sob. But she didn't say anything. She wouldn't give the young highwayman the satisfaction. Good girl, Panda thought. You keep those feelings inside. Don't give anyone the chance to hurt you any more.

'Right,' said Dick, brandishing his polished pistols once more. 'You two better start climbing down there. I want that treasure. And I want you to start dragging it out.'

Lilith and Panda had no choice.

They shuffled to the craggy hole in the ground and began to lower themselves into the hot darkness. Lilith went first, recalling her successful route from the previous day and Panda followed her down, muttering that, given his size, he had twice as far to clamber.

Dick shouted and goaded them on, standing close to the edge, tightening and checking the ropes. Lilith wished he'd let his two hostages use the ropes, but it was clear he was only interested in the safety of his precious artefacts.

'Do you know what he means to steal, Panda?' she whispered.

Panda was rather breathless. 'I suppose, the way he's talking, he wants the inner workings of the bus. The dimensional drive.'

'The what?'

'The gubbins that once allowed the bus to travel between all the dimensions,' said Panda. 'You don't know about that, do you?'

'I don't know about anything,' mumbled Lilith, feeling very sorry for herself. She looked down to see the sandy bottom of the ravine looming below her. She was level with the roof of the omnibus. Dick's loud imprecations were more muffled now. She could block them out of her mind and feel safe for a while. Still she felt like crying loud and violent tears at the loss of a one-time friend. She couldn't believe that Dick and Mary had merely pretended to be fond of her. She refused to believe anything so horrible.

Then, after a few more minutes' rapid descent, they made it to the bottom. Panda simply jumped the last bit, landing in Lilith's arms.

They both stared up at the scarred and dusty vehicle. Even under the damage the scarlet paintwork managed to stand out brilliantly.

'Whose omnibus was it, Panda?' Lilith asked.

'Ahh,' he smiled, sitting on her shoulder and feeling a little like Long John Silver's parrot. 'That's a long story now, Lilith. I'm not sure whether I should tell you. It might ruin things for you. All the things that are still to come.'

Suddenly Dick's voice rang out from above. 'What are you two doing down there? What are you up to?' He sounded wilder than ever. There was even the sharp ricochet of a bullet, bouncing off the shell of the wrecked bus.

'He's shooting!' Panda cried. 'The boy's a maniac! QUICK! Get inside, Iris!'

Lilith didn't even stop to complain that he'd got her name wrong. Instead she hurried to the doors and whooshed them open. Then she flung herself into the bus and the whole interior flooded with light.

A teasmade began pinging and producing steam. Five kinds of cuckoo clock called out different o'clocks. The stereo system burst into crackling noise and started playing Northern Soul. At the bar in the corner two automatic cocktail mixers shook into action.

And the engine of the bus was churning and grinding.

'What's happening..?' cried Lilith as the floor beneath her buckled and juddered.

Panda laughed out loud, bouncing up and down on a faded chaise longue. 'Can't you see? Don't you know? It's

151

coming back to life! It's all because of you! It's starting all over again, Iris!'

'What..?' cried Lilith, completely terrified by now.

Panda bellowed at her happily: 'We're setting off once more, my dear!'

PART TWO

Middles

1.

It had been a nothing kind of a day.

Terry spent the requisite time at his computer to make him feel as if a day's work had been done. He had fiddled around the edges of a new book outline. He had fended off a few emails. There was one very complicated one about ebook rights from his agent that he didn't really understand. And then there was a short and to-the-point message from Magda from *Magda's Mysteries* bookshop. He had seen her the other day on the train from Newcastle. She was reminding him of his promise to come to dinner that night.

He had to admit, his heart sank when he first read the reminder. He could do without the company tonight. Last thing in the afternoon he had a writing class at the Arts Centre to teach and all he could imagine doing afterwards is coming home to his flat and passing out on his bed.

Why am I so tired? He wondered vaguely. The hypochondriac inside stirred his sluggish head. Oh, it's probably just because I've spent so much time in front of the screen…

He'd worked on four different novel proposals since the day in Newcastle and his talk with Magda. He had been spending time pushing at four different stories.

There was no wriggling out of the visit to Magda. The thought of her prompted memories of her shop, *Magda's Mysteries* and all the many years since it became his favourite place in the world. She had, in her way, given him so much. He just wished she still lived in the same apartment block he did. Terry didn't relish the idea of travelling way into the countryside to this new place of hers tonight. Actually, the more he thought of that, the odder it seemed. Why would she move all the way out into the sticks, when mobility was presumably such an issue with her?

He mechanically got on with the rest of his day. He saved the current document – a storyline about Iris and Panda and an underground city that was getting out of control. Yes, another Iris, he sighed. And it wasn't even guaranteed. This was all speculative. Times were tough and even those with lots of experience on the franchise were having to compete for work. Somehow Terry had a feeling – a slightly paranoid feeling – that his brand of what they liked to call quirkiness – would prove to be expendable.

He packed his work bag – not forgetting to pick up the Wildthyme boxed set, as he had promised Magda – locked up his studio flat and hurried down to the street, where it was gusty, blustery and grey. Almost immediately he was just about knocked over by a tall woman in a long, black leather coat and wearing a monocle. 'Beg pardon,' she snapped, as she steamed past.

Great big splotches of rain started to fall. He was glad he'd put on his heavier coat.

He stopped on Posthouse Wynd at his favourite coffee place and there he went over his notes for this afternoon's teaching session, re-familiarising himself with his seven students' work. All were retired ladies and he had set them the task last week of *'Writing Something OUTSIDE Your Comfort Zone'* and the results had been quite surprising. Not just surprising – actually good. Unexpected. Odd. Better than all that stuff about grandchildren, wartime romance and continental holidays. He had asked them to write about things they would never usually dream of dealing with – spaceships, robots, detectives, dinosaurs...

And, as it happened, the session went rather better than he had been expected. They gathered in a modern, upbeat, trendy room with colourful padded walls and large windows looking out on the golden trees in the park.

One woman read out a story – a kind of space story – he felt sorely tempted to steal for one of his book pitches. But he nipped that thought in the bud and the others loudly applauded. They're getting really good, he thought. Not flattering himself, not taking credit. But it was true – they were getting better every week.

Before long he was at a bus stop at tea time with the shoppers as they waited to go home. The bus came and Terry was sitting at the very top, on the front seat of the double decker as it went down South Road and eventually out into the countryside. He looked again at Magda's directions from her email, and realized that his stop was imminent. Here it was. He bolted down the stairwell, banging into the walls as he went. Yes, he must remember that – racing down the stairs of a bus and lurching about. It would be good in an action scene for Iris.

He was alone at the stop at the edge of a field. The bus roared off and he saw that it was almost fully dark, now, with banks of violent purple cloud crushing the life out of the daylight. The horizons here were huge and grand – it was all crops and motorways for miles around. He realized with a stab of guilt he'd forgotten to buy flowers or wine or something.

Magda didn't mind. As she had told him, all he needed to bring was his good self. After another mile or two walking up and down rutted, filthy country roads and rough tracks, he was glad to hear it. He knocked at the stout wooden door of her farmhouse and she called him in.

She was in her chair, reaching up dangerously to stir something in a pot on the Aga. He glanced around briefly at the warm, comfortable space before he realized that she was just about toppling out of her chair. As he hastened to help her, he saw that her tartan rug was slipping off her knees. For a second he froze, thinking he had seen – rather than legs – a glittering mermaid's tail concealed under that rug.

She tossed the wooden spoon back into the pan and grinned at him. 'You made it!'

2.

Aunty Iris had a very nice flat inside the giant skull of Make Up Girl mountain. She had made a home for herself and her foxes inside the least ruined rooms of the old palace.

'Much nicer than that pokey old place I used to rent in Aberdeen,' she laughed, putting on an oven glove. 'I think this secret hideout is the nicest place I've ever lived, actually. I quite missed it, these past few years of living on Earth.'

'It's very homely,' Simon told her.

'Thank you, Simon,' she said, delighted. 'I've done my best. It used to be a very spectacular royal palace, years ago. But it was reduced to rubble during the Great Division, which was a kind of nasty, bloody revolution they had here. I had to do quite a bit of cleaning to make the place even halfway habitable...'

Each of the rooms we were led through was decorated in a very Aunty Iris kind of way. It was homely and comfy, but the colours clashed and the decor and ornaments were a bit busy. The living room had gold and red striped wallpaper and a chintz three piece suite. There were ceramic fish, china birds and some very disturbing porcelain dolls.

Aunty Iris whisked us all into the kitchen, which had black and white lino and cupboards she'd painted herself with vivid splashes of colour. The only weird thing was that there were no windows.

It was as if she had taken a very ordinary house from our own world, and hidden it inside Make Up Girl's stone head. The effect was disorienting and weird.

I wanted to ask her how she got all this furniture and stuff from our world into this one.

Aunty Iris obviously knew the secret of easy travel between the different worlds! She must do, I thought, if she could bring all her furniture and nicknacks with her...

Soon the three foxes and Simon were sitting at the wooden table and they were wolfing down fat bacon sandwiches and slurping hot tea out of mugs with rude slogans on.

I knew I was hanging back a bit. I was still gathering my thoughts and watching the others. Watching Aunty Iris, even though it was just ordinary stuff she was doing, like making tea and sandwiches.

'Pull up a pew, Kelly,' Aunty Iris said, slapping more bacon into the hissing pan. She had to raise her voice over all the chomping, snuffling and guzzling noises from the foxes as they tucked in.

'These are great, Aunty Iris,' Simon grinned through a mouthful of sandwich. I scowled at him. Who was he to call her 'Aunty'? He was just sucking up to her, I decided. But Aunty Iris was smiling back at him.

'It's very good that you're here as well, Simon. Keeping an eye on our Kelly.'

I felt my eyes flash at this. HIM keeping an eye on ME!

'Yes, she told me all about you and what a good pal you are to her.' Aunty Iris was taking a rather lopsided Victoria Sponge out of the oven and placing it carefully on the table. Then she flung herself down on a bobbly green armchair in the corner of the room. She sipped at her own cup of tea. 'Oh, do sit down, Kelly love. You're making the place look untidy. And you really ought to get more used to seeing impossible things, you know.'

I pulled up a wooden chair. 'Actually,' I said. 'We've seen quite a lot of stuff since we arrived here. Even before we saw your foxes. And me and Simon keep an eye out for EACH OTHER, actually.'

'Good,' said Aunty Iris, smiling at me. 'So, go on then. Tell us all about it. Tell us all about your adventures here in Hyspero so far. How long have you been here? It seems so long since Christmas... though, of course, time moves at a different pace here in Hyspero...'

So I told her. I recounted to Aunty Iris and her acrobatic foxes the story of our adventures here in Hyspero so far, beginning with how Make Up Girl was delivered to my house, and how we'd accidentally melted her face half off whilst worshipping her. Then, how her eyes had turned so weird and kaleidoscopic and we'd been sucked up through them, into a gateway to Hyspero itself. And then I described our arrival, without provisions or water or a map or anything, in the endless desert, and then our encounters with the desert people and how they'd been nice enough at first, but then how they'd given us over to the soldiers and the awful Vizier...

They were all listening very carefully. Even Simon - who'd been there, after all - was listening, agog, as if the whole tale was new to him.

'So you've had a few scrapes already,' Aunty Iris smiled. 'Just like you always imagined.' Then she looked sharply at Simon. 'And you, Simon? What do you think of Hyspero so far? I hear that you were very keen, just like Kelly, on getting to the other lands. Is it everything you hoped for?'

'I think it's fantastic,' he gulped, eyeing the cake greedily.

'Ha!' I said. 'He's done nothing but complain ever since we landed in the desert. It's too hot. It's too far. He's hungry. It's a bit tiring.'

Actually, as soon as I said this, I felt a bit mean. But Simon had got on my nerves, greasing in with Aunty Iris straight away. Calling her 'Aunty' and NOT being freaked out, like I was, that she was still alive.

Simon looked really stung and hurt by what I said. He was gaping at me and I felt myself blush. He looked so hurt that I wanted to take it all back and tell him what a great pal he was. That there was no one I'd rather be on an adventure with! But the words just wouldn't come out. And he carried on sitting there, looking hurt.

Aunty Iris was glaring at me. 'You should watch your mouth, girl. You should curb that temper when it flares up. You can't afford to lose any friends, you know. You'll need all the friends you can get, here in Hyspero!'

3.

Dinner was a kind of fish stew in a tomato sauce. Terry ate it happily, in something of a daze. He kept admiring the country-style kitchen and only half-listened to Magda burbling about her shop and the remaindered stock she had received today. She even remembered the names of his favourite fantasy writers from years ago, and hoped he'd pop in to buy their newer books. She had an incredible memory, he thought. But then, maybe she had no family, and no other complicated stuff to remember.

He showed her the Iris Wildthyme DVD boxed set and felt foolish as she admired it.

'Ahh, look, after all these years,' she laughed. 'And old Aunty Iris is still your favourite. I cannot tell you how proud I was when your first book about her was remaindered and came into my shop. My feeble heart glowed.'

After the bowls and dishes were sided up, Magda opened a bottle of chilled Sancerre and settled them both in her small living room, in front of a very old fashioned telly. Terry was fascinated by the objects and books on her shelves. It was like sitting in a museum of post-war fantasy fiction: dragons and unicorns and magicians and elves. Some of the ornaments glowed and sent out wreaths of dry ice or lit up with fibre optics. 'It's er, lovely in here.'

Smiling, Magda heaved herself out of her wheelchair, onto the settee, tossing the remote to Terry. 'Now, let us watch your show.'

*

Terry couldn't let go of the idea that there was an extra, unseen episode of the show. The idea had been planted last Saturday in the pub after the book signing at Timeslip, and somehow it wouldn't leave him alone. Obviously, it could easily have been a mistake on the part of the man from Timeslip. But what if it was true? What if there really was a script or unedited footage or a whole, complete episode out there?

He told Magda about it as they watched episode one.

'Well, that would be something,' she agreed.

'It would be the best thing ever,' he said.

Now she looked at him, along the settee, with a concerned expression. 'Would it really mean so much?'

'Of course!' he said. 'Well, to me, anyway.'

She frowned. 'You shouldn't put so much of your life into a thing like this. A television show. It isn't real, you know.'

He laughed. 'Of course it isn't real! Even I know that, Magda.'

'Hmmf,' she said, as if she wasn't convinced he had any sense at all. They settled down to watch more of the episode.

When he thought about it, Terry realized that this wasn't actually the first episode at all. When he focused on the action he saw that the right things weren't going on. There was a lot of running about amongst the main characters, and they were getting on and off the gleaming red bus rather a lot. There were guest stars and monsters galumphing about that really belonged to a later episode...

'I've put the wrong disc in the machine...'

'Have you?' Magda smiled.

In the first episode it was the story of how they all started out, wasn't it? It was set mostly on Earth in a very ordinary kind of place... a few ordinary streets and people and then the revelation of the big red bus. The Number 22 was unveiled only towards the end of episode one... that's how he remembered it. And that's how it was... he'd rewatched it only a matter of weeks ago, goosepimpled with nostalgia as he saw the episode again for the first time in thirty years.

But the story unfolding onscreen was quite different. Iris and Panda were already best friends and they were embroiled in an adventure that took place inside Roker Park football stadium in Sunderland. There was to be a concert by then chart-topping pop stars Boney M and the clock was ticking until the band played. But some dreadful creatures were lurking underneath the football ground and our heroes were running about in dimly-lit corridors, being chased by these sort-of scorpion men...

'This isn't right...' Terry said.

Magda was half-asleep, sitting up suddenly. 'Is this your missing episode? Have you found an episode you have not seen before?'

'No, no...' he said. 'This is a bit familiar... but it's changed. It's not the same. Boney M never appeared on *The Iris Wildthyme Show*, did they?'

But apparently they had. They were doing their song, 'Ma Baker' and the stars of the show were dancing beside them. It was a feature of the vintage scifi show that a pop group would appear at a random moment in each episode in order to plug their latest single. At least Boney M actually fit inside the plot. The thing was, Terry didn't remember this at all...

Perhaps it really was the missing episode... He snatched up the box set, dislodging the other discs and the commemorative booklet written by a TV expert. He scanned through other titles, other descriptions... There wasn't much light but, at first glance, he wasn't sure he recognized any of them.

Have I even watched this programme before? He wondered.

And if I haven't, how've I spent my working life writing sequels to it?

Even Panda's voice was different. More barking, even fruitier than Terry remembered it. He rolled his plastic eyes at every double entendre. And Iris herself, when you saw her in close-up, she wasn't the same either. Hadn't she been young in the TV series? Glamorous and eccentric and batty as hell? But hadn't she been a young actress aged up? This Iris was definitely older and less nimble. She crashed drunkenly into the furniture and the edges of the set. She stumbled very obviously once or twice as she dashed into action and some of the lines she spoke clearly came straight off the top of of her head in the heat of the moment.

'This is a very silly programme,' Magda told him, pouring them both some more of the cool, silvery wine.

'But… but…' he said. He was at a loss to explain to her. How could he say that someone had changed things? He had turned his back for a moment and someone had taken his childhood favourite and mixed it all around?

This Iris was completely different. This one even turned straight to the camera and talked to the audience at home. She did it almost jeeringly, as if breaking the device of the fiction was just a silly game to her.

'I need the loo,' Terry said, struggling out of the deep settee.

'Shall I pause it?' Magda asked, but he had already nipped out.

*

Magda's bathroom was incredibly impressive.

Once more Terry found himself being a bit uncharitable, and wondering how on earth she could afford a house this size, with all these amazing features. The bathroom was like something out of a palace, with glass pipes and tubes everywhere, and tanks that teemed with exotically colourful fish. There were photos in gold leaf frames that showed Magda in her wheelchair beside a number of rather odd-looking people. Terry squinted and he couldn't be sure... but was that a vending machine grinning beside the old lady? And here... surely that was a Panda she had on her knee?

Terry shook his head blearily. He was tired and mixed up. He was seeing Iris Wildthyme stuff everywhere.

'That's some bathroom you've got,' he told Magda when he returned to her TV room.

'Hm? Ach, well. We all deserve a little luxury, don't we?'

He shrugged and stared at her for a moment as she poured them another drink. He had a feeling that there was something important he was missing, that she hadn't told him.

They watched the rest of the episode quietly and, as it progressed, the story became more wildly different to what he remembered.

It finished with Iris and her friends convening in a moonbase that was also a shopping mall, and facing uncertainty as the moon lurched out of Earth's orbit.

*

Magda switched to the Special Features and found an interview with Charles Hardy, otherwise known as the Voice of Panda. He was wearing a military blazer and had an air of bafflement about him.

'Well, I hardly ever met the rest of the cast, of course. There was a launch for the show with the press, of course, as the end of shooting came near. That must have been during Christmas1978, in the Rainbow Rooms in Newcastle. That was a smart tearooms above a department store, yes. I remember that… and meeting the others. The girl who played Iris.. yes, Suzy. I remember her being rather uncertain… and she was somewhat worried, yes, that was it – worried. She seemed to think our little show would make us all terribly famous. Become a cult hit! And it would take over all our lives!'

Charles Hardy, the Voice of Panda, chuckled rather raucously then, and puffed on his cigar.

'I told her. Veteran, me, you see. Been on everything. Going way back. I can smell a hit. See it a mile off. And this wasn't it. This wasn't going to be anything much. Too weird, you see. Too quirky. Even for kids on a Friday teatime. No, none of us would get famous appearing in this nonsense. I was only glad you never saw my face! I was glad I was just doing a voice-over! But then I saw that Suzy was rather crestfallen at my words. When we rejoined the others for the big toast and the photographs she looked as if she was being brave. Poor girl was on the point of tears and, really, I could have kicked myself, you know. This was her first real part. And I'd crushed her. Her hopes. I'd squashed her hopes, you see. Nipped them in the bud with a few careless words over the buffet table.'

Charles took another puff of his cigar and looked lost for a moment. Lost and alone in the tiny studio with a cheap backdrop. 'Well, I've never told anyone this bit. Funny thing was… it was more strange, really, than funny. Before the launch event was finished, I nipped into the lav. Needed to, before the long taxi back to my flat, what. And most of the others were gone. The press people, the cast and crew… they were all shuffling towards the lifts. And I'm in the little boy's room, you know. And when I'm at the washing basin, I become aware of someone who's come into the room and is standing right behind me. And I feel something jutting into my back. A gun.

'I look into the mirror and there she is. Right behind me. Glaring at me furiously. Is it Suzy? I squint and stare back at her. 'Don't turn around,' she growls. 'Don't mess with me, buster.' Well, I am astonished. She looks about forty years older. Still the same girl, it's plain to see. But she's got all these terrible clothes on and lilac-tinted curls. Her face is squinched up like an old paper bag. The kind hobos carry their bottles in. And it suddenly hits me: this must be Suzy's mother! She must have been here at the beano. Surely that's who it is? But all of a sudden I can't speak! And she says, 'Just you stop heaving a go at Suzy. She's the star of the show here. Don't you go spoiling everything for her.''

'I manage to say, 'A-all right,' highly conscious of the gun barrel in my back. But I feel such a coward and a fool. Allowing this old woman with the crazy grin and the ginny breath to intimidate me so.

"You're no Panda,' she said then, jeeringly. 'Panda is kind and brave! Panda is loyal and never nasty! You don't deserve to be Panda!"

'And then she turned and bustled out, fast as you like. I caught a glimpse of the pistol she'd had up my back. Bright pink, would you believe it. The door clashed shut behind her. I almost fell over onto the tiles. I thought I was having a heart attack…'

Onscreen the actor looked discomfited all over again. He took out a large handkerchief and mopped his shining brow.

'There, there's an exclusive for you. I don't believe I've ever told that story to anyone before. Of how I was menaced by a person who was quite clearly our starlet's over-protective mother. Rather amusing in retrospect, what? I believe the old dear must be long dead by now, of course. Still, it was somewhat disconcerting at the time. And really, she needn't have bothered. For there were to be no more launches after that. No more night shoots or studio days or script readings. The show was already over. It had been cancelled even before the first episode was broadcast…'

The old man shook his head sadly and the interview ended.

I looked at Magda. 'Well! That was peculiar…'

But her mind was on other things. She stared at me intently in the flickering light from her old-fashioned telly. 'I've got something important to tell you, Terry.'

Oh god, I thought. What's this going to be?

She said, 'I work for MIAOW, Terry. Like in the books and on the telly, but it's real. I'm in charge, actually. Of MIAOW Darlington. I'm the one in command of the local branch!'

4.

Now that I'd told them I was looking forward to my adventure, it was time for me to learn a little more about how things in Hyspero worked. Specifically, how adventures in Hyspero worked.

And who exactly embarked upon them...

'All of them?' I gasped. 'EVERYONE in my family?'

'I was exaggerating,' said Aunty Iris. 'Nearly all of them.'

'Mum and dad? MY mum and dad? Are you sure they were here?'

'I told you they were. In the nineteen-seventies. They first met each other here, when they were supposed to deal with the blood-sucking badgers who invaded the city and... oh, well. That was a whole other story and they weren't all that good at adventures.'

'Huh,' I said. 'What about Nanna Beryl?'

'She's my sister, as you know,' Aunty Iris said with a strange, stiff smile. 'And she came to Hyspero in the nineteen-fifties, with me. The first few times I was ever here, she came along too. Oh, we had a marvellous time... We were younger than you are now and we used to come every school holiday... summer and

Christmas... having simply lovely adventures. Just like in all the books, I thought ... I always knew that stuff was real...'

I watched Aunty Iris's face go soft with nostalgia. The years seemed to drop away from her as she remembered her very earliest adventures in Hyspero.

I thought: So she felt exactly the same about the other lands, and about magic and adventures, as I do now. And so did Nanna Beryl.

Aunty Iris was saying: 'We had quests to go on and we had terrible hoo-hahs where we had to fight monsters and witches and nasty threats to the stability of Hyspero... and we met the good Empress Euphemia who lived in this very palace when it was grand and magnificent and... well, these were the old, old, golden days when it was peaceful in Hyspero... before all the troubles started...'

Oh, I thought. Here we go.

It was funny. Even in Hyspero, grown-ups still cracked on that the old days were the best. And that everything nowadays wasn't as good.

'We saw this world turn dark,' said Aunty Iris. 'We saw everything turn sour. That's how it went.' Her face clouded. 'This was the time of the Great Division, of course. And I'm afraid my sister Beryl and I got a bit caught up in that...'

There was that phrase again. The Great Division. I was about to ask about it, when Simon broke in: 'So it's like a family thing?' he asked.

'That's right, Simon. For some reason, members of Kelly's family are drawn to this land whenever the land has need of us. We've never known why the destiny of this place is so tied

171

up with Kelly's family. We don't know why we are all brought here… It was the Empress Euphemia who summoned Beryl and I all those years ago. She's no longer here, so I had to bring Kelly here myself. It's destiny. Kelly's destiny.'

I was pleased by this, but I still wanted to know where these magical powers of my Aunty's had come from. Did she mean that she had the powers of the Empress Euphemia herself? In that case, if she was that powerful, how come she needed me at all? I was just a twelve year old kid. Like I kept being told at home, there was nothing very special about me.

What did Aunty Iris need from me?

She'd certainly gone to some lengths to get me there.

'Anyway,' Aunty Iris was saying. 'What I have is a limited magical ability... to go back and forth between the worlds. I had to use much of my power to bring you here...'

'Make up Girl!' smiled Simon.

'And I think I've exhausted myself doing that much.' Aunty Iris shrugged. 'So I'm going to need every ounce of your strength and help, Kelly and Simon, when we travel into the Shrieking Forest...'

'Full of Irksome Parrots and Pigs Without Mercy,' I nodded. 'But you have to tell us more about this quest.'

'I don't want to fill your heads with too many details all at once,' she said. 'But what you must understand is that Hyspero, the land itself, is in the most ghastly peril. And you are the ones who will have to sort it out.'

'Good,' I said. 'Go on.'

Aunty Iris blinked, still surprised at how eager I was to face dire peril. She said, 'First of all, you both need to understand something about this land.'

'We've seen a bit of it,' said Simon. 'It seems a bit of a dusty, deserty kind of place. There's not much here really, is there, Aunty Iris?'

'What?' cried Aunty Iris. 'Why, you've only seen the tiniest fraction of the full extent of Hyspero. That desert you crossed? This mountain range we're hiding in? The Blasted Valley itself? Pah! They're nothing! They're just the size of ... a tiny, tiny back garden compared to the full extent of Hyspero. This is a VAST and HUGE land, Kelly and Simon. And it certainly isn't all boring old desert. There are florid jungles and forests and there are glittering ice fields and thrashing, boiling seas. There's everything you can imagine here, all jumbled up. You shouldn't go thinking it's all going to be like the little tiny bit you've seen so far. No, Hyspero can always surprise you with something new.'

Simon was glad to hear this. So was I.

'You see,' said Aunty Iris. 'Hyspero is constantly changing. It is continuously shifting and altering and evolving. We don't have any reliable maps. We never have. No sooner do you start using one and set off on your journey and WHOOOOSSH - everything has changed around. Cities can appear, just like mirages. Whole races of creatures can turn up out of the blue. No one ever knows what's coming next.'

'It sounds like a very confusing place to live,' I frowned.

'Ah, yes,' cried Aunty Iris, jumping up. 'But it's also the most fantastic place. Just imagine, never knowing what you might see next! Just imagine never being bored! That's why I could never settle back into ordinary life in England. Or Scotland, come to that. It's why I decided to stay here. It was just awful, back at home. You'd go out and everything would be the same as the last time you saw it. Things changed, only very very slowly, and usually for the worst. Oh no, I much prefer it here. Even if it is a little strange sometimes. And perilous. And now ... endangered, too.'

'How come it's endangered?' I asked. 'What's happening to it?'

'The land itself is revolting,' said Aunty Iris solemnly. 'I can hear it cry out every day. The land moans in protest as... something... drains its vital, mystical energies away. There is some kind of sorcery at work here, killing our world. Hyspero's deep, subterranean cries of pain become louder and more plaintive. It is becoming riddled with ruptures and gaps and... Corrosion.' She took a deep breath. 'Sooner or later... I suspect that this whole world may simply fall apart!'

We were quiet at this for a moment. It was as if we were all trying to picture such a terrible thing.

But I decided that the time had come to be practical. And to find out what we could do to help.

'What will we find in the Shrieking Jungle?' I asked. 'Beside parrots and pigs, I mean.'

I'd never seen Aunty Iris - in all our short acquaintance - look as serious as she did in that instant. 'You need to find a creature known as ... the Golden God. That is the only name I have been given. This 'Golden God' has knowledge... about what is causing the damage to Hyspero and how it may be stopped.'

Aunty Iris looked very grave. 'It's quite a lot of responsibility to give you...'

I thought so too, but I wasn't admitting that.

'No one knows what kind of creature he is,' said Aunty Iris, 'But he's in the Shrieking Jungle somewhere and he's stuck there... he can take you to a place where you'll find the knowledge that will save the world. That much I know. I can't be any less vague than that. Sorry, Kelly. That's as much as the Empress Euphemia ever told me.'

I gasped. 'Empress Euphemia told you...?! I thought she was gone!'

'In a dream,' Aunty Iris said smoothly. 'The old Empress came to me in a dream. Her spirit appeared just before Christmas... in a toyshop, in the middle of shelf after shelf of toys for girls ... The Empress Euphemia appeared before me, in the form of Make Up Girl. That's how I knew what to buy you for Christmas... And she gave me just enough power to get myself here - and to bring you two. She told me we have to search for the Golden God. Together. And, when we find him, he will know what to do. That is our quest.' Aunty Iris suddenly looked quite old and doddery, as if just telling us all this had tired her out. 'Will you help?' she asked.

5.

Panda led him on a midnight ramble. Sammy didn't want to leave the house. But he didn't even try to resist.

He knew it was wrong to release all the catches and unlock the back door, but he had no choice in the matter. From the moment Panda's head appeared through the catflap, Sammy was lost.

Panda had come for him.

Overstuffed bear and overgrown boy stumbled together across the scrubby wasteland at the edge of the estate. Under the sodium yellow and faulty pink streetlights they picked their way. Panda's feet were sodden and made squelching noises as he led Sammy under the stinky underpass and across the main road. Sammy drew in a sharp breath at how bold Panda was, dashing between the oncoming cars, almost causing accidents in order to reach the other side.

I always knew, didn't I? Sammy huffed and puffed, crossing in a quieter moment. I knew that someday he would come for me. Back in the schoolyard when we all gathered to talk about our favourite shows and enact our favourite scenes... I knew I had a strange connection with this show. The show that no one else really liked very much... They loved Starsky and Hutch, Buck Rogers, the Bionic Man... and I did, too, a little.

But none of those were the same as Panda and Iris Wildthyme.

I knew they were real.

He was sweating cold sweat and running harder and faster than he ever had before. 'I can't run, I can't!' he'd cried when his mum suggested they put in for the Great North Run together. She had trained like a demon for three months solid, trogging around their estate in her lime green tracksuit. In the end his torpor and general unwillingness had depressed her and she hadn't bothered either. 'We could have done it for charity!' she'd shouted. 'You could have shifted your fat arse for once, but no...'

He had tried to explain that he'd never been able to run. His heart always felt like it was forcing itself up through his throat. He was built all wrong inside and so he couldn't breathe, he would cough up blood, he would have a fatal heart attack if he tried too hard.

Yet now he was running... not smoothly, not that quickly... but he was jogging along in his dressing gown and pyjamas. His rolls of fat and his breasts were jiggling all over the place and, if anyone should see him, he was sure he would look grotesque. A monster. A loony on the run. Even a danger to the community. But that didn't bother him now. Not now that he was in hot pursuit...

Panda led him to the town dump. They passed through the tatty fringe of woodland and the end of the precinct of shops. There was nothing left of town after that save some pensioners' bungalows and then endless open spaces down the hills. Why was Panda taking him to the dump?

Panda stopped, and so Sammy stopped. And when he stopped his exhaustion hit him like a brick wall. He staggered and almost blacked out. Panda jogged back to help steady him with a sturdy paw.

'Where are you taking me?' he asked the small creature.

Panda didn't say anything. He'd said nothing at all since they'd left Sammy's house. At the thought of Mum's house, Sammy started fretting that he hadn't stopped to lock the back door. In fact, he had no key on him, so that was true. Mum would go spare, whenever she rolled home.

He squinted at Panda, and wished the creature would speak. Somehow his continued silence cast a little doubt on his identity. But there could be no argument about that, really. He was exactly as Sammy saw Panda in his head. His tidily-tied cravat, his fluffed-up ears. He moved along much less jerkily than the one on the TV. There could be no doubt that he was truly real. And living. And here.

On the breeze – he could smell old ash and burning rubber and tomorrow's rain. Then there was the whiff of rotting cat food and fish and chips. The skies over Tyneside were neon blue and pink… but here he and Panda could see the stars because it was so much darker and further from civilization.

Panda took a hop, skip and jump through oily puddles. Perhaps he wasn't even leading Sammy anywhere. Just round and round in circles. And yet he seemed so purposeful. Panda always did.

*

Sammy thought about the letters he once wrote to his heroes, and kept hidden inside his desk at school.

Dear Aunty Iris,

I really wish you were my aunty. My own aunts come round on a Sunday to see my mam and me. They smoke and cackle in the kitchen and then they all play darts together, saying vicious things about their husbands. And they tell me that I won't grow up like that. They tell me that I'll grow up special. But Mum looks cross when they say this and says I'll grow up just the same. All men are the same. Skidmarks and wet toilet seats and fag ends and chucking beer cans down just anywhere at home. Splashing on aftershave and all smiles and man-about-town when they're going out. That's what men are like.

I can't remember my dad being like how she says. In fact, I don't remember much about him at all. I remember him taking me aside, on the day he left, and begging me: 'Ask her in there if she'll let me stay.'

And the only thing I remember about his side of the family is being at their house when my grandmother got locked in the downstairs toilet. She climbed out of that tiny window feet first. Apart from that, nothing.

Mam says our family begins and ends with just me and her. It's me and her against the world round ours.

I wish we had a celestial omnibus like yours. Or that your bus could suddenly pull up at the stop outside our house. That's where we usually wait for the bus into town. Everyone sits squashed up inside the bus, breathing fog on the mucky windows. Watching the streets slide by into town. But if your bus came and stopped by ours, it wouldn't be like that, would it? There'd be like a party inside, like there always is. Or a holiday with bunting and streamers. And wonderful music playing inside as you pilot the Number 22 through the Maelstrom of all space and time… Mantovani and James Last and his Orchestra…

Dear Panda,

Please tell Iris to come and fetch me. One day soon. I've been expecting the pair of you to just turn up any day now… I've been expecting that for ages. So I thought I'd better prompt you, you know. Just to check that the two of you are still on your way…

*

It turned out that Panda was, in fact, leading him to a particular destination. By the dump there was a row of houses that stood alone in the wasteland. They stuck out like rotting stumps in a gummy mouth. Council houses that were bought by the owners in the old Thatcher days, and the owners had been holding on for years, expecting a pay-off.

One of them was a newsagent's. Sammy had been in there before, buying comics, crisps and pop. Inside it was warm and familiar. Bleachy-smelling lino and the hum of the refrigeration cabinets. A large bosomy woman called Barbra was marking up newspapers for the delivery boys. Was it that late already? Was it almost dawn?

She looked up at her two customers and didn't react in the slightest when Panda flew up into Sammy's arms. She and Panda were face to face over the newspapers and the pic-n-mixes. Panda nodded at her silently.

She pulled her massive, mustard-coloured cardigan tighter. 'He's waiting for you upstairs, Panda. He got your message. And, er, who's this?'

'I'm Sammy,' Sammy said, feeling faintly ridiculous as Barbra reached into a box of crisps past their sell-by and tossed him a packet for his breakfast.

Next thing, he was going up the gloomy stairs behind the shop to the flat above. At the top there was a door with rippled glass and a blind pulled down. Someone was up and about, because there was a light glowing. Someone was waiting for them.

Sammy tapped politely and the door burst open almost immediately.

A man in a military blazer and cravat glared at the two of them beadily. He understood at once what was happening, and he shooed them inside.

Inside everything was orderly and Spartan. G-plan furniture and a bookcase of Reader's Digests. The military man sat them down on his leather settee and turned to the wall unit. He brought them a tot of sherry each, plus an exotic-looking vase. It looked like something one of Sammy's aunts might have brought back from a foreign holiday.

The military man lifted the lid and a dark vapor issued out. It curled in arabesques around their heads, almost playfully, for a moment or two.

Panda lurched forward to inhale it and Sammy watched as it went up his nose. Panda coughed and spluttered loudly. He knocked back his sherry in one.

When he spoke at last he sounded rather grateful.

'Thank you, both of you, for understanding what was required.'

'Think nothing of it, old chap,' said the military gent in a very similar voice.

Sammy was staring at both of them, having just recognized the man as Charles Hardy, the actual voice of Panda on the TV, all those years ago. Also, he was gobsmacked to hear Panda speaking for himself. The small bear was standing on the glass coffee table and striding about, gesticulating... heedless of Sammy's awe.

'...Problem is, you see,' Panda was saying. 'The silly old fool thought she was being clever. She assumed she was protecting everyone from the consequences of the Ringpull being disabled. But, as ever, it was a lot more complicated than that. She got Euphemia, the original Empress, to help her out with the bits of the plan that should really, strictly, be called the magical parts, and that's what they did. They managed it. And then there was the funny business with the dragon's blood in the workings of the bus. Well, you know the funny things dragon's blood can do. And so the upshot was, they shunted you lot, and us, several dimensions apart. She pushed the world she knew here through a number of infinitesimal degrees into fictionality. You see? And that's why, in your world, we don't, erm, really exist in the ordinary, straightforward way...'

Charles, the Voice of Panda, had sat himself down carefully in his armchair. He ran a finger down the creases in his navy trousers. 'Yes, I do think I see, old chap,' he said mildly. 'Wasn't there an episode about that? About Iris shunting people into fictional dimensions? I seem to remember...'

'How would I know that?' Panda snapped. 'In my world, things don't happen in *episodes*. That's not how my world works.' He swung his head round to glower at Sammy, who up till now had been very quiet. 'In part, that's why I've brought geek boy here. He knows everything there is to be known about us. Or, us as we are in your world.'

Charles looked at Sammy and blinked. 'Really? Is this true?'

Sammy's voice came out scratchy and dim-sounding. 'I suppose I do. And the novels that came after.'

'Novels?' Panda gasped. 'They wrote novels about me, too?'

'Over three hundred and twenty four of them,' Sammy said.

Panda couldn't help looking rather pleased at this. 'And you've read them all, have you?'

'Of course,' Sammy said. 'It's... they are... well, you are, my favourite thing in all the world.'

Charles the Voice of Panda nodded sagely. 'Yes, I know about these novels, too. I've read some of them onto tape, you know, for Talking Books. Very strange things indeed. Couldn't make head nor tail of them, I'm afraid.'

'This thing you're talking about,' Sammy said, 'Sending people... into fictional universes...'

'Hm?' asked Panda. 'Well, that's not quite what she's done. You see, from her point of view, what she's actually

183

done is wrench herself and her own dimension – my dimension – several notches into fictionality. And leaving your dimension exactly where it is. Or was. Or perhaps her actions on Hyspero have summoned your whole world into existence. Do you see?'

Sammy was thrilled by all of this.

'Episode eighteen,' Charles said. 'The missing episode. The one we only half made before we were stopped. Didn't this strange thing happen in that one?'

Sammy squeaked. 'And in a book, too. In one of the novels. By whatsiname... I met him! Just the other day! Terry Kelly. He wrote about this kind of thing happening.' Then Sammy realized what the military man had said just before and stared at him. 'So there really was a missing episode?'

6.

Magda went quiet for a while, almost as if she regretted telling him quite so much. She hauled herself back into her wheelchair and went off to make coffee.

She's addled, Terry thought. She has to be, doesn't she? She works for MIAOW? How can she possibly work for MIAOW?

MIAOW was the secret agency of mostly female spies operating out of London in the TV show. They were also in many of the Iris Wildthyme novels. Not in Terry's, because he wasn't all that fond of the adventures that tied Iris down to Earth, as the MIAOW ones did.

After all these years, he thought, Magda has lost her mind. Perhaps sitting alone in that little shop of hers, surrounded by the strangest fantasy novels in the world, has driven her barmy.

They made small talk over coffee and he couldn't help feeling sorry for her. She once more described some of the latest books she had in the shop, and which she thought he might enjoy. Terry nodded and smiled.

After coffee she led him on a small tour of her lavish home, and all he could think about was wanting to get away. He longed to be on the bus heading back into town. But he marveled at the expensive touches, such as the vast swimming pool in her basement. The lights were out and the neon blue water pulsed eerily.

He asked, 'Did you mean it, Magda? About MIAOW?' Now he was feeling crazy, asking her this.

She sighed. 'What do you see when you look at me, Terry?'

He looked.

'The same old woman that you have known nearly all of your life, yes? Helpless, in a wheelchair. An ancient old crone with a funny accent.'

'Well, not quite,' he murmured.

'How could you ever expect me to have a life beyond my shop, hmm? What else might I be doing?'

'I don't know…'

'And MIAOW is something made up, isn't it? It isn't something real in our world, no?'

'I...'

'Come with me.'

He was reluctant to, if he was honest with himself. He watched Magda wheel herself to a metal door, which whooshed open at her touch.

It was a lift. A lift which, once they were safely inside with the door shut, sped them sideways suddenly, almost knocking Terry off his feet.

'Don't worry,' Magda said. 'It made me feel a little bit sickly at first, too.'

'But... where are we going?' he asked. From the speed they were going, they were surely well beyond her house now. Terry found himself clinging to the wall. What were they heading towards? And what kind of underground tunnel was this? Cut sheer through the wet, dark rock under Darlington? It felt like they had sharply swerved downwards two or three times, and so they were very deep down... Terry suddenly thought of stories he had read and watched set deep beneath the Earth's crust. Somehow it seemed this kind of thing was now coming true. But he wasn't as excited as he thought he might have been. Instead he was wondering how such a Pellucidar / whatever escapade might work out if he was busy looking after a wheelchair-user.

But soon enough they arrived at the destination Magda intended for them.

The sideways elevator jerked to a halt with an almighty screech.

'Are you ready for this?' Magda said, her finger hovering at the button that would open the door.

'Where are we?' he asked croakily.

'Underneath the indoor market in the town centre.'

His heart started thudding heavily. 'You mean, it's actually…'

She shushed him and the door opened to reveal a metal walkway and a system of metal gantries in the dark. There was an aroma of dank basements. Madga wheeled herself out quite matter-of-factly, and Terry followed, drinking in every detail. He trogged along behind her as she led the way to what appeared to be a very futuristic control room indeed.

'MIAOW headquarters,' she announced casually. 'Just as I say, Terry. I am in charge now.'

'This is incredible…' he whispered, gazing around.

'It shouldn't be here,' Magda nodded, turning to examine the banks of instruments. 'And by thinking that, you are correct in more than one way, my dear boy. But when Iris shunted this dimension and her own into opposite ends of the spectrum of fictionality… she forgot about the shielding placed about this headquarters and the Dreadful Flap. And so we sisters in MIAOW were exempted from her so-called helpful rescue. We live in a world where our friend Iris and her friends are fictional, but we remain operative here. It is ridiculous, but true.'

Terry gawped at her. 'I don't have a clue what you're on about.' He steadied himself against an angrily-flashing console. 'You're saying there's a dimension in which Iris... and everybody is real?'

Magda laughed good-naturedly. Suddenly she looked less severe. She was enjoying his confusion and his dawning realization. 'Tangential to this one, yes. That is how it was explained to me. Almost like something out of one of your peculiar books, Terry.'

He was trying to catch up fast. 'So she is out there... somewhere?'

'Oh yes, indeed. A very long way, however. She is on Hyspero. And it is events on that world that forced her to do this very strange business with the dimensions. She was trying to save us all, you see.'

'But... but is she all right, then? She is still alive?'

Magda shrugged. 'Communication is very difficult, Terry. As you can appreciate, we are talking about communications with a semi-fictionalised universe. It is not overly reliable, you see, the connection between.'

They were interrupted then by a tired-looking woman, who came tramping in from a separate room, carrying a roll of print-out. She was wearing a pinny and a hair net. With a shock, Terry recognized her as one of the women out of Greggs the bakers on the High Street. She saluted Magda wearily and handed her the roll of paper.

'This is all we've got, Magda, from a whole day scanning. We've probed as far as we dare through the

Dreadful Flap… if we go any further we don't know what might happen.'

'Very good,' said Magda, waving her away. She peered at the densely-printed text on the computer paper. 'I can't make any sense of this. Chapter One, it says.' She beckoned Terry to come and have a look. 'What do you make of it?'

Terry came closer and squinted at the print. He knew what it was at once. 'This is mine! I wrote this!'

7.

I carried on studying the weirdly-shaped parchment. One thing I had noticed was that, unlike maps I was used to, this one had no words on. There were no place names or names of anything at all. Only odd, indecipherable symbols. I guessed that must have something to do with the absence of books. They had all been taken away somewhere, is what Frank the Fox had told us. All the books in Hyspero.

Maybe there were no written-down words anywhere in the land … Only in my black notebook, in my backpack. I could almost feel it, like a presence, at my back … with my notes… just my usual scrawly handwriting… but that writing was unique in this land… the words squirming away on the page…

I turned my attention back to the map.

There was no mistaking the brilliant red triangular zone in the dead centre of the map. 'That's where the Scarlet Empress lives, isn't it?'

Aunty Iris played the torch beam right over the spot. 'Hmm. Yes. That's the ancient City of Central Hyspero itself. It's the capital city of this whole land. You'll not find a more hectic and tumultuous place anywhere in all the worlds. That's the Scarlet Palace... where she lives...'

I peered at the small, scratchy sketch in the centre of the red triangle. It was a representation of a horrible face, trapped inside what looked like a bottle or a jar.

Again, Aunty Iris didn't seem very keen on discussing the Scarlet Empress. She drained her coffee cup and clambered up onto her feet again. 'Oh, my aching bones. I forget I'm as old as this.'

As we set off through the level tunnel, deep underground, I was looking at the dark silhouette of my aunty, with that yellow nimbus of torchlight bobbing around her, turning all the crimson walls a bloody orange colour ... and I was thinking about how my dad had said she was a maniac.

We were following her deep underground in an unknown land... and we were hoping that we'd emerge into a place called The Shrieking Jungle. And there was a Golden God somewhere out there and it was our quest to find him and get him to help us... to save the whole of the world!

It was starting to seem a little bit too much to me.

Somewhere else there was a Scarlet Empress, who wasn't exactly wishing us well. She wanted to smelt us down... and she wouldn't be pleased that I had my black book with me...

We were very dependent on my Aunty Iris. She was dragging us out, right into the unknown.

I was really giving myself the creeps. Then I felt very disloyal and ashamed of myself, for having even the slightest doubts about my Aunty Iris. Aunty Iris was the greatest! She'd been on HUNDREDS of adventures before! Even back when she and her sister had been kids... they'd been running about here in Hyspero! Simon and I couldn't ask for a better ally and guide.

But still, Aunty Iris was lumbering along and wheezing quite heavily by then. She was tiring easily. She didn't seem all that nimble and healthy, all of a sudden.

Also there was something mysterious and shifty in the old woman's manner. It was as if she wasn't quite telling us the whole story yet. There was an odd glint in Aunty Iris's eye. There was a nervous flicker there, that she tried to hide while she smiled brightly and encouragingly.

I noticed all of this as we took our midday break and Aunty Iris opened up tinfoil parcels of cheese and pickle sandwiches. Something was going through Aunty Iris's mind. A thought that she didn't want to share yet with us, her fellow adventurers.

I was used to secretive grown-ups, though. Look at mum and dad! They'd not told me anything about Hyspero - ever!

Well... we all had our secrets. For some reason I hadn't mentioned my black book and silver pen to Aunty Iris. I don't know why. I felt a bit weird, having them with me, when I knew such things were forbidden in this land. I almost felt guilty about having them, and writing my notes down in secret... like I was doing something wrong.

I decided to put all these funny thoughts and suspicions and guilt to the back of my mind. We were all together on this journey, the three of us, and Aunty Iris would let us know *everything we needed to know, as and when we needed to know it. We had to trust her. There was simply no choice.*

As we ate our sandwiches we had come to rest at the side of an underwater brook. The water was black and bubbling and it looked (and smelled) like an open sewer. Aunty Iris flashed her torch up the tunnel, to where the stream became a river. And beyond that, the roof of the tunnel yawned wider and wider and it seemed that there was a whole lake up ahead.

'That's where we have to go next,' Aunty Iris said grimly. Then she tossed Simon an extra silver parcel.

'No more sandwiches for me, thanks, Aunty Iris,' he said as he neatly caught the package. I knew that he hadn't been keen on the pickle. It had bits in.

Aunty Iris laughed. 'That's not sandwiches, Simon. It's an inflatable dinghy.'

8.

Life didn't really begin for her until the day she found the bus.

She found a dying double decker bus somewhere deep in the desert and made it her own. She was just a child then, with no idea what or who she might turn out to be. And the bus was just an empty shell, flung down as if by some godly hand. However, when she saw it, she knew that the bus was her destiny and that it belonged to her in a way that nothing ever had before.

It was a magnificent beast, felled in its prime. It had lived in splendour, she instinctively felt. It had spent its life streaking through the mountains and skies. She sensed that it had come from afar.

Now it was crumpled, gashed, bleeding and dying all alone. Like some mythical beast, its sides pierced by enemy swords, it had plummeted out of the skies and come to rest on alien sands. Was that a whimper? A ghastly, drawn-out, hydraulic hiss as it expired?

The girl who was to become Iris found that she was drawn to it, to tend to it, to nurse it back to health. At first this seemed like an impossible task. What did she know of the mechanical innards of behemoths like the Number 22?

Until then she had never had anything to look after or nurture. She had barely learned to look after herself. She was still very young and her life so far had been a matter of accident and survival. The girl had ricocheted from place to place and had never felt secure, wherever she landed up. Now though, she was happy to draw a line under the whole sorry mess and declare the day she met her celestial omnibus as the day that her new life was begun.

Iris and the Number 22.

The rest of it – the time she had spent as an infant within the Clockworks, or the highway accident, or her imprisonment within the decaying walls of Wherewithal House – she would try to dismiss it all, and forget about it. These were just lurid shadows that filled up her dreams. None of those pasts would be real to her anymore. She was a strong-willed girl and could simply decide on these things. And now, she was resolved, her history would begin with this connection that she felt with the ailing vehicle…

She could feel it inside her mind. A slight thrumming at first. A continuous buzz of nervous enquiry. There was a sad, sickly feeling tickling away at her as she went up the spiral staircase to gaze at the messy remnants on the top deck. Almost a kind of nostalgia, though she was unfamiliar with that sensation.

As she explored the jumbled confines of the bus she realised that what she was in touch with must be the spirit of the machine itself and it was gently probing at her mind. She felt an immediate, indissoluble bond with the heart and mind of the Number Twenty Two… And all of a sudden it seemed to be promising her all sorts of things… if only she would help it to live again…

TING TING

A tinny bell sound. Deep inside her mind. A call to arms. A deep welling of memory. A distinct impression that she had heard this noise before.

Her companion, the aged and battle-scarred Panda, who had been so instrumental in helping her escape from her previous life, was rather mystified when his new friend told him she could talk with the bus. He boggled at her and then felt alarmed. He had brought her here. He was responsible now for what became of her. Then he wondered whether perhaps the girl was having a game with him, but he couldn't understand why. His small bearish head was befuddled as he tried to work out whether she was mocking him. Why would she do that? They were friends, weren't they? New friends, it was true, and they were still working out whether they would be loyal to one another...

He had crawled through the desert for her, and scaled the walls of the castle where she was imprisoned. He had presented his own, small self to her as her rescuer and her friend. Panda had done everything in his powers to make her understand.

She laughed at his confusion. Then she saw that he was somewhat hurt (she was only just learning what a sensitive creature he could be) and tried to explain to him.

She wanted her new, furry friend to understand what was happening to her.

'I can hear the omnibus inside my mind. That is what she calls herself. She is an omnibus. A celestial omnibus. The Number 22. And... somehow, she recognises me, Panda. She knew me the moment I climbed down into the earth and the wreckage to see her. She has started to explain herself to me. She says... she says that she has already had a lifetime among the stars. She has journeyed between dimensions for hundreds of years, and she longs to do so again. She feels it like a hunger, or worse, like a gaping wound in her side. This lying low here... this damage done to her... it's agony to her. She's holding back the waves of panic and pain through sheer force of will. But soon she must give in... she truly is dying, Panda.

'But maybe... no, not *maybe*. She is quite sure of this. And so am I. I know she is right. She can come out of this.

She can ride again. But she needs my help and yours, Panda. Before the blazing life inside her dwindles to a tiny spark… before she is snuffed out entirely in this dreadful, poisoned desert… She says that I can help her, Panda. I have the knowledge inside this head of mine… she can feel it. She knows that it's there… stitched into my mind. The knowhow of the Clockworks is sewn into the lining of my brain… all their secrets… the equations and formulae that we need in order to negotiate the spaceways, the timelines, the striations of the Multiverse… The bus is telling me that I can help her… that it's not the damage to her metal skin that is holding her down… it's the knowhow that's been knocked out of her head. And I am a kind of miracle, come to wake her. I'm like a prince in the fairytale, come to wake her with a kiss. I carry the numbers in my head, you see – the endless chant of them. By communing with me she can leap from this universe of ours and into the next…'

Panda stared at her. 'Can you trust this machine?'

She felt sure that she could. She was fourteen. The bus was millennia old. But they were equals and they were fated. Panda was just along for the ride.

*

The bus was unruly for quite some time. The girl didn't know what to expect, though, never having owned a transdimensional double decker before. Sometimes when she slept in her bed on the top deck it would rev its engines of its own accord. It would leap sideways through the dimensions and go exploring. Sometimes Iris would totter downstairs in the morning to find that she had been transported to another time and place. There might even be strangers from an unfamiliar era sitting downstairs, having tea with Panda.

The old bear (though he hated to be described as a bear) seemed very much more at home with the whole travelling lark. He took it all in his tiny stride. He encouraged Iris to embrace the whole cosmos, and relish those days when they stepped outside, not knowing where or when they might be.

Earth was a great favourite of Panda's, of course. Iris didn't remember the first time that she heard of the place, but pretty soon she and her furry friend were hanging out there a lot. Panda was keen on staying at the Chelsea Hotel in New York in the summer of 1966.

Using currency he apparently found in a drawer somewhere on the bus, he booked out a room for the whole of August and he and Iris would return there periodically. Iris bought a lot of clothes during those sporadic visits, and Panda became friends with a whole lot of rather earnest beatnik girls. The double decker bus would stand parked outside the Chelsea Hotel and people marvelled at it in an ironic kind of way. Panda explained to Iris that the bus shape came from somewhere called England, not too far away.

'So this is where the bus came from in the first place?'

He tapped his nose. 'Not exactly. Bits of it did, we could say.' He was rolling up a strange kind of cigarette with his bulky paws. 'The bus is a kind of magpie, Iris. She's picked up bits and pieces here and there... Bits of her transdimensional engines... and parts of her exterior... She's built it up over the years...'

Iris wondered how Panda knew so much about it. Sometimes his knowledge of the bus and how it worked discomfited her. She felt she was being led into something that she only partly understood. She had been dragged into this ongoing adventure by this Panda. He had even made her change her name...

They walked through Greenwich village one bright autumn morning, carrying orange juice and bread rolls for a picnic. 'Who was this Iris, anyway?' she asked him, all of a sudden.

The kids and hobos were out already in Washington Square, drinking in the sunshine. Panda had had a rough night and didn't want to be bothered by questions. 'What are you talking about, Iris?'

'You're making me into this other Iris,' she said. 'You make me talk like her, dress like her... Who was she, Panda?' The girl was struck by her own temerity. She hadn't articulated these thoughts even to herself yet. Others were watching now, as she stood arguing in the park with the tiny Panda.

'You're not copying anyone!' he roared. 'You're learning to become yourself!'

But Lilith / Iris didn't even know who that was.

But would she really be any better off if she'd remained on her homeworld? What if she was still living like a prisoner in Wherewithal House? Sickly and bad-tempered and cosseted by servants? Surely she wouldn't rather be there. She should be thanking Panda all day and every day for showing her the way to leave that life. She had left that whole world behind. And, if what Panda told her was true, she had left behind that whole universe.

'The Obverse is such a very small place, Iris,' he told her. 'You piloted the bus straight through the Cosmic Ringpull and out the other side.'

'I did?'

'Oh yes. Not many have ever done that before, you know. But there you were. Steady as anything. At the helm of your bus.'

'But how? I can't even…'

'You and the bus together, Iris. Together you cracked the Ringpull. And now we're in the vast universe beyond. You have left the Obverse behind.'

'C-can I ever get back? I mean, should I want to… can I ever return to that place? And… the Clockworks?'

Panda looked at her solemnly at this point. 'I don't know. No one has ever done that.'

'Oh..!'

'Why should you want to go back to that poky little place? You never liked it there very much…!'

'I know,' she said. 'It's just that…'

But she couldn't think of anything more to say to him. Panda had given her a new name, a new identity. And a whole new universe to be in.

That night he took her to the Factory to meet Andy Warhol and the others. Iris was in her element, looking on as Panda screentested for his very own movie. Even Andy – who managed to look both startled and jaded at the same time – was amazed by Panda, whom he said was absolutely made for black and white movies. All of his assistants, hangers on and groupie startlets gathered round to see the small bear.

'In the future,' Panda cleared his throat noisily. 'Everyone will be famous for precisely fifteen millennia!'

They all laughed at him. There was a kind of party then, and Iris wandered away from room to room to watch the lightshows and listen to the band. When she saw Panda again he was wearing a colourful plastic hat and a kind of cape.

'Hey, Iris,' he said. 'I was talking to some of the guys – poets, you know – and I happened to mention that we were thinking of heading to the Lake District next, to hang out with the Lakeland poets. Could we spare some room and take some of them along with us to the eighteen-hundreds?'

She didn't like the sound of any of this. She wasn't having Panda fill the bus with deadbeats. And she didn't like the look of these poets at all. They looked unwashed and spaced out.

'Oh, come on, Iris, please!' Panda whined. 'We thought we'd stand outside Coleridge's front door while he was having his famous nap on the sofa, dreaming about the most brilliant poem in the world and then we'd fling open the door and we'd all be tooting our kazoos and…!'

Iris yelled at him: 'I said, no, Panda! I'm not having a bunch of poets aboard! Forget it!…' And this was a moment of taking control for her. She wasn't about to be dictated to by Panda. He seemed to think the whole bus thing was like being in a non-stop party, whereas Iris was having bigger ideas. Or rather, she was starting to. She could see that there was a lot to think about… a lot to take on…

Later that night, as the party went on and on… she found herself up on the roof of the Factory, gazing at the derelict warehouses and rooftops of the West Village. Neon scarred the night sky and the stars could only be dimly seen.

Andy joined her up there and she saw that he was still wearing his dark glasses. His skin looked so pale when he was outside. The night air somehow made him seem less real than he was indoors, among his acolytes and artworks.

'Hey, it's a lot to take on,' he told her. Somehow he seemed to know just what she was thinking about.

'But a whole new universe…' she sighed. She lit a cigarette. She much preferred Earth fags to any she had known in her own universe. 'You know I'm not from round here, right?'

'I knew as soon as you stepped into the Factory,' Andy said. 'Lots of people who come in here look like they come from another planet. But you really did.'

She was amazed he wasn't alarmed by any of this talk. As far as she knew, no one on his planet had met aliens yet. The Earth had been bottled up all by itself throughout its history. Yet here was Andy Warhol, blasé as anything.

'Oh, that's because I've met you before. You and Panda. Christmas 1958. You were much older, he was much younger. I even came aboard the bus that year. You took me to the North Pole to see a man who said he was Santa Claus.'

'I did?'

He turned to smile at her and Iris saw her reflection twice over in his Jackie O glasses. 'Oh, sure, honey. You know, you have a really great time. You'll love it. Your life from now on… it's gonna be great.'

'Really?'

'Oh, yeah. Sure. Just enjoy your travels, honey. Don't take it so seriously.'

'And go with Panda to meet these Lakeland poets, whatever they are? In the eighteenth century?'

'Sure. It's already happened, you see. Panda interrupts Coleridge just as the old guy's dreaming of a poem about Xanadu. There's a knock on the door and Panda comes roller-skating in with you dolled up as Olivia Newton-John on roller skates, and all these guys dressed as the Electric Light Orchestra on roller skates as well. It's hysterical. It's really neat. And it's already history.' Andy patted her gently on the arm of her spacesuit. 'You'll get used to it all, honey.'

9.

'Handy I had a dinghy about my person, eh?' Aunty Iris seemed very pleased with herself.

The violence of the water settled down somewhat and she sat back elegantly, stretching out as we bobbed along. She looked as if she couldn't care less ... as if white-water rafting was something she did every day.

We settled into a smooth rhythm as the black stream unspooled deeper and deeper into the tunnels, broadening as it went. We paddled and bailed out, paddled and bailed out. Aunty Iris watched us and carried on talking.

'We have to try to keep out of her radar for as long as possible,' Aunty Iris said. 'We don't want the Empress sending her soldiers after us. We don't want her to know we're on a quest...'

I asked, 'But what about the nerve centre? How come the Empress doesn't know about that?'

'Ah,' Aunty Iris grinned. 'That's very clever. My base of operations is walled around by a force shield. Marvellous thing. The Empress has no idea that it's there or what goes on inside. It's the one place in Hyspero that the Empress knows nothing about. Technology, you see. Rather than magic. I don't think she understands anything that isn't magical.' Aunty Iris seemed very proud of her force shield. 'But now we have left the protection of the mountain,' she said darkly. 'And we have to be on our guard. She hasn't got to know where you two are... or that I am back here in Hyspero. That would be a very bad thing.'

'I always wished I had a secret base,' Simon said, taking his mind off the undulating water. 'But I wouldn't have built it in the shape of Make Up Girl,' he added.

Aunty Iris pursed her lips and narrowed her eyes. It was a look Simon and I were getting used to. She put it on when she was considering exactly how much to tell us. She nodded slowly and said: 'You know she isn't just a doll. That's just how you know her in your world. She was a real person. Once upon a time. Someone who lived here long, long ago. She guards this whole land and she is a sworn enemy of the Scarlet Empress, who she sees as a usurper. She's the one responsible for your being here, Kelly. In some ways, the person you call Make Up Girl really IS Hyspero. The spirit of the land itself... The Empress Euphemia! And one day maybe you'll meet her.'

Simon glanced at me. He didn't look like he'd be keen on meeting Make Up Girl in the actual flesh. But I was desperate to. 'You mean she could return to life?' I asked Aunty Iris. 'You said she's been dead for many years.'

'There are many things that are said in the old legends,' Aunty Iris shrugged. 'Some say that the Empress Euphemia will return to life. She will return to save the whole of her land. That's what was written down, at any rate. In one of the old books. The books that we no longer have...' Aunty Iris fell quiet then.

'There's so much to learn about Hyspero,' I said wistfully.

'It's your land now, Kelly,' Aunty Iris smiled. 'It always was. You belong here.'

The three of us sat in relative quiet and peace, thinking this over, with just the gurgling noise of the current to accompany our thoughts.

Then the moment passed as we hit a rougher patch of water and the flimsy boat bucked and jounced and threatened to throw us overboard. Aunty Iris let out an affronted shriek. 'Cling on, everyone!' she cried, unnecessarily.

We held on tight to each other and soon we were drenched right through by the foul-smelling water.

After the initial surprise Aunty Iris seemed quite exhilarated by it all. She whipped off her sopping hat and waved it around like she was riding a wild horse. 'Paddle! Paddle for all you're worth! We're coming to the lake!'

Our dinghy shot out like a cork from a bottle, into the more placid waters of the underground lake. Here, the smooth rock of the ceiling arched gently over us and we were aware of tremendous depths beneath. It was quieter here: just the dank sounds of ancient water pulsing and dripping.

It was the dingiest-looking lake that any of us had ever seen. Ahead, everything was gloomy and cowled in darkness. Aunty Iris got us to paddle over the sides with our hands again, first one side and then the other, and she probed the blackness with her torchbeam. The pale lancing beams reflected weirdly on the oily water.

Where were we going? Did she even know?

Simon yelped out once in shock, and then howled in pain and anger. Something must have nipped his hand! He jumped up as something underwater grabbed hold of his finger and pulled. He snatched his hands back and we were staring at him.

'Piranha fish!' he shouted. 'Sharks! Killer squid! Get your hands out of the water!' His voice was squeaky with fright.

'Don't be daft, Simon,' I said. 'It's your imagination. There's nothing like that in the water, is there, Aunty Iris?'

'Er, um,' said Aunty Iris. 'There could be just about anything in water like this. Maybe it's best if you stop dangling bits of yourself over the edge, Kelly love.'

I drew myself fully aboard and sat quietly, quite conscious now of how thin the bottom of the craft was.

'Maybe Simon made a mistake,' said Aunty Iris hopefully.

Suddenly there was a frenzy of thrashing and snapping around the dinghy. The water started to seethe and boil.

I jumped to my feet as the boat rocked and shuddered. 'What are they? What's attacking us?'

'I told you,' said Simon. 'Piranhas!'

'No,' said Aunty Iris. 'Look, I can see claws...'

Now there were holes appearing in the hull of the craft. The claws were scissoring and snipping through the tight skin of the rubber right next to us. The water churned and lashed over the sides and, at first it felt like sharp rocks were cutting through, but the pool was too deep for that.

'What are they?' I yelled.

'I wonder how close we are to the bank,' Aunty Iris was saying, quite calmly. 'Should we swim for it? Can you two swim?' She was on her feet and flashing the torch about.

I got an impression of terrible pincers lashing through the water. There seemed to be hundreds of the beasts massing around us, slashing at the boat.

'Ah,' said Aunty Iris. 'Lobsters.'

10.

In the MIAOW bunker deep under Darlington, Terry was still coming to terms with the fact that a great deal of what he had known to be made up was in fact fairly true.

Magda left him alone to absorb it, and she peered at the consoles for a while, though she found them all pretty mystifying. The two women from Greggs reappeared, bearing bagloads of pasties and cakes that had been left unbought the previous evening, and would only have been chucked out anyway. Terry accepted a sausage roll mutely, while a tiny part of his mind wondered if that's why Magda had brought in these operatives from Greggs: merely for the free stuff. It was an uncharitable thought, he realised.

The two women were poring over viewscreens and print-offs and working busily at their stations, so he gathered they were pretty expert in all this stuff anyway. One of them was shedding crumbs everywhere, though.

Was it all true, he wondered? Every single detail of it?

In his own Iris Wildthyme adventures he had created human characters, who lived here in Darlington. They belonged to a bookshop on the South Road called the Great Big Book Exchange. He had written a story in which a young man – one not entirely unlike himself, in another life, say – was given the chance to own the bookshop that he had loved the most as a child. Simon – that was the character's name (was Terry alone in forgetting the names of his characters? It seemed a silly thing to do – but they were so arbitrary, weren't they? And he made up so many of them... and so many of them were similar, too! He kept introducing youngish male characters who lived lives analogous to his own...)

There was Simon, who took over the bookshop from the mysterious man with two plastic arms, and there was the surly Gothic assistant, Kelly. And she got dragged along with Simon, too, in the adventures aboard Iris's bus. This was just how Terry had written it, and he added others, too... There was the obnoxious poet, Anthony Marvelle and his sinister poodle, Missy. Missy came from the notorious Dogworld, which had been introduced into what was known as the Irisverse several years ago in another book by someone Terry didn't know. That was how it worked in the Irisverse – it was all borrowing and swapping like that.

And they'd all gone to the world of Hyspero, hadn't they? Another theft on Terry's part. Hyspero had been in the original TV show, hadn't it? In the very final episode Iris and her friends had visited this vast, magical world at the very brink of the cosmos... it was a spectacular blend of the Arabian Nights and Oz and Wonderland and Narnia: it was every made-up world consolidated into one. And on a 1979 TV budget – by some kind of miracle - it had even looked amazing. It had seeped into the imagination of young Terry Kelly and it had drawn him back periodically to imagine it further and more fully...

Yes, he had written about Hyspero. And he had plonked all of his Iris characters there, right in the middle of the souks and bazaars, the deserts and the dunes...

But what had come next? He was frowning, hunting for a napkin for his sausage roll-greasy fingers. What had become of his heroes in his novel when he'd placed them at the end of the universe? They were on a quest, weren't they? They had the ancient old Empress, the original Empress, and she was stoppered up in a jar. They were taking her back to the palace from which she had been purloined, and they were keeping her away from enemies and villains... all because of some magic the old Empress could do. Something only she in all the cosmos could do...

The book had almost written itself. Terry remembered that. He had been up against the deadline, only six months ago, and he'd relinquished himself into the care of his own book. I give you this many hours per day: you do the rest. I will sit here in this trance and you just use me to transmit yourself through...

And somehow that had worked. The words had jerked out of his fingers, line by line (he typed with one hand, to his embarrassment – very fast, twisting his back, giving himself headaches)... and page after page scrolled upwards. When he read chapters back at the end of the day he was astonished. Things were happening to his characters... adventures were happening... but he wasn't even sure they had happened to him as well.

Reading back was often the first he knew of events in his novel. It was a very strange time for him. His mind was, perhaps, on other things. His boyfriend had left him for a job elsewhere, down South. He was drinking a lot of this green, almost fizzy wine his ex-boyfriend had brought back from abroad and it was giving him heartburn. And he sat up each night in what was supposed to be a luxury apartment writing stuff that even he didn't know how he was making it up. Or whether it was, in fact, making *him* up in turn.

Oh, and he fancied his lead character, Simon. Had he said that? Oh, it was true. And it had to be the lowest point he'd ever reached.

In the Iris Wildthyme fanzines and online fan forums, reviews of his books often harped on about the fact that he introduced what they called Mary-Sues. Apparently this meant that he deliberately introduced a character who was supposed to be himself. A wishwank fan fantasy, these readers opined. But Terry didn't really see it as he himself dropping a version of Terry into the proceedings… he had no special desire personally to run about fighting monsters and travelling through time. It was more a case of his handcrafting boyfriends in the shape of fiction – or vice versa, perhaps. This was more embarrassing than the fanwank idea of writing about himself, so he thought himself lucky no one had really cottoned on.

Simon was his in a way no one living had ever been… No one real, anyway.

This comingling of the dimensions that Magda was on about… now, that was interesting. Could it be possible? Could a being like Iris truly shunt worlds several notches away from their original position in the realms of likelihood?

Uncomfortably, Terry had to agree that she could. Certainly the Iris that had been created by successive TV and fiction writers would find such a task possible. It was just the kind of cosmic solution she would delight in – and probably accomplish using a heap of old electronic parts, a potted plant, a pair of old tights and a four-dimensional chess board. Or a vial of golden dragon's blood from Hyspero.

She could surely pierce those gaps between fictional dimensions, easy as anything. And, if a fictional character was as clever as that, there would be no holding her securely within any fictional space. She would be bound to bust her way out.

To Terry it now seemed entirely logical (but just what had been inside that sausage roll..?) and actually, it was surprising that she hadn't made an appearance yet in the dimension that Terry thought of as home…

This is what you get for working with tricky, slippery characters.

Magda called him over suddenly to where she was working. He hurried over, brushing pastry crumbs off his striped cardigan and felt woozy as he went to her. Somewhere he had lost a night's sleep (what time was it anyway?)… and he found it hard, at first to concentrate when she told him to

READ THIS

11.

How many hours had it been since Iris and Panda had disappeared over the top of that dune?

Simon didn't know. He'd been dozing aboard the bus in the midday heat and now he had no idea about the passing of time. He woke with a shock, and found himself sweating almost feverishly. Foolishly, he looked at his watch which was, of course, useless here.

Surely he should be used to that, by now? His watch had been no use to him in ages. It was a while since he had been working on Earth time.

He glanced around at the lower deck of the bus and its usual jumble of furniture and gee-gaws. He was quite alone. The blinds were down on one side of the bus, and the searing sunshine still came blazing through. The other windows were bare: and through their dust-coated panes he could see the desert stretching countless miles beyond.

It occurred to him that perhaps he ought to be worried. His friends had stomped off, up the hill ages ago. His head felt muzzy as if he had slept for hours. And the others – Barbra, Jenny and the Empress – had vanished also, it seemed.

Simon got to his feet woozily. He could be here all alone now. Stuck in the middle of nowhere on this double decker bus.

A very long way from home indeed.

Even as he teetered on the edge of panic it never occurred to him to wish he was still at home. Not for one second did he regret joining Iris on the bus. When he had joined her crew he had known that travels through the cosmos at her side would involve terrible dangers and calamities. He could tell that was the kind of life she lived. Since then, Panda had filled him in on some of their more hair-raising past adventures. And Simon had been involved in some terrifying scrapes of his own, too. But even then he never regretted coming along for the ride…

His moment of panic died down a little then, as he opened the bus's hydraulic doors and saw his friends gathered together on the multi-coloured sand, a little distance away.

'Have Iris and Panda come back?' he called.

Jenny turned back to stare at him. She knew he had been napping and he could see she didn't approve. Jenny – head of MIAOW Darlington and all round tough cookie – didn't really seem to approve of many people.

'They've abandoned us!' she yelled back.

Simon knew they would never do such a thing, and he also knew that Iris would never willingly abandon her bus. He knew at once that something must have happened to them.

Jenny had turned back to where Barbra the vending the machine was staring. Both were squinting at the distant horizon. When Simon followed their gaze he could suddenly see a dust cloud through the shimmering heat waves. Something was coming towards them.

He came to stand by Jenny. 'Do you have any idea what it is?'

She said tersely, 'We're sitting targets here. For whatever or whoever it is.'

Barbra looked alarmed. 'I don't like the look of this...' Simon stared at her, wondering what was different about the vending machine. Then he noticed that, amongst the cans of pop in her glass frontage was hidden away the ancient jar of the first Hysperon Empress. It seemed as good a place as any to hide the old dame, he supposed.

'It's a ship,' Jenny said, adjusting something to the monocle she habitually wore. Simon realized that device must be equipped with telescopic lenses and goodness knows what else. 'A sand ship,' she murmured.

In a matter of seconds they could see that she was correct.

It was a monstrous vehicle. Battle-scarred and rusty with the desert winds, it stood as fully tall as the Odeon Cinema in Darlington. As it sailed effortlessly across the sea of sand towards them, Simon could make out dark little slits all over the machine. He could feel hostile eyes trained upon his friends...

'Did you lock the bus?' Jenny asked him. 'Do it right now. We don't want Iris's secrets falling into anybody's hands...'

When Simon had finished securing the bus, the ship came to a halt. A ramp extended and doors flew up. There was a strange smell on the air all of a sudden. It was a tang of exotic spices, perhaps. A whiff of some strange elsewhere.

Soldiers in flowing robes emerged from the dark confines. They were tattooed from head to foot in elaborate patterns, Simon saw. Most of their coloured flesh was on display as they lined up intimidatingly before Simon and his friends.

'Don't move a muscle,' Jenny warned, eyeing the strange spearlike weapons these soldiers were carrying at their sides.

Simon heard Barbra moan, 'Oh my...'

The tattooed guards glared straight ahead and stayed motionless as another robed figure joined them on the sand. This was a much older, bulkier human form, swathed in billowing black folds of cloth and wearing a ludicrous, bulbous hat on his head. He cut an almost comical figure until he looked at his potential prisoners with an expression of such malign bad will that Barbra almost expired on the spot.

'I am Vizier to the Scarlet Empress,' he said in his nasal, whinnying voice. 'And this vehicle of yours is known to us. This... celestial omnibus... it is in our records. It is in our history. How does it come to be here now?'

Jenny elected herself as spokesperson and Simon found himself relieved. 'We are only travelers on board the bus. Its owner is not here. We are here for reasons of our own and mean you no harm.'

Simon could see the Vizier wasn't very impressed by this. 'The women to whom this... omnibus belongs is known to us. She is our enemy, or so the legends tell. You are her friends, hmm?'

'Oh.. no,' said Jenny. 'We are no friends of hers. Really, we were more like prisoners at her mercy.'

The Vizier's tone became much harsher. He was losing his patience with her. 'Where is Iris Wildthyme? Are you hiding her?'

'She went off exploring, over the dunes, several hours ago…' Jenny burst out. 'She can't have gone far…'

The Vizier stared over their shoulders, into the far distance. 'She went into the shifting sands on foot? Not so far, then… but she may be unreachable… The shifting sands can take you to all sorts of places… from which it may prove impossible to return…'

For a moment it looked as if he had gone into a reverie from which *he* may never have returned… but suddenly his attention snapped back to Jenny, Simon and Barbra.

'What is… this machine?'

'I'm Barbra,' said Barbra, sounding fearful and piqued at the same time. 'I-I'm a… snack machine.'

'This has no meaning for me,' sighed the Vizier. 'You are a living being, though?'

'Very much so,' said Barbra firmly.

Then, with a great sweeping motion, the Vizier instructed his tattooed guards to round these prisoners up. 'Bring them aboard the desert ship. They will come with us to Hyspero City.'

Simon and the others found that they had no choice in the matter. 'But… what about the bus?' he cried as the guards advanced.

'We will leave it here,' said the Vizier. 'But we will keep it under surveillance in case its mistress does return. But if she has walked into the shifting sands voluntarily, I fear that may not be any time soon…'

12.

'Where next?' I said, trying to look eager.

'Up there,' Aunty Iris said, peering up into the source of the soft light on this shore of the lake. 'We can go above ground again.'

We all peered up and, right above us, there was a disc of bright green daylight. It seemed to be a window, at the top of the walls around us.

We all drew in a breath.

'That's the Shrieking Jungle up there…' I said, quietly.

And, if you listened carefully, you could indeed hear a distant shrieking, far above.

We glanced searchingly at the walls of the cavern for a way up into the world above. You could see that the walls had been carved into, perhaps centuries ago, and they were decorated with all kinds of intricate statues.

There was also a network of staircases leading up to the window at the top. It was tangled in vines and seemed fairly easy for climbing.

'Maybe our luck's in,' Aunty Iris grunted, leading the way. Then she paused to pull a lobster out of her cardigan pocket. 'We'll get to the top, strike up a camp, and eat this fella for lunch.'

She grinned and waved the startled, blinded lobster in our faces.

Sometimes there was something very discomfiting about Aunty Iris and the almost heartless way she went on.

So, the next thing was, we went clambering up more steps. These were mildewed blue and green. It was like climbing up a very soft, old cheese. As we went we paused now and then to examine the carvings in the rock walls.

'These are ancient,' Aunty Iris mused. 'I wonder who did them.'

I was hauling myself up on the slimy vines, past a row of fierce-looking statues. They had vicious pointed teeth and very long hair. Or fur. Whichever, it was all over their bodies and their extra long arms and legs.

'I don't like the looks of these fellas,' Aunty Iris said, patting one on the head. 'Sloths. Horrible things! No manners! Lice! Bad breath! I hope we don't meet any of them!'

Somehow her jauntiness didn't inspire much confidence.

13.

Iris and Panda shuffled into the darkness behind the heavy curtains. They could still hear the muffled boom and chatter of the cinema... somewhere in the darkness... ahead of them, somewhere... They recognized some of the voices.

'This is what Hyspero is like, Panda, chuck,' she hissed. 'It throws up these perplexing and surreal moments... Very often, they're traps... '

The ground beneath their feet was sandy and strewn with pebbles, reminding them that they weren't really in the basement of a London pub. Panda seized his friend's sleeve just then, noticing that there were insects dashing hither and thither. Worse than insects... 'Scorpions!' he cried.

Iris seized him in her arms and plunged into the darkness ahead, crushing the creatures as she went under her plastic boots.

There was a span of darkness in the corridor ahead. A deep, inky blackness – and they halted just in time. It was a terrible pit; a chasm yawning before them. Iris took a running jump and managed to get clear to the other side.

Further along the tunnel there were creepers and vines. They clogged and choked the way forward and, when our heroes tried to slip past them, they stirred into unnatural life. Panda shrieked as he felt the slimy tendrils take hold of his furry limbs... Iris simply reached into her handbag and produced her trusty cigarette lighter. She flicked the setting to 'flame thrower' and incinerated the whole lot.

'My hero!' gasped Panda.

'Don't assume we're out of the woods yet,' she warned. Her voice had become all grim and determined, Panda thought.

And, indeed, there were other trials as they advanced into the tunnels beneath the pub in the middle of the desert. There were two gleaming robots holding scythes who suddenly appeared. They tried to ensnare our heroes in a game of logic and quick-thinking. Panda became rather muddled and almost doomed them both, but luckily Iris was still thinking clearly. Then, when they thought surely these trials must be coming to an end, there was a task involving two potter's wheels and the making of a nice vase in two minutes flat. This was followed by a very esoteric quiz, a rather long and complicated game of charades, and a vicious swordfight with several dozen animated skeletons.

After that lot, Panda and Iris were starting to wonder whether it was all worth it. They were exhausted.

'But if it's so difficult, there must be something worthwhile at the end of this tunnel, eh?' Iris winked at him.

Panda wasn't so sure. Sometimes he thought that Iris would fling herself into adventures for the sheer hell of it. She didn't care what was waiting at the other end.

He mulled this over as he watched her endure a weird challenge that saw her playing a baby grand piano that electrocuted her whenever she went wrong in following a fiddly score. But the music was obviously weird, alien, Hysperon music, and it was very hard to tell when it was in or out of tune at all.

Panda thought about the fact that he was following this woman into weirder and weirder escapades... and had spent so much of his life following her, with blind faith in her abilities...

Now that he furrowed his brow – and watched his friend plonking away and shrieking now and then as the keyboard became live – he realized that he couldn't quite remember how many years he'd been travelling with Iris Wildthyme. Things had become more than a tad hazy.

When she came to the end of the peculiar piece of music, a door opened up ahead of them and they were free to progress. Iris was miffed because Panda had gone off in his own thoughts and hadn't really appreciated her success in the musical challenge.

'You can't afford to let your concentration slip, Panda,' she said.

'I was just thinking,' he murmured.

'Thinking, he says!' she laughed. 'Typical – we're in the midst of deadly danger, and you're *thinking*.'

Luckily, their next task was something only somebody ten inches high with very small, dextrous and furry paws could accomplish. Panda got them through that one and looked rather pleased with himself.

At last, though, they came to the end of the seemingly endless corridors and entered what looked very like a projection room. There were dusty cans and tatters of celluloid film curled about on the floor. A projector machine was trained on a small hole in the wall and it was chugging away noisily, beaming brilliant light into the unseen auditorium.

'I wonder if *all* these films are about me,' mused Iris.

Panda had found a ten by eight glossy still pinned to the wall and was both pleased and disturbed that it showed himself in a rather glamorous pose.

'Hello..?' Iris shouted. 'There must be someone here to operate all this gubbins…'

And indeed there was. This was the point at which Iris and Panda came face to face for the first time with Fenster the dragon.

First there came the noise of heavily wheels inching along. Something went crash on the concrete floor. Then there was a muttering and a hiss of hot steam. Iris seized Panda to her and they both realized that someone was about to enter the room through the door opposite them.

What entered the room looked, at first sight, very much like a tall, thin-necked lizard with a bulbous body made of bronze and cartwheels for legs.

Iris and Panda blinked.

In fact, even on second sight, that's what Fenster looked like, because that's what he was: a dragon with glittering scales and tattered wings and tall, wooden cartwheels for legs. He was carrying a pile of heavy film cans and was staring at his visitors over the top of them. He looked only a little less startled than Iris and Panda themselves.

'Well, hello,' he lisped, flicking his elegant, purple tongue out of his tapered snout.

Iris greeted him coolly, introducing both herself and her companion.

'I am Fenster,' the dragon told her, looking for a clear space in which to put down the film cans. 'And I'm ever so glad you made it through all the way here to see me. I am instrumental, you see, my darlings. I am instrumental when it comes to what's going to happen to you next.'

'Oh, yes?' snapped Panda sceptically.

'Oh yes, my dear,' nodded Fenster earnestly. 'I'm the only one who can tell you what you need to know. The thing you need to know right now.'

'And what's that?' Iris asked shrewdly, careful not to give him any hints.

Fenster's stomach began to glow. 'Let me show you,' he said, and tapped his stomach with one gilded claw. Iris and Panda were startled to see that his stomach had a glass television screen set into the flesh. It was warming up and showing a luminous, black and white picture.

'What is it?' Panda muttered. 'I can't make it out...'

14.

Fenster's Story...
Hello, my darlings. I've been given this opportunity to try to explain a little bit about who I am and what my

origin story is, and somesuch, and perhaps you will learn a little about how I come to have an impact upon our heroine, Iris's life at this point.

Well, first you must know that I am a true Hysperon dragon. In the old days there were a great many of us, swooping about our world. We were all rather slender and svelte, and we cut rather a dash, zooming around the place. Everything went wrong with us when people began hunting us for trophies. They killed us and took our teeth, or wings, our skulls and our wheels. It was a terribly barbaric time.

Also, they became very interested in our blood.

The blood of the dragons of Hyspero is a very curious substance. We ourselves have always known how special it is. We have never quite understood its properties fully, but we knew it held a very great and valuable secret. Our blood glows, you see. When it is spilled and it pools it shimmers with many colours and seems to give off its own phosphorescence. Dragons' blood became a valuable commodity on Hyspero in the first place because people were drawn to those colours…

They painted their walls with the stuff, dyed their clothes with it. Our blood was every colour and no colour, all at the same time. But soon there were reports of very strange things happening… as these painted walls and fabrics started to take on a life of their own. Moving pictures slid out of the shadows, animating themselves… figures peeked out of the swirling hues and peered at the people in the rooms… People were horrified. What had they done? What was in this curious dragons' blood? How could it show pictures to them like this?

Worse things happened. These blobby, amorphous figures in the walls stepped into the rooms. The shapes came to life. Undistinguished, murderous life, it seemed. Even when benign, the characters who stepped out of the dried blood were horrifying; they lurched about mumbling indistinctly, bumping into things…

We should have warned them about the strange properties of our blood. We already knew about them, but we too were at a loss when it came to explaining. If we had told them, warned them, they might have stopped hunting us. But it was one of our secrets, wasn't it? One of the few things my people still had left…

Our blood was used as ink in a city far away from the capital. This was the library city of the professors. A legendary place, said to contain knowledge far beyond the scope of any Hysperon mind. The leopard professors – and yes, they truly were jungle cats, standing upright and wearing professorial gowns – even they were daunted by the vast array of texts their library held. The books were said to come from every end of time, and from universes beyond this one. No one knew how they had come to be on Hyspero: it was the leopards' job to transcribe them.

And they transcribed them using dragons' blood, because they knew that dragons' blood could bring those texts to life.

The big cats sat at tall desks, scratching runes and diagrams into thick parchment with their pens made out of old claws. They hunched forward on their furry elbows and bit the ends of their tongues in concentration. All was quiet in the halls of the spotted scholars. They dipped these claws into their wells of blood and filled up the scrolls with ancient languages they barely understood. For decades there was nothing but the sound of hollow scratching and the profound din of blotting. And then eventually they would sit back with a great big yowly feline yawn and survey their painstaking handiwork. The big cats would watch history unfold before them on scrolls and stitched folios and oddly-shaped charts. This was the secret magic that unfurled within those hallowed chambers. History itself came to life because it was written in blood that had been stolen.

Oh yes, indeed – the blood was stolen. It came transfused from a very particular source. Far from being benign and harmless scholars, the cats were vicious subjugators of another race. They had a subterranean farm, did the leopards. Cavernous dwellings were hewed into the dripping rock far beneath their elegant libraries. Here my people were placed in pens, lashed together and docile. Their wings and wheels had been sheared off. They were kept miserably alive for the sake of their blood. Their blood being the only substance in the galaxy that was known to be able to bring words to actual life.

As centuries passed, and the Hysperon city folk hunted and the leopards in the southern city drained us dry, the world eventually ran out of dragons. Our bloodlines petered out and dried up. Leaving only me. And here I am. Rather elderly and sluggish. Hiding out here in the middle of the desert, awaiting my destiny. Knowing one day a woman called Iris Wildthyme and her Panda friend would stray into my lair.

Oh, I'm unique, too – not only for being the last of my kind – but for having this television set built into my belly. It's very handy for demonstrating things. Much better than having to spill a whole lot of blood for scrying.

And that's what we're peering at now. The three of us. The long awaited Iris Wildthyme, her irascible Panda friend and myself. We're watching the picture settle in the flash and buzz of static and we're all three looking intently at my screen.

It shows a picture of a mountain. In the depths of an almost sunless valley, there is a mountain that has been lovingly fashioned into the shape of a woman's head and shoulders. It contains a secret base, the entrance to which is gained by making the arduous climb up the mountain woman's nose.

Panda gasps. 'But that mountain's in the shape of you, Iris!'

'My old secret base,' she muses. 'I spent a lot of time here, once upon a time. And I was a good deal more egocentric back then…'

As we watch, the viewpoint switches, taking us inside that secret base within the gigantic head. Iris tuts as she sees the dusty rubble and remains of her one-time home and all her high-tech equipment. 'It must be thousands of years since I was last here. It's all gone to rack and ruin…'

There are three figures in the secret base. We can see them now. One is a tall, rather handsome man. There is a pink poodle with hands. And an Earth girl, who looks exhausted and furious.

Iris identifies them in a flash. 'Anthony Marvelle! Missy the poodle! And Kelly from the bookshop!' She curses. 'We knew they were coming here, ahead of us. I should have known Marvelle would suss out where my base was, the creep. And poor Kelly, there, at the mercy of that ghastly versifier…!'

'They are lovers,' I feel I have to point out. 'And what's more, Iris, Marvelle knows that Kelly has a profoundly important role to play in the dramas ahead. He knows that she is the human key to the Ringpull…'

'She's the what?' Panda snaps. 'How can she be? Isn't the Ringpull some kind of cosmic phenomenon that separates this universe from the Obverse? How can its key be a shop assistant from Earth?'

'The one in the sky is a fake, I'm afraid,' I tell him. 'The real one has been disguised as a rather grumpy girl from Darlington.'

As they stare at me in horror I, too, am amazed at myself. This stuff just comes to me through the medium of my miraculous blood. No wonder my world nearly tore itself apart hunting my kind down. It's amazing stuff! My blood knows untold secrets!'

15.

'Have things changed much, since you were last here in Hyspero?' It was something I had meant to ask my Aunty all day, since setting off on our trip.

She huffed and puffed a bit before replying. 'With Hyspero, it's very hard to tell. The changes come in leaps and bounds. It's just how the world works here. But there's the breaking apart to consider, too... the damage being done. The Corrosion. I'm scared that I'll hardly recognise the place at all...'

She looked very gloomy as she said this, and I thought about those strange gaps and holes that had appeared in our maps.

By now we were getting quite good at climbing without looking down. Even though the staircase and walkways were mouldy and wet, they weren't proving to be that much of an obstacle.

Soon enough we were standing at the very top, some fifty feet above the dank and soapy lake, before the hole in the ceiling.

Quite high up. Nearly on steady land again.

And about to step out once more into daylight in Hyspero. But this time, into a completely different zone and a different environment altogether...

We saw that the glaring bright hole in the rock had once been a window, far above the temple. Aunty Iris snagged herself on some broken stained glass and cursed loudly.

Here the air was warm but it was fresh and alive with the sounds and smells of the brand new jungle. We breathed in deeply and the air felt steamy and heavy in our lungs. It was deliciously fresh, though, after the sulphurous reek of the darkness below.

'The Shrieking Jungle!' Simon said, as the three of us hopped through the broken window and shielded our tender eyes against the brilliant sun. It came dappling and trembling through the branches above.

And just at that moment there was an almighty shriek, from somewhere deep inside the jungle.

OOOiiinnnkkkkkk!

It was awful.

'Hm,' said Aunty Iris. 'That was probably one of the irate pigs. Apparently you rarely see them, but you know that they're about.' She was standing in the middle of the clearing with her hands on her hips.

OIIIIIIIInnnkkkkk!

'Hm,' said Aunty Iris. 'That's definitely the irate pigs.'

'It sounds more like 'oinking' than 'shrieking',' said Simon.

Aunty Iris asked him: 'Would you like to go and tell them that, Simon? Do you want to find the irate pigs and quibble over their pronunciation?'

OOOOOOIIIIInnnkkkkkkk!

'Besides,' she said. 'The Oinking Jungle sounds rubbish, doesn't it?'

Me and Simon dumped our bags of provisions in the tall, long grass and I realised that the damp was lifting off the three of us as a gentle - and slightly eggy - mist. Not very nice.

But here we were! In an alien jungle in our new world! With shrieking pigs!

'This jungle is a bit too lavishly coloured for my taste,' Aunty Iris sighed, waving her hand at a tall, lilac and lime coloured tree. 'All these plants are overdone.'

'Overdone?' I said. 'All the changes are natural, I thought. You said Hyspero makes changes every day ...'

Aunty Iris sniffed. 'I can detect someone's tasteless hand in the design. Does it feel natural to you? Hm? Look at these silver bananas! Golden figs! I've just caught a glimpse of a monkey out of the corner of my eye ... and it was heliotrope!''

Really, I had no idea what 'natural' meant in a land like Hyspero. But I wanted to know what my Aunty meant. 'The Scarlet Empress? You think she somehow ... invented or changed this jungle herself?'

Aunty Iris looked sly for a second. Like she knew more than she was saying. And that she wished she hadn't said anything of the sort. She nodded slowly, fanning herself with her hat. 'Yes. She has had some success, creating and changing parts of Hyspero. Some people, places, some buildings and animals. She has tampered with the fabric of our beloved land. With her magic.'

I gulped, and Simon shot me an anxious look.

'Well, anyway,' she said. 'However vulgar the jungle is, and whether the Empress had a hand in its design or not ... What we have to concentrate on is our mission. To find the Golden God of the Shrieking Jungle!'

Her voice rose on that last sentence, like a rallying cry delivered into the wilderness. It was met by all kinds of weird chirrupings.

And shrieking.

OOOIIIIIIIIIIIIIInnnkkkkk!

Simon started to examine some kind of plump fruit that was a livid blue with a hard nubbled rind. 'I think it's a smashing jungle,' he said. 'Do you think this fruit is safe to eat?'

'Shouldn't think so for a second,' Aunty Iris said and started waving her ready-cooked lobster about again. 'I'm going to wolf down this thing, once I've interrogated him. Would you like a bit?'

Me and Simon locked stares with the horrified shellfish and quickly shook our heads.

'Suit yourselves,' sighed Aunty Iris. 'There's some custard creams in that bag somewhere.' With that she stumped off into the trees for a shufti round. The captive lobster gave a nasty squeal as she yanked off a claw.

'Your aunty,' said Simon, 'can be a very peculiar woman.'

I gave him a hard stare. I sat in the shade of a massive fallen trunk and fetched out my black notebook and pen.

Something was nagging at me. A memory that had trickled into my head when we were looking at those old, worn statues. The creatures had been sculpted in various elaborate poses: prancing around and fighting each other. Aunty Iris was right: they were sloths, but of an unusually energetic type. But it was as if I had seen them before somewhere. Or dreamed about them ... or imagined them ... But that surely couldn't be true.

16.

Simon, Barbra and Jenny were spared a most uncomfortable journey through the desert by being invited to the Vizier's room. This was a great deal more lavish than the cell where the tattooed guards had shoved them. Now they were perched on silken cushions and drinking wine out of silver goblets. The plump Vizier passed round a pink wooden box containing sugary chunks of Turkish Delight.

Barbra's hydraulic knees were killing her. She found this kind of luxury hard to take, and had actually been much cosier in the hold of the sand-crawling ship. But she was prepared to sacrifice that for the sake of her new human friends. Plus, the Vizier was telling them all sorts of interesting things about this world of Hyspero and the palace of the legendary Scarlet Empress.

'I should have known Iris would be infamous here,' Jenny was scowling. 'That's how it was in the old days. No matter which far-flung world we visited, or which remote corner of time. They'd had word of her already. They knew exactly what she was like.'

The Vizier studied her keenly. His dark eyes were glittering with mischief. 'Ah, yes. Many of our old, old Hysperon tales tell of her curious doings. She was involved in some of the great old myths that have been passed down through the generations. She is – you might almost say – a kind of fictional, mythical being to us.' For a moment he clutched his damask napkin to his chest and looked bereft. 'How I dearly wish that she hadn't gone off into the sands with her friend, the Panda. I would have been most keen to get a look at her in the... er, actual flesh. I hear she was quite a looker, eh?'

Jenny shrugged. 'If you like that kind of thing. They certainly don't make them like Iris anymore.'

Simon smiled to himself as he took a swig of the strange-tasting Hysperon wine. Somehow it managed to taste like Christmas spices and fizzy and bright, all at the same time. He wondered how Iris would have reacted to this Vizier's smarmy ways. He imagined that she wouldn't have been taken in for a moment.

The journey seemed to be taking them in great looping circles around the mountainous regions of Hyspero. Simon drifted to the windows occasionally and peeped out at the monotonous features of the landscape as night settled in. He wondered what was going to become of them, once they reached the palace. The Vizier refused to be drawn on that topic, even when Jenny pressed him. He had merely clapped his fat, beringed hands together and chuckled. 'Why, the Empress loves to meet new people! She already knows everyone on her world. She has discovered every single thing about them! But new people... new individuals coming to her lands... Why, she is excited! She can't wait! She is longing to make your acquaintance!'

Jenny and Simon exchanged a glance at all this flim-flam.

'When do we arrive at the city?' Jenny asked the little wizard.

He waggled his fingers, boggled his eyes, and got up from his cushions rather clumsily. 'Ah, tomorrow and tomorrow and tomorrow, my dear. But first we must pick up some other visitors. There are others here in our world who are recent arrivals! Oh yes, and we must bring them to the city, too...'

This left the Vizier's guests mystified as they watched him shuffle out of his rooms in order to do his rounds through the sand ship. There were his guards to check on, and the pilot in the control room at the very top of the ship.

The visitors were left quite alone. Jenny told Simon off for eating so many of the sweets. She pointed out that it was best not to touch anything edible that was offered to you by your captor and potential enemy. Simon ignored her. She might have had more experience than him of travels in the Multiverse, but he wasn't prepared to be patronized by the former traffic warden.

Then all of a sudden they saw that Barbra was trying to get their attention. The vending machine looked rather flustered.

'It's the first Empress, Euphemia,' she said, calming down. 'She's been banging on my insides for ages, trying to get out. But I could hardly let her out when the Vizier was here, could I?'

Simon and Jenny assured her that she had been right to keep her glass front locked up and the tiny Empress out of sight. Goodness knew what the Vizier might have made of the sight of this monarch from the dawn of time. They opened Barbra up and found the ancient jar rocking back and forth behind a heap of crisp packets. Barbra gasped out loud when she realized that the Empress had eaten her way through most of her supply of comestibles.

The elderly Empress hopped out of her jar and surveyed them all critically. She was wearing a different silver fairy dress (where did she get all those outfits?) and her golden hair was frizzed up madly. 'What on earth are you doing getting mixed up with the Vizier?' she cried. 'Goodness me! I thought the one I had was oily and two-faced... but this one! Well, you mustn't trust him a single inch.'

'We didn't have much of a choice, your majesty,' Simon sighed. 'He had all those armed guards with him. We were bundled in here and had to leave the bus behind, and Iris and Panda...'

The Empress paced back and forth. 'That is very bad news indeed. The further away we are from Iris Wildthyme the less happy I am.'

'She went into the desert with Panda,' Jenny said. 'They never came back...'

Euphemia nodded. 'Yes, she's done that before. She thinks she can survive anything. Even the many conundra and chimera that the desert sands can show you... But she's wrong, you know. Back then, she was young. She could do anything. But not now... Iris is too old. She's too complicated and grumpy. Too full of stories. The desert winds and sands will make great sport with her... Oh dear.' The Empress looked at their large, concerned faces and told them: 'I think we must assume she is gone from us forever. And now we must look after ourselves.'

'No!' Simon burst out, surprising himself. 'Didn't someone say that the Scarlet Empress can see all? She knows everything that is happening on Hyspero! Isn't that what they reckon? Well, then… we can ask her, can't we? When we are taken before her, we can ask her where Iris is…'

17.

The noted poet Anthony Marvelle paced up and down the large room.

His poodle pal, Missy, stared at the gently curving ceiling, realizing that it was the curve of the interior of Iris Wildthyme's skull. This displeased the poodle quite a lot, since she loathed the Wildthyme woman with all her heart.

But needs must. Here they were – she and her master and her master's new floozy, investigating the one-time home of the loathed adventuress.

'Iris has always struck me as completely lazy,' Missy sniffed. 'How on earth did she carve a whole mountain into a likeness of herself? Surely her monstrous vanity never overcame her idleness?'

Marvelle stopped pacing and grinned at his dog. He was wearing a very smart suit in chocolate brown with a burnt orange tie. His outfit was rumpled and torn in places and Missy rather regretted that. It had been a *fucking* arduous journey across the sands and then up the face of this ghastly mountainous edifice. And then there had been the final indignity of the three of them having to crawl up the interior of one of the gargantuan nostrils of Iris Wildthyme in order to gain access to her one-time secret base.

'I doubt that Iris had much to do with the actual building of this murmur murmur,' said Missy's beloved Marvelle in his customary refined drawl. 'I should think she had it all done up for her when she murmur murmur…'

Ah yes, Missy remembered. Marvelle had taken unlawful possession of Iris's many volumed-journal, hadn't he? He had thieved the whole lot from under her witchy nose when he stole aboard her ramshackle bus on the world of Valcea. And now the many secrets of that old hag were his for the perusing. Anthony Marvelle had stolen a large number of important, impossible things lately and his poodle companion was extremely proud of him. Not only the journals and the time charts from Iris's bus, but also this human girl – this Kelly – who apparently was terribly important to their whole quest, even if Missy didn't quite understand that bit just yet.

To her, Kelly was just a rather cross and unhelpful young woman from Darlington whom Marvelle seemed to be sleeping with. She worked in a bookshop and was caught up in Marvelle's schemes because she had spent years in close proximity to a certain book that had sat neglected for years on an obscure shelf. This book had apparently given the moody girl some kind of fantastic power…

Or something like that. Missy was used to picking up titbits from her master's conversation, and trying to piece them together. Rarely did he actually sit down and explain things to her. And why should she? She was just his dog. She was there to follow him and unconditionally approve of everything he did. He was her favourite human being and at the moment she was grateful that he had brought them away from that dreadful planet Earth. Anthony and Missy were star-hopping and time-travelling again and Missy was very pleased about that.

Marvelle had resumed his pacing up and down. He was frustrated, Missy knew, because they had found this secret base mostly gutted and cleaned out. Anthony had imagined they'd find lots of useful gubbins and equipment here, left behind in the past by the Wildthyme hag. He knew she had some links with the Hysperon royal family and he was hoping to find something of use. There was talk in the journals of a room somewhere here, hidden away in all the tunnels, that somehow mirrored the map room in the palace of the Scarlet Empress… But after two days here inside Iris's stone head Marvelle had found very little.

At this moment Kelly reappeared, rubbing her hair with a towel and wearing a very glamorous dressing gown she had found in Iris's private quarters. She looked more relaxed and rested than Missy had ever seen her. Even the antagonistic poodle had to admit that her master's new girlfriend from Earth was attractive. Pretty, even. She just had this unfortunate habit of looking scared and complaining all the time, and wanting to be returned to earth. Missy also understood that the girl fancied herself as a poet, and Missy suspected that she was hooking up with Anthony simply to advance her lousy career.

Marvelle noticed her and crossed the room to give her a hug. 'You smell wonderful murmur cinammon and cloves murmur murmur…'

'There's an amazing bathroom back there in Iris's private quarters,' Kelly said. 'She might have cleared this place out of all her scientific equipment and everything, but she left all of her clothes and jewellery and personal stuff.'

Marvelle pulled back from kissing her neck and frowned. 'That isn't like Iris at all, actually,' he murmured. 'I wonder why she left here. It must have been in a hurry murmur murmur.' He shook his head. 'I bet not even her journals will yield up the whole miserable history of that awful woman. She's lived too long, and in too many lives for anyone ever to understand murmur murmur.'

When Marvelle talked about Iris Wildthyme like this, Missy's hackles went up and she felt a prickle of fear run through the shaved patches of her coiffed fur. It was almost as if her master's sneaking admiration for the Wildthyme woman spilled over into becoming something more. She would never go so far as thinking he was in love with the batty old hag, but nevertheless – there was something in his tone of voice that went beyond appreciation. He sounded… exhilarated by her at times. Missy would swear on it.

Kelly had obviously picked up on the same quality in his voice, because she switched the subject and said, 'Anthony, go and get cleaned up. Stop pacing about and angsting. Relax, will you? Look, I found the deep freeze. There's all sorts of supplies. I'll cook something. There's even wine…'

Missy tutted at this. 'Playing the little housefrau, eh? I expected you to be a feminist, Kelly. You're soon reverting to type!'

The girl glared at the dog with utter hatred. Already in her time with Marvelle she had grown to hate and distrust his dog and her slavish devotion. Kelly wasn't sure by which process she had started to develop feelings for the foppish poet – it certainly wasn't something she had planned or been conscious of. But she was damned if she was going to warm to his nasty poodle as well. 'If I want to cook dinner, that's my business,' she snapped. 'Someone has to, don't they? Otherwise we all starve.'

Anthony was too distracted to think about anything as mundane as food. He was over at one of the dusty, broken down consoles and fiddling with the controls. 'Hang on,' he murmured. 'I think I've got this working…'

Sure enough there was a low hum emanating from somewhere in the chamber. A few feeble lights flickered into life on the banks of machinery. Missy gasped and trotted over, just as a view screen opened in the rock wall, rather like a great fringed eyelid lifting up. It showed a view of the shoulder of the mountain and the scorched valley below.

'Well done, Anthony!' Kelly said. 'You've got stuff working again.' She was amazed at herself as she said this. Why was she so keen to shore up his ego with praise like this? What was happening to her? If this was love after all, she wasn't sure she liked it much.

Anthony was staring rapt at the screen. He knew that he hadn't succeeded in bringing this lot to life. This screen had opened up as part of the automated defence systems. They had been dormant for a long time, but now they were in action. And that was because something big and noticeable had arrived in the valley below Wildthyme Mountain.

It rumbled across the screen and ground to a halt right outside. It was a vast behemoth of a vehicle.

'They've come for us murmur murmur,' he said, with a flash of intuition. 'Someone knows we're here!'

18.

At home I was so used to feeling on the edges of things and that nothing I did was all that important. Here and now I was different. This whole weird, changeable land needed me.

Aunty Iris had made me feel that I belonged here, and that I had always belonged here. Hyspero had been waiting for me to turn up. To help out in its hour of direst need.

So of course I was starting to feel more serious about things. It just seemed right to me.

I felt special!

I looked at Simon then, in his scruffy clothes, and I realised that he was feeling left out.

Even though the three of us were heading off on this journey together, it was as if I was going in a separate direction altogether. I couldn't quite explain it. I just felt like I was changing.

And Simon could sense that too.

Some time after this Aunty Iris came crashing out of the undergrowth with her hair awry, brandishing the last remaining lobster claw.

'I didn't get very much out of our recalcitrant friend here,' she announced. 'Though I grilled him pretty thoroughly.'

'He could talk?' asked Simon, appalled. 'You ate something that could talk?'

'Values are different here, Simon,' Aunty Iris told him darkly. 'Before you leave this land you'll be very surprised, I imagine, by some of the things you'll eat and some of the things you'll talk to. Don't be so judgmental of hungry old lady.'

Simon's mouth snapped shut.

'What did you find out?' I asked.

'Well, the Scarlet Empress definitely knows that we are here in the jungle. She's furious that I'm back here in Hyspero, and that I've managed to hook up with you. The lobsters are equipped with these nifty little communications devices under their shells, and they managed to report our whereabouts before we squooshed them. Incidentally, the scampi weren't working *for the enemy, after all. They were just there because they like a good fight. Anyway, my erstwhile crustacean chum here reckoned that the Empress was especially interested to hear that you're here in Hyspero. She is desperate to hear more about you, Kelly.'*

'Me?' I said. 'Is it because we gave her soldiers and her Vizier the slip?'

'Partly that. But also because she thought she'd put up a barrier to prevent other members of our family coming to this land and dabbling in her affairs. She can't believe you've found a way to break through. She wants to know how. And she wants to know why.' Aunty Iris was grinning. 'She should have known that it was all down to me! That I brought you here! She must have guessed by now! Anyway, Kelly love, you've got the old beast of a woman all stirred up, it seems.'

The idea of the all-powerful Scarlet Empress thinking about me made me feel very odd inside. It was as if she was using her mysterious powers to spy on me, across hundreds of miles: through the mountains and swamps and seas of Hyspero. Those eyes were trained only on me.

Simon was suddenly at my side. He slapped me on the back. 'Never mind. We're with you! We'll protect her, won't we, Aunty Iris?'

I grinned at him. He didn't look so left out now. Simon had found his role in this adventure. He was my protector. My best mate!

Aunty Iris was beaming, too, as she tossed the lobster claw into the creaking jungle thicket. 'That's the idea, young man.' She tugged off her still-sopping cardy and tied it around her waist. 'Now I suggest a good afternoon's worth of walking and jungle-whacking and then we should find somewhere safe to make a den for the night. About thirty miles would be good going, I think.'

'Thirty miles,' Simon groaned.

'Whoever said that adventures were easy?'

I was gathering my stuff together. As I popped my notebook into one of the bags I realised that Aunty Iris was staring at me. Her eyes were wide with shock.

'What? What's the matter?'

'You've got a book!'

'I know,' I said. 'Simon bought it for me for Christmas. It's my journal of our trip.'

Aunty Iris looked as if she was going to keel over again. 'You mean you've actually been writing in it?'

I nodded slowly. I felt as if I'd been caught doing something dreadfully wrong.

Aunty Iris exploded. 'But people can't write! There AREN'T any books on Hyspero!' She reached out to take the book from me, and instinctively I yanked it away. 'The lobster was right! He hinted at such a thing!' Aunty Iris gasped, and stared at me in awe. 'That's why the Scarlet Empress is so keen to get her hands on you!'

'Why?' I said. 'I don't understand!'

'Because,' Aunty Iris dropped her voice, very ominously. 'You are the girl who can read and write. You have the power! You, Kelly ... are very, very dangerous!'

19.

Panda wasn't sure at what point they had started running, but that's what they were doing now.

Moments ago they had been in a cramped space – the projection booth in that weird cinema underneath the pub in the middle of the desert. He and Iris had been peering at that television in the belly of Fenster the dragon and there had barely been enough room to breathe. Panda had been on the point of feeling one of his turns coming on (he was never very good in confined spaces) but now…

Now they seemed to be running freely, smoothly, down some swiftly declining tunnel. 'Pick me up!' Panda roared after Iris. He was falling behind on his short legs and he knew they would soon be too far ahead. Iris was running full pelt after the dragon, who was rolling noisily on his brass wheels. 'What are we running from?' Panda howled. 'Why are we running away?'

Flustered, Iris suddenly stopped and hurriedly picked him up. She clutched him to her bosom and set off again, but she didn't say anything. I keep missing things, Panda thought wildly. It feels like I keep jumping tracks, jolting from one moment to another… Iris's ragged breathing made her seem panicked… but what by? What had Panda missed?

The metallic dragon, Fenster, called back to them: 'The leopard professors know where we are! If they find me, they'll drain all my magic dragon's blood and melt down my flesh and metal parts…'

Panda frowned and glowered into the deepening darkness. 'But why are we running with you?' he shouted. 'They won't do anything to us, will they? We don't even know them…'

But Iris kept running and Panda was surprised at how fast and fit she seemed to be. 'Fenster is our friend, Panda,' she told him. 'If he's in danger or trouble, we must help him.'

'He isn't our friend,' Panda snapped. 'We've hardly known him any time at all…'

There was a glazed look about Iris's sweaty face, he realized. Perhaps she had been hoodwinked or hypnotized by that peculiar golden reptile…!

'Why can't we just go back to the bus?' he asked her. 'Can't we simply turn around and go back to our friends?'

'It isn't as easy as that,' Iris puffed. 'Fenster tells me that they have all gone away and left the bus behind…'

'What?' cried Panda hotly.

'Yes! The poor old bus, left alone in the desert, with no one to guard it or look after it…'

'But what has happened to the others? To Simon and Barbra and…'

'They've bloody well wandered off,' Iris told him, still jogging along the rocky path and showing no signs of stopping. 'They went off with a bunch of people from Hyspero City, according to Fenster. And they're on their way to see the Scarlet Empress herself…'

Panda was alarmed. 'Shouldn't we get after them, then? They've got the tiny Empress Euphemia with them... shouldn't we be there to make sure nothing goes wrong...?'

Iris shook her head. 'I'm sure Fenster is right, you know. He knows what to do, and where we should be. He will take us to the right place...'

'Are you quite certain about that?' Panda snapped. 'Aren't we just fleeing aimlessly? As per bloody usual?'

A look of panic flashed across his best friend's face just then, and Panda realized that Iris was indeed under the control of some other influence.

Then, all of a sudden, Fenster ground to a halt. His cartwheels made a terrible grinding noise on the stone floor. Iris barreled into him, squashing Panda. 'Ooowwww!'

'We are here,' Fenster told them, whispering now and flicking his strange tongue at them triumphantly.

'Where have you brought us?' demanded Iris, and Panda was glad to hear some of her old gumption coming back.

A dark door opened up in the rock and Fenster chuckled. 'You should feel quite at home here, Iris.'

'Why..?'

He led them through the doorway and they found themselves on a small shelf of rock. There was a vast space ahead in the darkness and, as their eyes accustomed themselves, Iris and Panda saw that there was a dullish glow down there. A kind of subacqueous, greenish glow.

Soon they could pick out the shape of large, globular forms... buildings and domes, they thought...

'It's a city,' Fenster told them. 'Far beneath the desert sands of Hyspero. A city of the dispossessed.'

'This is where you come from,' Iris realized.

'Indeed,' said Fenster. 'I'm one of the few who are allowed to go up to the surface. In order to fulfil my mission for my fellow dwellers in the secret city, I am allowed to visit the upper levels of our world and brave the possibility of being discovered.'

'Mission?' asked Panda gruffly. 'What mission are you on about, then?'

Fenster turned his gaze on them, and they were astonished again by the beauty of the dragon, and the perplexing lights of his eyes. 'My mission has been to find you two. And I have been about that task for more than a hundred years. I was to look out for you two arriving on Hyspero again, and to bring you to the city of the dispossessed.'

'Oh!' said Iris. 'That's very flattering, but all you needed to do was ask nicely...'

'It isn't meant to be flattering, my dears,' sighed Fenster, and his thin tongue rattled against his metal teeth. Was that a touch of irritation, Panda wondered. He has spent so long waiting for us, perhaps he's disappointed with the actual thing.

'So what's so important about us?' Panda barked. 'And who are these underground city-dwellers so keen on clapping their eyes on us, eh?'

Fenster smiled at them both. 'Come with me. You will see for yourselves who your hosts are. But really, can't you guess, Iris? These buildings below us... the shape of the towers, look... the forms that the great halls take... isn't it all rather familiar to you, my dear?'

Iris peered forward, so intently that Panda feared she was about to drop off the ledge. Suddenly her face went slack and rather pale.

'What is it?' hissed her best friend. 'What have you seen?'

'The city reminds me...' she began, swallowing hard, and scrabbling in her cardy pockets for her cigarettes. 'It reminds me of a place I haven't been to for an impossibly long time...'

'Very good, my darling,' nodded Fenster complacently. 'Then it's all coming back to you...'

'What?' snapped Panda, feeling rather worried.

'It's nothing,' Iris reassured him, patting his head. 'It's just... for a moment... that city in the cavern below us reminded me a bit of... *home*. It looks just like... the Clockworks. Like... Saga City...!'

'Whaaaat?' cried Panda, again.

20.

THE UNOFFICIAL IRIS WILDTHYME FORUM
HOME

FORUM RULES

FAQ

NEW POSTS

SEARCH

CHAT ROOM

LOG OUT

UNOFFICIAL IRIS FORUM > ON THE BUSES > ON THE BOOKSHELF > IRIS WILDTHYME IN PRINT>LICENSED FANFIC

POST REPLY

4 NOVEMBER 2011, 18.48

DEMONQUEST

Reviewer!

This just gets worse and worse! I have been reading these books since they began and yeah, so I've not read every single one and haven't kept up to date maybe with all the plot arcs and so on, but I would expect as a reasonably intelligent human being to be able to follow these things. Never since the WHO IS PANDA? Arc fiasco have we seen such a car crash of monstrous proportions in the Wildthyme novel line. New editor Ivan Rosco needs to go. He has done this on purpose imho, alienating new fans and old by introducing his own agenda to the development of the novel line. I know for many Iris fans the books are simply not canonical and so they do not care what happens in them, regarding them simply as merchandising, but to some of us who have grown up with the books and to who they were their way in to the wonderful world of Wildthyme – I say we do care about them and even though THE BOOKS DO NOT COUNT and DIDN'T HAPPEN that still doesn't mean that a new editor should mess with the characters that we KNOW AND LOVE.

4 NOVEMBER 2011, 18.52

MONKEYBOY

Reviewer!

I reckon you shd cool it, Demonquest. It's only a TV show lol.

4 NOVEMBER 2011, 18.54

BUSDRIVER

Acolyte!

He's right tho they are terrible these days Iris is nothing like she was on the tv anymore. They are too long and complicate and what happesn to fans who do not like reading? Someone should write out what the stories are happening in the books in a straightforward way so that other Iris fans with betters things to do could read up what is going on in the irisverse imho lol lol

4 NOVEMBER 2011, 19.02

OWL

Reviewer!

Typical, this, of this forum. You lot simply don't appreciate what's going on in the world of Iris Wildthyme. Yes, so she began as the heroine of her own kids' tv show (and yes, it was for kids, before any of yours jump down my throat! Just look at the letters from the upper echelons of Tyne Tees television reprinted in THE MAKING OF

IRIS WILDTHYME book from 1980.) But in the years since, that transtemporal adventuresss disappeared from our television screens she has become that bit more sophisticated and the books about her adventures have had to grow up alongside their fans. Now the novels are even more intriguing and inventive than any of the Iris stories from the TV show and some are even a whole lot better! Yes, you might not be able to see the pictures or hear the voices, and yes maybe the story arcs get over-complicated and some of the books don't have all the answers (or even make much sense lol), but bear *('Bear!?!')* with them. They are great! I haven't read anything like all 324 of them but the ones I have read are fantastic!! Specially the more serious ones with guns and fighting and sexy ladies in them. Lol.

4 NOVEMBER 2011, 19.04

MAESTRO

Paying Member

THEY ARE RUBBISH! I'm sorry, but I have to say this – lol – but they are just licensed fan fiction. Some high profile fans have made it lucky and they are commissioned to write up their j*rkoff fanw*nk slash fiction and publish it as official Iris stories and most of them don't even fit in with Iris Wildthyme continuity as it ACTUALLY HAPPENED IN HER WORLD.

4 NOVEMBER 2011, 19.08

OWL

Reviewer!

QUOTE:

and most of them don't even fit in with Iris Wildthyme
continuity as it ACTUALLY HAPPENED IN HER WORLD.

Maestro, are you crazy? Are you seriously saying that you think there's a world apart – a shadow dimension, as Iris herself might say – in which there's an established continuity for her adventures?

There isn't even a Bible for the writers of the books! They are fairly free to invent, pick and choose and introduce and discard any elements they wish. THERE IS NO SUCH THING AS IRIS CONTINUITY! Apart from the obvious, that is – that she's a game old bird in a bus with a best friend who's a Panda. AND THAT'S IT!

4 NOVEMBER 2011, 17.20

MAESTRO

PAYING MEMBER!

But for any fiction to work and hold up, there has to be a continuity, doesn't there? And we have to imagine another world in which these things are happening in, don't we? It can't just be anarchy, can it?

4 NOVEMBER 2011, 17.25

OWL

Reviewer!

YES, it *CAN* be anarchy! That's exactly what I'm saying!

4 NOVEMBER 2011, 17.28

MAESTRO

PAYING MEMBER!

That's in your opinion, Owl. You can't dictate to others what their reality should be. And you can't enforce the view that it is anarchy.

4 NOVEMBER 2011, 17.29

MELKUR

FORUM MODERATOR

FOLKS! Calm it down in here! Owl – you must stop trying to enforce your version of the reality of the Iris Wildthyme universe on your fellow forum members. We live in a democracy and everyone's opinion is as valid as everyone else's. I will revoke your forum rights and eject you from this discussion board if you insist on this argumentative behaviour and tone.

This is meant to be a fun space, guys! Play nice!

8TH may, 1694

Ms Wildthyme

Listen – I don't have long. If there's anyone out there listening – can you help? They've got me banged up in some kind of prison cell and they reckon they're going to burn me at the stake at first light—

5 NOVEMBER, 2011, 6.03

IRIS WILDTHYME RETURNS TO HYSPERO

A REVIEW BY GEORDIE SAMMY

Followers of my reviews of the current crop of Iris adventures will recall my utter loathing of the direction this series has taken in recent years. However, this month's release by longtime Iris tie-in writer and one-time fanzine contributor Terry Kelly has proved to be a step in the right direction – for me, at least.

'IW Returns to Hyspero' takes us on a roller coaster ride aboard the beloved bus, back to the world of Hyspero – like in the final episode of the classic tv show which we all adore so much. Budgetary requirements of a 70s sf show being what they were, we never really saw much of the world of Hyspero – where magic and science walk hand in hand and legends come to life. All we saw were some sketchy backdrops and the admittedly impressive set for the throne room of the Scarlet Empress. That end of season climax finished with the theft of the very first Empress from the tunnels beneath the Scarlet Palace by a man with fake arms – and it was a cliffhanger that was destined to go nowhere, since the series was axed, back then in 1979.

It seems amazing that no one thought to sequelize that story in all the 324 original Iris Wildthyme stories which have followed – until now, that is. When Terry Kelly has our favourite interstitial adventurers return to Hyspero they are returning the stolen Empress Euphemia to the clutches of the ruling Elite for – as we are told in a rather heavy-handed piece of exposition from Iris herself, talking to Panda when they are first separated from their friends – the first Empress is the only one who knows how to operate the dreaded doorway into the Obverse – a small universe on whose brink Hyspero sits…

Keen Wildthyme fans will recognize 'the Obverse' as the mysterious dimension in which Iris originated! And that's what's so amazing about what Terry Kelly has pulled off here. He has returned Iris to her place of origin! Here are all the answers to the questions we have had about the enigmatic lady from another universe! They are all here, hidden away between the layers of the book!

All the regulars perform well here, and each are given their piece of the action. Rather too much time is taken up by the whimsical vending machine, Barbra, whose inclusion in the series was, I still feel, a badly judged mistake. Feeble puns about her outdated comestibles and her 'front slot' are becoming very tired now and I look forward to the day when she is written out. Much less is made of Jenny – head of MIAOW Darlington. I think there is much more potential for Jenny as a character. None of the writers seem keen to follow up on her character's emotional journey – now that she has returned, seemingly, to full-time travels in the cosmos with Iris. She is harder and more grown-up now – there should be allsorts of interesting things she will be thinking and feeling! And yet here she just comes across as grumpy! Simon from the bookshop is just cardboard, as are the ostensible villains of the piece – Anthony Marvelle (whose 'murmur murmur' verbal tick just infuriates this reader now) and the Vizier, who kidnaps many of the cast of characters fairly early on…)

Beware – much of the book consists of our heroes in various combinations wandering about the planet and encountering strange foes and deadly dangers. All the while they're chatting about the adventure they're on – and what it's all supposed to mean. In other words, it's disastrously LOW ON PLOT!! Until the very end, when many of the characters are reunited in the palace throne room of the Scarlet Empress and all the revelations take up the final twenty pages of the book – bringing the whole thing to an abrupt ending

SPOILER SPACE

*

*

*

Kelly – the girl from the bookshop – turns out to be crucial to the opening of the Ringpull into the other universe. This is why Marvelle was keen on finding her and bringing her to Hyspero. The old Hysperon book of legends, The Aja'ib (*'The Tales of Hyspero'*) was left untouched on a shelf in her bookstore for years and so she absorbed the magical vibrations. The book seeping into her head all those years also makes her think she had adventures in Hyspero as a child, alongside both Simon and Iris, who turns out to be her aunty. (Though this cannot be true according to established continuity in the Irisverse. I take it to be a piece of harmless whimsy on the part of the author.) Also, Iris rides in to the rescue of her friends, just as Marvelle and his colleague the Vizier are about to sacrifice Kelly in the station in space that houses the Ringpull. Iris has got together with a whole load of refugees from the Obverse, who have been living in secret exile far underneath Hyspero. Iris and Panda have befriended them all – including a masked Highwayman called Dick who, amazingly, Iris knew as a child (!). There is a great battle between the palace guard and the Obverse desert refugees, who firmly believe that the Ringpull into the Obverse should never be opened. The goodies win, of course – and the Empress Euphemia smashes her own jar in order to prevent anyone being able to use her powers. She has quite a pathos-filled send-off, dying in the arms of Simon, who she's become quite friendly with.

I'd give it 6 out of 10 and I'd recommend it with certain reservations. The prose is a bit flowery, however, and I feel that IT NEEDED MORE FIGHTING. You will like it if you liked Terry Kelly's earlier forays into the Irisverse. Especially if you like those books that hint at Iris's mysterious beginnings in a different universe. This implies all sorts of interesting stuff about that. Though there are continuity freaks on this very forum who will no doubt jump on this review of mine and tell me that NONE OF IT COUNTS. IT ISN'T CANONICAL. IT'S JUST FICTION. AND NOT AT ALL REAL, LIKE THE OLD TV SHOW.

He's a very Marmite writer and this is a Marmite book, imho. But for what it's worth, I liked it, though I'm not sure I followed it all.

21.

Aunty Iris was in a funny mood the next day. I thought perhaps all this walking and yomping through the trees was tiring her out. But she started talking that night about feeling old. She asked if we thought she was too old for all of this stuff. She said it was a long time since she went on any kind of adventure.

She said she had started to feel faint now and then. I thought she meant she felt like she was GOING to faint - like, pass out. But she didn't. She said, 'No, FAINT. Like, almost transparent ... like I'm fading away. Look!' And, there in the middle of the jungle, she held up one hand and ... it was weird, but I could see the trees right through it! She held her hand up and the light shone straight through.

'What's hapeening to you?' I said.

She looked very glum. 'I feel like someone's ... trying to write me out of this adventure,' she said at last.

But that was daft, isn't? I thought. That can't happen, can it?

'What if I really am too old for adventures in Hyspero?' she asked, aloud. 'What if it's really for kids and people your age, Kelly? What if I'm breaking some sacred mystic law by even being here? Maybe that's why I've started to fade away and become insubstatial...'

Anyway, by tea time she'd cheered up slightly and she'd grown a bit more solid. She even found some crumpets in her carpet bag that weren't too covered in bits of fluff. And she had a jar of Marmite, too! We had a lovely tea and Aunty Iris was cheery once more. But still Simon and I decided that we would have to keep an eye on her.

Something very strange was happening to Aunty Iris. Along with the colour and the substance, some of the fight seemed to be draining out of her. Some of her energy and her determination, too...

We had peach slices for supper again. We were all still hungry afterwards.

That night we heard music coming from the depths of the jungle and there was all this whooping and shouting, too. It sounded almost like a party...

PART THREE

Endings

1.

It was Fenster, the dragon on wheels who led Iris back to the Clockworks.

Deep beneath the blistering sands of Hyspero there was a system of caves and great hollow spaces and here the refugees had made their home. They had been there as long as anyone cared to remember and not even the Scarlet Empress herself knew that they were down there. Her all-seeing eye never penetrated their ancient security systems.

A small copter was sent out to fetch the visitors. It looked like an insect, taking off from the city and whirring towards their ledge. Iris watched it approach and swallowed down her panic. This was it: this was her reunion with her own kind.

Panda looked up at her. 'Are you sure you want to do this, my dear?'

She'd never seen him so serious. What did he know about the Clockworks, she wondered? How did he know what awaited her? She couldn't remember what experience he might have had of her kind... None, surely?

Iris blinked and swayed woozily on the spot. All of a sudden she couldn't remember how long she had actually known her furry friend. He had belonged to Tom, hadn't he? Tom, her old friend and companion who had left the bus so long ago, but whom she had visited once... Was that true? And Panda had belonged to Tom – or, rather, as Panda would put it – he had been living with Tom and working as his helper.

But Iris wasn't sure now. She had earlier memories of Panda... She could see him clambering up a stone wall, his clumsy paws finding footholds in the gaps and crevices. He was clinging to the withered strands of ivy and hauling himself determinedly towards a window... and beyond that window, like a princess in a tower, a little girl was sleeping and she was a prisoner of some kind...

'How long have we known each other, Panda?' she asked, as they watched the copter approaching.

He shrugged. 'I'm a little hazy on that myself,' he said. 'We've passed through so many dimensional gaps...'

But Panda was acting almost shifty, she thought. She reflected that he had always been a rather deep one. It was so hard to tell what was going on in his mind.

Fenster didn't seem as nervous as his two companions. He was studying the smooth, globular shapes of the city landscape below. It was as if he was drinking in all the details and taking careful notes for later study. That elegant lizard head of his was cocked on one side and his eyes were narrow with concentration. If he was telling the truth, he belonged in this city. It had been more than a hundred years since he had left it, however.

The copter was almost here. Iris fought away her rising pangs of terror. She felt panic constricting her throat. She fumbled with her cigarettes as the small vehicle circled them and chose a spot for landing on.

'You shouldn't be scared,' Fenster said. 'These are your people. They will be pleased to see you, won't they?'

She shook her head. 'I don't remember them. I got away, you see... when I was so young...'

Once the vehicle had settled and its blades were still, two figures hopped lightly out of its cab. They were almost identical: tall humanoid figures in close-fitting silvery outfits. As they calmly approached, it was obvious that one was male and the other female. They were both blandly beautiful, with almost translucent, pale skin. They came to a halt and bowed.

'We know who you are and we are honoured,' said the male.

Iris wasn't aware that her mouth had dropped open. 'You are, chuck?'

'We had hoped, you see,' said the female. 'We knew you were out in the universe. We knew that one of our kind had been brave enough… to be out there. But we had no idea how to find you, or contact you…'

Iris frowned. 'Look, are you sure you've got the right girl?'

They nodded. 'We lost you such a long time ago. The Clockworks knew at once you were gone. And then, when they Great Schism came…'

Panda held up one paw. 'Excuse me! Before we get into all of his, would you mind letting us sit down for a bit? It's been rather a busy and hectic day, as it happens.'

Iris patted his head, adding, 'Panda's right. We could do with a nice sit and maybe something to eat and drink. We've had quite a lot on today.'

The two elegant beings nodded again, and cast a quick glance at Fenster, who was busy taking everything in. 'And this dragon is with you?'

'Oh yes,' said Iris. 'He's our new friend.' Secretly, though, she was already wondering how he would ever fit aboard the double decker bus. Fenster, meanwhile, looked shocked that the Clockworks people hadn't recognized him. He kept his tongue still about that.

They were invited aboard the near-silent helicopter and squashed together in its seats as it flitted easily through the subterranean air. They swooped and soared across the city and saw that its shiny domes and rooftops weren't glass at all: they were formed from some gelatinous substance, like the soft eggs of underground grubs.

'And this is all that's left?' Iris asked the male. 'All that remains of… um, our civilisation?'

'We don't know,' he said. 'Back in the Obverse we may still have a great and flourishing society. We have no way of knowing what life is like back there. Beyond the Ringpull, anything could be happening. Millennia have passed since a handful of our kind ventured beyond...'

She was fascinated to hear all of this. She thought she had been the only one. But... thinking back... it had all been a bit of a rush and a blur, hadn't it? What they called the Grand Schism... it had been something of a bun fight. Would she had even noticed if a whole lot of others had escaped through the Ringpull at the same time as her? Iris had been so intent on rescuing the bus...

There wasn't that much time to think, though, in the hours that followed. Iris, Panda and Fenster were given a pleasant – if not exactly warm – welcome to the underground city. They were received civilly by a number of dignitaries and senior figures, all dressed in the same one-piece, silvery outfits. Still no one recognized Fenster, though and the golden dragon was starting to feel rather put out by this.

They were led through a series of translucent corridors into the heart of the Clockworks complex, where everyone they were introduced to received them politely and with minimum fuss.

After a while Panda grew grumpy. 'It's a bit dull, isn't it?'

There were fountains and potted desert plants that put them both in mind of shopping malls they had found boring on other, distant worlds.

'You don't come from here after all, do you?' Iris asked Fenster.

He shook his head, ashamed. 'I feel a fool for lying. But I just wanted to fit in…'

She frowned and Panda boggled at him. How far could they trust this strange reptile now? Suddenly he became effusive and excitable… rolling along on squeaky wheels. 'All of this splendour! All of this luxury! Deep beneath the blighted desert! Who'd have thought all this could exist?'

Iris felt like telling him to put a sock in it. Her weariness was catching up with her by now, and she was even starting to wish this reunion with her own kind hadn't even happened. The whole business might raise some awkward questions, after all. There were things lurking in her past that she didn't particularly want to explain, or have held up to scrutiny… And these rather pleasant, rather boring people in their shiny leotards were all being nicey-nice just now… but how could she tell what they were really after?

She was gripped by a sudden panic. We've walked straight into this with our eyes open! Straight into whatever trap might be waiting for us!

2.

In the jungle somewhere they were playing 'I Will Survive' and 'Yes, Sir – I Can Boogie.' At least someone was having fun, I thought.

What happened to cause all the bother was the arrival of the parrot.

We'd seen them flying around us, up in the trees, for the past few days. Parrots there were a bit bigger than earth-type ones and they had even more fantastic colours. This one was gold and pink and it landed right in the middle of the camp.

One of the irksome parrots, that Frank and his brothers had warned us about.

'Ahem,' he said and got all of our attention.

'I think it wants to tell us something,' Aunty Iris said.

And it did. It spoke in this squeaky, croaky voice, and its beady eyes flicked from one of us to the other. It had come to warn us.

'Irk! All of us parrots have been chatting and we've decided that we should give you a warning. We've watched the three of you gallumphing through the trees and - Irk! - drawing attention to yourselves.'

I was checking that the parrot's eyes weren't green. But they were golden.

He went on, 'Do you hear the music at night?'

'It sounds like a disco,' Simon said. He looked bewildered, having a conversation with an irksome parrot.

The parrot nodded. 'The music is coming from the temple of the - Irk! - Golden Sloths. You are hearing the sacred music of their midnight revels and - Irk! - ceremonies.'

'Oh, great,' said Aunty Iris. 'I suppose they're the savage-looking things we saw carved into the rock? Long daggerlike teeth?'

'That's them,' said the parrot. 'And they're covered in - Irk! - golden fur.'

'Fur?' said Aunty Iris. 'Or hair?'

The parrot blinked. 'Does it - Irk! Irk! - matter?'

She nodded.

'Well,' said the parrot. 'It's hard to tell. It's quite long and - Irk! Irk! Irk! - shaggy and bright gold. Anyway, the point is, these killer sloths have all these weird ceremonies that they - Irk! - hold in their temple and they like to dance around to their strange music and practice sacrifice.'

'Sacrifice!' Simon whispered.

'To their great god. Who they keep in their temple. A very demanding great god. He makes them shave off their golden - Irk! - fur and give it to him. That's another part of their ceremonials: cutting their - Irk! Irk! Irk! - hair off and shaving themselves all over. Except they're not that good at the - Irk! - shaving part. Sloths have very clumsy hands. Anyway, the point is, I came to warn you.' The parrot shuddered. 'They make do with sacrificing us parrots, you - Irk! - see. What they'd really like is a human sacrifice for their Golden - Irk! - God. They'd much rather have you than us.'

Their Golden God!!

I was desperately trying to catch my Aunty's eye.

We had found it! The place where the Golden God lived!

'Thank you,' said Aunty Iris. 'We'll keep well away from them.'

'I suggest,' the parrot went on, 'that you head north - Irk! Irk! Irk! - north - Irk! - east. That should take you right - Irk! - away from them. There's no danger at all in that direction.' He pointed one pink wing into a quite tangled-looking patch of trees.

'I see,' said Aunty Iris. 'That's very kind of you parrots. Thank you very much for your advice.'

'Yes,' said Simon. 'If you hadn't flown down and told us, we might have gone walking straight into the middle of their--'

But then he stopped in shock. That was because Aunty Iris had reached out quite casually with one hand, taken hold of the parrot and strangled it.

The bird gave one horrible IRRRRRkkk! and went limp.

'That'll do for our supper,' Aunty Iris grinned at us, and started plucking his gorgeous feathers off. 'Who's for Parrot a la Tinned Peaches, hm?'

Simon had gone white and was staring at her in disbelief. 'You killed him!'

'Pah,' she said, looking for a skewer for the barbecue. 'You're so gullible. He was sending us to our certain deaths! That route he pointed out was sure to lead us right into the clutches of the golden sloths. He was tricking us! And besides, we're all starving. It's been yonks since I tasted irksome parrot.'

'But that's where we want to go, isn't it?' I tried to interrupt them. 'That's where the Golden God is!'

But then the two of them were screaming at each other as the music got louder and louder (it was the Bee Gees at that point) and Aunty Iris roasted her dinner. Simon refused to eat any of it, and so did I.

And so, as the firelight faded, no one was talking, all we could hear were the distant IIIiirrrkkks of parrots and 'Night Fever', again and again and again.

3.

'And there doesn't appear to be a bar,' Iris added, once they were alone in the quarters that had been allotted to them and she had scouted around. She looked worn out and furious. Panda knew how fractious she could be at times like these.

'Look, Iris,' he said, going to her and patting her knee awkwardly. 'What is it we're doing here? I mean, really? Do you truly want to be reunited with the Clockworks people? You left all of that behind, such a long time ago.'

She blinked at him, astonished that he was even asking such a thing. 'What choice have I had? We've been bundled along like old baggage… No one asked me where I wanted to go! And besides, I'm quite fascinated by this… Seeing the kind of world I originally came from. Wouldn't that fascinate you…? If you could go back to your…?'

Panda shook his head solemnly. 'I've no desire to rediscover my roots, Iris. And you should know that! I've surely said that before. Origins, pah! I thought we were concerned about the very opposite? Weren't we? About going forward and trying to find out where we are going to end up! That's more our thing!'

She was rooting through her dusty carpet bag. 'That's what I always thought, old chum. But maybe I've hit a point in my life when I want to know more… And in order to know who I am now, I have to go backwards…'

'Poppycock,' Panda muttered, just as she hoisted out a small silver flask with a cry of triumph. 'Sentimental bobbins!'

Fenster creaked closer to them across the thick pile of the carpet. The constant squeaking of his wheels was grating on Panda's nerves and he was starting to wonder whether they were going to be stuck with this strange dragon forever. 'I sympathise with Panda, actually,' Fenster sighed. 'I neither know nor want to know where I came from. I thought it was here, in this very city, but it seems that I was mistaken about that. I was built, I suppose. Someone must have built me, once upon a time. I am a one-off creature of molten gold and a living heart… Someone fashioned me according to their own whims… But now I don't really want to find out who or why.'

'Interesting,' Iris said, and carried on drinking from her precious flask.

'It's no good getting drunk, Iris,' Panda grunted.

'Yes it is,' she said. 'When was it a bad idea? Seriously, Panda. When you think of some of the situations we've been in – would any of them be improved by our sobriety?'

'Well..' he said, and she grinned, as if her point was made.

There was a pause and, quite unannounced, the door slid open, allowing two of the slim and elegant Clockworks people access. They stepped in unison across the room and stared at Iris, who lit a cigarette and glowered back.

'You could have knocked before stepping into a lady's boudoir,' said Panda.

It was a man and a woman, that much was clear. Their faces had that unnatural calm about them that Panda already found infuriating.

'We have come to see our female relative,' said the male figure.

'Oh yes?' said Panda, instinctively getting protective and coming to stand between them and his best friend. Then the meaning of what the man had said hit him. 'Relative? What? You mean… Iris is…?'

The female indicated with a slow nod that Iris was indeed the relation they meant. 'She is our ancestor.'

Iris flinched at this. 'Ancestor? Just how old do you think I am?'

'We do not know,' said the man. 'We have been told that you are related to our genetic material, and that you are a time traveller. We believe you have come here from a time very different to ours.'

'Yes, but we should still be in synch, shouldn't we?' Iris gasped. 'I thought… no matter how far abroad I went, and whichever dimension… somehow I would remain in synch with the Clockworks and its folks…'

The two visitors smiled at her blandly. 'It is a matter of many millennia since the Great Schism, when we fled the Obverse,' the man said.

'Well, it is for me, too,' Iris shot back. 'Probably. But... erm, I can't be sure. And what's more, all my diaries were nicked by a dreadful poet from Earth.'

Fenster stared at her. 'Are you millennia old, Iris dear?'

'I suppose I must be,' she said. 'But I can't be sure. How can I be sure about any of it?'

The female figure stepped forward and held out her hands. 'All we can be certain of is that you belong with us. You are a part of our family, no matter how distant.'

Panda couldn't help gawping at the tableau before him. There couldn't be a humanoid figure more distinct from the hairless, gentle, almost golden-skinned beauties than the woman they were claiming kin with. After her recent exertions Iris looked even more disheveled than usual, in her curious motley collection of garments and her hair sticking up so messily. She was more like an interstellar baglady than ever before, and yet this didn't seem to faze the Clockworks people at all. Now they were holding out their hands to her...

'Will you stay with us, here in our city?'

'The Clockworks has missed you, Iris. Or rather... Lilith...'

'Lilith?' Iris frowned heavily, and sucked the last few dregs from her flask. 'Yes, yes... Lilith. I remember... I can remember being called... Lilith...'

Panda hurried over to her and flung his furry arms around one of her legs. 'No, no! Don't let these awful people brainwash you, Iris! You aren't Lilith or anybody else! You are Iris Wildthyme!'

She knocked him away, almost brusquely. 'Yes, of course I know that, Panda. Don't be daft. But these lovely people are talking about another me... an earlier me... a me that I only just remember being...' She was shuffling forward, closer to her putative descendents. 'I need to know more... I need...'

But Panda knew that this was all a very bad idea. 'No, Iris! They are up to something! I can feel it!'

'Hush, now,' she said. 'I'm curious. I'm fascinated by this whole business, Panda. And can't you be happy for me, now that I seem to have found my roots?'

'It's a trap!' he cried. 'Just as you yourself were saying about an hour ago!'

She shook her head. 'No, no... it's not a trap...'

The male descendent clicked his fingers and the door opened once more. This time a retinue of silver-skinned servants issued into the room. They brought trays of fruit and meats, and jugs of what Iris hoped was the local rotgut. She wasn't disappointed.

'You must relax and refresh yourselves,' the female descendent said. 'There will be plenty of time for all of your questions.'

'Yes,' said Iris. 'Thank you.'

Panda rolled his eyes. Fenster was quite still, watching all of this transpire but as soon as all the Clockworks people had backed out of the room, he said: 'I'm inclined to agree with Panda, Iris, darling. Can't you see what's happening?'

She was sitting on the circular bed amongst the satin cushions and exotic furs, gorging herself already on the Hysperon fruits and nursing a large goblet. 'Oh, you two! You're just jealous! Just because I've gone and found my place in the universe! Just because they're all so pleased to see me!'

'It's not that, Iris,' said Panda, in a deadly serious tone. 'I think we should get away from here as soon as we can. We should get back to the bus and go. What about our friends? What about the Empress? And the fact that Anthony Marvelle has a mad scheme to re-open the Ringpull into the Obverse?'

Iris waved him away and flopped down on the luxurious bed. 'Later,' she sighed. 'Let me deal with it all later on… I think I'm getting to like it here, chuck.'

4.

The three of us slept and the music of the sacrificial revels must have eventually stopped.

A kind of peace reigned throughout the jungle. A light dew came out on the long grasses and the mouldy vegetation. Simon lay muttering in his sleep, and I was having a very mundane dream about missing the first day of term back at school.

Meanwhile Aunty Iris slept soundly, as ever, covered in a smattering of pink and golden feathers.

It was at this still, quiet point in the very early morning that the savage golden sloths must have decided to attack. They might have been savage, but they weren't stupid. They wanted human sacrifices and they realised that their best chance of getting them was to catch the human interlopers unawares and as they rested.

We didn't know it, but for the past few days the sloths had been spying on us, and they knew that Aunty Iris would be a formidable foe. None of them fancied a walloping off the cantankerous old one in the floppy hat.

So, once the nightlong sacrificial fun had ended, a party of five slinky golden sloths stole away from their temple and into the jungle. They each took positions around the glade in which we adventurers were sleeping. They bided their time and grinned in anticipation of their triumph: at the idea of having human sacrifices that night for their terrible Golden God.

Then, at a signal from their leader, the golden sloths leapt into the camp and started shrieking and gibbering and waving around their lethal looking blades.

Aunty Iris woke up with an almighty scream to find clumsy, hairy hands all over her person. The sloths had gone after her first, knowing instinctively that she was by far the most dangerous. She yelled blue murder and thrashed about, panicking at the sight of these evil grinning faces bearing down on her. They pinned her to the ground and cheered at their own cleverness.

All this noise was the first that Simon and I knew about it. But we were on our feet in a flash. Simon almost died in fright at the hullaballoo and first he couldn't make out what was going on at all. It still wasn't fully light in the jungle and we got an impression of furry golden bodies dashing about and glittering hither and thither.

I think I had more presence of mind. I knew instantly what must be going on. I grabbed up my book and silver pen and stowed them swiftly in my backpack. Then I took hold of Simon, yanking him off the ground. The sloths were concentrating on Aunty Iris. All five of them tried to keep my aunty down. As she lashed out she screeched fit to burst: 'Unhand me at once, you beasts! I've never been so roughly treated in all my born days!'

The sloths simply laughed at her distress.

'Kelly! Simon!' Aunty Iris yodelled. 'Run away! Let them take me! You two have to get away!'

We barely had time to think about it. Simon stared at me. He was still cross with Aunty Iris for throttling and eating the parrot, but he'd never have abandoned her to the killer sloths. Yet the she was right. There was no point in all three of us getting captured. And now the sloths were turning their attention away from my desperately flailing aunty...

I made the snap decision. 'Come on!' And I shoved Simon ahead of me.

We piled recklessly into the darkness of the trees beyond the makeshift camp. Then we were running full pelt with the gibbering of the sloths ringing in our ears. I reckoned, someone must have noticed us escaping and they'd be on our tails in a matter of seconds.

The golden sloths would be much better at hurtling through the Shrieking Jungle than two human kids and as we dashed *headlong through the trees I thought: We don't even stand a chance!*

5.

Soon enough those slim, elegant aliens were back and Panda had to endure a kind of guided tour around their hidden city. Iris seemed to be quite happy to be led around. She was evidently enjoying all their bowing and scraping. Panda stomped along in their wake as she gazed at buildings and the underground folk going about their daily business. Wherever she went, the Clockworks people stopped and stared at her. They were polite, but clearly awed by her. Word must have spread that the prodigal daughter of the Clockworks was back in town.

Fenster came wheeling after them, wherever they went, squeaking all the while. His occasional lofty comments and hissing exertions soon got on Panda's nerves.

'It's all magnificent,' Iris declared, as they paused for refreshments in a well-lit piazza. 'What a delightful city you live in!'

Her descendents nodded graciously at her compliments.

Panda hopped into her lap and boggled his eyes furiously. 'How long do we have to hang around with this lot?'

She shushed him. 'Hopefully not too much longer.'

He felt a rush of pleasure at hearing her normal, cynical tone. She hadn't been brainwashed into bland acceptance after all!

'There's somewhere I want to see, that's all,' she murmured.

The Clockworks people had mentioned that, at the heart of their city, there was a wood. At hearing this Iris's own heart had leapt up and started hammering. She remembered at once the dense, dewy wood within her childhood home. She had become lost inside the forests within Saga City, hadn't she? She had found the tree – the oldest, wisest tree in the world. And there was something about a book… she had the image in her head of a book… growing out of the tree's ancient flesh.

Images… it was all she could think in; all that she could recall. Right now she didn't know what that book had contained, or what the importance of the tree was… But if they had a portion of that forest here with them, perhaps the Clockworks people also had that sacred tree… They might have brought it with them from the other universe…

'Iris?' asked Panda softly, as he studied her faraway expression.

'The tree told me what to do, Panda,' she suddenly said. 'It was the tree that told me how I should live my life. And who I was going to be…'

He wasn't sure what she was on about, but he was positive that she wouldn't want their captors to hear about it. He waved his stumpy arms in her face. 'Shush!' And then realized he'd thought of their hosts as captors, and he and his friends as prisoners... No matter how warm the welcome, that's what he thought...

They drank some kind of sticky, gloopy coffee from glasses, and nibbled at tasteless biscuits. One of the silvery beings attempted to engage Iris in conversation about her Celestial Omnibus, and where she had left it. Iris merely waved vaguely in the direction of the artificial sky and stars far above their heads. She waggled her beringed fingers as if her thoughts were still light years away.

'And how did you first come by your marvelous engine?' asked another of the Clockworks people. 'We have wondered for many years where you found such a thing...'

Panda was feeling very suspicious now. They were asking too many questions for his liking.

'A vehicle that can slip between dimensions and through time and space,' whispered the senior silvery being. 'It is a thing far beyond our capabilities. Even back in our own universe, when our civilization was at its height, we never could have invented such a thing...'

Then, all of a sudden, Iris was sitting upright and telling them in a loud, clear voice: 'I found her. Deep in the poisoned desert. She had crashlanded there... she was dying and her life force was leaking away into the burning sands.' She turned to look into Panda's eyes and he saw that her expression was wild and somewhat disturbed. 'And *you* were there, Panda, weren't you? You were with me... when I went to coax her back into life...'

He shook his head firmly. 'I'm sorry, dear Iris. But you've got it all wrong…'

'No, no,' she said. 'It's coming back to me… and you *were* there… you came looking for me… scaling the heights of the towers at Wherewithal House…'

As she pronounced the name of that place, there was a ripple of surprised recognition among the Clockworks people. 'We have a Wherewithal House, here in the city…'

Iris flinched. 'What..? Here…?'

The leader nodded graciously. 'It is a fragment of our former world that came here with us. It is still inhabited, though no one comes out or goes into that old place.'

Panda saw that Iris had gone white. 'What is it?' he said. 'Somewhere you know?'

She shook her head, as if to clear it of cobwebs. 'It can't be true,' she said. 'It can't be them…'

As the party finished their refreshments and gathered together to continue their tour, the leader was explaining how the house known as Wherewithal was wedged amongst a whole load of disused and dangerous buildings lining the banks of one of the rivers that ran down into their city. If you followed the rivers uphill you would eventually come to the surface of Hyspero again, though the going was perilous and naturally, it was impossible to sail anything against the tide. Personally, he advised against visiting those old mausoleums. Their inhabitants were ancient and mad. Best stay here in the gleaming city, under translucent domes, where nothing could hurt you… nothing could interfere…

And so they made their way to the woods in the heart of the city.

Iris remembered it as a wild place. Teeming with noise and ungovernable life. It was amongst her very earliest memories, and was the least cloudy of all: the day that she had chosen to run away into those dark woods. She remembered the sharp stink of decay and fecundity and freshness just as if it had been yesterday…

But this wasn't quite the same. It was a field perhaps half a kilometer wide. There were a number of straggly saplings lashed to stakes, and the rest was all yellowing grasses, about as tall as Panda. The tallest tree was a sickly, broken-down looking specimen, its thick bark pulling away from it branches.

'The glorious forest!' cried the leader of Iris's descendents. 'See how we have brought it from our native world? See how we have tended it and kept it alive! Is it not magnificent?'

Iris and Panda looked at each other and decided that they would have to be polite about this.

'It's terribly good,' Iris said. 'Well done! How on earth have you cultivated so much greenery down here under the surface?'

'We have wisdom and patience,' said the silvery man. 'And with these qualities, we can accomplish all sorts of things.'

6.

At first it went quite well.

The trail was easy to follow and there wasn't any sign of sloths. Simon and I crouched low, tried not to make too much noise, and were quite confident about creeping up on the golden sloth temple.

The temple was set into a natural, overgrown bowl in the earth. We hid in some bushes at the top and peered down at this impressive building.

'It's covered in hair,' I said.

'Or fur,' Simon pointed out.

Whichever it was, the elaborate building was decorated in masses of it, glinting gold in the meagre light that managed to penetrate this deep into the wilderness.

'Aunty Iris's going to be a human sacrifice in a hairy temple,' I said in a desolate voice.

'Actually, it looks more like tinsel from here,' Simon pointed out. 'It looks weird.'

I shushed him. I could see that there were sloths patrolling about in front of the grand furry building. They were gathering on the steps outside and chattering and gibbering enthusiastically, presumably about the news that at their next lot of revels they wouldn't have to make do with a lousy parrot. They had an old human lady instead.

'I wonder why their god demands sacrifices,' Simon said. 'It must be a terrible god.'

'Why do people do anything?' I said. 'They're just using this god thing as an excuse for completely awful behaviour. I'm sure it's not necessary to make sacrifices. They just want to do it, that's all. Because they're awful.'

'This Golden God is who we're looking for...' said Simon worriedly. 'He's supposed to help us on our quest. But if he's as awful as he sounds...'

I shrugged. 'We'll just have to see, won't we?'

We watched the way the sloths down there were gossiping and rubbing their clumsy hands with glee.

'What do you reckon we should do now, then?' I said.

'Well,' he said. He seemed pleased and amazed that I was listening to his ideas. 'I think we should sneak down there and find a secret way into the temple and ... maybe we should climb up the golden hair somehow and...'

And that's when we were captured.

We were set upon by two of the lithe and gleaming creatures. They jumped out of nowhere in a blur of gold. I let out a cry of outrage as we were both roughly seized.

Sloths' fingers are very skinny and very horrible.

We were led briskly down to the hairy temple, which looked more impressive and scarily forbidding with every step we took.

'What are they saying?' Simon hissed.

'How should I know?' I said. 'They keep talking in their grunty sloth language.'

We were marched smartly into an outbuilding to one side of the temple. This was less elegant than the rest and we were barged straight into the gloomy, stone-floored room. We were shoved in a cell, the doors were locked and the sloths stomped out again.

At first I was hopeful that we would find ourselves locked in with Aunty Iris. But when we poked around in the dim recesses of the prison we found that we were quite alone, apart from a heap of rotting straw and a human skull, which made Simon yell out.

'I wonder where they've put her,' I seethed. 'I'll never forgive myself if anything happens to her.' I slumped on the ground. 'I'd only just got her back,' I moaned.

Simon bent down and patted me awkwardly on the back. 'I know,' he said.

'She's an old woman,' I said. 'She's not as tough as she makes out.' I thought about how, in the jungle, she had, at times, seemed to be fading away.

'I think she could deal with anything!' said Simon. 'She's really tough!'

'She's not. She just puts on a brave face for us two. To show us she's not scared and not worn out or anything. But you heard her the other day, going on. The journey so far has taken it right out of her. She's too old for this.' I kicked at the floor-to-ceiling metal bars of our cell. 'Let's face it. The three of us are going to get our throats cut by a load of gaudy sloth-things who dance around to Seventies disco records.'

7.

Panda hated show-offs and those who seemed very pleased with themselves. They infuriated him and whenever he met people like that, he had to restrain himself from yelling at them. Or punching them up the hooter. This was particularly the case with these escapees from the distant Obverse, who seemed much too cool and collected for his liking. They just assumed that their captives would be terribly impressed with this underworld kingdom, and give up everything in order to join them down here.

That evening, once they had returned to the gilded building where they were quartered, Panda attempted to talk seriously to Iris about their plight.

'Plight?' she said, gazing dolefully at her empty gin flask and her last cigarette.

'Yes,' he insisted. 'They want us to stay here forever, don't they? Now they've got their clutches on you, they want you and the bus and you're never going to be let free again.'

'Oh, rubbish, Panda,' she said, whirling about in the gauzy gown her new friends had left out for her. 'We are honoured guests. We are free to come and go as we please. If we suddenly decide that we've had enough of this place…'

'I've had enough,' Panda snapped, a little rudely, she thought. 'I've had it up to here with this drippy lot. I want to leave right now.'

'Oh, I don't think we should do that,' she said.

'You're out of booze and ciggies!' he cried. 'What's the matter with you, woman? Can't you see? We need to get out of here as soon as we can..!' There was a touch of suppressed panic in Panda's voice, for he knew that he wouldn't be able to leave of his own accord. He knew – and Iris knew – that he was dependent upon her company to get back to the surface. His own little legs would never be able to carry him all the way back.

'We can't go,' she suddenly said. 'What about Fenster? We can't leave him alone here, and besides – only he knows the way back.' Fenster had been taken off by some of the silvery beings... They had been most interested in his workings and his endless memory banks, about which he had been bragging, in a pathetic attempt (Panda had thought) to endear himself to Iris's biggest fans.

Panda shrugged. 'I'm not all that keen on him, to be honest. He's too snooty. He's a liar, too. And anyway, can't we follow one of these rivers they were talking about? They flow up to the surface or something, they said, didn't they?'

Iris came up to him and stared him dead in the eye. 'We can't go now,' she said, making quite sure that he knew she meant it.

'But why..?' he thundered – though it came out a bit whiny.

'Because there's something we have to do tonight.'

'Tonight?' he frowned.

'We're going to sneak out of here, Panda!' she grinned. 'We're going back to that so-called forest of theirs to take a look at something…'

Panda's spirits lifted immediately as he watched Iris donning her heavier clothes again. He realized that she was still, in fact, her nosey, rebellious, fearless self, after all. She had merely been waiting for artificial night to declare itself over the city of the Clockworks – and then, all of a sudden, she was ready to go out and do some hunting around of her own.

'Are you coming?' she asked him.

'Of course!'

When they were wrapped up and Panda had donned his trusty night-vision goggles, they found that the door to their sumptuous suite had been locked from the outside.

'See?' Panda growled. 'We're prisoners here!'

Iris was hunting through her carpet bag for hairclips. 'I'm starting to see what you mean, chuck… Ah!' She grinned and produced one of her terribly useful and recently invented laser hairclips, which soon made short work of the door's electronic locks. 'Cheeky buggers! I'm supposed to be their honoured guest…!'

Luckily, there were no guards or stragglers hanging about in their building. They saw not a soul until they were down on the gloomy street again. 'How could you have even pretended to get on with such a dreary lot, Iris?' Panda hissed. 'You seemed so interested in them! You were so polite!'

She shrugged and murmured something about family.

'Family!' Panda laughed. 'They might claim to be related to you, but they're nothing like you! You've got nothing to do with them!'

'They're my descendents...' she said, as the two of them wove their way through the narrow, deserted streets, both trying to remember the route they had gone earlier that day.

'*I'm* your real family!' Panda burst out. 'Me! And the others, too... Simon and Barbra and... well, not Jenny exactly, and not that Kelly... but you get the point, don't you? You haven't forgotten your little gang aboard the bus?'

'Of course not!'

'Well, for a while there, I thought you were content to give it all up... and to let those so-called descendents of yours have the bus...'

'Yes, they seemed quite keen on learning all about it, didn't they...?'

'I wouldn't trust them an inch!' he said hotly. 'They mean you no good! They just want the Number Twenty Two!'

Iris sighed, and Panda knew then that his comments had hit home. They crossed the grand piazza silently, sticking to the shadows and avoiding the baleful glare of the fake moonlight. 'I just wanted to belong somewhere...' Iris said, rather pitifully. 'Just for once. It seemed too good to be true... Here are my people... I belong to them! And they to me! And they've been waiting for millennia to find me! It was very flattering... very enticing... I thought I could learn about my true past, and everything that's so long ago I've forgotten all the details…'

'Backstory!' Panda shouted. 'Exposition! Origins!' He growled warningly. 'That's all very well in books, Iris! But in real life it tends to get a bit over-complex! You don't really want people and things from your past turning up… and you don't want all your mysteries sorting out. That kind of thing can get a tad inconvenient, you know…'

She took her bearings sadly, working out the way to the somewhat spartan wood. 'Yes, I know you're right, really, Panda. These people have got me all mixed up, you see. They even had me confused over when I first met you, didn't they…?'

'You've been all in a tizz,' he said solemnly, 'ever since the bus brought us to this world of Hyspero.'

'Yes,' she said. 'And I warned us all, didn't I? Before we even came here? It all goes wrong when you travel to Hyspero! It's happened every time I've been here! It always goes tits up!'

And then they both noticed they had arrived at the wood at the heart of the Clockworks.

8.

Simon tried to take my notebook off me. I slapped his hands away. 'What are you doing? Don't touch that.' I was clinging onto the book and pen like they were the most valuable objects in all the world.

Perhaps they were.

'All right,' said Simon. 'You do it. I want you to try something. Since you happen to be the special one ...'

'What?'

'Get a fresh page. Write down what I say.'

'Not this again,' I groaned. 'I've told you. It won't work. I don't know how to do magic, Simon...'

'You can try,' said Simon.

I shrugged. 'What shall I put?'

'Well, you can't write, 'So Aunty Iris was safe and sound and the whole of Hyspero was safe again and everyone lived happily ever after.' That wouldn't work.'

I agreed with him sarcastically.

'Because,' he said, 'that would be rubbish. What kind of story would that be? There's no adventure or drama or fighting or anything in that. Now, I've been thinking about this, Kelly. And what I think is that somehow, that black book of yours is alive...'

I gripped the velvet of its cover even tighter. Weirdly, the fabric under my fingers was even starting to feel like fur. That must have been my imagination though. It felt like it was bristling at Simon's quiet words. 'Alive?' I said. I stared at him. 'Where did you say you bought it, Simon?'

He gulped. 'A little shop. Hidden away in our town. It's an old stationers' shop that looks ancient and a bit creepy from the outside.'

'I think I know the one,' I gasped. 'You went in there?'

'I wanted to get you something special. It isn't too bad when you get inside. It's a bit gloomy and the man behind the counter looks like Dracula … It was him who suggested I buy you the book and order the special silver pen…'

I nodded firmly. 'So… I was meant to have this particular pen and book. We've been stitched up. We're the pawns of destiny, we are.' I stared at him. 'I'm still surprised at you, going into that creepy shop alone…'

'I had to,' he said. 'I was drawn. It's like I say. The book is alive. As soon as I touched the cover I knew that it was the one that you were meant to have.'

The book seemed to be tingling again under my fingers.

'And,' Simon went on, 'the book wants to be filled with a really good story, Kelly. The one that only you can write. About saving Hyspero from whatever it is that's breaking it apart. And, like any good story, it can't have the ending come too quickly or too easily. That would spoil everything. If you just put, 'It was all over and everyone was safe and well and we all went home,' the book itself would be really disappointed. So it won't let you make these big, easy things come true. But …'

My heart and mind were racing. Maybe Simon was onto something here. 'But what?'

'Maybe little things. Small, seemingly unimportant things to alter the plot. Maybe you could make those come true. And they would let us move on and keep going. To keep the story moving. Maybe that's what the book wants. And maybe it'll let you write them down…'

I took up the silver pen and uncapped it briskly. 'Okay. I'll try it.'

I opened my book at the next fresh, black page, thought for a bit, and wrote:

9.

Under the artificial moonlight the tree was even more eerie and ruinous. It looked as if it had been struck by lightning, perhaps repeatedly, over the years, and still, somehow, it had struggled to stay alive – but only just. Its branches hung rather limply, and its few leaves were sickly, yellow things. 'Like scabs,' Panda pointed out.

'But it's still alive,' Iris whispered. 'It's clinging on…'

Panda saw the keen glint in her eye and he realized that she had seen something in the tree that he hadn't. Something that she recognized of old. She was standing there before the tree as if she was remeeting an ancient friend.

'Hello..?' she said, in a nervous-sounding voice. 'Are you still there?'

Panda almost barked out laughing. He wanted to scoff at her; to puncture the moment. The silly old thing was being absurd, talking to a tree like that…

'Hello there..? Once before… long, long ago… you talked to me, remember? Well, I was very different. I was just a little girl. And this was in a different universe, of course… But I'm sure it was you. I'm really, really sure that you are the same tree... the same entity... Eliot, wasn't it..?'

Panda grew hot with embarrassment, even in the wintry chill of night in the underground city. Here they were in this dreadful wasteland... and Iris was raising her voice, as if to summon up a spirit from the dead bark. They shouldn't go making too much noise... what if those silvery people heard them? And discovered them up and about in the middle of the night? Panda didn't trust those people at all. Iris may be vital to them... but Panda wasn't. He felt sure those epicene aliens would do away with him in a trice, should the opportunity arise.

When he looked again at Iris he saw – with some surprise – that she was getting results. The trunk of the tree had swollen somewhat, and there was a curious glow suffusing the lichenous and mildewy bark. Iris gave a cry of delight and stepped forward as the whole twisted body of the tree started to open out into...

What? A doorway? Another portal into yet another strange space beyond..?

But no... not a door. It was a book... the whole tree was opening up like a gigantic book, whose leaves were rustling with intense, uncontainable life.

'This is what happened before, Panda,' Iris told him excitably. 'I remember it now, so clearly. What happened to me... when I was so small... and I ran away... into the interior of Saga City, which was the city where I lived. I vanished into the forest that gave us air and I hid inside there, like a wild thing, like a feral child. And I found the tree at the heart of that place and it showed me… a book. Just like this. The book of the world.'

Panda wrinkled his nose. Partly this was because of the dank, bookish smell that was filling the gloom, but also it was some measure of disdain he was experiencing at that moment. 'The book of the world? Oh, dear, Iris. All of this sounds rather too mythological for me, dear. Rather earnest, in fact. Are you really telling me that you're having some sort of dreadful epiphany about your long-gone past… and it's all this hippyish mythical stuff?' He tossed his furry head. 'Christ almighty, lovey. Next thing, you'll be telling me that a voice spoke to you and gave you a mission…! A quest, in fact!'

Iris shook her head. 'I just remember this great big book… like this, look… and the pages were all maps and charts, like this. All these colours and complications… Somehow they were maps of times as well as places…. But more than that, too… they showed the short cuts and twisty secret passageways through the dimensions… and all the great off-the-beaten-track moments to go and visit.' She laughed. 'And there was something about… all the great parties to go and visit! Here, look…! And here, all the actual moments that myths begin…' She was actually touching the pages now, and turning them, rather less carefully than Panda thought she ought… They were thick and fibrous, almost fleshy, and they flipped one on top of the other too loudly.

Panda pressed his paws to his ears. 'All right! I believe you! When you were little, you saw these great secrets…'

'Wonderful secrets, Panda!' she cackled, turning the pages faster and faster. 'There I was – just a girl from the slums! Just a nothing and a nobody! A scrap of life from the wrong part of that fine city of the Clockworks. But somehow I had broken out of the dull routines and the set patterns… and I had been allowed to stray. The forest welcomed me… and the creatures I met there let me stay… and I found the tree and the tree showed me a book… and the book was all about how there was more to life than scratting and scrabbling about for existence in a world you didn't even like very much. The tree told me about all the great places in history and the wider universe… and how they could all be mine to explore…'

'That's all well and good,' Panda said. 'And I'm sure it's all true. But what I'm asking is… why is the tree here and now? And why is it showing you the book again? And why is it looking so dead?'

Iris stopped babbling excitedly to herself, and looked suddenly stricken. 'Now there's a point. Well done, Panda! You always hit the nail on the head! You always see through the moment into the essence of things…'

He beamed at this flattery. 'Can you think why? Why it is here now? Why have you been brought here, before it?'

Iris closed her eyes, thinking deeply. A cool night breeze skirled through the wasteland and she tugged her feathery collar up closer round her neck. Her eyes shot open. 'I think… I think it's because I need reminding, don't I?'

Panda didn't even have time to respond to that. The gigantic book was glowing a little brighter, then. A soft, tangerine glow, shot through with shafts of violet. They turned and it was if the tree and the book were after their full attention. Suddenly both Iris and Panda felt much lighter in their bodies... as if gravity was doing something peculiar just then, or their heavy, earthly essences were draining away into the sandy earth... They felt gossamer light and floaty... and Panda found himself wailing in a worried sort of way. He felt Iris patting his head in an effort to calm him. He could feel the cool of all those chunky rings she wore against his furry noggin... but then it was as if even that much bodily sensation was lost to him... and he was floating after her... rising through the murky air and into the bright, orange and purple pages before them...

'Ooh, and this happened last time, as well, chuck,' he heard Iris shout, with that raucous cackle in her voice once more. There was a pause as she lit up a ciggy (Even during an out of body experience she has to smoke...! he thought) and then she added: 'Poor Panda! Don't panic, lovey! Just give yourself up and go with the flow...'

10.

'That book and pen,' I whispered to Simon. 'They were the best present ever.'

'Even better than Make Up Girl?' he grinned.

'Even better,' I nodded.

The sloth was leading us outside, into the murkiness of the jungle. As the afternoon approached there was even less sun filtering down this deep: where it did, there were brilliant dashes of golden light.

Running between the prison house and the temple itself was like running through a dazzling strobe effect. The sloth led the way smartly and quickly, choosing the moment carefully so we didn't encounter any others of his kind.

We didn't know how we'd fare in a hand-to-hand battle with the savage-looking beings. They had those very long and bendy arms and legs. And their hands were those strange hooky shapes.

This close up, the temple was even more impressive. It was a weirdly organic structure, with that gorgeous golden tinsel hanging from every doorway and window frame. It must have taken generations of shaved sloths to cover the building so comprehensively with their hair.

Inside it was cool and dark and had a musty smell, quite like the monkey house in the zoo. It took some moments of getting used to, as the three of us inched into the shaded recesses. Simon and I had to hurry to keep up with our loping, lolloping friend. We crouched into the corners and darted through the thickest patches of shadow and saw only a couple of sloths who were moving from altar to altar, lighting candles to more of those ferocious-looking statues.

We were led to the central chamber where, we presumed, the sacrifices were to take place. In the centre of this circular hall there was a stone slab which was littered with a whole heap of multi-coloured parrot feathers.

Simon and I shared an anguished glance: what if the friendly sloth who looked like my Uncle Bill had just brought us here to be killed? And how come we had followed along so willingly?

But, no. The sloth turned to look at us. In the gentle, bluish-green light that came dappling through the ancient windows, he looked kindly and concerned. Though he didn't tell us so, we felt sure that he was on our side. He had brought us into the heart of this deadly temple because that was the best way of rescuing my aunty. He looked as if all he wanted to do was help us.

'This place gives me the creeps,' Simon said. 'I'm just thinking about everyone dancing around and some poor parrot having its head cut off on the altar for their god.'

'It'll be us tonight, if we don't get a move on,' I said. 'Where is their god, anyway?'

The sloth must have half-understood my words because he became all animated then. He hopped up and down and gibbered at us, spraying us both with flecks of spit.

'Ugh. What's he trying to say?'

'He's gone a bit excitable,' Simon said, drawing back.

Now the sloth was facing the altar and the shadowy area behind it. He was on his bony bare knees and waving his arms about.

'I think he wants us to move away,' I said. 'Maybe we're standing too close...' I was fascinated, though. There seemed to be some large, bulky shape behind the altar. It was draped in black cloths and, if you looked very carefully, it seemed as if some kind of faint blue light was flickering underneath...

'That's just a heap of old black curtains,' Simon said, nervously peering ahead.

I stepped past the prostrate sloth and up to the bloody altar. The sloth looked horrified at this sacrilege. 'I wonder what's underneath,' I said. 'Hang on.'

Before the others could stop me, I had darted right into the most sacred and shrouded spot in the temple. I didn't even give myself time to think. I just had to find out the secret of the temple.

I grabbed a handful of dusty black curtains and lifted it slightly. Simon was standing there, frozen.

At first I was disappointed. 'There's a pile of old junk under here!' My voice was voice echoing throughout the stone chamber, making Simon wince. 'Look!' I laughed. 'Here's an old TV set!'

I parted the hanging fabrics to reveal a black and white TV screen. It was muted, but its surface was buzzing and flickering with interference.

The Uncle Bill sloth shrieked in fear. Then he flattened himself to the ground, humming some kind of hymn in supplication.

'They're worshipping a heap of rubbish!' I yelled. 'This is what they want to sacrifice us to!'

I was so annoyed by this that I took hold of the black dust sheets in both hands and gave them a good strong yank. I wanted to expose the sloths' fake and bogus god in all its shabby glory. I wanted to see exactly what they were praying to.

The black curtains slid off the bulky shape. I had to tug a bit to get them all down and it took a few moments. Flurries of age-old dust came billowing around us. The sloth groaned and whimpered on the ground.

'Um, Kelly,' Simon said quietly. I was busy sneezing and shaking the dust out of my frizzy hair. 'It wasn't a pile of old junk under there after all.'

'No?' I said, rubbing my smarting eyes. 'What is it?'

'Look,' said Simon, and found that he couldn't move or say anything more at all.

Glaring down at us was a ten foot tall lizard.

He was a gleaming gold and covered with brilliant, oily scales. At first I hoped he might be a statue, but the creature flexed his glittering neck and rolled his fiery eyes in fury.

The television set built into his belly gave a crackle of monochrome irritation at being disturbed like this.

I tried my hardest to seem like I wasn't impressed. I stood with my hands on my hips and glared straight back up at the affronted creature.

'So you're the golden sloth god,' I said. I thought attack was the best form of defence. I made my voice as bold as I could and shouted up into his golden, leering face. 'What are you doing having everyone sacrificed all over the place? That's a horrible thing to do.'

The lizard blinked down at me, as if in astonishment. A forked purple tongue slid out of his mouth and experimentally licked his lips. When he spoke his voice sounded rusty with disuse. It welled up from inside him and emerged in a dusty hiss. 'I never asked them to kill parrots on my account, dear.'

'Well, now they're going to kill my Aunty Iris! And us as well, if they can catch us! What do you think of that, oh, Great Golden God of the sloths?'

The lizard sighed unhappily and said, 'Do I look like a sloth god, little girl? Look at me. I'm a reptile. I'm not even a sloth.'

'So what are you doing here?'

'Can I help it if the sloths want to worship me? I've told them, no more parrots. No more sacrifice. And I can't stand all that awful disco music every night. But they just nod and gibber and bang go a few more parrots. I think they like all my golden scales and my television set.'

I frowned. 'Why HAVE you got a TV set in your belly?'

'Don't be so rude, dear,' snapped the lizard. 'You seem a very impetuous young lady. What's your name?'

'I'm Kelly and he's Simon. We're here on an adventure and, so far, we've been quite busy. There's been quite a lot to get on with, and you're next on our list. Who are you?'

The lizard coughed grandly and said, 'My name is Fenster. And, quite honestly, my dear, I'm as much a prisoner here as your poor aunty. I can't help what these foul creatures get up to. I can't stop them.'

'Can't you just walk away?' Simon put in. 'You're bigger than anyone here. And they're completely terrified of you. Look at Uncle Bill.' The sloth was still face down on the flagstones, quivering in fear.

'This is your Uncle Bill?' Fenster asked.

'No, he just looks a lot like him,' I said.

'Oh,' said Fenster. 'The thing is, you see, I've been clamped. I can't get out.'

'Clamped?' Bravely Simon inched forward and saw, with a shock, that the lizard didn't have any legs at all. Instead he had two metal wheels, almost like cartwheels, appended to the sides of his body. It was these that were clamped securely to the ground in vicious-looking metal vices.

'I'll never get out of here,' Fenster sighed melodramatically. 'I'll be forced to watch sloths having ceremonies until the end of my days. And I was built to last a good long while, you know, my darlings. I'm already several centuries old. But now, this is it. I have to watch these dreadful hook-handed creatures shaving off their hair. They bring it in tribute to me, you know. Heaps and heaps of the dirty stuff. What I'm supposed to do with all this golden fur I don't know. They seem to think I'd like it. I have to say, 'Oh yes, very nice. Just chuck it in the vault with the rest.' It's quite hard work being a sloth god. They're very demanding, you know...'

11.

A Story about a Tree

He was gnarled, but that was okay. He'd expect to be that way, after so long alive. Those heady days of swaying, supple arms and freely-gushing sap and tender little buds and leaves were far behind him now. He was gnarled, elderly, and stuck in his ways. His roots were far beneath him now and he could barely hear or feel their endless questing and probing into the thinnish soil of this subterranean world.

Yes! Subterranean! What a terrible thing for a tree of his pedigree and his august standing... To be placed underground and hidden from the sun and the sky and the mercy of the elements. It was his incarceration down here that had stunted his growth and made him sickly. He poured curses on the heads of the people who had brought him here... so far from his native soil. Into a different universe, they said.

A different universe! What did a tree care for universes and cosmic whatnots such as that? He knew it was true... he was familiar with stars and their merry circling round and the intricate patterns they made... his branches would stretch to their fullest when the stars were out... He was forever reaching and grasping after them... at least – that's how it had been when he was young and over-reaching had seemed so easy...

They transported me on their space ship... Yes, I remember those Clockworks folk digging into the precious soil around my trunk. They startled me from my slumbers... the woods were alive that night with curious shriekings and moans of dismay... The forest was invaded by well-meaning people who were determined to rescue me and to take me away.

I never understood... what tree could? It seemed so impossible, too disastrous... I was too mature, surely... they'd never lift me... surely they'd never succeed in transporting a tree such as I...

But I was their world tree... the source of all their knowledge. I was practically a god to those people of Sagacity. If they were under attack, if their world was doomed and they had to flee... then they would never leave me behind. They were quite determined to take me with them. I was aware of all the other trees in that forest at the heart of Sagacity watching these nocturnal exertions. They watched with scorn that disguised their horrible fears. They would be left behind when the Clockworkers fled...

And so he remembered being stowed away in a great big, filthy tank in the hold of the spaceship that travelled out of the Obverse and into the wider universe beyond. The journey lasted... how long? He knew only that he grew... he actually flourished in that rich soil and he was grateful for being rescued as the world behind them went up in flames. His gift to his heroes was, of course, the gift of air. He flexed his many delicate leaves in the artificial light of the ship, and he pressed them firmly against portholes when the ship was passing by the pale yellow suns of their new universe... and he was glad to make oxygen for them and to keep them all alive...

But that was all a long time ago. Since then – those wonderful days when they escaped certain doom in the Obverse – life had all been downhill.

They had come here. This arid world of Hyspero. Mostly desert, mostly sorcery and strangeness. A world ruled by a dynasty of cruel and crazy women. The ruling Empress had detected his superior mind, his bizarre magic and she had declared him her enemy. She wouldn't rest until the world tree was chopped up and burning in her grate in her throne room within the Scarlet Palace.

That was the way with Scarlet Empresses. No one could be cleverer, more beautiful, more magical than they. Anyone coming even close to that must be disposed of and, in the world tree's case, splintered into firewood and matchsticks.

But his people had hidden him here, deep beneath the crimson soil of his adopted world. And here he grew sickly, bored and lonely.

Generations passed. The Clockworkers who had survived the transplant even forgot where they had come from. They thought they had always lived here... their legends and their wits were scrambled... they struggled merely to survive day to day in the gloomy shadows... and only their world tree recalled that they were once rather powerful and could travel through dimensions and space and time...

He kept all of these secrets of all alive inside his book of many pages. His book was his very self, it could be said, in that it was written on the many delicate skins he had grown around his essential core. With each layering of woody, pulpy skin he had accreted more detail, more knowledge, more *story*...

But it was rare that he shared this storehouse of knowledge with anyone. Over the years he had grown to distrust the children of his rescuers. They were silly, lazy and greedy... almost barbaric down here in the underground Clockworks. They were a far cry from their noble ancestors...

He kept his book to himself.

Except one day... somebody approached.

Someone he was shocked to realise that he recognized.

From another time, another universe. Someone who, in the strict, chronological placement of things, should be long dead and buried. Her shrewd old skull should be picked clean and white – a dessicated bone lost in the ruins of a long-abandoned world…

She approached the tree cautiously. With great respect… just as she used to… just as she once had… back when she was a child…!

How strange to think of this ancient harridan as a young girl. This coarse old floozy with her thick skin, stringy hair and layers of garish clothing… this had once been the skinny, rather sickly, impossibly young girl from Sagacity. She had been the only one truly interested in the world tree for himself. Not just for his amazing book and everything he kept recorded there. She had seen past that and realized that he was really alive – thinking and feeling – with opinions of his own… longings and ideas of his own…

Back then – walking in that gorgeous garden at the heart of Sagacity – Lilith was the girl Iris had once been and she had said to the tree: 'You must want to move around… you're stuck in once place… you can't go anywhere you want to, can you?' And she'd added: 'There are so many places I want to go! But right now I feel like you. Too rooted… too dependent. But one day I will! I'll go anywhere I want! Impossible places! If they don't exist anywhere but inside my head, I'll still find a way to get there…'

He'd been so touched by her thinking. And her thoughts about him.

And he knew she was right.

She was walking towards him again. She knew him at once, as he did her. She brought with her a small, furry Panda, who she introduced as her very best friend and travelling companion.

They greeted each other as long lost old friends. The old woman put her arms around the tree's rough, scarred bark and hugged him hard. His gnarled, green skin was ungiving... and yet – somehow - he still felt her hug.

'You said you would get away from Sagacity,' he whispered. 'And you were right.'

'Oh, yes!' she said. 'I've been everywhere, dear Eliot. Name any place, any time, any party that there's ever been – anywhere worthwhile and fabulous, I mean... and I was there! I took heed of what you said... and what I read in your book all those years ago. I knew there was a whole universe out there... a Multiverse, in fact! And it was one I will never grow weary of, no matter how old I get, or however, suddenly young I may become... There'll still be enough to keep me occupied. And you were the one who told me. You were the one who sent me off on this... this wonderful quest.'

Panda sighed. 'See? I *knew* it was a quest. We have to find something, right? Some powerful object or a missing person or a maguffin of some curious kind?'

Iris looked back at her black and white pal and shook her head happily. 'No, that's not it at all, chuck. You've misunderstood this time. When I say 'quest' I don't mean any of that stuff at all. I'm just talking about the adventure of ourselves. Our lives. Having fun. Avoiding disasters. Learning how to be just us – to the best of our abilities. That's what the tree told me… all that time ago. Really – that was it – he just said, 'Have fun, dear.'

'*Have fun?*' Panda frowned.

'Oh, of course there'll be other quests,' Iris went on. 'Searches and rescues, invasions and investigations, and mysteries and quandaries and terrible to-dos to sort out. But they're all incidental and just the day-job, really. No, the biggest quest and the important one – that's quite simple, straightforward. '*Have fun.*' It's the meaning of everything – that's what Eliot the tree said.'

'How profound,' said her companion drily. 'Like that was something you never knew.'

'But it wasn't!' she said sharply. 'Really, it was the first time anyone had ever said that to me. Seriously, Panda! I was brought up to be a proper little lady… quiet and well-mannered… Speak when you're spoken too – and all that jazz. And then it was all about getting educated just enough to prove that you can learn to accomplish tasks when you're set them… but don't learn too much that you start to ask tricky questions and undermine things and see past the boring illusions of everyday life. Just learn to fit in and be like everyone… don't stand out in any way whatsoever. Don't draw attention to yourself. Don't show off. Don't mess about. Fit in. Be the same. Keep quiet. Be decorous. Wear nice clothes. Live blandly. Don't step out of line. Prefer neutral colours. Don't fill your house with garish, nonsensical garbage. Grow up past the need to talk to stuffed toys...'

She was on a roll now, ranting a little as the two of them stood before the withered tree. Her voice had become rather shrill...

'Stuffed toys...?' asked Panda, boggling at her.

'Yes!' she cried. 'Don't believe in magic! Don't believe in serendipity! Or ghosts and monsters! Believe in the evidence of your own senses and nothing more! Believe in rationality and science! Believe that time moves in one direction only and the past cannot be altered! Do exactly what your family and ancestors did! Don't steal a bus! Don't talk to it like a person! Don't go crashing through the dimensions having fun! That's what was drilled into me, Panda... from a very early age! And yes...! I did need someone... some glorious someone... to tell me that I need to enjoy myself. That my life's mission, if you like, was to take that idea and embrace it and obey it with every fibre of my being. I was born in order to enjoy myself and really enjoy the life I was somehow given...'

'Enough!' Panda cried. 'I understand!'

'And now,' said the tree. 'It's time for you to leave me again. Now I have reminded you and you have reminded me... Dear Iris...'

'Time to leave?' she shouted. 'No! Surely not? Already?'

'You must leave this place... these stultified remnants of the Obverse, hiding down here. They can't help you. They have nothing to do with you anymore. You must seal your past back up and return to the universe, Iris… which needs you…'

'Funny,' she said. 'I don't remember you being able to talk before… back there and then, in the heart of Saga City…?'

'But I did!' laughed the tree. 'We talked and talked. We shared dreams and ideas and we spoke them aloud. I've kept the echoes of those talks close to my heart in all of that time… they were all I had to console myself at times in my long and sometimes horrible life. I thought… at least *she* is out there… somewhere, I'm sure… enjoying herself…'

'Yes…' she said. 'You're right. I do remember the sound of your voice. You were the first impossible thing I remember encountering…'

'Most everything can talk,' said the tree. 'If you listen closely enough.'

Panda was starting to feel a little creeped out by the conversation. He understood that Iris was having some kind of epiphany about her past and all, and that was fine with him. It just didn't need to go on all night, surely? And now that this tree had told her – and convinced her, he hoped – that this dump underground was bad for her, Panda hoped it would soon be time to get out of here.

'Excuse me,' he piped up, addressing the tree. 'Would you please direct us to the best way out of here? Seeing as you think we ought to make a move?'

The tree rustled his dessicated branches thoughtfully, causing a few faded leaves to fall. Iris popped one inside her capacious carpet bag.

'Yes, I'll tell you,' said the tree, and started giving them a very long and complicated series of directions for returning to the surface.

'But first you must pick up your other friend,' he warned. 'The lizard, Fenster. He is crucial in the unfolding of this tale, Iris.'

'Really?' Panda pulled a face. 'I found him insufferably pompous, actually. And rolling about on wheels like that – he'll only hold us up.'

Iris said, 'The world tree knows what he's on about, chuck. If he says we need Fenster... Besides, we can't just leave him...'

'It's his blood,' said the tree. 'Very precious substance, you see. His blood – like the blood of all the dragons of Hyspero – has the ability to... well, you'll understand. Don't forsake him!'

Panda sighed and started stomping off as Iris said her emotional goodbyes to the tree. How ridiculous, Panda thought. A tree commanding us not to abandon a dragon on wheels! Also, he thought – so now I know a little more about the origins of my best friend. It was all very interesting, really – but he was tired and mucky and wanted to be back aboard the bus. He'd heard quite enough revelations for a while.

Quickly the two of them left the wasteground and went back the way they had come, through the city streets, bathed in false moonlight.

No one saw them. They were glad. The really didn't want to explain where they had been... and who they had been talking to...

They hurried into the tower where the Clockworkers had housed them. They hastened up the stairs as they heard, behind them, bells ringing for the dawn. They had been out all night!

And in the room at the top of the tower – amongst all the luxurious soft furnishings – they found the remains of the golden dragon. His wheels had been sawn off and lay useless on the carpet. Someone had sheared off both vestigial wings. His stomach had been cut into and the television set and its workings had been pulled out. His head was disconnected and part of it was removed. The narrow fork of his tongue lolled pitifully at his discoverers.

His oily green blood was splashed liberally about the place.

'Someone has siphoned it off,' Panda said, in a strangulated, horrified tone. 'They've stolen his blood, Iris!'

She was rooted to the spot, unable to believe what she was seeing. 'How could they do this? He was harmless... he never meant them harm... Why have they done this?'

'Remember what the tree said... about his blood...'

'But... but *Fenster!*' she gasped. 'They've killed him for it.'

Panda didn't mention that he'd never trusted that spooky lot in the first place. It wouldn't do to bring that up now. Instead he said, 'We've got to get out of here. Right now.'

12.

'You were built? You're a robot?'

Fenster frowned. 'I'm a cyborg. Only half of me is a robot, as you so indelicately put it. The rest is lizard. And it's all good.'

'Huh,' I said.

'I was built far, far away from here. And I was sent on a very important mission, many years ago. I've been rolling around all over this land in search of something extremely important. Except that these sloths suddenly got me. And that's put the kybosh on the whole thing.' Fenster sighed and tutted with his long purple tongue flapping in irritation. 'Which means that Hyspero is completely doomed, I'm afraid. My mission was that important, you see.'

'Same here,' I said gloomily. 'We're very important to the destiny of this world, too.'

'Oh, yes?'

'Yes!' I said defiantly. 'You don't know the half of it.'

The lizard nodded. 'Then I wish you the best of luck. Believe me, I've no great hankering to see you two or your aunty sacrificed on that stone slab this evening. Nasty, messy business. I imagine that, once they've finished hacking bits off you, they'll chuck you in their fiery pit over there. Awful, aren't they? Sheer barbarians!'

'Will you help us rescue Aunty Iris?' Simon urged.

'My dear boy,' Fenster chuckled, 'I might indeed. But I'm quite useless clamped here to the floor, aren't I? And those silly sloths don't listen to a word I say.'

Both Simon and I must have been looking at him doubtfully. I know I was wondering what use he was - this great big golden creature - if he couldn't even budge from the spot. He was meant to be the object of our quest ... but so far, he didn't seem to be much use at all.

'You're suspicious of me, I know,' he said suddenly. 'But I shan't be offended. You two are right not to take things here in Hyspero at face value.'

I thought for a moment and said, 'You reckon you're on a mission to save Hyspero. You're not working for the Scarlet Empress are you?' That terrible thought had only just struck me.

Fenster laughed throatily. 'Oh, dear me, no. What a ghastly person she is. No, my masters want nothing to do with her. No, my mission concerns someone quite different.'

'Your masters? Who are they?' And I thought: perhaps this is it. Perhaps he's going to tell us what we've come here to find out...

But, of course, with Fenster - as with everyone we met in Hyspero - the answers were not straightforward in coming.

'I shall regale you with the tale of where I came from, who sent me and how I came to be incarcerated in this abominable dump.'

I tried to be patient as I started to listen to Fenster's tale, with Simon and the Uncle Bill sloth both crouching by me. We were right next to the worn metal wheels of the cyborg lizard, trying to conceal ourselves in the shadows for when the sloth priests happened by.

At first we weren't all that bothered about listening to Fenster's wittering on. As his story developed, though, we were gradually pulled in. Even the Uncle Bill sloth looked up from his abject position to earwig and soon we were all hanging on the lizard's every word.

And so the afternoon went on, with Fenster telling us about the city where he came from, which was hidden on the other side of Hyspero, far from prying eyes.

'The city, my city, from which I set off on my travels, so many years ago ... was one huge university with no students, only professors. Everyone in the university used to work at the same endless task. I dearly hope that they are still busy at that task. They tended the books that contain all the true history of the land of Hyspero.'

'All of it?' asked Simon.

'Every scrap,' Fenster nodded. 'Everything from the most exciting bit, right down to the most mundane thing that ever happened. The whole of history, past and future. All of the secrets, hidden away in books.'

'The secrets of the future?' I said, my ears pricking up and a shiver going down my spine.

'Every secret you can possibly imagine. Every secret there has ever been, and ever will be. All written down in those millions of books.'

Millions!

The books! I thought, though I stopped myself from shouting out. Fenster's city was where all the books were sent to! That's where they ended up!

This was why we'd been sent to find Fenster, then. Because he knew where the city lay, that contained all the books of Hyspero.

My pulse was starting to pound.

Fenster went on: 'Every single room in every building of the city houses these precious books. It is the only place in the land of Hyspero where, to my knowledge, books still exist at all…'

13.

Let's sidestep for a moment to the city of Hyspero. Here, the Scarlet Empress was waiting in her throne room. She crouched inside her giant jar, squelching and luxuriating in her unguents and life-sustaining jelly. As ever, she plotted and schemed and looked forward with great relish to meeting new people.

Her Vizier had sent a messenger ahead of his transporter vehicle to inform her that he had taken most of the prisoners she wanted. Of course, as far as they were concerned, they were merely honoured guests. He was a shrewd and oily rapscallion, her Vizier, and she knew she could rely on him. He would have the earth people eating out of his hands. His rubberized plastic hands…

Ah, yes.

The Vizier had two plastic arms. Kelly – the girl whom the Empress was most keen to see – had already noticed that the man in the turban had these curious appendages. On seeing them, lifeless and insensate as he poured out the wine and lifted his own goblet in their honour... she set to studying him carefully. She peered at what could be seen of his face through the thickly-curling beard and the oddly-shaped hat he wore. She listened hard to his thickly-accented voice and wondered if she had ever met him before, a long way from here. Had she once worked with him, in a shop a million light years from here? A book exhange in Darlington, from which he had abruptly disappeared?

But no... she was seeing mysteries and solutions where there were none, surely. She was staring at their host and captor and hoping that he was Terrance, nothing more. Kelly was fiercely hoping for rescue and a return to home... but that wasn't on the cards...

The Scarlet Empress had her painted lackeys wheel her jar before her magic window, through which she could see anything at all as it transpired upon the surface of her world. Simply by focusing her thoughts she could light upon any unfolding scene and observe undetected. And so she eavesdropped easily upon Kelly and the others aboard her Vizier's sand ship as it approached the city.

There was the boy, Simon, and the vending machine Barbra, the woman from MIAOW called Jenny (the Scarlet Empress knew all about MIAOW, it turned out); and there was also that seductive poet, Anthony Marvelle and his

Dogworld companion, Missy. Marvelle, of course, fancied that he was the most important member of that luckless party. He assumed, with all his scheming and temerity, that it was he who the Empress hankered for. The preening nitwit thought he could outwit them all… and yet he was just another pawn. He was as clueless as Jenny, and Barbra – as any of them.

Only two were missing from the Vizier's haul. Two very important visitors to Hyspero. The Empress was furious that they were missing. The transtemporal adventuress and her Panda friend. She had no idea where they had got to. She sensed that their bus was still standing empty and alone in the desert wastes, so she knew they had not abandoned their friends. They had seemingly removed themselves to another realm, where they might not be detected… perhaps they were underground. The very thought of that and what it might entail gave the Empress the shivers…

She bade her guards prepare for the arrival of her prisoners. She commanded them to check and double check the instruments aboard the small bathysphere in the tallest tower of the palace. Yes… yes… they assured her. All was well. All was ready for the experiment… She allowed herself a smile at the thought of what was going to happen pretty soon. And how the visitors would simply have to do her bidding…

She watched them from afar – the boy and girl who wanted to come home; the fearful machine; the poet, the leader of women, the savage hound and… and someone else... Yes, she sensed that mind again. The small party had another soul with them. Someone hidden... shielding her mind against the Empress... but who could that be?

I am all-seeing! All-knowing! cried the Scarlet Empress inside her jar. Who could be hiding their mind from me?

She would find out soon enough, as the Vizier's lumbering, massive vehicle approached the city walls...

14.

He was on the top deck, shouting his commands. There was an awning up, protecting his prisoners and himself from the noonday sun.

'Look! Look! Behold the ancient walls of Central Hyspero!' bellowed the Vizier impressively. And then he was yelling at the guards on top of the walls to winch open the gates: the Empress' favourite servant had returned!

Simon and the others huddled together, oppressed by the heat and the dust.

'Oh my,' Barbra said, 'Those walls are huge! Imagine the city within! It must be colossal... And look at the towers rising high above!'

They were like gigantic talons, clawing their way into the cerulean blue. Scarlet talons of the palace of the Empress, deep in the heart of the seething city...

'It'll be all right, Barbra,' Kelly reassured the vending machine. 'They won't harm us. If they meant us harm, they'd have done it by now…' Though, even as she said this, Kelly wasn't at all sure. She was aware that they were all caught up in something they didn't understand…

It was all the fault of Anthony Marvelle. It had been his meddling that had brought them all here.

'I've read Iris's journals about Central Hyspero,' he said. 'About her visits to the Palace and so on murmur murmur…'

'Journals that you stole!' Simon accused him.

'Can't we forget our differences murmur murmur? And pool our resources murmur?'

'You got us all into this,' Jenny told him savagely. 'It's all down to you!'

'And not your precious Iris, murmur? She abandoned you all, didn't she, murmur murmur?'

'Something must have happened to her,' Simon snapped back. 'If she could, she'd be here, helping us. Something must have prevented her coming after us… Just wait! Any minute she'll arrive with Panda, in the bus…'

The poet's snide poodle, Missy snickered at this. 'I hope she's been squashed or eaten or expired from thirst,' said the dog with hands.

There was no time to carry on the argument as, just then, the vast doors of the city started to open with a deafening screech. A gap opened up and there came even more noise: the raucous, joyous hullaballoo of the largest, most densely populated city on the face of the planet. A city dedicated to pleasure, as Iris's journals had put it. A hectic and hedonistic place that had drawn her as surely as a lit flame will tantalize a moth and send it crazy with desire.

Music spilled out of the city; and chatter and screams. There were a thousand exotic scents, too – not all of them appetizing or pleasant.

The small party huddled together – even Marvelle and his dog – as the Vizier turned to them and waved his plastic arms in triumph. 'You are so very fortunate! To be conveyed into the city aboard my vehicle! To have the honour of being brought before the Empress herself! Why, the denizens of this city enter a lottery each weekend in the hope of being brought to a meeting with the Scarlet Empress! She brings them their heart's desire – as she pledged to do, so many years ago. This week, it is your turn, my friends. This week, it is you who have won our lottery!'

15.

Fenster continued with his tale. His golden face was gleaming with pride. 'The greatest intellects amongst the keepers of the books decided to work together in order to build a servant. One who would be able to live for a very long time, quite safely in the sometimes perilously chaotic land of Hyspero. To this end they took all the metal they could find in their city - even melting down all their valuables - rings and necklaces, goblets and clocks - and this boiling liquid was poured into a gigantic lead mould.

Even though they could neither read nor write, they were very skilled in the ancient arts of alchemy, bionics, micro-surgery and cybernetics. These precious techniques had been passed down by word of mouth like magic spells and so, working in secret, the leopard professors were able to put together a huge lizard who ran on indestructible brass wheels. He was an emissary who would never tire as he rolled around the world, seeking out his target. They equipped him with a TV set so he could communicate with his feline masters and they gave him a hide of glittering scales so that he would be impervious to ice or fire or any of the more inhospitable elements in the land.

'And so ... many, many years ago I was despatched to search for the one that their legends had spoken of. It was my job to eventually locate her and return with her to the university of leopards. There, in the many hundreds of corridors crammed with dustless books, she had a lot of reading waiting for her. The whole future history of Hyspero to read...'

Fenster shook himself out of his storytelling reverie then, and blinked at us, remembering where he was.

'So you see, my dears, to be locked up here, superintending the barbaric rites of these sloths, has been something of a bind.'

Fenster looked down at us sadly. His tale had taken a while to unfold and the light through the temple windows had grown murkier.

IT WAS ME!

This was MY destiny he was talking about. I just knew it.

I was the only person in Hyspero who could read and write. And I would have to go with him to this city of leopards where all the books in this world were kept...

I was the Reader!

It was just like Aunty Iris had said. The Golden God in the temple would take us to find out how to save the world.

The answer must be in one of those books. Somewhere in the city of books was the secret we needed to know - about why Hyspero was corroding and falling apart. And we'd be able to save it. It was all down to me!

I looked at Fenster, now he was finished his tale. Simon was looking at me with his eyes all wide. He looked as if he was about to burst out with: 'Tell him! Tell him you can read and write! Tell him it's you he's looking for, Kelly!'

But I gave Simon a funny look. He seemed confused by my reaction. But I wasn't telling anyone anything yet.

We'd play it more carefully than that.

I said to Fenster. 'I think we should join forces. We can free you from your clamps and get you out of here.'

He licked his golden lips thoughtfully. 'Indeed?'

'My Aunty Iris will be able to free you. She has a laserized hat-pin that can cut through any lock or bolt.' Actually, I didn't know if that was true or not, but Fenster was nodding appreciatively. 'So...' I said, 'If we can find her and free her, she can set you free in turn...'

Fenster seized upon the hole in the plan. 'If she's so good with locks and bolts, why doesn't she free herself?'

I frowned. 'Because she isn't well. I'm afraid for her. Something weird is happening to her... we were in the jungle and she would fade away every now and then ... as if the life was being drained out of her. But I'm sure that she can help you. Do *you know where they are holding her? Where would the sloths have put her?'*

Fenster nodded quickly. 'I believe that they dragged her past me earlier on. This morning, in fact. I was meditating under my covers and suddenly there was all this yelling. I had a peep out and there was this terrible old woman clapped in irons, bawling at the top of her voice.'

'That'll be her,' Simon nodded.

'Was she wearing a lumpy old cardy and a dirty-looking sun hat?'

'Yes,' I nodded. 'Where did they take her?'

Fenster raised one pointed claw into the air. 'Up there...' he said dolefully.

At first we didn't know what he was on about.

Then we looked up into the hugely tall, arching ceiling of the temple of the sloths.

If you craned your neck and stared really hard, you could see that right up there, at the very highest point of the ceiling, suspended in murky mid-air... there was a metal cage ...

16.

Iris decided that they couldn't hang around much longer. Gingerly she picked up what remained of Fenster's golden skull and placed it inside her carpet bag for safe-keeping. Then she drew off some of the green ichor of his

327

blood, still dripping from his dismembered body, and stoppered it up inside a glass vial. 'Poor Fenster,' she murmured, absently.

'It's too late to worry about him now,' said Panda worriedly. 'Surely this proves to you that your alien friends are a whole lot nastier than they seem? Hmm?'

'Yes, yes,' she nodded sadly. 'You were right not to be swayed by them, Panda. I should trust you more: your instincts are always right.'

'Indeed!' he beamed.

'It's just that... for once... I wanted to belong to the beautiful people! Look at them, they were so composed and pretty and... and *thin!*' Now Iris was crashing around the room, fetching the gorgeous outfits and fabrics and bottles of scent she had been given. She threw everything into her capacious bag, hunting around for everything not nailed down... her eyes alighting on the weird, alien mini-bar beside the bed.

'We haven't time for this!' Panda cried. 'They'll be after us!'

Soon the two travellers were tottering and stumbling down the polished steps of the tower, back into the quiet street. As they hastened away they noticed that the city was coming to life, with several of the lissom inhabitants moving about... fixing their calm golden eyes on the escapees and frowning puzzledly. Who would want to leave their peaceful city? Who would want to rush about like that?

Panda wondered if these Clockworks folk were perhaps telepathic, and already news of their running away from the tower was being reported back to head office...

And then... when they were caught... what had happened to Fenster would happen to them, wouldn't it? Perhaps not to Iris, whom they clearly revered. But it would happen to me, Panda thought. They would chop me up gladly, I suppose, in order to see how I tick. Off would come my woolly head! They'd snip off my fluffy ears. They'd peer inside to see if I had little organs and a brain. And I wonder how disappointed they will be if they find only stuffing inside me. He shuddered with a superstitious dread at the very thought of anyone probing inside him, trying to understand the secrets that gave him life...

But in the meantime he pelted after Iris, as fast as his short legs could carry him. He really didn't want to ask to be placed inside her carpet bag, as he usually would. He didn't want to be pressed and jostled against Fenster's brain and those miniature bottles of booze and scent...

They ran for the outskirts of town and the weird, gelatinous skin that formed a greenish barrier over the city. Iris shouted something about getting through that barrier, about piercing that skin... but her words were drowned by the cries of the locals, who had just realized what was going on. Their raised voices were more frightening for being so calm and unperturbed, Panda thought. All in all he found the underground Clockworks people very disturbing and unnatural.

Iris paused, heaving in great lungfuls of air. 'They're after us now,' she said. 'We'll never outrun them, will we?' She fumbled in her pockets, produced her golden box of cocktail cigarettes, and swiftly lit one.

'Come on!' Panda yelled. 'Let's make for the river! Look, I can see it, between those tall buildings. Remember dear, just like they said? The rivers flow upwards, to the surface…'

She snapped her fingers. 'You're right! Of course!'

Now there were louder shouts from the skinny pursuers.

'Do you think they'll harm us if they catch us?' said Iris.

But Panda was already leading the way down a narrow alleyway. It was rather damp and slippery here as the walls grew closer and the alleyway more cramped. There was a dinginess and a brackish smell of dark waters moving sluggishly.

'Oh, cripes! Oh bloody hell!' screeched Iris. She hoiked her pink pistol out of her cardigan pocket and started firing with more enthusiasm than skill at their assailants. She hit one and he toppled sideways, collapsing onto the pathway. His fellows took no heed of him as they marched remorselessly onwards.

'How could I ever think I was related to this lot?' Iris shouted wildly, still taking potshots and sending pink laser beams richocheting down the alley. 'Why would I ever want anything to do with them? They're a rotten lot!'

'We're almost at the river!' Panda panted, chucking aside boxes and discarded items of rubbish which were clogging the way ahead. Through the narrow gap between the ramshackle buildings he could see the enticing silver ribbon of water... and there were boats there, some moving with great forcefulness and speed uphill and others were tethered at the riverside... Surely we could steal one, he thought...

But Iris was still looking backwards. She picked off another of their enemies, and another, but it seemed that there was an endless supply, and they were catching up...

'What we need now,' she thought grimly. 'More than ever before... is a rescuer.'

Iris hated to admit this kind of thing.

And suddenly, here he was. In a whirl of activity and a swirl of black cape... A broad and muscular figure interposed himself between quarry and prey. Iris cried out at the sight of him, and her pursuers fell back at once.

He wore a mask that covered half his face, and his hat was clamped down over his tangled, silky dark hair. Even as he raised his flintlock pistols and jeered at the Clockworkers, Iris knew at once who he was. Someone she had never expected to see again. Not in this life. Not in any life.

He chuckled to see the Clockworkers flee, and turned back to Iris and the astonished Panda with a handsome grin.

'I don't know why they're so terrified of me,' he laughed. 'But I'm glad. Now, say thank you.'

'T-thank you!' Iris gasped, gazing up at him.

'Iris, who is this?' Panda asked, tugging at her coattails.

'I'm not sure, lovey…' she said. 'But I think… that I've met him before…'

'Come inside,' the highwayman told them. 'Come indoors. They can't come after you there. Not inside the house. They won't go anywhere near Wherewithal House…'

Their handsome rescuer swirled round to lead them to a portico'd entrance and a relieved Panda trotted after him. Iris, meanwhile, gave a horrified gasp. She looked up at the back of the building, and recognized at once the pale, butter-coloured walls and green tiles. She knew at once its narrow, mean little windows and swags of sickly ivy. 'This… is Wherewithal House?' she whispered.

'Yes,' said the highwayman as he pushed open the heavy door.

'But it used to be in the middle of nowhere,' Iris said. 'It was once in the middle of a radioactive desert…'

The man took off his hat and mask and laughed bitterly at her words. 'But isn't that the truth of everything? Isn't that the secret that we all learn as life goes on, Lilith? That nothing ever stays in one place? Nothing at all? Wherever you think a person or a thing belongs… it's never where they started out, is it?'

'Hmm…' She followed him and Panda into the cool chamber within. 'Perhaps you're right. But… I'm not Lilith any more, you know. I haven't been Lilith for a long time, Dick.'

He patted her shoulder. 'I know. I know more about it all than you can imagine. We've been keeping up with your exploits for quite some time, you know.'

She stared at him. She stared into those bright grey eyes of his with awe, just as she had once done as a little girl. 'You've been... keeping up..?'

'Oh yes,' said the Highwayman – or Dick, as she had once known him. 'Come and see. Come and meet the Aunties.'

17.

Once the music started up it didn't take long for the sloths to swing into action.

They flailed around their extra long arms and legs and soon they were filling up the central circular space of the temple. Even the shyer ones had started to contort and gyrate their slender, furry bodies. The disco music was quite deafening. It was even louder than me and Simon had expected. It almost made our ears bleed. The bass was thudding so much it set the dangling vines and festoons of golden hair trembling on the walls, and it sifted down mortar and dust from the ancient ceiling.

Our attention, though, was fixed on the spectre of Aunty Iris in her cage, high above the barbaric proceedings.

She looked terrified. Her clothes were ripped and her face was dirty and bloody. The way she looked at us at first, it was as if she hardly recognised us.

There was a seemingly endless space of empty air between the banister where we stood and the cage in which she was trapped.

I fought hard to keep my voice steady.

'Aunty Iris,' I called out. 'It's us! Kelly and Simon! We're here to rescue you!'

She blinked and wiped her eyes with both hands, as if unable to believe what she saw.

'Um, Kelly...' Simon murmured, nudging me in the side. 'Have you thought about how we're going to get across to her? It's quite a drop, you know...'

And as Aunty Iris moved about in her suspended cell, it was swaying sickeningly in mid-air.

'Kelly, love?' came Aunty Iris's cracked, dry and terrified voice. 'Is it r-really you?'

'Yes! Now, just you hold on, Aunty Iris. We're going to find a way out of there for you...'

'I don't think I'm going to make it, Kelly,' Aunty Iris was saying. 'I think my number's come up at last!'

'Rubbish,' I said, thinking furiously. How on earth were we going to get her safely down?

It was the Uncle Bill sloth who had the brain wave. He came up with a solution that only a sloth could. He started jumping up and down eagerly, and then grunting and pointing at the festoons of golden hair hanging down off the stonework.

'What's he saying?' asked Simon. 'He's gone a bit funny.'

'What is it, Uncle Bill?' I asked. Then I realised he was miming something.

Grabbing hold of some of that golden hair and twining it into a thick rope. He was miming swinging on it ... across the gap to the suspended cage.

I gulped.

'What's he doing?' Simon frowned.

Our sloth friend was working busily at making his rope and testing its strength. All of a sudden it became very clear to both Simon and I that we were about to take our lives into our own hands.

We were going to have to TRAPEZE ourselves across to Aunty Iris!

18.

Barbra had a fit of nerves about carrying the jar that contained Euphemia – the earliest of the Scarlet Empresses. As they entered the city of Central Hyspero she begged Kelly to look after the precious cargo instead. 'All my insides are jumbling up together,' Barbra moaned. 'I'm scared of smashing the old dear to bits.'

Kelly hugged the jar protectively under her jacket, glad of something to look after, in the midst of a situation where she felt so out of her depth.

Kelly was the reluctant space and time traveler. When Iris had been offering passenger seats aboard her crazy bus, Kelly had felt herself backing out instinctively. A single trip to 1890s Montmartre had been quite enough for her. She had been appalled to observe Simon's excitement at the whole thing.

The jar of the Empress was burning hot now against her side, as if Euphemia within could sense that they were inside her native city. Her magical senses were bristling and burning with the feeling of being on home ground...

But here Kelly was – in the thick of it – surrounded by strange companions. She could hardly conceive of ever seeing home again. It seemed impossibly far away. Home seemed more like somewhere made up than even here did...

The Vizier's ship of the desert groaned a halt in a dusty dry dock. Immediately it was set upon by scores of alien mechanics, and its crew and passengers were led out into the burning heat of the city. They all gathered together with robes pulled about them and hoods over their heads. 'It's best if we don't advertise our presence,' the oily wizard advised. 'If the denizens of the city know that we are about the Empress's business then we will be vulnerable to attack. The Empress isn't popular with the hoi-polloi these days...'

Even with the tattooed guards to protect them, Kelly wondered. But the guards were marching off elsewhere, and would provide no protection for the Vizier's guests.

The small party set off into the seething streets of the city, held back by the surging crowds and also by the slowness of Barbra. The vending machine brought up the rear, embarrassed under her dark blue cloak. Simon and

Kelly walked with her, matching her pace and whispering amongst themselves.

'Can't we break away and escape?' Barbra asked.

'I'm not sure what's for the best,' Robert said. 'Remember, the whole point was to bring the jar and Euphemia back to the Scarlet Empress, to stop Marvelle opening the Ringpull into the Obverse...'

'You're right,' Kelly nodded. 'We've come this far.'

'Iris knew more about it than we do,' Barbra sighed. 'I wish she was here.'

'That goes without saying,' Simon snapped. 'But she isn't, is she?' Actually – though he would never voice this – he felt annoyed at Iris and Panda this time. Surely they could have found their way back to their friends by now? But, since they hadn't, he guessed something truly horrible must have happened to them... and this was a thought he didn't dare entertain.

'Kelly...' came the winsome, silvery voice of the first Empress.

'Can you hear that?' Kelly asked the others. 'That's Euphemia... is it just inside my head, though? Can you all hear her?'

Simon frowned. The noise from the markets and little shops and cafes they were passing was very intense. The streets of Central Hyspero were bustling and seething with life and chatter in languages of all kinds. Off-worlders and every kind of native Hysperon species were in evidence here in the sandy, shady souks and backstreets. They were haggling after bargains, striking deals, sightseeing, arguing and laughing. He certainly couldn't hear the quavering, glassy warble of the Empress in the jar. 'What is she saying to you?' he asked Kelly.

But Kelly was quiet. She carried on walking as the voice spoke to her, trying to take in what it was telling her...

'You mustn't let anyone know I am with you,' Euphemia warned. 'Smuggle me into the throne room, my dear. Only then can I help you. You see, you are the one whose life is at stake, dear Kelly. They are going to try to make use of you. The poet Marvelle and the current Empress. Because, in your bookshop, you absorbed the energies and the life force of the Aja'ib – the sacred book of Hyspero – only you have the power to unlock the Ringpull and open up the various universes...'

'Yes...' Kelly replied calmly inside her mind. 'I do know that... deep down... though no one has ever told me until now. Thank you, Euphemia. I knew I had a bad destiny all wrapped up in this. I felt sure that I should keep away from the adventure. This is why I backed off from the bus... I wasn't just scared... I also felt the sting of... well, it sounds silly, but... *foreboding*. Destiny. Fate.'

'Your instincts were correct, my dear...'

'Bugger and fuck,' Kelly thought. 'Here I am on this ancient planet, calmly walking to my terrible fate...'

'But I can help, my dear,' said Euphemia. 'And I will. You'll see. Just be brave. And have faith in your friends.'

'Anthony was... he was... my *lover*,' Kelly said. 'I let him seduce me... I did! I'm such an idiot! I thought I was falling for that bastard... and all the while he was after

338

me simply because he needed me… to take part in some weird kind of ritual thing…'

'Yes…' said the first Empress. 'A very old ritual. Very dangerous. One that hasn't happened since… ooh, since my time as the ruler of this world. The opening of the Ringpull into the next universe. It was something that should never have happened in the first place. And it's something I simply won't allow to happen again…'

At this point the tiny voice of Euphemia faded away inside Kelly's head, and the jar inside the folds of her coat started to cool. She gained the impression that the tiny remnant of a woman had exhausted herself in giving this warning.

Kelly shook her mind clear, trying to absorb the lessons she had learned. Okay, I'm doomed and caught up in this inextricably… and everyone wants their piece of me… but Euphemia is with me and says she can help… She's like Glinda the Good Witch… and suddenly this made Kelly felt a whole lot better.

She remembered watching *The Wizard of Oz* on telly, Christmas Day, when she was seven. In the flat. Her dad was asleep on the settee, his boots on the cushions, he was stinking of lager. He snored all the way through it – though he'd meant to watch it with her. He knew she would love it. And Kelly *had* loved it – and every Christmas since. She had to feel brave like Dorothy. She had to believe in her friends…

They were emerging from the coolness of the markets now, and walking into a sun-baked square. Here there were small encampments of beggars and those who sought an audience with the Empress. There were also gaggles of people seated around the proud figures of story-tellers, who chuntered on, all day and night by smouldering fires… telling tale after tale after tale…

'The Endless Tale Spinners of Hyspero,' said the Vizier disdainfully. 'That's what's wrong with our culture. Too much talking and imagining. Not enough of the real.'

'Ahh,' said Anthony Marvelle. 'But only our imaginations can set us free murmur murmur. How else would we dream up marvelous schemes murmur? How else would we decide on our fabulous plans murmur murmur? These unfolding events are – I must point out – all down to the brilliance of my own imagination murmur. Where would we all be without my amazing capacity to dream murmur murmur?'

'Darlington!' shouted Barbra, in a harsh, mechanical voice. 'That's where we'd be! Safely at home in Darlington!'

Simon had never heard the vending machine sounding quite so pissed off. He gently asked her for a can of pop, hoping that would cheer her up.

'We are here!' cried the Vizier grandly. He swept up his arms to encompass the massive edifice before them.

And it was true: the palace with its soaring towers was truly incredible. It seemed to be composed out of bright red ice that shone in the noonday Hysperon sun.

'And now,' said the Vizier, 'We have an audience with the Scarlet Empress herself!'

19.

CLLAAANNGGG!

As the three of us smashed into the side of the suspended cage.

We scrabbled and grabbed hold of the bars. And held. We were safe. Panting and delirious with fright and excitement ... but we were alive!

'Kelly! KELLY!' Aunty Iris squawked. 'Are you all right? Are you okay?'

She was on her feet inside the cage, peering up at the three of us.

'Yes!' *I gasped, feeling a bit winded.* 'We swung ourselves over, Aunty Iris!'

'I feel sick,' *Simon moaned.*

'We made it, Simon!' *I was shouting out jubilantly.* 'We made it across!' *I pounded the Uncle Bill sloth on his back and he grinned at me.*

'Aunty Iris,' *I said.* 'Have you got something that will unpick locks?'

She fiddled about with her hair, which had gone a bit wild and unkempt by now. 'I've got a hairpin here somewhere,' *she said.* 'It's my special one. It's got me in and out of a few places I shouldn't have been in...'

'Good,' *I said.* 'We—'

Then I blinked, peering through the cage bars, because Aunty Iris was doing that awful thing again, when she faded away and came back again.

'Oooooh,' she said. 'I don't feel very well at all, Kelly chuck. In fact, I feel decidedly dicky.'

'Just hold it together, Aunty Iris. We'll get you down from here and then we can go and get Fenster and all of us escape together...'

'Who's Fenster?' she frowned, producing her lockpick from her tangled hair with a shout of triumph.

I explained very quickly who Fenster was, and how he was the Golden God of the sloths. He was the one person who could help us find out what was causing all of the deadly Corrosion and the gaps and fissures in Hyspero!

Fired with a new determination, Aunty Iris was working busily at the lock of her cage. 'But can we trust this lizard? I was going to be sacrificed to him! I still might be, if I can't get out of here!'

'He reckons he's looking for me, Aunty Iris,' I hissed through the slick golden bars. 'He says he's been searching for many years, for the girl who can read! Well, that's me, isn't it?'

Our cage lurched then, and we had to cling on tighter. Simon cried out in surprise.

'We're moving!' he yelled, right in my ear. 'I think they've noticed us! And they've started to winch us down!'

We all looked down, to where the flames were licking in the pit and the sloths were still dancing and flailing around. I could also see that, trapped in his holy spot behind the altar, Fenster was rolling his brass eyes and they were blazing with frustration and pent up fury. His beaten gold wings were flapping and his wheels must have been itching to roll...

The cage lurched again and the chains that supported it clanked and slithered. We were definitely going down.

The Uncle Bill sloth grunted in fear. I knew why. He had been helping us to escape. They wouldn't show him much mercy.

Clank! Clank! Clangclangclang!

We were going down... back into the temple...

Then Aunty Iris was saying: 'My time is up, Kelly. I knew, when I came back to Hyspero, that I was too old, really, to have adventures like this. I knew that I couldn't survive here long, really. But the important thing was to get you here, Kelly, love. To make sure that you could fulfil your destiny!'

'She's fading away again...' Simon said, and it was true. My Aunty was turning ghostly and faint and pale. Her beseeching expression vanished completely and returned, looking wilder and even more frightened.

'You shouldn't have bothered trying to rescue me, Kelly chuck,' she hissed. 'You should have freed Fenster and ran off with him. To this University of Leopards. That's where your journey will take you next! You should never have bothered trying to take care of me! You should just have left me here...' She handed me the hairpin through the bars. 'Set your golden lizard free. Run away with him! Find the books that will save all of Hyspero!'

20.

The Aunties? Iris pondered. Surely Highwayman Dick couldn't really mean those three sisters who had owned Wherewithal House in the old, old days... ?

But here was Dick himself, full-grown and still alive. Even here, in another universe and another time. He was still himself. Couldn't the three sisters in the upper tower be alive still?

'You've gone very quiet, Iris,' said Panda worriedly, as they scaled the wooden staircases of the ancient house.

'I've been knocked a bit bandy, Panda, love,' she said. 'This is the house where I was a prisoner... when I was just a kid. This is where they kept me...'

The place still smelled the same. A dampness, a rottenness that invaded her senses and made her feel sick. The old wood was familiar, too: banisters sticky and too slick with honey-scented polish. The windows were multi-coloured glass, depicting scenes from legendary Obverse tales.

'But you were here, too, Panda,' she said. 'You were the one who rescued me from all of this!'

He shook his woolly head, looking confused. 'If I did, dear, then I've forgotten. I don't remember what you're talking about...'

They climbed and climbed, with Dick leading the way. It grew darker as they went higher, and suddenly the brawny highwayman was holding aloft a candelabrum blazing with light.

'But, Panda,' Iris said. 'Don't you recall it? How we found the bus in the desert... it was the first time I ever saw my bus... and then you followed us home to here, to Wherewithal House...'

'Wasn't me,' Panda frowned. 'Or if it was, it isn't me *yet*...'

'Oh dear,' sighed Iris. 'I think the continuity of my life is more buggered up than I ever thought...'

Soon they were at the highest point of the tower, and Iris remembered the carved, jet black door well enough. It looked rather like it should be the doorway into hell: with those carvings depicting twisted limbs and agonized faces... She took a deep breath as Dick pushed it open...

And within were the three Aunties. Conjoined, as ever, of course, and sharing a single chair. Their skinny, wasted bodies were clothed in some kind of purple, velvety drapes and their faces were just as keenly alert and simian as she remembered them from her far distant youth.

Panda exclaimed at the sight of them.

'Be polite, Panda,' Dick warned him. 'These are the three sisters who were responsible for Iris' well-being as a child. If they hadn't taken her in, she would never have survived out in the wasteland beyond the Clockworks...'

'Well, then, I'm grateful to them,' said Panda gruffly.

'These are my aunts,' Iris said, her voice quavering. 'Faith, Hope and Susan.'

The withered, almost bald heads of the three sisters nodded all together at her words. One of them was humming tunelessly, and all were trying to focus on the shabby figures before them.

'The girl has come back to us, at last,' said the middle one, whom Panda assumed was called Hope.

'H-how did you get here?' Iris said. 'You came through the Ringpull into this universe… How did you..? I mean, *why* did you?'

'They knew you had come this way, Iris,' said Dick. 'We knew you had led the way, in that bus of yours. When it came to the mass exodus from the Obverse, your aunts decided they would come after you. They feared for you. They wanted to see you again…'

'Millenia have passed,' said Faith. 'And we've been waiting.'

'But I've been here before,' said Iris. 'I've visited Hyspero numerous times over the years, and I never knew… I had no idea you were here…'

Dick was moving over to a tall wooden cabinet under the attic eaves. 'Yes, we know! Didn't I say that we had been keeping a watch over you? We've been monitoring all of your activities, you see. For such a long time.'

Iris watched as he opened up the cabinet door. Actually, it looked more like a wardrobe to her. Perhaps even a Valcean wardrobe, as she had encountered in her previous set of adventures.

Within the wardrobe there lay shelves and shelves of old-fashioned video tapes, cd's and paperback books, all of them gathering dust.

'What are these?' Panda frowned.

'This is your life,' Dick told them both. 'Not quite everything – but then, I suppose you never know the full story, do you? But everything we could get our hands on is here... and everything in strict chronological order, as best we could figure it out.'

'You've got books about my travels?' Iris demanded. 'My diaries..?'

'Better than that!' cried the smallest and youngest of the sisters. 'Novelisations! Written by the finest scribes of an alternative earth! You've got your own novel range in that universe, Lilith! And you once had a TV show, but it wasn't very good and got cancelled. Though it does have its fans.'

Iris found that she was standing with her mouth open, looking rather shocked. 'You've been keeping tabs on me by collecting cultural tat about me from an alternate dimension?'

'Oh yes,' enthused Hope. 'We've become rather good fans of yours, you know. And Panda. Haven't we, ladies?'

'Oh yes!' grinned Faith. ''Have a little splishy-splashy, Panda!' and 'I'll punch you right up the hooter!''

Now the three sisters gave in to gales of laughter as they all started to impersonate Panda. Panda himself was feeling rather put out about this.

'They're completely mad!' he told Iris. 'Plus, they're disturbing me!'

'Me too,' said Iris.

'It's simply because they have missed you,' Dick told them. 'You've been away from home for such a long time. Can you blame them for keeping faith, and trying to keep up with your movements and your exploits? This was the only way they could do it, you see. By using their arcane magical powers to poke a little hole through the dimensions... and keeping an eye on your fictive self.'

'My fictive self?' she blinked.

'You're famous in several dimensions,' Dick told her.

Panda laughed. 'And rich and famous too, eh?'

'I'm not sure about that,' Dick frowned at him. He didn't seem to be that fond of Panda. Iris had noticed that already. Perhaps it had something to do with how Iris and Panda had run away from him in the first place. They had left him back in the Obverse, in the wastelands beyond Wherewithal House...

'Is Mary still alive?' Iris asked. 'Your sister?'

Dick shook his head quickly. 'She wouldn't come through with us. When everyone was fleeing the Obverse and getting aboard whatever transport they could... she refused at the last moment to come along with us. Even though the House and the sisters and everyone was coming along... She wanted to stay where she was... she was convinced that you would return one day... to see how we all were... and she wanted to make sure that someone was there waiting for you.'

Iris felt ashamed at this. Back when she was a kid, Mary had been one of the few to care anything about her. The Aunties certainly hadn't. All they'd been bothered about was collecting a possible reward from the Clockworkers. But Mary had been loyal to Iris, and Iris had let her down. As the world emptied around her – and even the towers of Wherewithal had removed themselves... Mary had stayed alone...

'Mary was good to me,' she said.

'This is all very fascinating,' Panda said (the gloomy mood in this attic was getting on his nerves). 'But are we finished yet? I thought we were in the process of getting away from this subterranean dump. We need to return to the surface and to find the bus...'

Iris nodded briskly, agreeing with him. 'Yes, of course. The others will be needing our help. I do hope they haven't wandered away from the bus... or tried to move it...!'

'They're bound to have done just that,' Panda sighed. 'We've been away for days, haven't we?'

'Look,' Iris began cajoling her old guardians. 'It's been smashing to see you all again, but, as you know, my life rarely slows down for a moment and, well, it's time for my small furry chum and myself to be moving along. All right? Dick, would you show us back out again?'

The three Aunties looked alarmed at her peremptory manner. 'But... won't you stay...?' gasped Susan. 'We've learned so much about you... we've pieced it all together so carefully... please... let us see you for a while longer...

tell us… explain to us… what it's like to be *you*… to be as free in the world as you are…'

Panda was tugging at Iris's coat tails once more. 'Don't listen to them! It's a trap to make you stay here forever! We have to keep moving, Iris! We have to move on!'

'Wait,' Dick said, moving towards her. 'The Aunties deserve more respect, surely? We all want to hear about your life. You left us all that time ago. You left without a backward glance… Can't you find it in your heart to stay a bit longer with us…?'

Iris dithered for a moment. Their voices were so plaintive. She felt guilty. All these years of freedom since her escape from this house. All the fun and adventures she'd had. And what did they have? Nothing! They had sat here in an attic… wondering how she was getting on. Learning everything second hand… And she herself had given them hardly a moment's thought.

'I should stay,' she told Panda. 'Just for a while.'

'No!' Panda growled. 'It's a trap, Iris! They are messing with your mind…! They'll keep you here forever in this nasty, dusty space! Don't look at them! Avert your eyes…! Take hold of my paw, Iris, and let's get out of this bloody dump…!'

21.

The fierce noise from below was increasing in hellish volume and pitch. Disco music and the unholy gibbering of sloths.

Aunty Iris was flickering and fading ... and I thought: but what if she turns completely intangible, and slips right through the bars ...? What if she slips through and into the blue furnace below? And what if she keeps on falling and falling into the centre of the world?

The dancing sloths were jeering at us as we came down low enough for them to get a good look at us.

Aunty Iris seemed to recover some of her former spirit then. She started ranting back at them, and shaking her fists: 'You wouldn't dare touch me! You horrible, mucky lot! Don't you realise who I am...! Don't you realise who we are..?'

There was only one word that we could make out in all their noise. They chanted it gleefully and mockingly:

'Sacrifice! Sacrifice! Sacrifice!'

The dancing mass of sloths were demanding their traditional entertainments.

And as we were dangling and holding on for dear life ... I couldn't see any way that we could deprive them of their show.

22.

On their way into the Scarlet Palace, Jenny the ex-traffic warden tried to take charge of their small party. She started issuing instructions to the others about not being scared or speaking out of turn when they were in the presence of the monarch.

Kelly snapped at her, 'You're not in charge of us, Jenny. You might have been the head of MIAOW in Darlington, but that doesn't give you the right to tell us all what to do now.'

Simon took hold of Kelly's hand, trying to calm her down. He knew that Jenny's bossiness was just her way of controlling her own nerves. As they were led by tattooed guards through the blood-red corridors he was feeling pretty worried, too. But at the same time he was excited. This place was everything he had expected it too be. Grand, superb, drafty, alien, ominous… and echoing with the noise of their footsteps and the whirring and shunting of Barbra's hydraulics. They were dwarfed by the magnificence of the place… and this only made Simon feel even more excited… by the very idea of entering a royal palace on a distant, alien world…

Anthony Marvelle and his obnoxious talking poodle trotted ahead, as if they did this sort of thing every day. The poet kept pace with the Vizier, as if they were already in league together. Simon could hear the ingratiating murmurs of Marvelle as they insinuated themselves in the dumpy wizard's ear.

'I do wish Iris was here,' Barbra sighed, not for the first time. 'Somehow I always feel braver when she's with us.'

Then they were before the tall doors that led into the palace throne room: the very heart of this whole complex. It was a room some fifty feet in length and breadth and height. Its crimson walls were unadorned and lit by icy chandeliers. The guards drew open the doors and the party of Earthlings and others shuffled across the sheeny floor.

'At last! At last! Murmur! Murmur!' cried Anthony Marvelle, scooting ahead in his Hush Puppies. 'Empress! Empress! Here I am! I have come to you across the immensity of the Multiverse…! I have succeeded in my task! I have brought them all to you!'

The others stopped short of the gigantic jar.

Kelly and Simon exchanged a look. The jar was exactly like a giant-sized version of the one Kelly concealed within her jacket. It was a thick-walled glass some twenty feet high and wider than any of them could stretch their arms (except, perhaps, for Barbra – whose arms were telescopic.) The jar was filled to the brim with a thick, gelatinous substance – purplish-red. And, squatting within that jelly – indistinct at the moment, but clearly alive and moving its limbs… was a woman.

'It's hideous…' Simon heard Jenny mutter. He remembered Iris once saying that Jenny never coped well with the sight of anything too alien. Which wasn't a helpful trait in a space-time traveller…

'Empress, Empress, murmur murmur…' said Marvelle, prostrating himself.

Something stirred violently within the jar. There was a convulsion in the sloppy jelloid substance and, all of a sudden, a hideous face was peering out at them. It had thin, pointed, witchlike features and its eyes were burning with fury.

'She's awake! Murmur murmur!'

'I should think so,' said Missy. 'We've come all the way across the Multiverse to see her…'

'Get him away from me,' sighed the Empress. 'He gets on my nerves, the way he goes on.'

Her voice came from speakers placed all around the chamber. This had the disconcerting effect of making her seem omnipotent, which was probably fair enough, Simon thought.

Two tattooed guards moved forward, picking up the prone poet and transporting him further down the room.

'Phew, thank goodness for that,' the Scarlet Empress said, shuddering in her aspic. 'I can't abide crawlers. The rest of you aren't like that, are you?'

They all shook their heads hurriedly. The Empress came closer to the curved wall of glass and peered at them intently. Her eyes were bright green, it seemed and they shone with intelligence and amusement.

'Ah, I know you lot. I've been monitoring your progress ever since you arrived on my world. I can do that, you know. I see all! I control all! I am the supreme being on the whole of Hyspero!' She laughed maniacally at this, and Simon thought that she was probably putting on a big act just to impress them all. 'Actually, it's true,' she added. 'Being the Empress and sitting in this jar at the centre of the world… it means that my will is magnified magically and impossibly… and everything has to dance to my tune! And I'm aware of every single thing that transpires everywhere on the planet. Which can actually be rather wearing, you know. Anyhow, I'm rather enjoying this conversation of ours. It's nice to have new folk visiting, so thank you for that.'

There was a lull just then as the Empress gave them a ghastly grin, displaying stumps of sugar-rotted teeth. Simon jumped in with a wobbly voice and asked, 'W-well, if you can see and hear everything that happens on Hyspero… can you tell us where Iris and Panda have got to? They've been missing for ages and we'd like to find them, if at all possible.' He was rather pleased at himself, for speaking up so bravely before such a terrifying being.

The Scarlet Empress's mien darkened at once. Her face became a rigid mask of horror. Even the lights in the throne room dimmed and flickered as she vented her sudden fury, thrashing about in her life-supporting unguents. 'Iris Wildthyme! You're asking me for help in finding that terrible floozy! That reckless harridan! That monstrous old whore from space and time…?!'

'Er, yes,' said Kelly, stepping bravely to stand next to Simon. 'She can get us home. She's our friend. And we want to get her back.'

Simon was surprised to hear Kelly talk like this. He felt proud of her. 'That's right, your Scarlet Majesty!'

'Hmmm…' rumbled the Empress. A flood of poisonous-looking bubbles filled her jar as she ruminated. 'And if I agree to help you locate the Wildthyme woman – who, remember, has already caused her fair share of trouble here on my world – what will you give me in return?'

The visitors all turned to look at each other. What could they possibly offer the Empress of all Hyspero?

Missy and Anthony turned their backs brusquely. 'I won't give anything,' said Marvelle. 'I don't want the nasty woman back. Why would I?'

Jenny implored the Empress, 'We could persuade Iris to leave your world at once, and never come back! Would that do?'

Barbra shuffled forward, 'I have so little to offer, Majesty. But you could take all of my comestibles. My pop and my crisps…'

The Empress sneered at all of these suggestions.

'Anthony Marvelle has the Aja'ib!' Kelly cried, accusingly. 'He has the book containing all the secrets of this world! He stole it from the Great Big Book Exchange in Darlington!'

Everyone looked at Anthony, who acted shocked. 'I have no such thing!'

'He does!' Simon shouted. 'He's stolen all sorts of valuable stuff – even Iris's diaries!'

The Empress shook her head. 'I've got at least thirty copies of the Aja'ib hidden away in my secret library. One more doesn't bother me. And anyway, I've read it. I know what's in it. Of course, I do. I'm omniscient, remember! And omnipotent!'

As if we could forget, Simon thought. The Empress was beginning to seem a bit neurotic to him.

Then Jenny suddenly standing between the Empress and their party then. She spoke in cajoling tones, thinking she was acting for the best... 'Ah, Empress, but we do have something with us – something we have brought from our distant world of Darlington – and it is something that I think you will be very interested in... A thing that rightfully belongs to you. A jar that contains something infinitely precious. And the girl Kelly has it in her possession right now...'

The Scarlet Empress inside her jar perked up at this. 'Is that a fact? Then give it to me! *At once!*'

23.

It was a terrible, oily voice booming through the temple. Simon and I exchanged a quick glance. We recognised that voice...

Below our swaying, suspended cage, all the surviving sloths were frozen in shock. It was like a bizzare game of musical statues down there.

And then the source of that booming, taunting voice appeared in their midst. Now that the soldiers had done his nasty, murderous dirty work, the Vizier appeared. He came tripping lightly into the sacred space, sweating and panting, with his turban slightly awry. He glared at the shocked and frozen sloths in utter contempt. And then he looked up at the hanging cage that held Simon and I, and the Uncle Bill sloth and Aunty Iris.

'It's very tempting, of course, to let the sloths have their way with you. Or to simply cast you out of that cage and into their burning pyre.' He was sneering at us. Real and vicious hatred flashed in his piggy eyes. 'You would deserve it, too. Running away from us! Leading us a merry dance! Actually having the nerve to abscond from the loyal servants of the Scarlet Empress!'

The sloths all around him moaned and chattered at the mention of this name.

'But, no!' barked the Vizier. 'I am afraid that there will be no sacrifices here today. These human beings are now the prisoners of the Scarlet Empress! They are ours.'

The sloths were terrified and many of them were wounded or dead, but they still didn't seem very pleased about that. They weren't used to having their revelries interrupted.

'Don't you mutter at me,' the Chief Vizier cried out, affronted. 'How dare you! You awful, smelly, primitive creatures. Muttering and gibbering in my presence! Why, you will do as I say! You will obey me!'

From our vantage point up above, we could see that the sloths were about to revolt. They were absolutely furious and they had nothing to lose by now. The pompous Vizier and his soldiers had broken into their holy of holies and the sloths were getting ready to fight. You could feel that tension in the air.

'Get back! Get back at once!' cried the Vizier. There was a note of panic in his voice. 'Get away from me, you stinking, golden brutes! Do as I command and bring those prisoners down here at once!'

And that was when the bravest of the temple sloths darted forward and sank his teeth into the Chief Vizier's leg.

That was the signal.

All of them went crazy after that.

The sloths attacked the Vizier and the soldiers and it was only then that the Scarlet Guard realised that there were a thousand or more sloths in the temple ... and there was only twenty of them.

Suddenly things looked horribly hairy for the tattooed soldiers as those lithe and gleaming bodies descended upon them...

'Kelly!' Simon shouted. 'What do we do? We're stuck here!'

It seemed that, for the moment, there was very little we could do. We were still about twenty feet off the floor.

From inside the cage Aunty Iris was shouting out bloodthirstily as she watched the terrible, pitched battle below. It wasn't quite clear which side she was urging on. 'Kill them! Slash them! Bash them! Mash them!'

24.

Iris and Panda were running. She had gathered him up into her arms and they were running away together, just as they had from countless disasters and cosmic menaces in the past.

They clattered out of the attic where her conjoined aunties sat squawking and squealing, and they clattered down the wooden stairs of Wherewithal House. The venerable place hadn't seen so much activity in ages, and great puffs of dust came billowing out from tapestries as our heroes fled. Dick the Highwayman came charging after them, yelling as he did so – and Iris remembered suddenly how ruthless he could be. She remembered her horror at him, when he had shot those innocent people in cold blood. He was never the boy she'd thought he was. She redoubled her effort and ran even faster.

Down, down through the house that had once been her place of captivity. As a child she had felt entombed there. Forced to wear stiff, formal black clothes, as if she had been forever in mourning... And now the place was reaching out to her again, seeking to drag her back into its shadows... those almost palpable shadows that lay enticingly in every corner... How easy it would be, simply to give in and live out the rest of her life, languishing here, underground... with the last few, crazy survivors of her home world... She need never be in danger or confusion again...

She felt Panda squirming in her arms then, and the leaden weight of Fenster's golden head in her carpet bag, and she reminded herself savagely that her true place was among the stars. She belonged on that zig-zag path between the dimensions, and nowhere was home to her really, apart from the big red bus.

Soon enough they were down on the ground floor, and her boots were stamping noisily across the marble floor. She struggled with the heavy locks on what seemed to be the front door, and soon made short work of them with her laser corkscrew.

The doors swung open to reveal the surging river outside. There was a mildewed jetty out there, and a sturdy black boat seemingly waiting for her. It must belong to Dick, she reasoned, before hopping aboard and slashing the ropes that tethered it to Wherewithal House. Panda thrust his snout out, sniffing the air and looking appalled: 'I hate boats! And you can't sail, Iris! You're a menace on the water!'

'We've got no choice, chuck,' she said grimly, and turned to mess about with the motor. Soon there were great plumes of black smoke choking them both as the boat shuddered into life…

And soon they were out in the middle of the wide river. The mean, dark windows of the buildings that lined the bank glared down at them. Iris took them into the middle of the uphill river and gave a yell of triumph.

'Whoever heard of a river that flows uphill?' Panda cried.

'Who cares?' Iris laughed. 'If it gets us out of here, who cares?'

But she broke off in that second, as there came a hideous hullaballoo from behind them. They both turned to see that they had a monstrous pursuer. A gigantic batlike creature with unfurled claws and veined, purple skin stretched to its utmost. It had three fanged heads and was bearing down upon the small, vulnerable boat. Iris couldn't let go of the steering wheel, for fear capsizing the craft, and so she shouted at Panda: 'Grab something! Chuck something at it!'

Panda jumped down from the dashboard and hunted around in Iris's boot for her laser pistol. He whipped around with it at the ready, training it on the creature, and aiming for one of its heads…

'B-but Iris…!' he bellowed in shock. 'It's… your Aunties!'

She turned around in dismay, catching a glimpse of that trio of revolting heads with their lizardlike tongues and flashing fangs. She saw at once that the faces were those of her three aunts – Faith, Hope and Susan. Distorted by rictus-like grimaces as they came swooping after their errant niece.

Panda was firing bolt after bolt at them, clipping their wings with bolts of pink lightning. The Hydra-like being screamed as it was scorched and struck, but the noise was almost lost in the fierce howls of the motor engine and the thunderous churning of the river…

'Go away!' Panda shouted. 'Leave us alone! Iris doesn't want to stay with you, and neither do I!'

The Aunties still came flapping their grotesque way through the hectic air.

'Could you Aunties always fly, Iris?' he asked her. 'Were they always one giant vicious harpie like this?'

25.

Aunty Iris gave a terrible howl of dismay.

A terrible black mood stole over me. I stared down at the Vizier, who was hopping about gleefully at the chaos he had managed to cause.

He looked up and caught my eye.

And even though he was looking up at a girl of twelve... a girl who didn't have a sword and couldn't use one if she tried ... I saw the Vizier flinch when he caught my eye. Something he saw in my expression made him turn pale.

Then, the battle was stopped abruptly by a great booming voice.

'There will be no more killing here!'

'What's that?' cried Aunty Iris.

'Who is it now?' asked Simon.

'It's Fenster!' I gasped. He was flapping his gleaming wings and putting on his best Golden God voice and the whole vast chamber shook. Fenster flexed his talons vengefully.

'You must all stop this horror at once. There will be no more sacrifice. No more fighting or killing in my name. I never wanted any of this. You must all cease at once!'

The soldiers and the sloths were so alarmed by the volume and vehemence of his tone that they did exactly as they were told.

Fenster went on. 'I never wanted to be your Golden God. You sloths have held me prisoner here for years now. I really never wanted living creatures - parrots or pigs or anybody's Aunty - beheaded and thrust into the flames! And I was never keen on your tributes of golden hair...'

The sloths seemed very downcast and confused by this.

'And I certainly don't want people fighting in my temple! Who are these ghastly soldiers and where do they come from? Send them away at once! And free me from my bonds!'

At this the Vizier turned crafty. 'You are a prisoner too, eh?' He chuckled evilly. 'So you aren't quite the divine and all-powerful god of the sloths, hmm?'

'I've told you already!' thundered Fenster. 'I am not their god! I haven't got any powers like that!'

'And you're quite helpless here, are you?' asked the shrewd Chief Vizier.

'Yes! That is why I need to be set free!'

The Vizier sneered. 'Then I really don't see how you can tell us what to do. Why should we listen to you?' He laughed. 'Guards! I think we have another prisoner to take back to the Scarlet Palace. We have found a delightful clockwork toy for the Empress!'

'Clockwork! Clockwork!?' Fenster bellowed.

He was drowned out by a series of grand crashing noises that came from outside the temple. It was as if the tallest, oldest trees in the jungle had just collapsed.

Aunty Iris was shouting down at Fenster: 'No! You mustn't let them take you prisoner. You have to keep away from the Scarlet Empress. Fenster, you have to help Kelly. You have knowledge that she needs. Only she can save Hyspero from the Corrosion. The Scarlet Empress is your enemy! She's the enemy of all of us!'

26.

Euphemia was back in the throne room that had once been hers. She wasn't entirely sure how long ago that had been. Her memory of such things had frittered away through the years... but as soon as Kelly took her out from her hiding place, and set the jar upon the smooth floor, the original Empress knew where she was.

Everyone drew back with due reverence.

'We thought she was gone forever...' said the court Vizier. There was fear in his voice. He was wringing his two plastic arms in consternation.

Anthony Marvelle pushed himself forward, beseeching the current Empress in unctuous tones. 'Your Majesty, murmur murmur. Oh great and bountiful ruler of Hyspero... I have struggled mightily against the odds to return to you your antecedent, who was stolen from the vaults beneath this very throne room... murmur...'

The eyes of the Empress were blazing within the jar. 'You, Marvelle? You alone have brought her back?'

He nodded humbly. 'These other humans and personages, murmur...' (He nodded briefly at Kelly, Simon, Barbra and Jenny) '...have been of some assistance and, at some points, it must be said, hindrance, murmur murmur...'

Simon found himself stepping forward, rather bravely, he thought. 'Your Majesty, you mustn't listen to a word this man says. He's a liar and a cheat, and he's been up to all sorts of...'

'ENOUGH!' roared the Empress, and it seemed that the very air shook as her voice echoed out of her speakers. 'I will not have quibbling in my throne room.' She eyed them all beadily. 'Now, what makes any of you think I wanted this earliest Empress back, hmm?'

They stared at her, dumbfounded.

'But..' gasped Marvelle, his voice cracking. 'Surely... you wished to be reunited with your stolen great great great grandmother... Surely that's what you wanted? It was a great crime, murmur murmur... to take her away from your secret vault... murmur...?'

'Who told you that?' the Empress shot back.

'Why, the Dogworlders, murmur,' said Marvelle. He turned to Missy, his poodle, who was looking a bit shifty at this point. 'It was the dogs who told me, murmur murmur... that there'd be a terrific reward, murmur...'

Missy looked away. 'You needn't believe everything you hear from poodles,' she murmured.

Simon laughed out loud. 'So, you've wasted your time, Marvelle! All this effort to return something and someone who wasn't wanted!'

The poet was furious. 'You *wanted* your great great great grandmother sent to the other side of the galaxy murmur?' he shouted at the Empress. All of the others could see that he was getting himself too worked up, and was stepping out of line.

'I did,' said the Empress simmeringly. 'It's too dangerous to keep her here. With all of the Empresses in one place... there are too many dangers. We are too powerful when we are all together... and so I sent my Vizier... he stole her away and sent her to a place we felt was obscure and far away enough...'

'The Great Big Book Exchange,' said Kelly. 'On the South Road in Darlington.'

'In the early twenty first century,' added Jenny. 'And right under the noses of MIAOW.'

The Empress shrugged. 'I don't know what this MIAOW is that you speak of. But the point is, the jar should never have come back to me. And I still don't understand how it did...'

There was a rushing noise then, of smoke issuing from the small jar in the middle of the floor. Evidently, the tiny, ancient Euphemia had decided it was time to manifest herself. She appeared, moments later, with a gentle popping noise. She was dressed in her very finest silvery frock, with all of her golden hair floating out around her. She surveyed everyone critically.

'Don't believe her!' she cried. 'This great great great granddaughter of mine is a slippery one! She's a liar. She's tricked you all. Marvelle was working for her the whole time. She wanted me back – of course she did – because only I can open the Ringpull for her. Only I have the requisite magic at my dainty little fingertips…'

Simon and the others didn't know what to believe. At that moment Kelly realized that all eyes were on her.

'It was you she sent Marvelle to fetch, Kelly,' said Euphemia. 'You are the key to the Ringpull itself.'

'Great,' Kelly sighed. 'I know. But… what are they going to do to me?'

Suddenly the scarlet guard were surrounding them. They drew their daggers and looked extremely menacing.

'We're sending you up in the bathysphere!' the Empress caroled. 'Everything is prepared! You mustn't worry, and you mustn't resist!'

'No!' Simon shouted at her. 'Leave Kelly alone!'

'There's nothing you can do to stop it, murmur murmur,' said Anthony Marvelle, who was relieved that things seemed to be going his way again. 'The Ringpull will open! The way to the Obverse will be open once more!'

27.

The Vizier was on his knees beside the altar. He was battered and bruised as he surveyed the scene of ongoing disaster. He held up his hands in defeat and supplication: 'Empress!' he howled. 'I call on you! I call upon Your Gracious Gelatinousness! How can you let your servants be defeated like this? How can you let us be destroyed? Come! Come to us and lend us your protection!'

'He's lost it,' said Simon. 'He's gone barmy.'

'She's the one doing it!' Aunty Iris cried. 'It's the Empress who's turning everything to glass and causing the Corrosion!'

Then, by the altar and the ravenous blue flames of the sacrificial pit, something very alarming shivered and shimmered into existence.

Two malevolent orbs.

They appeared out of nowhere, hovering in the air and surveying the scene of wreckage and carnage.

The eyes of the Scarlet Empress herself!

They appeared magically and hung there in the air: gory, veiny and bloodshot. They took us all in at one glance and all of us who saw them were stilled and silenced by the evil in their stare. I was in no doubt that these eyes - with their brilliant ice green pupils - belonged to the legendary Scarlet Empress.

Her chilling voice rang out, and it seemed to come from nowhere.

'Do not think, any of you, about approaching these eyes of mine and attempting to injure me. These are a mere projection. None of you can harm me. I am many thousands of miles away.'

'That's disgusting!' Simon muttered. 'She sent her eyeballs!'

'I demand that you all give yourselves up to me. None of you can escape the might of the Scarlet Empress!'

Great wrinkled claws appeared then in mid-air, some height above those horrible eyes. Two shrivelled hands that came scything through the hot air towards our cage, reaching out to us...

I shrank away instinctively, pulling Simon with me.

So this was the Scarlet Empress at last!

Her voice came hissing into my ear. It seemed closer to me than anything. 'Kelly...' she sighed. 'I am glad you are here. You have something I need. Something all of Hyspero needs!'

Aunty Iris saw at once that the Empress was speaking to me. She became livid and shook the bars of her cage again. 'Leave her alone, you old witch! You leave my Kelly alone!'

The Scarlet Empress roared with laughter. Her hovering eyeballs turned a livid, bloody crimson. Somewhere below, hiding in the rubble, the Vizier joined in sycophantically with that laughter.

'You shouldn't listen to your Aunty Iris, Kelly. Haven't you guessed by now how mad and deluded she actually is?' The Empress laughed again.

'No!' I yelled out. 'No, she's not!'

'She thinks I cause the Corrosion. She thinks I am the cause of the whole land being about to break apart. But I am not. She must be mad, to suspect me of such a thing.'

'You aren't harming Hyspero..?'

'She is!' Aunty Iris cried out. 'She's behind everything! She's evil! She's the cause of all the badness and corruption and Corrosion in Hyspero! We should kill her! We should--!'

One of those huge, clawed, scarlet hands reached out towards the cage. It wrenched open the metal door with a bone-jarring screech and it groped its way inside to take a hold of Aunty Iris. My Aunty howled and kicked, backing away into a corner of the cage.

There was nothing Simon or I could do. He kicked and I kicked and we both struggled to grab through the bars to take a hold of Aunty Iris's extremities as that huge hand pulled her out of the cage. But it was no good.

She was in the monstrous grasp of the Empress.

'My old enemy!' laughed the Empress. 'After all of these years! I have a chance to destroy you properly at last!'

Aunty Iris wriggled feebly in the colossal claw's grasp as she was hoisted through the air.

'You can't kill me! You can't! Not after everything we've been through...!'

'Oh...' sighed the disembodied voice of the Empress. 'I think I can, you know.'

Then, the savage claw of the Empress lifted my Aunty Iris much higher into the sizzling air and, almost casually, hurled her down into the blue sacrificial flames.

It was over too quickly for any of us to yell out or do anything.

One minute she was there - the next, my Aunty Iris was gone!

She had been swallowed up by the hungry blue flames.

We hadn't rescued her at all.

She was gone forever and we were stuck there ... still at the mercy of the Scarlet Empress!

28.

The river rose in a great arc, high above the crumbling buildings of the underground city. Iris and Panda clung to each other as fizzing, hissing, foaming water poured over the sides of their frail vessel and threatened to capsize them. As the upwards torrents bore them through the soft, gelid shielding of the Clockworkers' city, they saw the last of the three-headed creature that had once been Iris' Aunties, and they both heaved a great sigh of relief.

But their boat was out of control, as if the workings were frozen and locked into place. They were zooming crazily through the cascading water...

'Is this it, Panda?' Iris squawked. 'Are we both going to die?'

Panda was gargling and spitting out streams of the nasty-tasting water. He shook himself fiercely, and yelled, 'This is what comes of reunions with long-lost family members! Remember this for future reference – you should never go back anywhere, Iris!'

His next words were drowned in a crashing wave that broke over their heads. Iris clung to the wheel and her carpet bag, desperate not to lose any of the vital stuff it contained.

'How much longer?' she screeched. 'How far up does this go..?'

She was answered almost at once, as the two of them became aware that there was a mist gathering about them. A foggy layer of freezing air formed a kind of ceiling and they were plunging through it…

And then, there was the sensation of being popped out of a bottle like a cork… and the wooden boat seemed to shudder and splinter into a million pieces.

All of a sudden they were out of the boat and out of the river.

They were soaked to the skin, but on dry ground.

They were no longer underground.

Iris lifted up her head and sniffed cautiously. There was heat. Baking heat. And an actual sky above them.

She stretched her arms and legs. Panda and the carpetbag were lying next to her… on the glittering sand. The bag was open and, rather disconcertingly, Fenster's disembodied head was staring back at her.

She sat up. The sky above her was cobalt blue.

She was sitting on a sand dune in the desert above ground on Hyspero. When she craned her neck round stiffly, she saw the welcome shape of her double decker bus waiting for her. Her heart leapt up excitedly at the sight of it.

'We made it!' She shook the soggy Panda awake. 'Panda! We made it back to the surface!'

He sat up groggily. He patted himself and gave Iris a hard stare. 'I mean it, Iris. No more digging around in your past. It's much too dangerous!'

She was on her feet now, not really listening to him. Now she was doing an absurd dance in the sand, joyous at the sight of her bus. 'We can go! We can leave this dreadful place behind!'

'What?' Panda cried. 'But we have to get after our friends. Remember? We need to rescue them!'

For a second Iris looked irritated. 'Really? Can't they look after themselves, lovey?'

'We brought them here, remember?' Panda bellowed. 'They are our responsibility!'

Iris started to sulk, stomping her way through the sand towards her beloved double decker. 'We're so tired, though, aren't we? We've been in hair-raising peril, and we need a rest and a lie-down and a little drinky, don't we?' She brightened for a second. 'Anyway, they're probably still round here, somewhere. They won't have wandered far, will they?'

But they found the bus completely abandoned.

Panda told her, 'We have to find them.'

'Just let me get washed and brushed up first,' Iris groaned. 'And pour us a couple of drinks, chuck.'

Panda toweled himself dry and hopped over to the cocktail cabinet. Fenster's head was glaring at him from the chaise longue, where Iris had chucked him.

'Remember, Panda. The Clockwork people took my blood. That's a dangerous substance in the wrong hands, my dear.'

'Oh!' said Panda, and called up to Iris on the top deck. 'That dragon's head is talking! It's saying cryptic things on the chaise longue.'

Iris's voice came back muffled from her dressing room. 'What was that?'

The dragon's head continued: 'The blood of Hysperon dragons makes false things real, remember. And it can have the opposite effect, Panda. Imagine what the disappointed Clockworkers might do with it…'

Panda frowned as he listened and popped ice cubes into their gin. As far as he was concerned, the remains of Fenster were talking gibberish.

'They can turn us all fictional, Panda,' warned the head, who was quite getting used to the idea of the chaise longue as his new body. He attached himself to it more firmly. 'That's what they will do now. They will use my blood to nudge us several notches into a fictional universe. That's the kind of thing that the people of the Obverse delight in…'

Panda thought that Fenster's brains must have been addled by being carried around in Iris's bag. She had enough strange old junk in there (as Panda knew all too well!) And now the poor golden dragon was doo-lally as well, poor thing!

'I've got your drink, dear!' he shouted up the stairwell.

'Could you tie my head down to this chaise longue?' Fenster asked him, breaking out of his more portentous tone. 'I think I'll adopt it. Do you still have my wheels?'

'Sorry,' Panda sipped his drink. 'We had to make a quick getaway, and all we could manage was your head. But the chaise longue's on castors, you know.'

'Oh! Good,' said Fenster, easing back and forward gently, hearing them squeak beneath him.

Then – fortified by a fiendishly strong G+T – Panda set about discovering exactly where the devil all those friends of theirs had got to.

29.

'You will come to me, Kelly,' the Scarlet Empress said. 'One day. You will come to my palace because you need me, or because you have decided you must destroy me. But we will meet again, Kelly.'

At that moment, all I could think about was getting away from her. I was wriggling free of my backpack, and fumbling to get out my black notebook and my silver pen. Simon saw what I was up to and he helped me.

The crashing and screaming of the sloths and the soldiers was still going on, through all of this. But I had become deaf to it. The shock of seeing my Aunty flung into the flames had made me feel very still and very quiet...

I flipped to a blank page in my book.

'Ah,' the Empress sighed. 'The girl who can read and write. Even in Hyspero. The girl for whom Hyspero has waited.'

I was going to try to banish her.

That seemed like the only thing to do. I barely stopped to think. I uncapped my pen and, in my book, I wrote, in large, looping letters: 'Empress - begone!'

I concentrated. I waited. I willed the magic to work with every fibre of my being.

It didn't work.

I looked down into those veiny, horrible floating eyes and waited for them to vanish.

The Empress shrieked with laughter. Her pupils turned mostly to black. 'You aren't that powerful yet, little girl! Not yet!'

So that was it! My best idea! A horrible feeling of doom sank through me.

'And besides,' she gloated. 'You don't really want to banish me from here, do you? If you succeeded in sending me away, what would happen to the jungle? To the remaining sloths and pigs and parrots? And do you know what would happen to you two..?' She laughed harshly. 'You would all be Corroded! If I wasn't here, using my magic to hold back the onslaught of the Obverse!'

'She's lying,' Simon whispered.

'It's true!' boomed the voice of the Empress. 'You have a choice! To surrender to me, or send me away and commit this entire temple, this whole jungle zone ... to the Corrosion!'

'Send her away!' hissed Simon.

'You must choose!' screeched the Empress. *'Come with me! Surrender! Let me take you away to my palace! Or let the Corrosion swarm over this land!'*

30.

They were taken to the top of the palace. Bundled roughly by the guards, with the Vizier at their heels, giggling nastily, Iris's friends had no choice in the matter. The Empress stayed downstairs in her throne room and her shattering laughter rang out behind them.

Marvelle and Missy looked mightily pissed off at being lumped with the others. They were all being sent off together to this bathysphere thing at the top of the tallest tower. The Earthlings were all being dispatched together.

Simon was holding Kelly's hand, in a futile attempt to reassure her that everything would be all right. She knew that it wouldn't be, however. The girl had a dreadful feeling in the pit of her stomach. She knew that this was the peculiar fate that had been marked out for her since she was born... All her life she had harboured the secret knowledge that she was somehow doomed. Never would she have been able to guess exactly what that would entail, but now she was getting a much clearer picture.

She thought glumly about her poetry. It had been primitive, jagged and quite incomprehensible. When she had joined the women's poetry group in Darlington everyone had been rather impressed, and a bit discomfited by all the cosmic imagery in her stanzas. The words had simply flowed out of her, and she had been amazed. But now she knew that it hadn't actually been her own writing. The Multiverse had been speaking through her, tossing out clues about her ultimate destiny. Not even her poems were her own…

Kelly felt rather resigned and glum as she climbed the many winding stairs with the others…

Barbra was labouring with all the many staircases. She tottered bravely, not quite understanding where it was they were heading to, or why. She simply knew that her place was with the other Earthlings, and she was more than content to share their fates…

Unlike Jenny, whose eyes flicked warily about, waiting for a moment in which she might seize the advantage, overpower her guards and escape… Though that moment never came. There was no escaping this. It was too late.

The bathysphere turned out to be a somewhat ramshackle-looking vehicle on the highest landing of the tower. It was incongruous there in the sumptuous setting of the palace. It was a greasy hunk of ironmongery, studded with rivets and festoons of piping and tubing. There was a single porthole and, peering through, Simon saw that it was going to be cramped inside for all of them, and none too comfortable. It looked like the kind of thing that would be used for exploring the seabed…

'They're going to send us up in that?' he asked Jenny, and she nodded tersely.

Send us up where, though, he wondered.

The Vizier wasted no time in opening the dangerous-looking contraption and ushering them inside. There they found alcoves all around the sphere's interior, into which they must be strapped.

A single viewscreen opened up and displayed the Scarlet Empress's gurning, wicked face. She glared down at them and explained that they mustn't let her down.

'I've waited centuries for this. The Ringpull must be opened. Unimaginable riches and possibilities lie beyond this universe, inside the Obverse. And destiny has ordained that you are the people to make this possible. Now, go with my blessing. And know that, if you fail, you will face the wrath of the Scarlet Empress!'

Everyone had had quite enough of her ranting by now, and were quite relieved when the screen went dead again, and the engines started up.

'The engines are rather quiet,' Simon observed.

'They're just the life-support systems,' snapped the Vizier. 'They don't have anything to do with the vehicle's propulsion. That comes about through a special substance that the whole sphere is covered with – the precious and rarefied saliva of the Empress... plus the sheer force of the Empress's mighty will...'

Before anyone had the chance to react to the idea of a saliva-coated bathysphere, they experienced the gut-churning sensation as the machine lifted up. It lurched about a bit, and then there was a great howl as it flung itself upwards...

Smashing through the highest spire of the palace…

There was an almighty crash… and then silence…

The sphere turned end over end as it plummeted upwards into the hot blue skies above Central Hyspero…

Everyone aboard passed out for a few moments… their consciousnesses crushed and crumpled like little paper balls as they were propelled out of the atmosphere and into the rather more prosaic regions of space surrounding the impossible planet of Hyspero…

31.

'I have searched for you for a hundred years,' Fenster cried. 'You are our Reader. You must come with me at once, to the city of leopards.'

'That's what I'm saying, Fenster. But first, we have to--'

'Uh, Kelly,' said Simon. 'I think we'd better hurry. I can hear some very nasty rumbling and grinding noises … I think this whole temple might be about to collapse. The Corrosion … I think we're going to see exactly what it can do…'

'Fenster!' I shouted, taking aim with Aunty Iris's hairpin. 'We need to get out RIGHT NOW!'

I didn't actually see if he caught it.

We were all distracted by the Vizier. He was cackling with glee and standing at the winch controls. 'Where did he come from?' shouted Simon. 'I thought he'd vanished at the same time as the Empress's eyes…!'

'The little creep was hiding!' I cursed and yelled down at him: 'What are you doing?' But it was too late. He was wrestling with the controls and the cage was moving about in mid-air. The chains were clanking and grinding and it was all too obvious that he was manoeuvring us until Simon and I were suspended right over the pit of blue flames.

They flickered, sapphire and emerald. But if you looked closely, there was a heart of deadly blackness in that sacrificial pit...

'Let us down, Vizier!' Simon shouted.

'Let them down at once!' Fenster bellowed.

The Vizier simply laughed maniacally. 'Sacrifice!' he screeched. 'Sacrifice! Sacrifice! Sacrifice!'

It was clear that he had gone absolutely bonkers.

'You children have brought chaos down on Hyspero! You have ruined this land!' He was frothing at the mouth by now. 'And so I condemn you both! To the sacrificial pit!'

As he threw one final lever I heard Fenster cry out in anguish: 'No, don't, you fool!'

He severed the chains that held us suspended.

And then the cage dropped away beneath us.

I heard Simon squawk out indignantly and I think I gave a scream, too. But the next thing was ... we were plummeting.

Straight into those ferociously hungry flames.

32.

Soon Iris was back on the bus's lower deck. It had taken her a matter of minutes, but she looked refreshed, immaculate, and ready to face the universe again. She had even done her hair up in her favourite Farah-Fawcett 'do. She had donned a piratical outfit in pink and purple. Panda reflected that all she was missing was the cutlass between her teeth, but he guessed that would interfere with her smoking.

As she stomped down the gangway of the bus, she looked hell-bent on something or other. She spared barely a glance for Panda, nor for Fenster, who was still shuffling about on castors.

'Where are we going?' Panda called after her, as she made for the driver's cab.

She flung herself into the driver's seat and started flicking all the buttons at once. The good old Twenty Two hummed into life at once, as if glad to be obeying its mistress's instructions once again. The engine roared happily. The defensive shielding crackled into being. The windows rattled and the pneumatic doors made themselves secure. Iris switched on the telepathic circuits and flooded them with info about her missing companions.

'Hello..?' shouted Panda, trotting down the bus after her. 'Can you hear me? Are you talking? I was asking you, Where are we going now?'

She surveyed the panels of instruments, and fixed for a moment on a tiny, dirty screen that showed some interesting blips of light. It was a view of what was going on in space, right on this world's celestial doorstep. Most interesting...

'We're going to the Brink, Panda, old chum!' She grinned. She clamped a fresh cigarette into her mouth and prepared to yank the final lever that would send them spinning off into their travels again.

'The Brink?' he frowned.

'That's where our friends have gone!' she cried. 'They've been sent to the Very Brink! And we haven't got a moment to lose!'

With that, she gave an almighty yank on the lever... and the whole bus reared up...

And leapt into the impossible... once again!

33.

Dazzling, endless, swirling blue, licking at us.

Simon and I kept on falling through it. Head over heels and over and over ... and the flames, it turned out, weren't in the slightest bit hot.

Some very confused part of my mind couldn't figure that out at all. Why hadn't we been burned up into a crisp? What had happened to us?

We smashed through the flames and they splintered and broke.

They were glass.

And beneath them ... only Corroded blackness.

It was cold. It was just nothing. And we dropped through it, yelling.

We dropped through the Corrosion into the emptiness beyond. We fell through a gap in the fabric of Hyspero itself.

We kept on falling and falling and the overwhelming darkness of the Corrosion eventually became the spangling and revolving of a kaleidoscope of every colour imaginable.

And then...!

We crashed to a halt.

A bone-jarring, skull-crunching jolt.

And we found that we were sitting side by side.

Outside. On a bench. On a freezing cold day.

In our own town centre.

About lunchtime, according to the town clock.

A crisp packet went blowing past us in the frosty breeze. A woman in a headscarf with lots of shopping and two toddlers went hurrying past. She gave the two of us startled, horrified, messy-looking kids on the bench a very funny look and tottered away on the slippery pavement.

Simon and I waited for a few moments before we dared to look at each other.

Then Simon said, 'Kelly...' He blinked, looking dazed. 'I think we're home again!'

34.

They woke up a bit sore and cross.

Simon was the first to be fully compus mentis… and he looked around at the others, lolling in their alcoves. Barbra had come free of her safety belt and had rolled into an instrument bank, but as far as he could tell, the vending machine hadn't sustained any serious damage, thank goodness. He had become rather attached to Barbra in recent weeks.

Everyone else seemed okay in that dingy little craft. With moans and groans they were waking up, and remembering where it was they were supposed to be. Steam hissed through the darkened air and the various control panels were blinking like mad. Simon shook his head to clear away the fuzziness, and suddenly became aware that the Vizier was hopping about in the middle of the room.

'We did it! We made it! We actually managed to get here!'

The smug little man started helping Anthony Marvelle to free himself from his alcove. Even Missy the poodle was helped out before the Vizier turned to the others.

'Where are we?' Kelly demanded. She, too, was standing now, and clutching the jar that contained Euphemia. Her fingers were tingling and strange after the short flight through space. She must have let her guard down momentarily, because Marvelle reached forward and neatly snatched the precious item out of her grasp.

'We'll be needing this, thank you, Kelly, murmur murmur. It was good of you and Jenny and Barbra and Simon to look after the jar for so long, but now is the time when the earliest Empress is needed most of all. By *us!* Murmur murmur!'

The door of the sphere opened up at once, and mercifully fresh air swooshed in at once. During its flight, the ship's interior had become rather stuffy.

'We've landed somewhere!' exclaimed Jenny, who had banged her head in transit, and hadn't really kept up with developments. 'Are we back on Hyspero?'

'Oh no, murmur murmur,' said Marvelle. His poodle snickered horribly. 'We're in space around Hyspero. We've docked at the small space station on the very Brink. The fabled location of the Ringpull itself.'

All at once he reached out and seized Kelly by one arm, twisting it roughly behind her back. 'You are coming with me, young lady, murmur.'

But no one was giving in without a fight. Simon flung himself at Marvelle, as did Jenny, and then Barbra. They were furious at Marvelle's attempt to manhandle Kelly. Soon quite a scrap had broken out, and spilled out of the saliva-coated bathysphere and onto the metal platform where the ship was resting and cooling down. Marvelle tossed the jar to safety, and the Vizier neatly caught it. Just in time, before Jenny clouted Marvelle about the head.

'STOP HITTING ME MURMUR MURMUR!' he yelled. 'Can't you see? You've all lost! We're here! At the Ringpull! And we've got Kelly murmur murmur, and the Empress Euphemia murmur murmur! And so it isn't really any use you lot fighting me or struggling against the inevitable murmur. Why don't you all just give in and go along with the ride murmur murmur? I'm going to open up the Obverse whether you like it or not!'

Simon stepped bravely forward. 'And we're going to stop you!'

'For heaven's sake, why?? Murmur murmur?'

'Because Iris has told us that it's a very bad idea, that's why,' said Simon, astonished by his own steadfastness. 'And, oddly enough, all of us lot believe in that old transdimensional baggage. We trust her and everything she says.'

Marvelle sneered. 'So where is she, then, eh? Why isn't she here to help you?'

Simon felt uneasy, and looked around at his friends. In fact, Marvelle had a point. Iris wasn't there. They hadn't seen her in ages. Both she and Panda had abandoned their travelling companions in the desert quite some time ago…

He looked at the exhausted faces of Kelly, Jenny, and Barbra… and realized that they were on their own with this. But they still all believed in Iris – even Jenny. Even if Iris had been discommoded elsewhere, and was unable to help them out… it didn't mean that she wouldn't if she could. Simon still had faith in the flaky old bag.

'We're going to stop you, Marvelle,' he told the triumphantly foppish poet. 'You'll just see. You can't just make use of Kelly and Euphemia like this.'

'You're going to stop me, murmur murmur?'

Simon took a step closer. 'Yes!'

'Then, murmur murmur,' said Marvelle, giving a quick nod to Missy. 'You'll have to get through this lot first.'

And, all at once, a dozen poodles appeared out of nowhere. They had hands and blaster guns and very nasty expressions. And they had the Earthlings surrounded.

There was barely time for anyone to react before Marvelle seized Kelly once again, and disappeared through a side door.

'No!' Simon yelled, but they were gone.

35.

I couldn't believe Simon had accepted our return so easily. To this place. This same old shopping precinct!

'We made the choice that the Empress put to us,' I said. 'We refused to surrender to her, and let the Corrosion take over the temple. It's our own fault that we were catapulted back home. We've ruined our own chances of ever saving Hyspero now!'

Simon nodded grimly.

I knew that, right now, he was keen to get home to his parents and to tell them that he was okay. Well, so was I, but we had another world and its welfare to think about too.

And that was a world as real as this one.

As real as the shopping precinct we were hurrying through right now. As real as the pedestrians around us, the cars parked at the kerb, the supermarket and charity shop.

And as real as Nanna Beryl, who we saw outside the Everything-Costs-a-Pound shop, lying in her iron lung. She was being pushed by her nurse - that skinny woman in a headscarf, called Jenny. Jenny looked worn out from hauling the metal contraption round the shops.

'Nanna Beryl!' I yelled, and dragged Simon across the precinct, over to my Nanna.

She was blinking in confusion and trying to focus on the mirror above her face. Her breathing was even worse than usual and she took some moments to recognise her own granddaughter. When she did realise who I was, she looked alarmed.

'Nanna Beryl!' I said. 'We've done it! We've actually been there! We've been to ... you-know-where!'

Nurse Jenny was looking furious. 'Hey, you two. Stop bothering her. She isn't well.'

'She's my Nanna Beryl!' I shouted, shrugging the woman off. 'We've just returned to Earth, Nanna Beryl. We fell back through a gap in Hyspero!'

Nanna Beryl was struggling to speak. Her eyes were blazing intently and her lips struggled to form the words. 'Back to...' she gargled.

'Yes!' I said. 'We have to get back before it's too late. We know it can be done. You used to go there all the time. How did you do it? We need to know!'

Simon said, 'Don't rush her, Kelly. You're getting her confused...'

'I'm going to call the police if you carry on like this, young lady,' said Nurse Jenny.

But then Nanna Beryl startled us all by bursting out very loudly: 'You have been to HYSPERO!? How did YOU get there? What did you do? Why aren't I there? Why can't you take me with you, Kelly--? Why don't you take me with you, to Hyspero..?'

Then she started making some terrible noises and warning lights began flashing on the side of the iron lung.

'That's it!' cried Nurse Jenny. 'That's enough. I'm taking her home. She doesn't have to put up with rotten kids yelling at her outside the Pound Shop!'

'She's my Nanna!' I protested.

Nanna Beryl was groaning now.

'Come on, Kelly,' Simon urged. 'Calm down...'

'You two have been missing for weeks,' said Nurse Jenny suddenly and sharply. 'You ran away from home. Oh, you two are in for a right walloping!'

'You know about us?' said Simon. 'My parents ... What do –'

But then Nanna Beryl burst out in a much larger voice, which made the whole iron lung rattle:

'YOU MUST GO BACK!

'THEY NEED YOU, KELLY!

'THEY NEED YOU IN HYSPERO!'

And then she fell silent.

We all stared at her.

'Right,' said Nurse Jenny darkly, taking a firm grip on the iron lung. 'That's enough excitement for one day. I'm taking this poor old dear home immediately. You've exhausted her. And I suggest you two get yourselves home, too. You've both got some explaining to do!'

Simon and I watched the skinny, headscarfed woman wheel Nanna Beryl away uncomplainingly across the shopping precinct.

There was no point in running after them. The rasping, booming words from Nanna Beryl were still ringing in our ears.

'YOU MUST GO BACK!

THEY NEED YOU, KELLY!

THEY NEED YOU IN HYSPERO!'

36.

Panda was clinging on tightly to the cocktail cabinet. He saw himself reflected madly, many times over, in the jagged glass panels of the Art Deco interior. Everything else aboard the bus was rattling free and tumbling through the stiff, juddering air of the Maelstrom (that curious space-time region where just about everything is buggered up.)

'Hang on, everyone!' Iris shrieked. 'The telepathic circuits are causing quite a rumpus! They must be a bit rusty!'

She was homing in on Simon, whose brainwaves were strongest in the bus's memory. But still the whole vehicle shuddered violently and bucked madly as it tore through the coruscating tunnel of noise and clashing colour. Panda gave out an ululating cry of dismay and that was nothing compared with the affronted howl from Fenster's head. It was Fenster's first voyage about the Number 22 and it all came as something of a shock to what remained of him.

But at last everything died down. There was a dark, pensive pause aboard the bus.

Then Iris said, 'We're going in!'

And the Number 22 to Putney Common materialized aboard the Ringpull space station.

Right at the very moment Iris's friends needed her the most.

It was just as Simon and the others were bracing themselves to be shot by poodles.

They fired..!

Mercilessly, as poodles always do.

But…!

Instead of eliminating everyone at once, those dazzling, sizzling laser blasts bounced harmlessly off the sides of Iris's bus. There was a horrible smell of burning pompoms. The armed dogs howled at this vast apparition and the human beings simply stared in wonderment.

'Iris!' Barbra shouted at last with jubilation in her tinny voice. 'She came after us after all!'

The poodles were frozen in shock. Three of them had fallen under their own laser fire, and the others were staring in dread and dismay at the being that their race knew only as *'The Evil One in the Wonderbra and Sensible Shoes.'*

The hydraulic doors whooshed open and suddenly Iris was there – looking amazingly glamorous and unruffled in her pirate costume and with Panda at her side. 'You lot again!' she yelled at the poodles. One of them whimpered. She bellowed at them: 'I should have known! Marvelle's been working with you the whole time, hasn't he? Trying to get into the Obverse! Well, it's no good, you know. There's nothing out there to interest you lot!' With that she plucked out her own laser pistol and started firing shots, seemingly willy-nilly about the room. Every single dog dropped the weapon they were carrying with a frightened yelp.

Iris turned on her friends, 'Don't I get a hug?'

They gathered round her and everyone was hugging everybody else and shouting. Fenster had rolled his chaise longue body up to the doors of the bus to see what was going on (he hated being left out.)

In the rush of laughter and explanations, Simon suddenly remembered himself. 'Iris! They've got Kelly and the First Empress! And they're opening the Ringpull *right now!*'

Iris hoisted up her belt and clutched her pistol tightly. 'Not if your Aunty Iris has got anything to do about it!'

At that, she sent the submissive poodles scattering, and ran for the side door, with all of her friends following after her.

37.

It was actually a bit further than they thought.

The space station that was poised on the very Brink of the Obverse was done up inside like something out of Las Vegas. Or, more probably, Blackpool, commented Iris. She led the charge, clutching Panda and her carpetbag, while all her friends hurried, trundled or lollopped after her. Even Fenster came squeaking on his new castors and plush, cushioned body through the casino rooms.

'It's like Christmas in here,' Iris yelled back at them, taking in the splendid chandeliers and other somewhat gaudy decorations. She was also wondering vaguely how she had ended up with quite so many companions, all of whom she felt responsible for. Wasn't it rather easier, in the old days, when it was just Panda and herself?

'Are you sure you know where you're going?' Panda asked her, still clutching her drink for her.

'I know which way Marvelle has gone,' she growled. 'I can smell his cologne, can't you? It's sickly sweet and insinuating…'

Now they were hurrying through what appeared to be the foyer of an old cinema, complete with dusky lighting and hot dog stand. There were no staff members in evidence, and the whole place had an air of desolation and abandonment.

'Funny old place,' Iris said. 'Aha! Look!'

She had spotted a black curtain that had been pulled aside. Behind it was a not-very-obvious door, which had been left ajar. All at once she knew that that was where her quarry had gone.

'We've got him!' she hissed, and ducked through the curtain and the door.

Everyone else came galumphing at various speeds after her.

As it turned out, the Ringpull room was a very ordinary-looking place. It was metal-walled and looked as if it was a kind of maintenance cupboard. There was a bucket and a mop in the corner and a somewhat inconsequential-seeming control panel on the blank wall.

Anthony Marvelle and the over-excited Missy were standing there, seemingly pushing the terrified Kelly through a narrow doorway. It looked something like a bank vault she was being placed inside.

'Wait!' Iris yelled.

They all turned to look at her. She stopped in her tracks just as all her friends caught up with her, even Fenster.

'You!' Marvelle shouted. 'What do you want?' he idly flipped a few switches on the control panel, and the whole room filled with an unearthly light. It was a nasty shade of apricot that made Iris instantly nauseous. There came an ominous humming noise and the thick metal door started to close on Kelly…

'No!' shouted Simon, bursting forward. 'They're shoving her in there! Into the whatsit..!'

As he raced to help, Missy set upon him with her teeth bared and, in a surprising show of strength, he was wrestled to the ground by the nasty poodle.

Everything seemed to happen at once then, with his friends surging forward to help, and the noise of hidden machinery intensifying. It was as if the cogs and wheels of the universe itself were starting to shift and rotate and to move into new configurations... And perhaps that actually *was* happening, Iris thought wildly... If Kelly truly is the key to the barrier between dimensions...

As the air darkened around her she swung round to give Marvelle a final warning.

'You really don't see, do you?'

'What?' he snarled. 'All I see – murmur murmur – is a past-it ratbag who keeps running after me through space and time, trying to put a stop to everything I want to do, murmur murmur!'

'That's because I know best,' Iris bellowed. 'You should listen more to your Aunty Iris! I know how *all* these things work!'

'You won't stop me opening up the Ringpull between universes murmur murmur!' Marvelle screeched, flicking the last few switches.

'But you can't do that,' said Iris. 'You've no idea what lies out there! It's a terrible idea! I should know! I know what that universe is like! I was born there...!'

But there was no reasoning with the crazy poet. He was in the possession of an intractable idea. Now he was reaching for the murky jar that contained the tiny Empress,

Euphemia… and all his horrified onlookers knew that this was the final part of the ritual…

'No, you can't!' Jenny screamed. 'You can't sacrifice both Kelly and Euphemia to your terrible schemes!'

She launched herself forward, pushing brutally past her friends and, before anyone knew it, Jenny had her hands around the poet's neck.

'Let me go at once murmur murmur!' Anthony Marvelle croaked and choked. His arms swung round and his eyes just about popped out of his head as the ex-traffic warden increased the pressure of her fingers on his throat. 'Axxccchhrruugghhh murmur aagghccjjkkyy murmur!!'

And then everyone held their breath as the glass jar flew out of his hands and described an elegant arc through the air. In the apricot light it looked rather pretty, turning end over end…

Then there were hands reaching out to grab it. Everyone leapt up in order to catch Euphemia's jar…

But they were too late.

It went CRRAAASSHH on the metal floor.

What emerged from it was a fine, hissing mist. Bright green. Not the viscous fluids and jelly that everyone was expecting. The shards of glass lay scattered and the contents of the jar were issuing into the air… dissipating…

'Oh, crumbs,' said Panda. 'What have we done?'

Jenny had Marvelle in a headlock, just as Simon was being held down by the poodle. Everyone was fixed in position, staring at the mist that gathered above the smashed jar.

And just then – the tiny Empress appeared. She was in her finest frock, all sparkles and gold on ivory white. She looked stricken, dismayed and… in some terrible way… almost triumphant.

'Oh dear…' she gasped, and her face was very pale. 'That's torn it! Who dropped me? You've fucked it up now. You've really gone and blown it!' She turned her tiny, lilac eyes on Marvelle – whose face was purple with rage and incomprehension. 'Do you hear that? You foolish scribbler! You versifying ninny! You venial shithead! You great lanky cosmic fuckwit! In your desperation to have what no one else can ever have… in your furtive, futile desire to peek into the next universe – the forbidden universe – you've gone and fucked it all up! You revolting fop! You stupid sod…!'

'Empress Euphemia, please… murmur murmur!' gasped Marvelle. 'I was doing what your descendent… the current Empress, would have me do murmur murmur… We worked together and we thought you would be pleased…'

'Pleased..!' shrilled the miniature Empress – and she was starting to fade away by now. Everyone could see that this was the case. Her voice was becoming fainter under the grinding gears of the Ringpull machinery, and her exquisite features were becoming transparent… 'Of course I'm not fucking pleased! You've destroyed me, Anthony Marvelle. In your rapacious greed and unseemly hurry, you have rendered extinct that which has survived for countless millennia! You have severed the sacred

Hysperon line from its earliest beginnings and, in so doing, have ensured that the Ringpull will remain shut forever! In short, you absolute idiot… You've fucked it royally… forever…!!'

Marvelle let out a ghastly sob and, for a terrible second, Jenny thought she had inadvertently choked the life out of him. She released her grip on his windpipe and he slumped to the metal floor… only inches from where the glass shards were scattered… and the Empress in her wreathing mist was fading out of existence…

Iris flung herself to the ground and inched closer to Euphemia. The tiny woman was like a phantom… like a wisp of an Empress… a memory or a rumour of a long-gone era…

'Euphemia… we tried. I'm so sorry, lovey. But we thought we could do this… we could stop him, and return you to the vaults beneath the Scarlet Palace… and to safety again…'

The Empress gazed up at Iris… looking almost fond of the irrepressible ratbag. 'I know you were trying, dear. But it wasn't to be. And it's better this way. The current Empress is a crazy lady and I'd hate to see what she comes up with next… Hyspero is changing… perhaps it's doomed. I'd rather fade away now, to be honest, than see what the future holds. All right, dear… I think that's me done, now. I'm just about completely faded away, aren't I?'

Iris stared at her evanescence and nodded tearfully. 'Yes, I'm afraid so…'

'Don't look so mournful, dearie! Life will go on! And you will go on, too. Just keep a keen eye on my Hyspero, will you? And remember to rescue Kelly out of the machine. She thinks she's in a dream, you know. Poor Kelly… she's in a dream of a book she once read, bless her… Oh, and that sneaky Vizier is still lurking about on this space station, remember… And he's a wily one! He's a sneaky little fucker! Right now he's trying to steal away on board your double decker buuuuusssssss…'

And with that, the Empress Euphemia was gone.

There was a single beat of silence that hung heavily in that room.

Then Iris jerked into violent action. 'My bus!!!'

38.

The others followed Iris back through those plush space station rooms that were got up like a sleazy nightclub and casino. They would all be glad to see the back of this place… though, as Simon pointed out, unless they prevented the Vizier from stealing Iris's bus, they would all be stuck here for the foreseeable.

Simon led them all at a run - Kelly (shaky but unharmed), Panda (furious), Jenny (with her dander up), Fenster (confused and clumsy on his castors) and Barbra (clunking along expertly, wondering when would be a good moment to pass out some fizzy drinks.) Marvelle and Missy were stumbling after them, as were a number of other poodles, all of them keen to shoot their blasters at Iris's party. But Marvelle never gave the order. He looked terribly shocked at what had happened today.

'It was all my fault, Missy, murmur murmur,' he was heard to say. 'The Ringpull is closed forever, the Obverse is sealed away… and the Empress Euphemia has faded away out of existence – and all because of me!! Murmur murmur.'

Missy the poodle shrugged. None of it was any fluff off *her* pompoms. She just wished Marvelle would hoik out his Subtle Pinking Shears and open them up a new slash in the fabric of space-time. Missy reckoned it was time to be away from here.

'What do you say, Anthony?' She put this proposal to him, as the others went haring after the bus. 'I don't reckon you'll get a warm welcome from the Scarlet Empress now. Not now that all her plans are shagged to bits. And all because of you.'

Anthony Marvelle was distraught and, for once, lost for words. 'Murmur murmur,' was all he had to say. He dug around in the deep pockets of his silk-lined blazer, and found that the sharp points of his magical pinking shears had snipped away at the lining… A curious shower of cosmic fairy dust came lifting upwards out of his blazer and he gasped.

'It's already happening, Missy,' he cried. 'Murmur murmur! We're leaving this ghastly joint murmur murmur! Right now!'

And then they were gone.

But no one in Iris's party was there to see them.

The friends had caught up with the mistress of the transdimensional bus to discover that it hadn't gone without them after all. The bus was still there – big, bold and beautiful. Bright red and glowing with cosy, colourful light within.

Iris was outside, giving the Vizier a sound thrashing. 'How dare you lay your plastic hands on my bus! Don't you ever try to steal it again! It's mine, do you hear me? We've been together a very long time, this double decker and me! And it'll take more than some skanky sorceror from a distant world to prise it out of my grasp!' She kicked him roughly up the behind for good measure, and he collapsed into a heap of his silken robes.

'Quickly,' Iris told her friends. 'Take him and drag him aboard the ship that brought you all here to this station. We can send him spinning back down to Hyspero. And there he can explain to his Empress just what happened to her ridiculous plans!'

Kelly, Barbra and Jenny carried the Vizier to the bathysphere. While they did so, Simon and Panda did their best to help the cumbersome Fenster back aboard the bus.

Iris flung herself into the driver's cab and studied the various readings that were flickering across the dials.

'Everything okay?' Simon asked, catching the concerned look on her face.

'Hm? What?' She turned on a grin. 'Of course everything's okay, lovey! Everything's tip-top, shipshape and Brighton fashion!'

'Erm, Marvelle didn't cause any damage when he was messing about with the Ringpull, did he?'

Iris looked deeply serious for a moment. 'I think we stopped him just in time. But if he had succeeded... he would have unleashed *my* universe into this one, Simon. And then we would all have been really, terribly buggered up. We had the narrowest of escapes.'

Suddenly Panda was with them. 'Hurray for us! We arrived just in time, as per usual!' He clung to Simon's neck and kissed him noisily.

This was rather effusive for Panda, Simon thought. Then he saw that Jenny, Barbra and Kelly were returning from the bathysphere and about to get aboard. 'Kelly is all right, isn't she? Marvelle didn't harm her?'

'She's fine,' said Iris quickly. 'Well, relatively speaking, she is. She's got a lot going on, that girl! But she'll be fine, I think.'

Then Iris shushed Simon and pushed him away, so that she could concentrate on the controls of her bus.

Everyone was aboard the by-now rather cramped lower deck, and the hydraulic doors swooshed shut behind them.

'Are we all set?' Iris yelled down the gangway.

'I think so...' said Simon. He watched her pour a little vial of dragon's blood into the workings of the bus... No one else seemed to notice these rapid and furtive repairs, however.

'Yeeeesss!' shouted the others.

'A-are we returning to Hyspero?' Barbra asked quaveringly, giving away the fact that she wasn't at all keen on the idea.

'Our work there is done!' Iris cackled, and gave the stereo system a thump. There was a nasty crackling sound from all the many speakers throughout the bus, and then her favourite Northern Soul compilation burst into life.

Fenster was having second thoughts about joining the noisy crew. 'Could you perhaps drop me off…?'

But it was too late. As The Three Degrees hit their first chorus, the others were dancing in the close confines of the Number 22. Iris stamped her foot on the pedal and they accelerated madly into the Maelstrom, while Panda toddled off to pour everyone a drink.

PART FOUR

PART FOUR

Beginnings Again

1.

On the morning of the convention, Mr Charles Hardy turned up at their house bright and early, looking his most dapper. He was in his best blazer and tie, and he'd even put the Rover in for a valeting. The car waited for them, gleaming burgundy, in the road.

Sammy answered the door to him while his Mum was busy readying herself upstairs. She was in a bit of a panic, truth be told. 'What on earth am I supposed to wear at a function like this?'

Mr Hardy raised his eyebrows as Sammy let him into the dark and messy hallway. 'Your mother is well, I take it?' he said in that oh-so familiar, cultivated voice. Sammy could still hardly believe it – even though Charles Hardy had visited round here more than a dozen times in recent months… Sammy was still amazed that there was a living legend coming into their house!

'She's absolutely fine,' Sammy said, and he could hear the excitement in his voice. 'She just wants to look the part. Dressed up nice, like. She asked me what people wear at these things! And I had to say, well, often they dress up as characters from the show…'

Charles rolled his eyes. 'I hope you told her that anything she puts on will be absolutely splendid, Sammy. Your mother would look a treat in anything she wore. And besides, she isn't attending as a fan, is she? She is there as my guest. You both are.'

'Right,' nodded Sammy, leading him into the kitchen. 'I've told her all of that.' Sammy himself was sporting black jeans with a black and white T-shirt – and two black furry ears on top of his head.

Charles Hardy scooped a heap of library books and newspapers off a kitchen chair and sat himself down. 'She should have more confidence, your mother. She's a lovely looking women. Haven't I always said so, Sammy?'

It was true, Sammy thought, as he set about making coffee for all of them. The first time that Charles had popped round, a couple of months ago, it must have been – he had been gobsmacked at the sight of Sammy's mum. She had come bursting into the house – bringing bagloads of stuff from the pound shop in the precinct – more stuff they didn't need – and she had been in a proper narky mood. When she realised that there was company she suddenly switched moods and put on a more la-di-dah accent. It had been a long time since there had been a man in her kitchen. And this was a rather refined-sounding one.

When Mr Charles Hardy had explained that he was one of the actors involved – such a long time ago – in that TV show Sammy was obsessed with, his mother had been appalled and amazed. She shot a glance at Sammy as if to say, 'What have you gone and done now?'

But Charles was friendly and amused and, even though Mary could hardly credit it, he was friends with Sammy. This much older man who had once been a TV star was friends with her son – her useless, homebound lump of a son. At first Mary couldn't help but be suspicious. But then, Sammy was a grown-up (although he hardly ever acted it) and it was up to him what he got up to.

But then Mary had received another surprise, when it turned out that the gentlemanly actor kept coming round to visit, sitting at the kitchen table chatting – and it turned out that it was *her* who he was coming round to see. Oh, he was friendly enough with Sammy, and he seemed to enjoy the lad's attention and even his endless questions about his starring role in that daft old show – whatever it was called. But it seemed that Charles' ulterior motive in coming here was to court Mary. Yes, that was just the right word for it. With all his olde worlde charm he was courting her…

And that was how she came to be accompanying Charles and Sammy on this trip to Manchester, to this convention thing. IrisCon, or whatever it was called. She packed everything she had been trying on into her overnight case, and decided on a new, floaty peachy-coloured top and some white trousers with strappy shoes. Not too over the top for travelling and arriving in.

Charles had made the arrangements and he had promised that she would have a lovely weekend, even if the hotel was full of fans. It would be a little citybreak for them. She wondered if that meant they'd be sharing a hotel room. Well, of course it would. Their first weekend away together. It made her feel a little nervous, truth be told.

She hurried downstairs and dumped her bags in the hall, then flicked out her hair (newly-done yesterday at the salon) and strode into the kitchen, all smiles.

Charles embraced her and, at once, she had that wonderful feeling he somehow gave her. She felt safe and lifted up. 'Now, are you going to mind all these fans dressed up as…things?' he asked her, with that gentle edge of mockery she was so used to by now.

'Oh, I'll be fine,' she said. Then she looked over at Sammy. 'Like him, you mean? Dressed up as his own Panda?'

Panda himself was sitting pride of place in a chair next to Charles – or Mr Charles, as Panda always insisted on calling him. My representative in this dimension, was the other term Panda sometimes used for the actor.

Panda was sitting very still. He had agreed some months ago not to move around or to talk when Sammy's mum was about. It might freak her out completely – and even Panda could see that Mary was happier these days. He had vowed not to do anything to rock the boat at Sammy's house.

'How are we doing for time?' asked Mary.

'Time for coffee and then we must be off,' said Charles. 'It's a fair distance, and the weather isn't marvellous.'

Sammy clicked the radio on for the weather report. It was mid-December and those low, menacing clouds over the Pennines were only to be expected. There were delays on the major motorways that ran through the hills and the moors of the north… and there was more snow on the way…

'Are we mad to be setting out in this?' Mary asked, accepting her coffee from Sammy gratefully.

'Of course we aren't!' Charles said, putting on Panda's gruff and pompous tones. 'This is the first major Wildthyme convention in over ten years! We simply have to be there!'

Mary nodded and sipped her coffee – glancing out of the back kitchen windows and seeing that the clouds looked even heavier and lower now. A few hesitant snowflakes came whirling by, plastering themselves on the glass.

2.

Further south, in Darlington, the snow had already begun to settle. The fields beyond the town limits were already coated in several hardening layers that had fallen

411

through the night. Down in the MIAOW base beneath the town centre, Magda was studying the weather reports and clicking her tongue.

Maybe it would be better simply to stay at home. It was comfy down here in the secret base. And those two operatives from Greggs were due on at eleven. They always brought hot sausage rolls and doughnuts with them.

Then her mobile trilled.

'Magda, it's me, Terry.' He was speaking in a muffled rush, as if he was wrapping himself up in scarves and all sorts. 'I'm just leaving my flat. Where are you?'

'In the base,' she said. 'Will you call a taxi to the station? I'll meet you upstairs, outside of '*Magda's Mysteries.*''

'Okay. How are the readings?'

At first she thought he meant the weather reports, and she was about to tell him about the train delays and all. Then she realised he meant the other stuff.

'The bus, you mean?' she said.

'Are the sensors still saying the same thing?'

She leaned forward in her wheelchair to examine the perplexing array of dials and displays. 'Oh, yes, indeed. That is, if we can rely on such things.'

'I think we have to, Magda!' said the young man eagerly. She heard the noise of him setting his burglar alarm, and slamming his front door behind him. 'We've just got to hope and believe this is true. It seems completely impossible, but...!'

Then the line went crackly and his voice disappeared. Magda sighed and looked once more at the banks of computers and the lit-up map of the North of England at the heart of the MIAOW base.

'Is it true, Iris?' she asked. 'Are you really on your way?'

Magda stared hard at the pulsing point of lime green light on the map. It was centred on Manchester and the Palace Hotel.

There was another light blinking on the console nearest her, Magda noticed. A communiqué direct from the top brass. She hesitated before taking the call, but she knew she would have to.

Mida Slike's hateful visage filled the largest of the view-screens. That livid silver scar down her face caught the light and flashed as she grimaced at Magda.

'We at MIAOW know what you are doing,' Mida began, with no preliminaries. 'And you must understand that this… expected incursion comes not from our own dimension, Magda. It comes from an unauthorized source. The woman who is entering our space-time does not belong here…'

'But she does!' Magda protested. 'She belongs everywhere! That's the point!'

Mida Slike shook her head quickly and her helmet of bobbed hair quivered with fury. 'It is a breach of fictive etiquette, and it will not go unpunished.'

'You can't punish her for…'

'We can,' snapped Mida. 'I have heard tell of other worlds in other dimensions where this personage and her

413

friends are real. And I have heard about the chaos that follows in her wake. The Ministry cannot and will not let the Wildthyme woman cross over into this reality. It cannot be countenanced.'

Magda was worried now. Mida was deadly serious. 'W-what are you going to do?'

'Anything necessary,' Mida gloated. 'Absolutely anything necessary to send her spinning back into her own ridiculous reality. She isn't real, Magda. And even if she is real elsewhere, she doesn't belong here.'

Magda was just opening her mouth to reply when the image of Mida suddenly vanished. This didn't sound at all good. Iris thought she was returning home to a lovely heroine's welcome. She didn't even know yet that she was headed for the wrong dimension… and a distinctly unfriendly reception.

Now it was even more imperative that Magda and Terry attend this convention thing. She had to get her skates on. She wheeled her chair quickly to the lift, but not before sending out the recall signal to the operatives in the bakery on High Row. They would have to come by earlier to start their shift at the MIAOW base.

Ten minutes later Magda was sitting outside her shop munching a steaming sausage roll and brushing flaky crumbs off the tartan blanket over her knees. Her luggage was by her side and she was pleased to see Terry hurrying up the street towards her through the crowd of eager shoppers.

The snow was falling thick and fast. 'Thank goodness we're going by train,' he said. 'I would hate to be driving in this weather…'

Magda nodded and then told him quickly about Mida and MIAOW's attitude to the advent of the visitors from another dimension.

'Oh, that's awful…' he said. 'But are you sure, Magda?'

'Yes!' she cried, shocked that he would doubt her. 'I've just had her yelling at me down the viewscreen…'

'Ah, here's our taxi to the station,' he said, taking hold of her handles and pushing her to the kerb. 'No, I meant about what the instruments were saying… about, you know… the nature of this incursion… this materialisation from another dimension…'

'Oh, that,' she said, as the taxi driver got out and hurried around to the pavement to help with her wheelchair. 'Well, of course I'm sure. Now, wrap my blanket round me securely, Terry. We don't want everyone to see my mermaid's tale.'

In the back of the car – which smelled of pine trees and fags – she murmured to Terry as the car swished through the snowy slush: 'I am alert to these dimensional flickers, you see. These sparkling moments of iridescence, as the boundaries of the dimensions are breached… I don't need the computers and so on to tell me what is going on. I, like Iris herself, am a liminal being and I am sensitive to these matters. And so you needn't doubt that she is on her way… as impossible as it seems. And isn't it typical of her, to choose as her point of arrival, the location and the time that she has…?'

Terry nodded, and thought about this all the way to the railway station. He had been going to this convention anyway. He remembered doing the signing at Timeslip and saying to Bob Fordyce – the genre tie-in king - that he would see him there, late in the year. It was to be a great gathering in Manchester – of the friends of Iris.

And now this. No one knew what was heading their way. No one quite knew what to expect.

At Darlington station Magda had a great fuss made of her. As their train pulled in under the vaulted roof, the platform manager and his helpers made a big show of being ready with a ramp. Magda sat there with a heap of magazines and bags of sweets and let all these kindly men tend to her needs. Terry followed on smiling – remarking that he'd never been in First Class before.

'Ach, let MIAOW pay the extra,' Magda chuckled, as they settled at their table. She spread all her mags out and glared at all the other passengers, who came shuffling down the aisle. 'We deserve a little luxury, we do. Do we not, Terry?'

'Oh, yes, we do,' he smiled. And he thought about his year. He'd written two full-length novels this year. One of them had been about Iris and Panda… and Simon and Kelly and Barbra… It seemed so long ago now, he could hardly recall the details. But that was happening a lot just recently, wasn't it? When he turned his attention away, it seemed the Iris stories – even the ones he thought he knew well - even the ones he had written himself... were warping and morphing into new shapes and configurations.

Now he knew that wasn't him going crackers or stressing from deadlines or anything of the sort. Now he knew it was to do with the fact that the dimensions were fucked up. And that seemed rather reassuring.

Now he was on the train across the country... about to hurtle through the hills and over the plains of whirling snow... for a rendezvous with people from another world.

Magda saw him settle back and relax, but noted the somewhat strained look on his face. She knew how to deal with that. Snapping her fingers, she called the trolley lady over. 'Gin and tonic,' she called. 'Two doubles, please. We're both going to need it.' She swished her mermaid's tail under the table and nudged Terry's knee. 'What say we get pissed, eh?'

3.

After a couple of hours the passengers in Charles Hardy's Rover were wondering whether this had been such a good idea. Now they were on the Moors and the weather was ferocious; the snow clouds seemed a matter of inches above their heads and the car was crawling through a howling tunnel of freezing wind. As Charles Hardy struggled with the wheel, they were inching along, and the others were ducking down in their seats...

At least it was warm inside the car. They were listening to Christmas tunes and Sammy's mum was passing around mints.

'Shouldn't we just give up and turn back?' she asked Charles nervously.

'Oh dear, no,' he said, glancing round briefly. The car wobbled nastily just then and he yanked the wheel. They could even hear the squeezing and crunching of the thick snow beneath their tyres. 'We've come this far,' he added. 'It would be just as bad to turn back and return. We must go forward… it's all downhill from here… you'll see! We'll be in Manchester soon!'

Sammy stared out at the wild, white wilderness, rubbing at the condensation on the window with his gloves. For the first time he had caught a note of fear in Charles' voice and he felt the panic starting to rise up in him. What if they were trapped out here? What if the car battery died and they were left in the freezing cold all day and all night as more snow settled over the top of them? It had been twenty minutes since they had seen another car on the road… everyone else had simply turned tail and gone home a long time ago…

But Charles Hardy was determined. There was a bullish and determined set to his shoulders as he sat hunched at the wheel.

Panda was sitting between Sammy and Mary on the flip-down arm rest. Naturally, he hadn't said a word the whole journey. But Sammy could sense his trembling with agitation. He knew Panda was bursting to say something…

'I wish we'd never bothered now,' Mary said quietly. 'We could be all cosy at home…'

Just then Charles let out a great cry of triumph. He was peering hard at his rear view mirror. 'Someone is coming up behind us! Can you see, in the back? Look… there are lights… it's something big…'

Sammy was craning round. Yes… he could see the dark shape, too. It was tall… and it was moving much faster than they were…

'It's a snow plough!' Charles shouted joyfully. 'I bet you ten pence it's a snow plough! We're saved!'

But Sammy and his Mum weren't so sure. They twisted round to stare into the whirling vortex of snow to see what was about to overtake them.

'It's a double decker bus…!' Mary yelled, as the vehicle went by them in a flash. All of its windows were lit up and it seemed to be relatively inconvenienced by the blizzard. 'What the hell's a double decker doing out on the Yorkshire Moors?'

Charles Hardy, Sammy and Panda were all silent at this. All three of them simply stared as the bus roared past them. It was almost like a snow mirage, seeing that bulky shape hurtling into the invisible road ahead. They had its lights directly in front of them… and then… it was fading away. For a moment it even seemed as if it was lifting into the air… and taking off for flight…

Charles Hardy, realising he'd removed his hands from the wheel, grabbed hold of it again, hard, before he sent them trundling into a ditch.

'It didn't stop!' Mary cried. 'It just went streaking by…'

'I-it was…' Sammy stammered. 'It was l-like…'

'It's done the work of a snow plough for us,' said Charles with great satisfaction. 'Look!'

And it was true. The road ahead had been cleared. The M62 was smooth and dry all the way to the ring road around Manchester, and they had that mysterious bus to thank.

'We're going to make it!' Mary laughed, as Charles turned the Christmas music up again.

'Hurrah!' shouted Panda, forgetting himself.

Mary glanced at the stuffed toy in shock. 'Did he talk?' she asked Sammy.

'Don't be daft, Mum,' said Sammy. 'It was you throwing your voice, wasn't it, Charles?'

'Oh yes,' said Charles, in Panda's voice. 'Did you really think the little chap was alive?' He laughed.

'I don't know,' said Mary warily. 'With you two, I'm never sure what to believe…'

4.

Terry and Magda's journey passed in relatively uneventful quiet. The train hurtled through tunnels under frozen mountains and through valleys where tiny villages lay under mounds of heavy snow. The countryside seemed to be hibernating through winter and the sight of it made both Terry and Magda sleepy – especially after their second Gin and Tonic.

The first class carriage was empty apart from them, which was disconcerting. It was as if no one else had dared to venture out today. Nothing was important enough to get them out and about.

While Magda dozed Terry attempted to read. Then he fetched out the IrisCon brochure from his bag and tried to make sense of it all. It seemed like a whole lot of panels scheduled against each other, at which various people connected to Iris Wildthyme the TV show, plus the various spin-off media, would present work or have discussions in front of audience members. There was a formal dinner, a screening of rare footage, a dealer's room packed with goodies, and a masked ball and disco in the evening. Terry perked up a bit as he read about it all. It might even turn out to be fun.

Soon their train was pulling into Piccadilly station in Manchester and Magda woke with a sudden cry. 'Oh! Are we here, Terry?'

It was a struggle to get everything together, and to unfold her chair and help her onto the platform, but soon they were ready to face the world.

'Oh, they've got potted palms in the station in December,' noted Magda. 'It's a bit more cosmopolitan than Darlington, eh, Terry?'

He pushed her chair to the taxi rank and asked the driver to take them straight to the Palace Hotel.

5.

Aboard the Number 22 there was chaos.

Everyone had been flung about the place, along with all the furniture and fixtures. Barbra had rolled backwards into the galley kitchen, windmilling her arms and scattering neatly-stacked crockery everywhere. The others were crushed under falling cabinets and the contents of cleverly-hidden overhead lockers as the bus bounced and careened about the skies over Yorkshire.

Panda was yelling blue murder at Iris, and the others found they could barely find room to stand up in all the mess. Fenster the dragon was moaning pitifully – though that could have been because Jenny had fallen heavily onto the chaise longue he had adopted as his body.

'Where are we?' Simon yelled, crawling over to the nearest window and staring at the hectic storm outside. 'Are we out of the Maelstrom?'

At the front of the bus, with her pirate's hat clamped down about her ears, Iris had managed to block out the hullaballoo of her passengers. She was at one with the workings of her miraculous engine, and staring at the eye of the storm.

'So this is another new dimension…' she whispered to herself, and lit up a gold Sobranie to celebrate. 'A new dimension I've never been to yet!' She grinned madly and gunned the engine. 'Come on, old girl! It's up to you! Where are you taking us…?'

The Number 22 lurched and leapt, higher into the skies above Yorkshire and then toppled over the heights into Lancashire. They emerged from the tumult of the blizzard and soared high above the clouds. For a while they sailed in peace under the darkening winter skies and, as Iris let the bus soar where it wanted, the others started picking up furniture and inspecting the damage.

'Is anything permanently ruined?' she yelled at them.

Her friends were battered and bruised, and her favourite capodimonte angel ornaments were smashed to bits, but no one felt like telling her that while she was still driving.

'Where is she taking us?' Kelly asked Panda.

'I can't tell,' he said. 'And neither can she, I think. You see, Marvelle stole our maps and charts... and anyway, I don't think they'd be much good in this new dimension...'

'New dimension?' Kelly asked, peering out of a window. 'But that's Britain down there. Look! There's a city and it's...'

'We're back home!' Simon shouted happily.

Then Iris's voice came from the front of the cab. She warned them: 'Not quite, lovies! This isn't home as you remember it!'

Then the bus started its rapid descent. Inelegantly plummeting through fathoms of frosty air. Through bands of frozen cloud and blankets of virgin snow. Everyone screamed, convinced they were being flung to their certain deaths.

'We're about to land!' Iris shrieked. 'In Manchester! It's December! Happy Christmas, everybody!'

And after that it went a bit dark and noisy for a while. Simon gathered that the bus was trying to put its brakes on and somehow cushion their impact in the centre of the city.

They landed smack bang in central Manchester, a few streets away from the Palace Hotel.

Snow was falling so quickly that flakes were landing on the outer shell of the bus already. But they sizzled and melted in the heat generated by the sudden descent.

The Number 22 was standing in an alleyway between a multi-storey car park and an All-You-Can-Eat Chinese buffet. There had been no damage, even after a drop from several thousand feet onto rock hard frozen cobbles. Iris took a bow while the others applauded her.

'What say we pop out and get a drink, eh?' She looked around the interior of her bus, which the others had done their best to tidy. 'It's looking a bit cramped in here. Come on you lot!'

And she led them out into the wintry streets. The closest bar (according to the handy monitoring device she always kept stowed away in her carpetbag) told her that the nearest and nicest bar was downstairs in a hotel just a block away.

6.

The Palace Hotel was a grand, imposing edifice with towers of red brick, lording it over the busiest road in town. The clock in its tallest tower was bonging out the hour: it was evening in Manchester and very few folk were out braving the streets tonight. Traffic had dissipated and, miraculously, no one had noticed the sudden arrival of a London bus through the clouds. Which was just as well. Iris and the others were in no mood to explain themselves tonight. They all felt that they deserved a little peace and fun.

They made a surprising-looking bunch as they hurried, slithering down the snowy street. Iris took the lead, followed by Simon and Kelly, who didn't particularly stand out here, in a dimension not-their-own. Jenny, too, looked relatively normal, even in her long dark coat and monocle. But then came Panda, riding on the cushioned back of Fenster, and chatting away to Barbra, who was finding the going difficult on her hydraulic legs. 'It's so chilly,' she moaned. 'It's chillier than my refrigerated insides!'

Panda hoped she wasn't about to start offering her warm, flat orangeade around again.

Simon asked Iris, 'Erm, don't you think we're going to stand out a mile in a public bar?'

She shrugged happily. 'Let them deal with that. It's Christmas! We all deserve a night out, don't we? Even those of us who don't look right.'

It took some doing, getting them all through the revolving doors. There was a man in a top hat, with braiding on his uniform, who proved to be very helpful in easing Barbra into the hotel. Fenster had to be stood on one end to get himself indoors.

Inside it was luxurious and very festive and...

'Have you noticed anything funny?' Kelly asked Simon, as they made their way to the bar.

He frowned. 'I'm not sure...'

Iris was leading them with single-minded determination to a vast bar area that was decorated in old colonial style, with bamboo furniture and a lot of exotic plants. The whole place was packed to the rafters.

'Oh, crikey,' Simon said.

'See what I mean?' asked Kelly.

'What is it?' Jenny demanded.

Panda hopped onto Simon's shoulder to see. 'Bugger me!' he cried, and burst out laughing.

No one could hear their various expostulations over the noise of the music. No one paid much heed to their astonished expressions as they stared at everyone in the bar.

In fact, no one paid much attention to the newcomers at all.

'Everyone is dressed as *us*!' Fenster laughed. 'Look, there's me! And you, Iris… I can see four, five, six of you…! And every one of them has their own Panda…'

'I can see a lot of me,' said Jenny, eyeing up her competition.

'And even a few Anthony Marvelles and Missy the Poodles!' Kelly choked. 'What the hell is this, Iris? What on earth have you brought us to?'

They were all watching a large lady wearing a cardboard robotic body topple past them, pretending to be Barbra. 'Fizzy pop! Crisps! Have some fizzy pop!' she shouted.

'I don't know what it is!' Iris said, amazed. 'But I love it!'

7.

Dear All,

Hello there, again! It's me, Panda!

I thought I'd drop you all a little line at the end of this book of ours, just to say that… well, we all came out of it unharmed and had a jolly nice time after all the upheaval and everything! Amazing, really, after all the scrapes and difficulties the whole lot of us experienced, what?

How nice it was, to finish up at a disco at the Palace Hotel, in a Manchester from another dimension. It turns out (and I had to have this explained to me – by Barbra the Vending Machine, of all people!) that we were accidentally attending an Iris Wildthyme convention! (Or rather, an Iris Wildthyme *and Panda* convention.)

Now what are the chances of that? We slip into a new dimension and the first thing we find is a great big party and celebration *in honour of our very own selves!*

At first Iris advised caution. 'Don't go telling them that you're the real thing,' she said. 'We don't know anything about these people yet!'

Instead we milled about in the bar as Iris shoved her way to the front and ordered a bottle of champagne for us. Pushing the boat out there, I thought!

Already we were getting some approving looks from the other guests at the convention. I must admit that I – sitting on Iris's shoulder as she poured out the bubbly – was attracting a good deal of attention myself. I thought: have they never seen a fully-articulated and sentient Art Critic Panda before?

What these fans clearly thought of as our 'costumes' were drawing quite a lot of attention by then. We mingled for a while, until Jenny found us a corner table in the bar. Simon was approached by a young man in a spotted shirt, who engaged him in a rather involved conversation. Accompanying this young man was a woman in a wheelchair whom we all recognised at once.

'Magda!' Jenny cried. 'What are you doing here? Shouldn't you be at home at the MIAOW base?' She looked confused then. 'Er, you do *have* MIAOW in this dimsension, don't you?'

Magda smiled and nodded, and accepted a glass of champagne (Kelly was sent to fetch some more.) 'I am an alternate universe Magda,' Magda told us, rather tipsily as she clinked glasses with everyone. 'Hello, hello, welcome to our dimension! You know, don't you, that none of you really exist here, in our world? You are all made up!'

'Yes, yes!' Iris grinned happily. 'Isn't it wonderful?'

Marvellous woman! She's never fazed by anything!

I overheard a fragment of conversation between our Simon and the other young man just then. It seemed the gist of their exchange was similar – with Simon being told by the other young man – Terry – that he was a figment of his imagination. Terry was a novelist, apparently. He said he had written three hundred and twenty four novels – all about me! (But that can't be right, can it?) Simon didn't look all that alarmed to be in the other man's novels, truth be told. If I wasn't mistaken, the two of them were taking something of a shine to each other anyway. They had a little dance and were seen holding hands as they sat on high bar stools. Then a little later on that night they vanished off together in each other's company.

I myself was somewhat startled to meet a youngish man dressed in a ludicrous approximation of my own look – fake ears, a cravat, etc. He was accompanied by a very distinguished gentleman called Charles, who claimed to do the voice for my character in the TV show all about me. I received these fans graciously and let them burble on for a bit. They also had another version of me with them – from *yet another* alternate dimension. This Panda – though terribly handsome - was rather surly and wouldn't say a single word to me. I was ashamed at having a counterpart so rude! Instead I took a twirl around the dance floor with a rather attractive lady – Mary – who had travelled all the way from Gateshead with them. In a blizzard, no less! Just to be at *my* convention!

Too bad there were some snipers from MIAOW hanging around that bar. Disguised as fans and apparently enjoying themselves. Coming over ostensibly to say hello, they whipped out laser pistols in a very peremptory manner and tried to assassinate Iris on the spot. Oh, there was a terrible to-do as they surrounded her banquette. She was horrified and then livid at having the party mood disturbed. Anyway, there was a punch up and the leggy, glamorous MIAOW assassins were put swiftly out of action by Iris and her friends.

The would-be assassins' being wrestled to the ground and dragged away was almost an unfortunate blight on an otherwise marvellous evening. Not so much the violence (Iris enjoys a good barney) but the nasty taste it left afterwards. MIAOW operatives! Assassinating Iris! And after she's done such a lot of good work for them, too! Luckily, my good self wasn't bothered by would-be killers that night. I'd have been most vexed indeed, had they tried.

And so the night went on. Rather drunkenly, it has to be admitted. And we had a lovely knees-up at the disco that lasted for much of the night. Even Barbra joined us on the dance floor, energetically lifting up her hydraulic legs in time to the music, and flapping her telescopic arms. Fenster couldn't be persuaded. He was still learning to coordinate his flung-together new form and didn't feel up to boogying yet, he said.

Iris was right in the middle of the dance floor, kicking up a storm as usual. The two of us danced like crazy that night. Surrounded by all our friends.

And by a room full of people who would be startled to discover that we truly were exactly who we were pretending to be.

We'd survived our ludicrous adventures again!

And come out dancing at the end!

Plus, it was Christmas as well!

THE END.

THE END